Cookie Honey

"You've got to love a book that calls itself
SWEETIE BABY COOKIE HONEY."

Waldenbooks

"THE MOST SIZZLING PROPERTY TO COME
ALONG IN YEARS."

Liz Smith, *New York Daily News*

"Compulsively   readable...unabashedly
sexy and bursting with realism and vitality."

Booklist

RICK FIRESTONE
To a boy from Brooklyn,
friends were the reason
for stardom...and the
means to survive it.

Sweetie

HEDY HARLOWE
To "The Heavenly One,"
friends were for
forgetting in a haze of
drugs and in the arms
of hustlers.

Baby

JOYCE HELLER
Her friends would help
turn a life of torment
into one of triumph.

Cookie

Honey

You've got to have friends...

RICK FIRESTONE

He opened his heart and soul to the world and learned the hard way just how cold that world could be...

HEDY HARLOWE

Born Lois Rabinowitz, she used her talent to soar to the heights of ecstasy, then compromised it to sink to the depths of drugs and despair...

DAVID BARRY

He sold his soul until he earned enough to buy—and sell—anyone and anything he wanted...

JOYCE HELLER

She overcame the worst humiliations a woman can suffer to make herself a force to reckon with....

Please turn the page for the critics' praise of

Sweetie Baby Cookie Honey

Sweetie Baby

Sweetie
Baby
Cookie
Honey

A Novel by
Freddie Gershon

BALLANTINE BOOKS • NEW YORK

Copyright © 1986 by Freddie Gershon

All rights reserved under International and Pan-American Copyright
Conventions, including the right of reproduction in whole or in part in
any form. Published in the United States of America by Ballantine
Books, a division of Random House, Inc., New York, and
simultaneously in Canada by Random House of Canada Limited,
Toronto.

Library of Congress Catalog Card Number: 86-13981

ISBN 0-345-34638-6

This edition published by arrangement with Arbor House Publishing
Company, a division of The Hearst Corporation.

Manufactured in the United States of America

First Ballantine Books Edition: October 1987

CONTENTS

A very special thank-you to

John Dodds,

*without whom I could not have
endured and persevered in my
writing task,
and to*
Andrew Karp,
*for his invaluable
assistance*

Dedicated to **Myrna,** *my pal*

my partner,

my wife . . .

my love

ACKNOWLEDGMENTS

Wayne Bickerton
Peter Brown
Dr. Robert Cancro
Allan Carr
Al Coury
Peter Dekom
Jim DeMeaux
Nina DePass
Roseanne Ehrlich
Roger Englander
Joyce Frigon
Dan Gershon
Miriam Gershon
Allen Grubman
Lois Wyse Guber
Victor Irving
Mitch Julis
Robbie Lantz
Owen Laster
Morris Levy

Tony Lutz
Myrna Masour
Peter Noone
Monti Rock
Henry Rogers
Leba Sedaka
Neil Sedaka
Joe Smith
Gloria Stavers
Robert Stigwood
Dick Taylor
Dr. Kenneth Unger
Vivian Vance
Dr. Herbert Walker
Phyllis Wesley
Walter Yetnikoff
Alexander & Dinah
Abraham and, mostly,
Grandma Becky

A VERY SPECIAL THANK YOU TO MY FRIEND
AND MENTOR THE GREAT ATTORNEY HARRY E.
WEISS, FOR A TREASURE-TROVE OF TRUTH.

BOOK

1

Rick

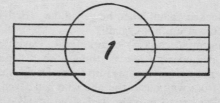

1981

THE CRAZY LADY OF LAUREL CANYON LIVED IN A HOUSE that was closer in spirit and look to the Bowery than it was to Hollywood. Filthy and unkempt, it looked like the shambles of a burned-out tenement. The lawn was a tangle of weeds, the white stucco was cracked and faded, even the car parked in the driveway—a '73 Olds—was a rusty, beat-up has-been.

David drove the Lagonda into the driveway and checked the address again. There was no mistake. Stepping out of the car, he walked up the stone path over intertwined brambles, vines, and overgrowth, over piles of unopened newspapers and mail, over empty beer cans and broken glass, all of which reminded him of Grey Gardens. He straightened the Windsor knot of his Sulka tie, strode up to the door, and knocked. This wasn't going to be easy.

From her hiding place in the living room, Hedy lifted the filthy *shmata* she called a curtain, pushed aside the blackout shade, and looked out. The man at the door was in his early forties, six feet tall, distinguished-looking with black hair tinged silver at the temples. He wasn't a salesman, a lost soul, or a tourist. He carried himself with a sense of purpose, as though he knew where he was and what he was doing. Hedy didn't recognize him.

David knocked again. Then he yelled out, "Hedy! Hedy, it's me, David. Open up, it's urgent!"

At first her mind couldn't comprehend "David." The Cointreau and Quaaludes made everything fuzzy and played tricks with her memory. Then it came into focus. David was her friend and lawyer from way back, the one who had saved her career by introducing her to movies, Rick's old friend, the one who collected her dwindling residuals and doled out what little remained of her trust fund. She hadn't seen him in so long. She hadn't seen anyone in so long. She knew he was much more than a lawyer today—that during the eight years since she had fallen to oblivion, he had risen to power and prominence.

The David of old had a gentle face and sensual lips that curled slightly and gave the impression of openness and good humor. Now something had hardened his face, straightened the curl of his mouth, and turned the twinkle of his eyes into a deep, piercing glance. His lips were tighter and narrower, reflecting anxiety and the inner tension of an overly controlled man.

She became genuinely excited. Rushing to the door, she fumbled with the many locks until the knob finally turned in her shaking hand and the door swung open. Even through the smog, the glare of the California sun blinded her. She winced and held both hands up to her eyes.

David stared at her incredulously. For a moment he thought he was looking at Hedy's mother. "Hedy?" he asked hesitantly. "Is that you?"

"Yeah, it's me, David. Come on in."

David couldn't believe his eyes. Was this really *the* Heavenly Hedy Harlowe? Once she'd been the hottest and raunchiest of stars, a singer and performer without compare, a living legend of the stage and screen. Now the bloat of drugs, booze, and self-abuse had distorted her features until she'd become grotesque and unrecognizable. Her once wildly exotic dark hair, now flecked with gray, was matted and dirty, done up in an ugly, matronly bun. The once firm, plump, and frequently exposed breasts now resembled those of a fat buddha. Gone were the dazzling flashing eyes, Persian nose, and glamorous air. Now she looked like a fishmonger on the streets of Beirut. Her tawny skin was marked with scabs. Her unbathed body was fat, flabby, and shapeless.

Most of the women of southern California looked ten years younger than their years, but Lois Rabinowitz, once known to the entire world as Hedy Harlowe, looked twenty years older. At forty-one, Hedy had lost her voice, her looks, and everything that had once been her life. She thought she had nothing left to lose. She was wrong.

Despite his shock, David willed himself to retain his composure. When he entered the house, though, the odor was so overpowering that he couldn't disguise his revulsion. He'd seen a lot of stars go down in his day. It was never pleasant. But this was the worst. Hedy had sunk below rock bottom, down into a self-imposed hell.

He stopped in the hallway before she could offer him a seat on the stained and encrusted couch. "Hedy, listen, I had to come. I've got bad news." His voice, like his movement, was slow and deliberate.

She looked at him blankly. Nothing he could say would hurt her; she was beyond pain. "What is it, David?"

"Rick is dead."

Hedy just stared at him in disbelief. Then she began to breathe in and out, in and out, deeply, as if she were hyperventilating. After a massive breath, she let out a wail. It was more than a shriek or a scream, more like the cry of a mother at her own child's grave. It came from her guts through the very vocal cords that had stopped singing years ago. It echoed through all of Laurel Canyon, bouncing off each rocky hill like a muezzin's call to prayer. When the last echo died, Hedy Harlowe collapsed unconscious on the filthy floor at David Barry's feet.

Hours later she awoke in a private nursing home in the Valley. No Quaaludes, no booze, nothing to protect and envelop her. She felt naked. No matter how hard she tried to forget, she still remembered. It was no dream. Rick was dead. By his own hand.

On the table beside her bed, she found an envelope addressed to her. She opened it and read:

Dear Hedy,
I'm sorry I upset you so. As the executor of Rick's will and as his friend, I came to ask you to comply with his final

request. He asked that you attend his funeral. Please read
the attached page describing the special provision of his
will.

I'm counting on seeing you tomorrow at Mount Hebron
Cemetery. Clothing, car, and driver have all been provided. It would be a mitzvah if you could make it, but if
you can't, I understand.

Thank you for loving Rick. I know you loved him as
much as Joyce and I do. Never forget that he loved you
and cared for you very deeply throughout his life.

Warmly,
David Barry

Hedy couldn't believe it. *She* was the one who was supposed
to be dead, not Rick. Dead to her friends. Dead and buried as
far as show business was concerned. As dead as Mama Cass and
Janis Joplin, as Jim Morrison and Jimi Hendrix, as dead as John
Lennon, Elvis Presley, and all the others in rock-and-roll
heaven.

At one time in her solitude, she had lived in the past. But
thoughts of her past no longer brought her solace or warmth.
The memories only depressed her. There was no one to remi-
nisce with and no one to hear her cries of agony and frustration.
No one to care. No one to listen. The servants and the paid
companions had all quit, unable to tolerate the Crazy Lady and
unable to find anything of value left to steal from her.

She lived in a bleary-eyed stupor, her body crisscrossed with
black-and-blue marks from her drugged-out, drunken lurching.
She couldn't remember how long it had been since the so-called
psychosomatic laryngitis had caused her "lost voice." All she
knew was that there were no more interviews, no more curiosity
seekers, no more nothing. Just loneliness.

There was a time when she used to order pizzas and hope. But
she had ordered so many pizzas looking for some delivery boy
to fuck her silly that she finally got sick of smelling cheese and
tomato sauce. Years had passed since she'd had a hustler. Now
she had no one.

She'd stopped trying to quit the ludes. She never wanted to
stop. Why should she? There was nothing to be up for. Nobody
remembered her anymore, and even if they did, they wouldn't
recognize her. Hedy had no need for wigs or sunglasses. She was
her own disguise.

Loneliness, anonymity, and depression had become her way of life. If there had ever been a Hedy Harlowe, she'd evaporated, regressed back into plain old Lois Rabinowitz, an unattractive, middle-aged, fat Jewish broad.

Once she had been bitter about the record company, the promoters, the agents, all of the people who'd made money off her and lived off her talent. The press had called her the Judy Garland of rock-and-roll, and they didn't mean it to be flattering. She was known as "Miss Uncongeniality" or "Miss Hedy Unreliable." Still, they'd labeled her unique blend of talent and flamboyance "stylish," "outrageous," even "adorable"—until they jumped on the bandwagon and turned against her.

When her movie *Immaculate Conception* bombed, the press lambasted her without mercy. The critics tore her to shreds with their cruel, scathing reviews, until she had nowhere left to go and no place left to hide. That's why she became invisible and anonymous. Driven into hiding, she was sentenced to oblivion. Her life became a tortured existence filled with excesses and self-pity. Her humiliation was so unbearable, the sight of her own pleading eyes so painful, that she shattered every mirror in the house. Only by turning off her brain and succumbing to the numbness had she finally stopped feeling the sting.

Until now.

Now the fact of Rick's death sent shock waves rippling through her body. Rick was dead. Gone forever. She didn't know how or why. But her self-pity and fear seemed fake next to that harsh reality. Rick *had* loved her, David said so. And deep down she knew it was true.

She opened the extract of the will and read Rick's words, hearing his voice the way it had sounded years ago, when they were just starting out in Brighton Beach:

"And it is my fervent and most profound wish that my dearest, most special friend, Lois Rabinowitz, professionally known as Hedy Harlowe, sing 'How Can I Go On Without You?' at my funeral."

Sing! "No!" she screamed out loud, flailing her arms and knocking over the glass of water on the nursing home bedside table. She couldn't do it. She wouldn't do it. Even if she wanted to, she wasn't able to sing anymore. Even if she could sing, she wouldn't do it in front of the hypocritical music industry. The fuckers would all be there, laughing at her, judging her . . . Those bastards—she was terrified of them.

Hedy started to cry, but they weren't the tears of self-pity that had filled her eyes for so many years. This time she cried for Rick. She cried for the love she'd lost. Her Rick. Her dear, sweet Rick. Rick, who'd never intentionally hurt anyone in his life. In the end, he had remembered her and called out to her while she had forgotten him, caught up in her own self-absorbed and self-destructive cycle.

It had been over twelve hours since she'd popped her last pill and Hedy was cold sober. She got up off the bed. No one would stop her. She could return to her Laurel Valley hovel and forget about David and Rick and the entire world. She had run away before, she could do it again. Hedy Harlowe was dead, and the dead couldn't and shouldn't be resurrected.

She reached down to pick up her clothes, then stopped, suddenly overwhelmed with revulsion and self-hatred. She couldn't just run away, not this time, not when Rick had called to her from his grave.

She finally sank back down onto the bed and fell asleep. It was a natural sleep, unlike any she'd had in years. And she dreamed about Grandma Becky and about Rick's first hit, "How Can I Go On Without You?"—the song he had written for her, the song that had become an anthem for ill-fated lovers.

She slept through the night. Awake at six the next morning, she soaked luxuriously in a foam bath for an entire hour. Two nurses medicated her body, then helped with her hair and with the enormous, tentlike, steel-gray dress that Rick's Grandma Becky would have called a *fahtik*. A large gray hat, a veil, and dark glasses, all thoughtfully provided by David, completed her attire.

Hedy felt shaky but alive with resolve as she settled awkwardly into the back of the limousine and watched the chauffeur close the door. When the car approached Mount Hebron, however, her newfound confidence drained. The scene was a nightmare of pandemonium, just like the funerals of countless other stars: TV, newsreels, crowds of frantic, sobbing fans; traffic snarled for blocks; hawkers selling Rick Firestone memorabilia; hordes of police and security guards struggling to control the chaos; flashbulbs popping; helicopters hovering noisily overhead.

Waved on by the police, her limousine rolled through the gates and came to a stop behind the line of black Mercedes, Lincolns, and Cadillacs parked along the cemetery grass. When the driver opened her door, Hedy froze. She couldn't go through with it. Not alone, without even one of her ludes as a crutch! She hesitated but wasn't given the opportunity to make a choice.

"I'm so glad you made it, Hedy," David said, leaning into the back seat and offering her his hand. "It's what Rick wanted more than anything."

She clutched his strong hand and felt a resurgence of inner strength. David Barry was not just a lawyer—he was Mr. Power. He wasn't a star, at least not one the public would recognize. He'd become something bigger: the man who owned and controlled the stars. From lawyer and manager for recording artists and occasionally movie stars, he had risen to the chairmanship of L.O.L., Levy Organization Ltd., one of the largest entertainment conglomerates in the world. And now he had come to Hedy, to escort her personally.

As she emerged from the limo, an additional arm supported her gently but firmly. Hedy turned to her right and stared at a gorgeous, sophisticated-looking woman whose glorious figure, shoulder-length black hair, and penetrating green eyes were as startling as any movie star's. The woman was smiling benevolently, engaging Hedy's arm and patting her hand in a comforting, reassuring way. Hedy looked quizzically at the lovely lady, her lack of recognition registering on her face.

"It's me—Joyce," the woman said.

She had only heard about Joyce Heller's transformation. Now Hedy saw it for herself. The once skinny, dykish assistant producer had actually been transformed into the first woman of show-business executives, a liberated movie and music video mogulette who ran the movie division of David's company. Hedy would never forget how Joyce had stood by Rick through the bad years, helping him cope and grow and survive. How, in fact, they had helped each other.

Joyce had been there for Hedy, too. She was strong and tough as nails but had been understanding and compassionate when Hedy needed it most. Especially out in the desert when Joyce tried to get Hedy back together with Rick. Even though she'd been through her own hell, Joyce always found time to reach out, to give of herself, to be a friend. And they did have Derek the hunk in common.

Hedy became teary-eyed and choked up. On either side of her were Joyce and David, holding her up, supporting her, encouraging her. She realized they were the two remaining musketeers, there to bury Rick, the third musketeer and their very best friend.

They were all here now. All her friends, living and dead. David and Joyce . . . and Rick.

She held tightly on to their arms and walked bravely through the crowd and across the grass to the open grave on the hillside. The southern California sun shone through the bright haze, illuminating the oil wells in the distance and casting deep shadows on the rectangular hole that was to be Rick's final stage. Why hadn't God had the decency to make it a gray, rainy day?

Although David and Joyce were known to everyone at the gathering, no one bothered Hedy. Certainly no one recognized her. To the crowd of over a thousand people, she was simply another faceless, fat relative of the deceased. But Hedy knew them all.

The old woman next to her was sobbing, her head bent, her face covered with a black veil. It had to be Rose Feuerstein, Rick's mother, whom Hedy hadn't seen or spoken to in almost twenty years, not since the split with Rick. No longer a tough blond stage mother, she was a bent, arthritically stooped old lady. It was hard for Hedy to hate her still.

Next to Rose was a tall blond Viking, Thane Crawley. Cold but brilliant. Snobbish, aristocratic, and contemptuous. Impeccably dressed, forty-three years old, single, with patrician features and deep gray, penetrating eyes from which emanated power and control. As head of L.O.L. Records, he was probably the single most powerful man in the American music business. Back in the Sixties, before his first scandal and fall from grace, he had signed both Hedy and Rick to recording contracts with Apollo Records. Then had proceeded to drop them both.

Hedy would never forget the roses or the compilation albums. Nazi pig. Hateful, evil prick, she thought. You, I'll never forgive. All you see are dollar signs in that grave.

The rabbi began softly with prayers in Hebrew. There were mumbled responses from the crowd. Then he spoke aloud in English. "We are gathered here today to mourn the passing of one of our great artists. Like all of us, Richard was only a visitor in this life. During that time, he enriched all of our lives in ways none of us can measure, but 'All things must pass; all that lives must die; all that we prize is but lent to us. The time comes when we must surrender it. We are all travelers on the same road that leads to the same end. . . .' "

Hedy looked around her at the artists and executives, the press and opinion makers, each one making his own "special guest appearance" at the ultimate rock-and-roll funeral. They were dressed up in black silk, black leather, black suede and velvet. Dressed to be seen, as if they were attending the Grammies. These mourners were the very people who had made and unmade Miss Hedy Harlowe. These people didn't love Rick. They were too wrapped up in their own egos to love anybody but themselves, just as she had once been. Even the fickle fans screaming outside the gates loved only some cardboard Rick, a fantasy creature created by the record company.

They were the users and the takers. Using and taking the creative juice of talent and exploiting it for their own selfish ends. She knew that Rick's death would make some of them richer; that the music industry would find some way of feeding its greed and avarice off his corpse.

She would never believe he'd killed himself. If he had, they'd either driven him to it or driven in the stake. Either way, she knew that, somehow, they had killed him.

The crowd suddenly stirred expectantly, shifting uncomfortably from leg to leg, looking about. David turned toward her and lightly touched her arm. Then she heard the rabbi's words: "Miss Hedy Harlowe, if you are present amongst us, please step forward and fulfill the request of the deceased."

As if at a séance, her spirit was summoned forth to reveal its presence.

The moment was at hand. It felt worse than all her opening nights. If she took that step forward, the eyes and ears of the music world would focus on her once again. They'd be expecting a ghost, or at the very least the same unchanged, outrageous creature with pushed-up tits, a lot of attitude, and body-hugging costumes, the consummate performer who always "gave good show."

Hedy suddenly realized why Rick had made his special request. He hadn't done it *to* her, he had done it *for* her, to help her regain her self-respect. To force her, even from the grave, to live again, to do for him what she wouldn't do for herself all these wasted years.

Hedy moved forward very slowly, like a child taking her first steps. She didn't care how she looked. She didn't care what any of them thought. She walked very deliberately toward the open grave, ignoring the stage whispers of disbelief, curiosity, and shock. When her shoes touched the pile of freshly turned earth that would cover Rick's coffin, she stood still, holding herself as tall as possible, and waited like the pro she was until the murmurs of the mourners turned into the absolute silence of expectancy. She took a deep breath, closed her eyes, and prayed.

Then, perfectly on pitch, with crystalline purity and bell-like tones, the greatest popular voice of two generations emerged once again, without amplification or gimmicks or backup singers or musicians. She sang her heart out, finishing for her friend, her lover, Rick, what he had started twenty-two years earlier at the grave of his Grandma Becky, doing for him what he could not do for himself. She sang his song, her song, the song only she and Becky knew he had written for her—"How Can I Go On Without You?"

When she finished, the sound of her final note hung suspended in the air. No one, not even the rabbi, dared to break the spell. Many in the jaded crowd sobbed. But Hedy's eyes were dry. Behind the veil and dark glasses, she was smiling. She had sung. She had felt. And to feel even grief was better than eight years of numbness.

"Thank you, Rick," she whispered. "Thank you for making me live again. I will go on, Rick, but I'll never be without you."

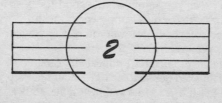

1956

ROSALIND FEUERSTEIN AND HER SON, RICHARD, walked into 1619 Broadway with mother leading the way. Rick followed reluctantly, clutching his homemade lead sheets in his sweaty hand.

She marched through the first door on the left, the one with the name Moss Publishing inked in black on the opaque glass, and walked smartly up to the receptionist. "Hi, I'm Richard Feuerstein's mother. We're here to see Mr. Moss." She felt her son's insistent tug on her jacket.

"Firestone, Mom," he whispered. "Rick Firestone."

The young brunette behind the desk continued filing her nails, blew on her fingertips, and slowly raised her head to look at the statuesque blonde standing tall before her and the skinny kid hovering behind her, near the door. "Listen, deary, it's like I told sonny last week. No meetings. You leave the sheet music and we'll get back to you. Got it?"

"You listen to me, *deary.* I think Mr. Moss should meet my Rick. It'll be good for him. Believe me."

"Really, sweetie? I think *I* know what's good for Mr. Moss, and it ain't your son."

"Yeah, I'll *bet* you know what's good for boss Moss."

"And what's that crack supposed to mean?"

"Just that everybody knows you're the woman behind the man, if you get my drift."

"You bitch!" the brunette squealed. "I oughta . . . "

Rosalind finished her sentence: " . . . oughta keep your mouth shut before I visit *Mrs.* Moss and have a little talk about you and your boyfriend. Why don't you do something smart for once, honey, and show us right in."

Rick couldn't believe his ears. He'd never heard his mother talk like that before. When they'd first walked in, he'd scrunched down in the background, his cheeks burning with embarrassment, feeling even shorter than his five feet, five inches and younger than his sixteen years. Now he stood up a little straighter. Maybe it hadn't been such a bad idea to let his mother accompany him. It sure beat having doors slammed in his face.

"Well, Mr. Moss is . . . ah . . . busy."

"Busy doing what? Picking his horse? Picking his nose? Go tell him I'm here," Rose ordered, leaning over the desk and glaring at the brunette. All the way on the sweaty, noisy, shaky BMT from Brighton Beach to the Brill Building she hadn't come just to have some *fehkokteh* receptionist give her the brush-off. Not when her baby, Richard, was a musical genius.

The intimidated girl sauntered into the back room with her hips sashaying as if to runway music. Two minutes later T. P. Moss opened his office door and swept his hand in with great panache.

"Sweetie, honey, come in, come in, welcome. Take a seat. Well, kid, what have you got for me?" Moss said, flopping down into a Naugahyde chair and putting his feet up on the edge of his desk.

Rick screwed up his courage and spoke out boldly. "I've got lead sheets, Mr. Moss, but no demo. If you'll just let me use the piano . . . "

"Go ahead, go ahead, darling, but I haven't got all day." Moss shook his head, gritted his teeth, and pursed his lips, all the while eyeing the busty bombshell, Rose. At age forty-two, her breasts were still big and firm and she'd dyed her hair almost white, like Jean Harlow's, and teased it so she looked like a gun moll.

Rick played his songs on the rickety piano and looked up for Mr. Moss's reaction. There was none.

"Rick . . . please, leave me alone with your mother for a few minutes, so we can talk business."

When Rick closed the door behind him, T.P. dropped his feet to the floor, pushed aside a pile of sheet music, and propped his elbows on the desk. "Look, Mrs. . . . "

"Firestone," she said, remembering her son's tug and reluctantly using the professional name that he'd spent so many months agonizing over. "But just call me Rose."

"Look, Rose, cookie, your boy shows great promise. With the help of the right publisher, he could develop. I think I could make him commercial."

"So?"

"So, we'd have to rent studio time, prepare a demo, put together a whole package. The costs, sweetheart, are very high."

Rose knew what was coming. She didn't answer. No reason to make it easy for the *gonif.*

"Sweetie, baby, here's what I'll do for you. I'll prepare a full kit, a presentation with real professional musicians performing on the demo, and I'll sign Rick to Moss Publishing. All this I'll do for you, darling, as a personal favor because I like you and your boy, for only, let's say, three hundred."

"Let me get this straight, Mr. Moss—"

"Please, T.P. Call me T.P. All my friends do."

"Let me see if I understand this right, T.P. You want me to pay you for the privilege of publishing my son's music?"

"Now, it's not quite like that, Rose."

"It's just like that, and I don't like it one bit. Even if I had three hundred dollars, I wouldn't waste it on bribing you."

"Bribe? Darling, who said anything about a bribe?"

"Cut the shit, T.P. I may look like an easy mark but I'm not."

Moss smiled lasciviously at the feisty woman. He stood up and walked around the desk until he was directly in front of her, his paunchy stomach level with her eyes. "Rose, listen to me. I understand three hundred dollars is a lot of money. So, maybe we can make an . . . arrangement. There are other ways of showing appreciation. You get lonely sometimes, don't you, sweetie? I know I do. Sometimes I crave companionship, someone to help me relax."

Now it was Rose's turn to be chagrined. This fat, balding slime wanted a "quickie" in return for what? For a promise to do nothing and get paid for it. If it was a quickie he wanted, she'd give him a quickie, all right.

"So you want to relax, T.P.?"

"Yeah, sure, Rose."

Rose slid up from her chair and gave T. P. Moss her most smoldering look. Then she quickly kneed him in his gazoobees, smiling disarmingly all the while. As he fell to the floor, doubled over in pain, she flung open the office door and rushed out into the hallway with little Rick hanging on to her for dear life.

Outside, in the warm September sun, they ran into the corner Chock Full O' Nuts to catch their breath. They sat down at the counter and ordered. The black waitress slammed down a white mug and filled it with coffee, then reached under the counter and tossed a whole-wheat doughnut on waxed paper in front of Rick.

When Rick bit into the tiny doughnut, and crumbs tumbled onto the counter and into his lap, he could see his mother was shaken. "Mom, let's call it a day. It's no use."

Rose sipped her sweet, creamy coffee. Although she was revolted, she wasn't about to give up. She hadn't gotten this far by being a quitter. Not when she'd managed to raise four kids on her own, with only her momma, Becky, to help, after her husband had passed away. She'd worked her way up at the Foundation Creations factory until she was forelady of 200 seamstresses. She was still a knockout, as T. P. Moss had just proved and as her new slick friend, Joey Gold, was going to prove to her again tonight. She had faith in her son's talent and she'd be damned if she was going to let the *meshugeneh* music business make her little Richard lose heart. "No, we go on. Today especially."

They started the rounds again.

On the second floor of the Brill Building, Rick noticed a man painting gold lettering on one of the doors. The first line read WORLDWIDE INT with the second word still unfinished. "Mom, let's try this office. It looks new. They haven't seen me yet."

Rose wet her fingers and tried to flatten Rick's hair into place. "Smile, Richard. And stand up straight!"

They maneuvered past the sign painter and into a room so tiny that they both barely fit. The "reception desk" was really a slab of plywood propped on old cartons, inadequately concealed by a piece of felt cloth. There were two folding chairs jammed against the desk and nothing on the walls. There was no receptionist.

Rose edged tentatively into the small room with Rick following. Since the door to the inner office was ajar, they couldn't help overhearing the conversation.

"Please, Mr. Norman, I have terrific credits. I've sung at every coffeehouse in the village."

"Baby, darling, we don't represent singers. I'm not an agent, I'm not a booker."

"And I'm not a singer. I'm a stylist, a performer. Just give me a chance to show you what I can do."

"I don't care if you're Fanny Brice or Edith Piaf, honey. I manage songwriters and publish music. I don't get bookings for singers. I'm not an agent. I can't get you work. I wish I could, but I can't. My audio equipment hasn't been hooked up yet, so I can't listen to your demo. Furthermore, cookie, your piano arrangements are illegible and there's no one here to accompany you, so you can't sing for me now." Despite the words, the man's tone was sympathetic and respectful. He wasn't coarse or rude like T. P. Moss and the countless other publishers Rick had visited. This man was doing his best to be polite, and Rick liked him instantly.

Before Rose could stop him, Rick squeezed past her and stepped forward two paces into an inner office no bigger or better furnished than the reception area. He looked down at a sixty-six-key minipiano that had seen better days, and up at an elegantly dressed man sporting a beautiful silver toupee, and a very big-bosomed, unkempt girl in a frayed cloth coat. She looked about his age.

Rick cleared his throat. "Uh . . . excuse me . . . "

The girl shot him a look that Rick recognized and understood immediately. "Asshole," her eyes were saying. A lot of nerve this pipsqueak kid had, walking in on her time!

"Excuse me, but I can read any music. I'd be happy to accompany you, miss," Rick offered in his alto voice.

"Thanks, kid," the smooth-talking Al Norman said, "but my company doesn't need singers."

"Oh, but, sir, you *do* need singers," Rick piped in. "You need professional singers to properly present the original music you publish. It'll help persuade real singing stars to record your songs. Most songwriters—except for me, of course—can barely croak the songs they write. Give her a chance."

The harsh expression on the young girl's face changed to a warm smile when she realized she had an ally.

Al looked the kid over. Hell, wasn't this what the music business was supposed to be about, giving young kids breaks? Where was the harm? He had nothing to lose and nowhere to go anyway since he wasn't exactly on top of the world at the moment. He nodded and smiled. "Go ahead, kids, you talked me into it. I'll listen. But I ain't promisin' you nothin'." The publisher motioned to Rose. "Come on in, sweetie. There's plenty of room!"

Rose squeezed into the little office as the girl beamed with joy and handed Rick some crumpled pages of sheet music. She wasn't beautiful or svelte by any means, but her face was interesting and loaded with expression. The big brown eyes, dark hair, and Egyptian nose gave her a kind of off-center appeal—as if she were a cross between Nefertiti and Keely Smith, with Sophie Tucker tits.

Those breasts. Rick had to struggle not to fix his eyes on the enormous mounds.

"I'm Hedy," she crooned. "What's your name?"

"I'm Rick," he said, sitting down at the piano. He started opening the sheet music, trying to find the beginning. It was torn at the edges and held together by strips of Scotch tape. He kept spreading it out wider and wider, like a Cinemascope screen, until it was longer than the width of the piano. On it were scrawled directions like "Go to section B," "Return to section A," "Repeat section D twice." He wouldn't have been surprised to see "Go directly to jail. Do not pass go. Do not collect $200," since it read more like a Monopoly board than sheet music.

Rick studied the music. It was an old tune from the Twenties, but the tempo arrangement read, oddly, "Lento Romantico." Sight-reading even a mess like this was a breeze for Rick after the grueling musical training he'd received at Juilliard. He looked up at Hedy for a cue and began to play the intro very deliberately.

Hedy stood suddenly transfixed, staring out the single dirty window that opened onto a gray air shaft. She let her ragged coat fall slowly and provocatively off her shoulders onto the floor. Her face and body assumed an eerie, sexual glow, as if she'd suddenly been possessed. Then, as the piano intro ended, she turned to Al Norman and began to sing very, very slowly, pronouncing each word softly, breathily enunciating and pausing between each word.

"I . . . can't . . . give . . . you . . . any-thing . . . but . . . love, ba-by. . . . "

The publisher shifted uncomfortably in his chair, feeling the effect of the sensuous, erogenous, unique delivery Hedy was directing at him. She ignored all the traditional phrasing, breathed in all the wrong places, but somehow managed to create a style that brought new life and double meaning to the old tune.

It took Rick only a few seconds to realize what she was after. Playing off her arrangements, he began improvising a new, supportive accompaniment, one that accentuated the lusty mood this white Billie Holiday was creating.

Hedy sang with her heart and with her body, with her lips and with her eyes, in the pleading, anguished wail of a woman who had absolutely nothing more to give her man than her love.

"That's . . . the . . . on-ly . . . thing . . . I've . . . plen-ty . . . of, ba-by. . . ." The way she told it, her love was more than enough for any man.

When Hedy finished, she saw Rose was riveted. She clutched Rick, kissing and hugging him excitedly. They had made magic together.

"That's not singing, little lady," Al Norman said softly. "That's what we call a performance."

Hedy beamed with pride at the lovely words, knowing they were the supreme compliment.

"I'm out of my mind, darling," Al continued, "but you're such an incredible performer, I'll do what I can for you. You're much too special to sing for me, or even for my songwriters. Baby, you could overwhelm any song. But let me ask around, see what I can dig up for you. Remember, though, no promises, no guaranties. I don't book acts."

Hedy glowed, and smiled as Al turned to Rick. "And you, kid. You two make quite a pair. You're a top-notch keyboard man. Anytime you want, I can find you piano work, no problem. How many shows you cut, kid?"

"Cut?" Rick said quizzically.

"The kid doesn't know what cutting a show is? Am I dreaming? It's what you just did, kid. Like when you play a club or the circuit and an act shoves their music in front of you two minutes before they walk out on stage and you play it cold. Then you're in the business, you can cut it."

"What's the circuit?" Rick asked naïvely, figuring it was better to ask than pretend he was some smart-ass pro that he wasn't.

"The borscht circuit, the belt, the mountains."

"You know, Richard," Rose chimed in, "like Schwartz's bungalows in Loch Sheldrake where your rich uncle Abe goes for the summers."

"Excuse me, Mr. Norman, but I'm not just a piano player. I'm a songwriter."

"So, what are you waiting for? After what I've just heard, I'll listen to anything. Limber up those magic fingers and that squeaky voice and let's hear some tunes."

Relaxed and encouraged by Al Norman's enthusiasm, Rick launched into four original Firestone tunes with Hedy leaning over the piano, listening with rapt attention. They were ballads, slow and rhythmic, and Rick sang them with surprising beauty in his melodious, high voice. It wasn't a performance, but it was a display of some solid, catchy tunes.

When he finished, Rick held his breath and looked up.

Al rose from behind his desk. "Kid, you got a publisher and you got a songwriting deal, if you want it."

"Want it! Are you kidding?" Rick screamed. He jumped up from the piano and hugged first his mother, then Hedy. He'd show those kids from Juilliard. He wasn't going to spend the rest of his life playing somebody else's old, dead music.

"No hugs for me, kid," Al Norman joked, waving Rick away when Rick turned to face him. "Just put 'er there," he said, offering his hand.

"Hey, what's the name of this company, anyway?" Hedy asked.

"Worldwide International Talent Consultants," Al announced proudly. "Al Norman, president, at your service."

Worldwide International? Why not Global Worldwide International? Rose had to hold back her laughter at the incongruous name. The last thing she wanted was to be rude to this man after he'd been more than civil to her son. Full introductions were finally made all around.

"Come back tomorrow, Mrs. Firestone. I'll have our standard contract ready. And to show you how much faith I have in the boy, I'll give him an initial twenty-five-dollar songwriter's advance. How's that sound?"

"Just fine, Mr. Norman."

"And don't you worry, Hedy. I sure as hell won't forget about *you*," Al reassured her. "By the way, what'd you say your last name was?"

"Harlowe, as in Jean," Hedy boasted.

"Yeah, and Hedy, as in Lamarr, right?"

"You got it."

When they walked out the door of Worldwide International Talent Consultants, they were all on cloud nine. "Come on, kids, it's time for a treat," Rose declared mysteriously. "Follow me."

Rick and Hedy shrugged to each other and followed obediently. Ten minutes later they were standing in front of Lindy's, looking at the eight-by-ten glossies of stars in the window. Hedy looked longingly at Patti Page, then Teresa Brewer.

"In ya go, it's my treat," Rose declared, giving her nervous son a push and stopping her ears to Hedy's halfhearted but polite attempt to resist.

The place was jammed. After waiting a few minutes, they were seated at a little table toward the back of the big room, near the swinging kitchen doors. While Rick and Hedy searched the room for stars, Rose looked at the menu, then counted her money surreptitiously in her lap, under the table.

A tall waiter in a yellow jacket came up beside Rose, pencil and pad in hand. "Order?" he asked.

"Yes," Rose said firmly. "One order of Lindy's strawberry cheesecake, with three forks and three plates, please."

When the cheesecake arrived, Rose, Rick, and Hedy all clicked forks, pretending they were fluted crystal champagne glasses. "To future stars, may God let us be so lucky—my own Rick Firestone and Miss Hedy Harlowe," Rose toasted, beaming with pride.

* * *

The rehearsal in the brightly lit gymnasium wasn't going well at all. The girls kept trying to kick in unison like the Rockettes, but they were pathetically out of sync. Their kick extensions never reached beyond waist level, and they seemed to be fighting against their developing fifteen-year-old bodies. The boys were even worse, tripping over themselves like self-conscious clods, then giggling and making wisecracks at the sight of high-flying skirts and budding, shaking bosoms.

The dance captain, Joyce Heller, was firmly and valiantly trying to keep the crew of high-school sophomores under control.

"Come on, cut it out, creeps. If you want to make fools of yourselves, that's okay with me. But not in this show. Not if you want to win the competition. Now settle down and let's try it again."

"We need the music," one of the boys griped.

"Gimme a break, will ya? I know it's harder without the music, but we'll just have to manage until Rick arrives. If you keep complaining, *I'll* sing the music."

They all shouted back "No!" in unison and broke into laughter.

Joyce smiled warmly. "Now that's more like it. If only you could dance together like that. Come on, girls only this time. Over there," she said, pointing to one of the countless red basketball-court lines painted on the shiny wooden floor. "Position. Now ready . . . one, two, three, *kick.* Two, two, three, *kick.* Three, two, three, *kick.* Side two, three, *kick.* Reverse, two, three, *kick* . . ."

Standing three feet in front of her line of would-be dancers, Joyce cajoled, connived, kidded, and encouraged, trying to squeeze a performance out of the row of similarly attired, makeshift dancers. All the girls wore rehearsal outfits of sneakers, bobby socks, wide flannel skirts, and angora or cashmere sweaters. The fellows were still decked out in their school white bucks or saddle shoes or cordovan penny loafers, with crewneck sweaters on top of button-down shirts and cuffless, pleatless khaki chinos with tiny belts and buckles between their two back pockets. They weren't in costume, but they were certainly in the unofficial school uniform of Sheepshead High, 1956. All very Henry Aldrich and Archie Andrews.

In marked contrast, the fifteen-year-old director/choreographer looked shabby and shapeless in her adopted "Village" beatnik attire—red beret, torn jeans, black sweater, and sneakers (dictated more by poverty and a limited wardrobe than by any profound philosophical or political leaning). Because she was different but never threatening, smart but always open and friendly, and never seemed interested in stealing anyone's boyfriend, Joyce was uniformly liked. They all knew she had no parents but lived mysteriously with relatives, off in the bad section of Brighton, and that she was a self-taught ballerina with grace and an instinct for the stage. She was so arty and dressed so drearily that no one felt competitive with her. Instead of reacting to her take-charge attitude with jealousy or resentment, the students usually responded with enthusiasm and support.

They didn't know how much she kept bottled up inside her, how much strength it took just to keep going, knowing she'd been abandoned but never knowing why. Her aunt Ceil and uncle Al were doing their best to raise her, she realized that. But she also knew they never had wanted her and had taken her only reluctantly and temporarily on that fateful day when her mother drove off after her drunken father, promising to return but never returning.

Her own feelings of guilt and inadequacy were the worst part, even worse than the poverty and her aunt's resentment. She carried the burden of responsibility around her neck like a ball and chain, weighed down by the feeling that she was to blame; that if she'd been a better little girl, everything would have been different. As she approached high school, however, the pain had turned to grim determination and she threw herself into work and play with an unquenchable vigor and intensity.

The double side doors of the gym swung open and a tall, bulky presence entered. As he walked deliberately toward the rehearsal for the Sophomore Show Competition, Joyce turned and called out to him. "Hey, David, any sign of Rick? I really need his music."

"Nope. He was making the rounds again in the city. He said he'd try to be back by four."

"It's four-thirty already."

"So he's late. Come on, I'll help you." David walked to the upright Knabe piano, theatrically flipped the back of his Harris tweed jacket (with the worn suede elbow patches) as if he were wearing tails, and took a seat at the bench. He straightened his invariable knit tie, smoothed his hand-me-down corduroy pants, then opened the music and began to play his way more than adequately through Rick's arrangement of the George M. Cohan medley. David had a passion for music even though he lacked Rick's talent.

David Barry was the president of the student body and the BMOC—big man on campus. He exuded a sense of cool, confidence, and control far beyond his sixteen years. When most kids were anxious to blend into the crowd and not call attention to themselves, David wasn't afraid to be different. He liked jazz and R&B music when no one else did (traveling to shows at the Village Vanguard in Greenwich Village) and wasn't ashamed to admit it. Funny and self-deprecating, bright and outspoken, he was the school charmer, the boy with the golden tongue. It was David whom mothers adored and teachers enjoyed. Without being at all nerdy or too straitlaced, but with a certain hip style and élan, he was able to win the affection and respect of most of his classmates, even though some kids thought he was an a.k.—an ass kisser. Everyone knew he was "Most Likely to Succeed" and bound for glory.

At sixteen, David knew things that many of his fellow students would never know. He knew how to play "let's pretend" to the hilt, cover his flaws and make the most of his assets. He used his humor, his intellect, and his keen awareness to charm and seduce. Manipulating students and adults alike, without their ever realizing it, he generally got what he wanted. He *made* them love him. He *made* them want and respect him. He thrived on the admiration and needed it for his own self-respect.

Like Joyce Heller, David Barry stood out from the crowd. And like his close friend Joyce, he wasn't embarrassed to be different, to be a shepherd rather than one of the flock.

Suddenly, screaming in a high-pitched prepubescent voice, Richard Feuerstein came running through the gymnasium's swinging doors, past the folding chairs, and right up to Joyce, hugging her while he continued screaming.

"I did it! I got it! I did it! I got it!"

David jumped up from the piano and ran over to his two best friends. "Did what? Got what?" he and Joyce asked in unison.

"You owe me a Coke," Joyce whispered first, following the ritual, because they'd spoken the same words at the same time.

"A deal! I got a deal!"

"You're kidding!"

"No! I'm being published. I'm a professional. I'm really in show business!" Rick shouted exuberantly. "I got a publishing deal with a real publisher in the Brill Building and I met this incredible girl and I went to Lindy's for cheesecake and I'm signing contracts tomorrow and I'm officially joining ASCAP or BMI or whatever. From now on, I'm gonna be Rick Firestone and my name's gonna be on sheet music and in *Billboard* magazine, and I think I'm gonna shit in my pants 'cause I can't believe this is really happening," he said without seeming to take a breath.

No one could believe it. Here was little Richard Feuerstein. Rick the Stick. Short and skinny, with one weak eye that tended to rove but was getting stronger. Forever excused from phys. ed. with a note from his mother or his doctor. In a world where athletic prowess was the measure of a boy's worth, Rick was nothing short of worthless. The kind of kid who always got picked last—"Odd finger gets Richie." Except for David and Joyce, essentially friendless.

Rick came to life only when he was at the piano. He brought culture, class, sensitivity, and classical training to Sheepshead High—in other words, he was the class nerd. That is, until he began writing pop songs, and David and Joyce made him use his musical talent to help out with the school shows. That's when Rick began to emerge from the shadow of David, alongside of whom he was always walking, as if hoping that David's "big man on campus" imprint would rub off and stick to him like Silly Putty. Add Joyce to the mix, with her beatnik attire and tough, radiant teenage charm, and you had a pretty odd but inseparable trio of musketeers.

As Rick's announcement sank in, a wave of deferential admiration spread through the students. A few applauded spontaneously for the new mini-celebrity, displaying a newfound respect.

"That's so keen, Rick," Joyce said sincerely, wrapping him in her arms and trying, in vain, to lift him off the ground. "I'm so happy for you." She was too embarrassed to ask the "pro" with the stage name to run to the upright and play music for the rehearsal. "Okay, that's it for today," she called out, knowing that his announcement had effectively ended the rehearsal anyway. "Tomorrow, three o'clock sharp."

David pulled Rick away from Joyce and put his arm around him. Although he was genuinely happy for his friend and felt the contagious air of excitement, David also felt a tinge of jealousy. He knew he'd never have Rick's musical talent. And he knew that his position at school had just slipped a notch and that his dream of being the first to succeed was about to be shattered by the most unlikely candidate of all: the late, not-so-great "Richard Feuerstein."

Quickly, David forced the unworthy thought from his mind and yelled out loudly, "Okay, everyone to Schmidt's for ice cream sodas, on me! We're gonna celebrate. We've got a star in our midst."

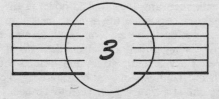

1957

7HE TRAFFIC CRAWLED BY ON FIFTY-SEVENTH STREET, horns honking and motors humming, as Joyce and David saw their friend off on his first business adventure.

"Good luck," Joyce whispered, hugging Rick's overdressed frame. "Don't be nervous."

"Nervous? I'm practically peeing in my pants. What if I mess up?"

"You won't mess up, come on. Tell him, David."

"You're a cinch. She'll love the song. Now go break a leg, isn't that what they say?" David added, patting his friend on the shoulder and pretending to trip him.

Rick looked pale and his palms were wet with sweat. "Thanks for escorting me, guys. I don't know what I'd do without you."

The door of the white Cadillac opened and Big Tony emerged, towering over little Rick. "Come on, kid, get in. We gotta go," he growled. "Can't keep the lady waiting."

Rick waved goodbye to his friends and slipped into the back

seat of the Cadillac. He let his hand run over the soft tufted velour fabric. Noticing a little leather hook protruding from the seat next to his shoulder, he pulled on it and jumped when an armrest came tumbling forward. As Big Tony, in black shirt and thick white silk shantung tie, plunked down in the seat beside him, Rick nervously pushed the armrest back into place.

"Okay, let's get outta here," Tony said, leaning forward toward the driver. They pulled away from the curb in front of the office on West Fifty-seventh Street and headed southwest toward the Lincoln Tunnel. Tony sat back and began cracking his big knuckles, one at a time. "Ever been to Teaneck?" he asked, his eyes concentrated on his fingers.

Is he talking to me? Rick wondered, pulling at the tight, starched collar that Rose had forced him to wear. "Uh, no, I've never even been to New Jersey before."

"Well, there's a first time for everything."

He could say *that* again. There'd been a lot of firsts since that first day in Al Norman's office, but none as big as this one. Mostly, there'd been disappointments. In the beginning, Tin Pan Alley had turned a deaf ear to Rick Firestone's songs, despite all of Al's efforts. Still in high school but ready to take the music world by storm, Rick had been forced to take on "gigs" playing piano whenever and wherever he could. Cocktail parties, recording sessions, auditions, recitals—he did it all.

It was the Juilliard of the streets for Rick. As though by osmosis, his sensitive ear absorbed information about vocal ranges, show tunes and accompaniments, arrangements, charts, and musical figurations. At late-night recording dates, he watched the producers and the engineers, how the tracks were laid down, the mixing and the mechanics of making records. He was amazed at how much of it was trial and error, and as he watched the tedious process of recording, he realized that he could hear the finished sound in his head in a way even the musicians and the engineers couldn't. It was a far cry from Mozart, but it was still music, and that was a passion Rick heard in his head and not simply a collection of notes on paper or in the air. He said nothing, though; he just watched and listened.

Now, when he wrote his own music, he no longer heard simple, unaccompanied piano, he heard tambourines and bass, horns and strings, a full musical production. In his head he embellished and orchestrated and heard not only how it *could* sound but how it *should* sound. But that wasn't what Tin Pan

Alley heard. They were hearing only a hollow, empty piano-and-voice demo. They couldn't hear the essence of the song without the trappings.

The breakthrough came when he persuaded Al to let him make a real demo. He'd pulled it off for $200, getting cheap studio time, working the mixing board himself, playing all the instruments, singing harmony with himself. It sounded great and the song was placed immediately, as a "B" side for Steve Lawrence. At one cent per side and sales of 300,000 singles, Rick made himself a tidy $3,000, plus the performance royalties. Other "B" sides followed, and a couple of album cuts, but no opportunity like this one. This was a biggie.

After a forty-five-minute ride, the Caddy pulled up to a large suburban house with a circular driveway. The manicured lawn along the driveway was scattered with plaster of Paris statuary depicting Greco-Roman ladies draped in togas with water jugs on their shoulders. Rick followed Big Tony into a spacious living room filled with fancy gold brocade couches (covered in plastic), Formica tables with gold flecking, and, in the center of the room, a white grand piano, gold-spray-trimmed. Rick found it all staggeringly impressive, so clean and showy it reminded him of the Castro Convertible showroom at Broadway and Forty-seventh Street, where Rose had once taken him to get a taste of imagined luxury.

When he saw Rina Constance, Rick's stomach did a somersault. A star, a real pop singer! She was hot now, her last single, the oldie-but-goody "Don't Blame Me," still high on the charts. She'd struck gold with a number of traditional ballads but was desperate for a new contemporary song.

Despite being overwhelmed by the lush surroundings, the star, and her tough manager, Rick felt confident. He'd done his homework, he was sure of his musical touch, David and Joyce had approved. Now, if only his gimmick worked.

"Pleased to meet you, Miss Constance," Rick managed to blurt out, offering his hand to the overdressed, youngish woman on the couch. Rick noticed that she wasn't nearly as pretty as her pictures; the pocked skin had been airbrushed perfect on her glossy photos. Since she was talking on the phone, she ignored his outstretched hand and Rick awkwardly withdrew it, trying to be nonchalant, reaching up to rearrange his hair.

When Rina hung up the phone, Big Tony tried to introduce

him. "This is the fellow you asked for, Serina," he said. "What'd ya say your name was again?"

"Rick. Rick Firestone."

"Take a seat at the piano, kid," Tony ordered.

Rick did as he was told. The piano bench was too high, but he resolved to make do, stretching for the pedals, rather than call attention to how short he was. Rina walked up beside him. "So you're going to write a song for me 'on the spot,' are you, young man?"

"I'm going to try, Miss Constance."

"I like what I've heard of your work, Rick, but nothing was really just right for me. I need something special, something written just for me and my unique voice."

"That's just what I plan to do for you today, Miss Constance. If you could start out by singing some standards for me, let me get a feel for your range . . . "

He ran through a number of songs, changing keys to accommodate her voice, accompanying her with a facility and style that couldn't help but impress the singer. Of course he already knew her range and everything else about her from listening to all her recordings and getting Al to do some digging. In fact, he'd already written the song for her. Only she didn't know it, and never would. She'd auditioned numerous other songs from a variety of writers, but Rick was the only one who'd offered to write a song just for her "on the spot."

"I think I've got a pretty good idea of your range and style, Miss Constance. Can you tell me something about the kind of song you're looking for?"

"Nothing slow and traditional, Rick. I want something new, light, up-tempo. You know the kind of song."

"Something that'll appeal to a younger audience?"

"Yes, exactly. Light and frothy."

"And the subject matter?"

"Love, what else? Something cute, maybe about teenage love or something like that."

"Something with a story, perhaps. You're crazy in love with a guy, can't get him out of your mind. You're not sure he's good for you. Maybe your parents don't approve. . . ."

"Yes. That sounds good."

"Just give me one minute to concentrate," Rick said. Theatrically, he closed his eyes, he hummed just audibly, he feigned consternation and concentration, then said, "I'm ready, Miss Constance."

He played the intro, then began to sing "You're the Devil in My Life."

Rina couldn't wait to get at it. It was light, it was romantic, just a touch sexy but completely inoffensive. Perfect for her limited range and somewhat nasal delivery. He'd hit pay dirt.

"My driver will bring you back to New York, kid," Tony said when Rina had finished going through the composition. "I'll take care of strikin' the deal with Al."

During the air-conditioned ride back to the city, Rick was in ecstasy, his mind racing. He imagined himself cruising through Brighton Beach behind the wheel of a white Chevy Impala, the top down, the wind blowing through Hedy's hair as she snuggled up to him in the front seat, Joyce and David lounging in the back. Rose and Grandma Becky would be showing off the mink stoles he'd buy them "for a song" at the Ritz Thrift Shop. He was on his way.

When he got back to Brooklyn via the BMT—he didn't have the nerve to ask the limo driver to take him to Brighton Beach— Rick bounded up the stairs of 711 Ocean Court. Grandma Becky greeted him at the door, picking him up and hugging him like the professional wrestlers she watched on TV.

"Come, come, Rickeleh. Sit. Eat. I made you a *glasel* tea *mit* rugelah."

"Nana, I did it! Rina Constance liked my song!"

"And why shouldn't she like a good song after the dreck she's used to? Come, we'll celebrate. Put 'Tico Tico' on the Victrola for old times' sake."

"It's called a 'hi-fi' now, grandma. I just bought it."

"Hi-fi, schmi-fi, it plays music, yes?"

"Yes, grandma."

Becky and Rick proceeded to samba, laughing and giggling as they used to do when Rick was younger. Even though she was nearly seventy-nine, Becky was still the most glamorous grandma in Brighton, unlike any of the other *bubbas* and *nanas*. They were stout, matronly, hair in buns, wearing dark shawls and housecoats.

Becky was a tall, full-figured, Rubenesque woman with pure white hair braided in exotic knots and interwoven with brilliant brocaded ribbon. Large, bright, inexpensive earrings hung from her ears and she always wore colorful, intricately embroidered

peasant blouses. A dirndl, a sash, endless clanking bracelets—
there was always some *schtik.* Born of Rumanian peasant stock,
she claimed she was half gypsy and half Jewish. She read palms,
forced everyone to eat a yellow cornmeal gruel called mamaliga,
and looked so dark and exotic that everyone in Brighton Beach
called her the Gypsy Grandma.

Then the loud, concussive knocking started.

"Oi vay—that *meshugeneh,* Mrs. Gitlin. She doesn't like the
noise of dancing on her head. My luck, a screwball neighbor
downstairs. Because I'm an old lady, she doesn't like to see me
dance. What can you do, Rickeleh? Everybody's got his own
meshugaas. "

Rick laughed and laughed. If anyone had her own idiosyn-
crasy, it was Grandma Becky. Forget all his formal music training; Grandma Becky was his true mentor. He remembered how
she used to dance when she was younger. Like a gypsy princess.
The samba, the rhumba, the cha-cha, the mambo. It was almost
nine years earlier, around 1948, when Becky was singing
"Miami Beach Rhumba" and making him sing melody "like the
Andrews Sisters." Even then, without understanding what he
was doing, Rick sang in perfect harmony exactly one-third
above his Nana, just like he heard on the radio, reproducing
perfect tonality.

"I started out to go to Cuba. Soon I was in Miami Beach—
that's not so very far from Cuba. Oi, vat a rhumba they teach!"
Rick would knock together two big wooden salad forks, making
"*mit* the sexy rhythms" like Xavier Cugat while Becky shook
the *pushka,* an old pickle jar filled with loose change, as a
substitute maraca.

Times and music had changed a lot since then, but Becky
always managed to keep up. Now she sang along with Buddy
Knox and the Rhythm Orchids ("Come along and be my pa-arty
doll, come along and be my pa-arty doll, come along and be my
pa-arty doll, and I'll be true to you, to you, and I'll be true to
you") and made Rick spin her around and dance the way the
kids did on "American Bandstand."

The dancing stopped when Rose and Joey finally arrived. In
his silk shantung suit, custom shirt with embroidered *JG* (for
Joseph Gold), and star sapphire pinkie ring set in white Floren-
tine gold, Joey was the closest thing to a "gentleman" Rose had
ever laid her eyes, or her hands, on. They'd met at Foundation
Creations, where Joey was a "financial consultant." Thanks to

Joey, the girls Rose supervised were turning out girdles by the gross on their newly financed Singer sewing machines. On Kings Highway and on Ocean Parkway, that meant only one thing: Joey was a loan shark. Between the Gypsy Grandma, Rick the young songwriter, and Rose's downright risqué affair, the Feuersteins were the talk of Brighton Beach.

Rick's youngest sister, Selma, the only one of the three sisters still living at home, followed her mother up the stairs and into the house.

"Home already, Richard? So, tell me everything. How'd it go?" Rose asked anxiously, kissing her boy on the forehead.

Rick told her the whole story in vivid detail, answering question after question—most of them from Selma—about Rina, her house, and her car. Even if the music was taking a back seat, he was glad to tell all.

"I'm so proud of you, Richard. It's just the beginning and don't you forget it," Rose said, beaming with joy. "Wait till I tell the neighbors!"

"Now, ma, don't go telling anyone anything until Al strikes the deal. You never know."

"Smart, talented, *and* careful. Didn't I tell you, Joey?"

"Hey, Rose, maybe I should talk to this Al guy. I know a thing or two about finances. Maybe I could help him swing a better deal for your son."

"Uh . . . I don't know, Mr. Gold," Rick said. "I think Al can handle it pretty well himself."

"Well, if you ever need me, kid, don't hesitate to ask. I got a lot of connections in show business."

Grandma Becky quickly passed around the plate of poorly made rugelah, her "belly bombs." Then she turned on the radio and started singing.

"A white sport coat and a pink carnation, I'm all dressed up for the dance. . . ."

* * *

When they walked by Balducci's on Sixth Avenue the next day, Hedy stopped and stared at the outside stall of fruits and vegetables. Rick was almost ten feet ahead, talking with Joyce and David, before he realized Hedy was missing.

"Hedy! *Now* what are you up to?" he called out, shaking his head and smiling. She was irrepressible, just like Becky, and she'd even taken to dressing like the Gypsy Grandma. In

wooden platform shoes and a wild, multicolored blouse, she
looked like ZaSu, Pitts. All in all, they were quite an incongruous crew, with Joyce in her slovenly beatnik outfit of ratty
secondhand shirt, torn jeans, and beret; David in his white shirt
and tweed jacket; and Rick in his khaki slacks and nerdy madras
shirt with the top button buttoned.

"Look at this fruit! It's fantastic!" Hedy shouted, first pointing
at, then picking up, a huge display basket. "Hey, wanna see me
give head to a banana?" she shouted lewdly. Before Rick had
time to blush or say "Carmen Miranda" (whom Becky used to
call "the lady with the fruitcake head who shows her *pipik*"),
Hedy had the basket atop her head and was dancing wildly in
the street, singing "The Lady in the Tutti-Frutti Hat."

Rick ran after her, with Joyce and David not far behind. As
usual, she needed an accompanist. Picking up two pineapples,
he started shaking the soundless maracas, clicking his tongue
against the roof of his mouth to make like castanets.

They attracted a crowd in no time. "Beatniks," someone whispered.

"Hey, bring that back!" the manager shouted, running out
from inside the fancy store. "Police!"

As Hedy looked at Rick in terror, she caught her high heel
on the curb. The basket tumbled from her head, spewing apples,
bananas, and pomegranates onto the street and sidewalk, under
everyone's feet.

"Go on, get out of here!" David whispered urgently, pushing
Rick forward with his hand.

Rick hesitated. "But—"

"Now! Get her out of here now! We'll meet up with you
later."

Heeding his friend's good advice, Rick grabbed Hedy's hand
and pulled her through the crowd. In a flash, she whipped off
her shoes and began running up Sixth Avenue behind him.
When she looked back, she saw a familiar scene from a silent
movie. As the Balducci man lurched after them, David and
Joyce bent down, on cue, pretending to pick up stray fruit, and
blocked the path of the rampaging grocer. Trying to avert a
collision, the grocer stepped aside onto a banana and landed,
splat, on his hands and knees.

Hedy and Rick squealed with laughter as they made their
getaway, giving silent thanks to their accomplices.

Hedy hadn't felt this zany in months. It had taken her that

long to recover. After that fateful day at Al Norman's, she'd survived by waitressing and singing backup "doo-wop" at recording sessions. Then, last winter, she'd gotten what she'd thought was her big break.

"Oh, shit, another cattle call," she thought to herself when she opened the stage door off Shubert Alley and saw the crowd milling about inside the theater. She had no choice but to wait. God, she wanted the part so bad she could taste it.

Stomping the snow off her shoes, Hedy tried to make herself comfortable for the wait, but it was fucking freezing. Everyone was shivering. It was Monday morning and the goddamned Shuberts kept the heat off on Sunday, so it would take all day for the theater to warm up. A nice assistant stage manager passed around a large container of Irish coffee from Sardi's, but Hedy was tired and unhappy and the only thing that kept her there was the knowledge that Hal Prince, out of the George Abbott School and straight from his *West Side Story* success, was casting for a new show and she was made for the part.

"WANTED: one crazy-zany female singer, must look 20–25, with pipes like Merman." That was her, to a T.

Fifty other girls thought the same thing, though, and they each had five minutes to prove it. Now, after five hours of waiting, five hours of studying the lead sheet until she knew every note of the song, the chill was in her bones and she just wanted her shot, even if the director noticed her only enough to make up an index card for future reference. Just when her spirits were hitting rock bottom, she heard her name called.

"Miss Harlowe. Can we have Miss Harlowe next?"

She made her way onto the stage, her knees shaking.

"First, we'd like you to sing something you've prepared. Then the song from the lead sheet."

Although the rehearsal pianist was no Rick, Hedy moved into her special rendition of "I Can't Give You Anything But Love." She kept waiting for the usual midstream "Thank you," i.e., "We've heard enough," but it never came. She was allowed to finish the entire song. She was encouraged, even though there was no applause.

As torchy as the first number was, that's how brash and brassy the show number was—and she sang it for all she was worth, belting her brains out to the second balcony.

A very dry "Thank you" was all she heard when she finished.

Life wasn't like the movies, after all. They were supposed to
come running down the aisle, jump onto the stage, and embrace
her. The pianist was supposed to hug her. The director was
supposed to say, "The role is yours, baby!" Instead, she walked
off to a cold, faceless "Thank you."

When she walked into the wings, however, one of Mr. Prince's
assistants called her aside. "Miss Harlowe, under no condition
are you to leave this theater. Mr. Prince would like you to stay
till the end of the audition."

Her heart pounded. This was it—her big break.

She got the role and two weeks later was in rehearsal. It was
only one song, but it was one song in a Broadway show headed
by a living legend of the theater, an aging Eve Harrington.

Four weeks later they opened at the Colonial Theater in Bos-
ton. After a two-week run, the show was on the verge of closing.
But every night that Hedy walked out on stage, her song stopped
the show. When a new director and a new writer were brought
in to revamp the show, Hedy got brash and went a step too far.
Boasting about the success of *her* number, she asked for—
almost demanded—a second song.

The next development was inevitable. The cast turned against
her and the star threw a fit. What choice did the producer have?
It was a simple $500,000 decision. A happy cast and a happy star
were indispensable; an ambitious, albeit talented, upstart like
Hedy Harlowe was not. So Hedy was fired.

She'd blown her big chance, and it took her months to cool
down and regain her sense of humor. In her depression, she
turned to Rick for help, and began sleeping on the Feuerstein
couch. Now she was accompanying him to Al Norman's to find
out about Rina Constance.

"Hey, wanna bite?" she asked, producing a salvaged banana
from her pocket as they walked uptown.

"Not in the mood, but go right ahead."

"Don't mind if I do, big boy," Hedy drawled à la Mae West.
Then, looking Rick right in the eye, she began slowly peeling
back the skin and sucking on the yellow fruit. It was downright
obscene and Rick was embarrassed and mesmerized at the same
time. Hedy might not have been the most beautiful girl in the
world but she sure could be the sexiest when she put her mind,
her voice, or some other part of her body to it. Rick watched her
lips curl around the banana and imagined himself in her mouth,

or his lips sucking on the nipple of her huge breast. If only he could find out what it was really like.

When they reached the Brill Building, Rick's hands were jammed protectively into his pants pockets and he was afraid to look Hedy in the eye. For a moment he'd forgotten why they were there.

"Rick, Hedy. Sweetie, honey, baby. Come in, come in," Al Norman said, hugging the kids like long-lost children as they entered the office of Worldwide International. "Sit, sit. So there's only one chair, so share."

Hedy sat. Rick stood, leaning over the desk impatiently. "Well?"

"Well, the good news is that Rina Constance wants to make 'You're the Devil in My Life' her next single 'A' release on RCA."

"Rick, that's great!" Hedy shouted, wrapping her arms around Rick's waist.

"Don't celebrate yet, children. There's a catch."

"A catch?"

"Yeah. A condition. The bad news. Miss Constance will record your song, but only if Regency Music publishes it and you sell your writer's share outright and abandon your songwriting credit. In return for which we get five thousand cash."

Rick's mouth dropped. "I don't understand, Al. Why would they want to do that?"

"It's the business, kid. Who do you think owns Regency Music?"

Rick shrugged.

"The fellow with the Cadillac, the one you rode to New Jersey with. Remember him?"

"Tony, Rina's manager? He can't do this to us, can he, Al? It's got to be illegal or something," Rick pleaded, the disappointment showing in his voice and in his face.

"Legal, what's legal got to do with it? He can do whatever he wants, sweetie. He's one of the boys. We don't agree, his underworld family gets nasty. I'm sorry."

Rick sat down on Hedy's knee. She stroked the back of his head. "So what does it mean?"

"It means I lose the publishing and you lose any writer's royalties, but we end up five thousand ahead, and I know we both need the money."

Rick thought of the finance payments due on the hi-fi and the used Sohmer baby grand piano he'd bought. And the help he wanted more than anything to give Rose and Becky. "Yeah, I sure could use the money, but what about my song?"

"I got an idea, kid. Listen. We'll take the five Gs, we'll give up the publishing and the writer's royalties. We'll get that stuff next time, but we'll insist on credit. I'll play tough. I'll tell Big Tony that we'll make the deal but only on the following two conditions. One, that you're credited as the sole songwriter on all records and sheet music. And two, that everywhere your name appears, it has to say that you're an exclusive songwriter of Worldwide International. So if it's a big hit, we don't get rich but maybe we get famous."

Rick stood up and started pacing around the cramped office.

"Hey, kid, sit down, you're making me nervous. Don't worry so much. It could be worse, lots worse. Look, talk it over with your beautiful mother and give me a call tomorrow."

"I don't know, Al. It just doesn't seem fair. If the song's a hit—"

"And if it flops? We end up ahead. Hedy, darling, take the star home, will ya, before he wears out my carpet. Go on, get outta here," Al said, patting Rick on the shoulder.

Hedy took Rick by the arm and led him to the door.

"By the way," Al said, "I almost forgot. What are you two doing a week from Saturday?" He didn't wait for them to answer. "Well, keep it open. I may have a gig lined up for 'Hot Hedy Harlowe' and her songwriting accompanist. I'll know by next week. Call me, sweetie."

Rick was quiet on the subway ride back to Brooklyn. He wasn't sure how he felt, torn between joy and disappointment. They got off the elevated BMT line, walked past Mrs. Stahl's Knish Store and down to the boardwalk. They walked toward "the ridge," where Hedy insisted on buying a round of Nathan's hot dogs in celebration. They ate silently, the taste enhanced by the Coney Island ocean breeze blowing grains of Brighton sand into the yellow mustard.

"Come on, Rick, cheer up," Hedy said, wiping a smudge of mustard from his chin and twining her arm into his. "Let's go back home and make some beautiful music together."

"Okay, good idea," Rick said, looking forward to sitting down at the piano.

When they got home, they discovered a note from Rose. The

three generations of Feuerstein women had gone shopping at Loehmann's and wouldn't return till late afternoon. For once, they had the house to themselves.

Rick sat down at his piano and started practicing a new tune. As Hedy began singing in her husky voice, Rick felt a familiar tingle through his spine. He loved working with Hedy. They interacted well. Ever since she'd come to him, they'd spent countless hours together at the piano. He reworked old tunes for her, created undershadings for the special nuances of her voice. She needed his arrangements, his choice of material, his taste and his instinct, his time and his talent. He understood her vocal limitations and her abilities better than anyone, and she seemed to understand things about him, things he didn't even understand about himself. They made a great team.

After about an hour, Hedy called it quits. "Come on, Rick, I've got something to show you," Hedy offered, walking back toward Rick's bedroom and beckoning him to follow. He got up from the piano and followed her wiggling ass into the room. "Shut the door," she said, flipping on the radio. The Del Vikings crooned about whispering bells in the background. "And lock it."

Still somewhat puzzled, Rick did as he was bid. When he turned around, his eyes nearly popped out of his head.

Hedy was standing there, unbuttoning her blouse. With each deft touch, the red blouse opened further. Rick watched her hand slide down from her neck to her waist, her brassiere showing more and more clearly. When she undid the final button, she pulled the blouse off, dangled it in front of her, then let it drop to the floor. It seemed to take forever to hit the ground.

"Can you help me with this?" she asked in a southern drawl, turning around.

Rick's knees wobbled, but he managed to take several steps forward and come up behind Hedy. His hands were shaking. He reached for the clasp of her bra and jiggled it, the way he'd seen his mother do. Miraculously, the clasp came undone. Then he reached up and slid the straps off her shoulders and watched the bra tumble to the floor.

Hedy turned around.

Oh, those glorious mounds! It was an erotic dream come true. Huge breasts, naked, like his mother's, staring him in the face! Hesitantly, he ran his fingertips over her white flesh and touched first one nipple, then the other, between his thumb and index finger. They were soft, yet taut. Better than he'd ever imagined.

She sat down on the edge of the bed. Encouraged by her smoldering look, Rick fell to his knees and buried his head in between her luscious globes. The smell, the feel, the darkness—it was ecstasy! Just like he remembered as a child, sucking on a mammoth nipple attached to a soft, warm, life-giving breast. He picked up his head and ran his tongue round and round Hedy's dark nipples.

She pulled him down to her and licked his ear, whispering, "Rick, do it now."

He did. It was the best. In fact, for the rest of his life, it never got any better.

1957

"**I** KNOW I'M DESPERATE, AL, BUT DID YOU HAVE TO book me into a fucking freak show?"

"Sweetie, baby, they'll love you."

"If I was a guy in drag, they'd love me!" Hedy exclaimed into the phone in exasperation. "But I'm not. When you said the Baths of Caracella, I thought you meant a restaurant downtown in Little Italy. I thought it was some fabulous deal—a private party. I mean, three hundred dollars for one night, for me and Rick—it's the most we've ever gotten. Tell me you're pulling my leg, Al."

"It's no joke, honey, we got a deal, we got a date. The guy at the Morris office set it up for us and I gave my word. It's union and you're gonna have to do thirty minutes at midnight Saturday for the boys, whether you like it or not."

Hedy hung up the phone and shook her head in Rick's direction. "The fucking baths! Jesus Christ, what the hell's gotten into Al?"

Rick wasn't about to complain about his publisher, not with Big Tony having agreed to Al's two conditions and the contracts freshly inked. He had the lion's share of $5,000 coming his way, although most of it would go to pay bills, and Rina Constance was about to make his song into an "A"-side single. That, on top of the memory of Hedy's tits, was enough to keep him flying high. "Come on, Hedy, it's a gig. That's better than nothing, isn't it? Hey, if I can take it, you can take it. Let's just do it and get it over with."

At 4:00 P.M. that Saturday afternoon, Rick and Hedy made their way down the steps of the Baths with great trepidation. There was no steam. In fact, the place was empty. Sound check coincided with cleanup time. Fresh towels, fresh linens in cubicles, disinfectant on the tiles in the steam room, fresh chlorine in the pool.

They couldn't believe the facilities. Built in 1921 and converted from a health club, the place even had a lavish restaurant, with everything done in old tiles, mosaics, mirrors, beautiful arches, and elaborate Moorish-style architectural detail. It was all too too elegant, more like the City Center than a downtown bathhouse.

Rick sidled up to the upright Baldwin. The sound system was nice, the acoustics good, and, surprisingly, the piano was in tune. They did ten or twelve minutes, met the lighting man to work out some simple lighting cues, chatted with the manager.

Rick began to relax. Hedy began to relax. Still, they both wished it were over. They knew what this place really was. It wasn't an auditorium or a nightclub, it was a sex palace. In a few hours, 500 men would be cruising each other and "carrying on."

They made a pact. "Eyes front, don't stare, be cool, just act normal," Hedy said, trying to reassure herself as much as Rick.

"Okay." It was agreed.

They arrived back that evening at 11:30. Music was blaring, lights were flashing, the restaurant was packed, the pool was filled. Everyone was male. The attendants wore hospital white ducks with white bucks and T-shirts that read, "The Baths of Caracella." Everyone else was either naked or wrapped in a small white towel. Keys to lockers or cubicles dangled from wrists.

Hedy smiled through clenched teeth and whispered, "Be cool,

Rick, be cool." Rick couldn't keep to the pact, though. The harder he tried to resist, the more his eyes were drawn to the nakedness parading about the room. He was glad when Hedy squeezed his hand and hurriedly led him into the kitchen. Behind closed doors, they both prayed for a reprieve, a fire alarm, anything that would force an evacuation, abort the evening, and cancel their performance.

After what seemed like an endless wait, the white-clad manager of the Baths popped in. "Okay, folks, I'll be announcing you in a couple minutes. Are you ready?"

No! Hedy wanted to scream. But she didn't. She smoothed her short taffeta skirt and adjusted the scarf in her hair. Rick straightened his tie nervously and fastened the middle button of his black jacket. The loud pop music over the P.A. system suddenly died and there was silence. Then they heard the announcement.

"Gentlemen, the Baths of Caracella are pleased to introduce, in her first appearance here, Miss Hedy Harlowe, the Heavenly One!"

Rick pushed open the swinging kitchen doors and waved her through. As she kissed him on the cheek, he whispered, "Be cool."

She stepped out and walked directly to the microphone, Rick several steps behind her. Most of the seats were empty. About seventy boys were sitting around the piano. The rest of the patrons were still playing in the pool, sitting and chatting with each other at the restaurant tables, or simply roaming about. There was a smattering of polite clapping hands. Hedy was practically ignored.

She kept her eyes closed so as not to laugh, not to cry, not to be distracted. Ignoring the boys, she immersed herself in the music and the lyrics. In her mind's eye she wasn't at the Baths; she imagined she was singing at the Blue Angel and everyone was wearing sequined gowns and silk tuxedoes.

She heard Rick and felt his supportive presence. They had worked out arrangements for fifteen songs, going back almost thirty years, mostly film tunes, show tunes, with a few pop songs mixed in, all integrated into a twelve-minute supermedley. A little Berlin, a little Gershwin, a little Cole Porter, Rogers and Hart, arranged as they'd never been arranged before, sung as they'd never been performed before. Hedy sang for herself, and for Rick.

When the medley ended, Hedy opened her eyes. Now, before her, were 500 practically naked guys on their feet. They stood. They applauded. They were respectful. No one was eating, no one was swimming, no one was screwing around. Something special was happening and the boys knew it. They knew the songs and they appreciated what she was doing. This was no ordinary singer, this was a *chanteuse*. She was jazz, she was blues; she stressed the lyrics, she gave them new meaning. She was someone special, someone just for them, and they all converged, worshiping her, her loyal subjects, shouting, "More, more, more!"

She felt good. She felt high. Looking back at Rick, she smiled and he nodded knowingly. He, too, felt the exhilaration and was happy for Hedy. The adrenaline flowed.

Although she had them, she wanted to cinch it, to make sure. Her right hand reached high above her head and pulled down twice on an imaginary cord. Rick moved into the "Trolley Song" and Hedy segued into nine solid minutes of Garland hits, ending with a sexy, smoky version of "The Man That Got Away."

The crowd went totally crazy. Now they were standing on their chairs. Hedy immediately picked up on their reaction to the lyrics. It meant something special to these men, many of whom had lost their own man. Before the applause could die down, she leaned over, whispered to Rick, and was cued in for her next number, "My Man."

When Hedy sang the last line—"It cost me a lot but there's one thing that I got . . . and whatever my man is, I am his, forevermore"—the boys were crying and she was too. She could do no wrong. She was heaven—Heavenly Hedy Harlowe.

The screams and applause died down. The room turned silent. They were waiting expectantly. Hedy looked out at the adoring faces and the sea of lean, well-cared-for bodies and white towels. She had yet to speak and wasn't sure what to say.

Making like Clara Bow with her lips, she placed her hands beneath her very ample bosom and pushed up. Then she set her hands on her hips and swaggered, shifting her weight from side to side. With her left hand on her left hip and her right hand behind her head, pushing her hair up and forward, she drawled in vintage Mae West tradition, "Boys, are you all carrying concealed weapons in those towels or are you just excited by my singing?"

Roused by their reaction, Hedy let loose all the pent-up *schtik* that she'd held back for years. Surrounded by a captive, loving audience, for the first time she felt free to let herself go, to forget all her compromises. The boys screamed in adoration. She was not only talented, she was funny. She was one of them. There, that night, without hype or hoopla, Hedy Harlowe became heir apparent to Judy Garland as the boys' number one *chanteuse*.

* * *

"Oh, that'll be the day-ay-ay, that I die . . . W . . . A . . . B . . . C," the radio sang out, holding the final high *C* as the station promo cut off Buddy Holly's final notes. Then the resonant, raspy, familiar, and frenetic voice of Cousin Brucie jumped in before silence invaded the airwaves.

"This one goes out to Sally and Tommy in Queens, to Joe and Judy on their first anniversary, and to all the kids at Sheepshead High"—the music started up in the background—"alma mater of Brooklyn's own cousin Rick Firestone, who wrote this new sure shot by Rina Constance."

David jumped up from his seat, turned up the volume, and dialed the phone.

"Hello?" Rick answered.

"Your radio on?"

"No."

"Well, why not? Hurry up, *putz*, turn on ABC. They're playing your song. Cousin Brucie announced your name."

"Hold on." Rick rushed across the living room and turned on the radio, already set to WABC, then ran back to pick up the phone. "What he say?"

"Something about dedicating the song to Sheepshead, alma mater of the great songwriter Rick Firestone."

"Really? He said that, really?"

"No, I'm making it up. So, can I have the star's autograph?"

"Maybe. If you help him with his history homework."

"Later. When Joyce comes by. We'll all do it together."

"Okay." Rick hung up, beaming, and flopped down on the couch beside Grandma Becky. "Hear that? I'm a celebrity, grandma. Cousin Brucie mentioned my name on the radio." He popped a packet of Sen-Sen into his mouth. The little granules tasted like soap.

"Celebrity? You hear your son, Rose? In Brighton Beach

maybe you're a celebrity. So where's the car and the minks, Rickeleh, and all that *chazerei* you talk about?"

"Come on, grandma. It takes time. I've got credibility now. Al can walk into any record company, agent, or manager in New York and they listen. I'm breaking into the big time."

"But, Rickeleh, listen to Rina Schmina singing your song! Her voice, it's in her nose. Not like when you sing it. An angel don't sing as good as you. Pitch, uh, so perfect. A falsetto like a bell. You know I'm telling you the truth, my darlink. Happy you won't be till you sing yourself. One-half of Richard Feuerstein, that's what you are now. Only when you sing your own songs will you be yourself, one hundred percent."

"Nobody sings their own songs, Nana, unless they're folk singers, like Woody Guthrie. Real stars sing other people's songs," he said halfheartedly.

It was true, but that didn't make it any easier. Once again Becky was telling him what he knew deep down but hadn't wanted to admit. Although he loved the songwriting, and he loved accompanying Hedy, he still felt unfulfilled. The Gypsy Grandma was right on target, as always. Just like she'd been last time, three years earlier, when he'd stormed out of Juilliard, fed up.

"Miss Goldstein, I don't think I want to go on. Maybe a semester's sabbatical would be a good idea." The dreaded words, rehearsed hundreds of times, were finally spoken. Rick sat at the piano, his face buried in the keys. He was afraid to look up at his teacher.

"Rick, you can't. You have talent, even potential greatness. It's a God-given gift. Six months away from our daily discipline and your technique will slip, the nerve synapses will forget, you'll lose the touch essential for concert performance—"

"But I don't want to be a concert pianist," Rick said, squirming uncomfortably on the hard piano bench.

"Rick! You don't know what you're saying!"

"But I do. I'm not driven enough, Miss Goldstein. I can live without piano concerts but not without music. I don't want to end up bitter, teaching finger exercises to drippy-nosed kids. . . ." The end of the sentence, "like you do, Miss Goldstein," remained unspoken but understood. "I've been playing for you and for my mother, always for others and always other people's music. I just don't feel right. I feel trapped, unfulfilled . . . I don't know what.

"It's like I'm surrounded, with everyone pointing a gun at my head. The passion and love I once had for the music—it's not there anymore. I don't want to play for anyone else. I just want to play for *me.*"

She blanched. Her heart sank. She couldn't speak and had to hold back tears. Frances Goldstein couldn't bear the thought of losing her star pupil. She'd invested so much of herself in him. He was destined for greatness, she just knew it. She thought back to one particular lesson—an exercise that had started out as a game and had become progressively more difficult and challenging.

"Richard, now I want you to stop talking about Mozart—stop rattling off what you have memorized. I want you to *become* Mozart. Do for me what he would do—prove to me that you *are* Mozart."

He never knew whom she would choose, which composer, which style. As part of his learning process, he had to keep building his repertoire and his understanding of the great composers. How else would he become a great concert pianist? After all, it was a foregone conclusion in Brighton and at Juilliard that that's what he must be, what he should be, what he would be.

The fourteen-year-old hesitated at first, then turned to his teacher. "All right, choose a Mozart sonata. A piece I've never played."

Miss Goldstein smiled to herself. She knew what he was about to attempt: to perfectly sight-read and memorize a difficult composition. Until the day she died, she regretted not having tape-recorded that moment, so she could reconstruct and relive it over and over. She handed him a heretofore untried Mozart sonata.

He played it creditably, at sight. Then he continued with variation after variation, improvising imaginative, creative chords, moods, key changes, and styles, all based on the sonata but all original with Rick, all sounding exactly like late eighteenth-century Wolfgang Amadeus Mozart without a tinge of Bach or Beethoven or anyone else. He built fugues and minuets, each variation becoming more complex and more technically challenging until he finally returned to the original sonata, this time closing his eyes to prove that he had memorized it completely from having played it only one time, some seventeen minutes earlier.

He had become Mozart.

Miss Goldstein sat rigid, mesmerized. Then with great restraint she said quietly, "Well done."

She'd always known he was special. But it was in that lesson, when she saw the creative composing side of Rick for the first time, that she fully realized his taste and uniqueness, his ability to absorb and reconstruct everything he had seen and heard and learned about music. She knew she was right—she felt validated. All she had to do was keep driving him, keep testing the depths of his talent, his resilience, his strength of character. More than anything, she wanted him to "go for it." Until he stabbed her in the back and walked out of Juilliard.

Rick dragged his feet as he walked the two blocks from the station to Ocean Court, oblivious to the sights, sounds, and smells of Brighton. He prayed no one was home. What would he say to Rose, who had slaved away at the girdle factory to pay his tuition? And to Becky, with her dreams of his bringing glory to the family? He was letting them down just like he'd let down Miss Goldstein and her embarrassingly profound belief in his "talent." They'd never understand.

After investing years in learning about touch tonality—about Becksteins and Baldwins, acoustics, conducting, arranging, Béla Bartók and Villa-Lobos—now he was about to turn his back on it all.

He had to be alone. He had to think.

As he approached the apartment, second floor rear, he heard the blare of the radio. He opened the door, saw the silhouette of Becky bent over the hot stove, smelled her infamous and dreaded *holishkes* and *mamaliga*. The loud pop music—it was the Teen Queens singing "Eddie, My Love"—grated on Rick tonight. It was noise. Crude, harshly executed sounds emitted by strange people from strange places with stupid words. Kay Starr he liked. He could tolerate Patti Page, the "Hit Parade," Kate Smith, even vintage Jolson, but not "doobie-doobie," "shaboom-shaboom," simple chord structures, simple lyrics, simple hooks, all formula.

Not tonight, please, not tonight, Nana, he thought as he walked through the door. There was no sign of Rose, thank God. But it was Becky who was going to drive him over the deep end.

The cooking cabbage stank and the music stank even worse and Rick wanted nothing more than to be left alone.

That wasn't possible.

Becky grabbed him as he passed the kitchen and held him close, a little longer and a little tighter than usual.

"*Vos machtir?* The world is not over, my little *vontz.* You *think* it is, but it's not. It's all just beginning for you. Talk to Nana and I'll tell you *emmis,* the future of Richard Feuerstein."

"What are you talking about?" he said, feigning ignorance.

"Becky knows, Becky always knows, Rickeleh. Something terrible you think has happened, I know, so don't pretend. Terrible, it's not. Tell me, I'll help you. Trust me."

He couldn't hold back, not in the face of Becky's mind reading. He told her everything: what had been going on in his mind and what had happened at Juilliard.

She listened and showed no surprise. "Don't mope, Richard. Grow up. You're following your instincts, keep it going. Listen to me, you got *shpilkes,* you know what it is?"

Rick shook his head.

"You're restless, Rickeleh, and that's good. Now is the time for you to stop playing other people's music, to stop trying to please *other* people. Those old composers you play, they're all dead. Their music, though, it lives on, in pianos, in violins, in orchestras. They're immortal. Do you think, my darlink, that Bach's music will die? Your Mozart, will he be forgotten? God forbid! Their music lasts forever, longer than the singers or the patrons and even longer than the monuments the pharaohs built to themselves.

"For eight years, Rickeleh, you taught me about the music you were studying. You practiced on me and I listened. Now you must learn a new lesson. You're young. Start to write a little. No more exercises. Your lessons are over. Now write whatever comes into your head. Get yourself out of other people's heads and start being Richard Feuerstein. They wrote their music, now you write yours. This is no *bubbe mayse.*"

He was shocked. Becky wasn't as old-fashioned as he'd thought. She was perceptive, articulate, assertive. She was "with it."

Rick never reenrolled at Juilliard. Instead, he decided to give writing a shot. He'd show the Juilliard crowd, he'd show them he could be somebody.

Becky kept him from feeling sorry for himself. Becky kept

Rose from bugging him about leaving Juilliard. Every day, though, she nudged him. Every day she kvetched to him. Every day she rode him. "Become Richard Feuerstein, not some guy who plays piano better than the next guy. Don't pretend to be Mozart, be Richard."

At first he tried composing in the classical vein. When he showed the material to his old Juilliard colleagues, they called his pieces "derivative piano configurations, eclectic and without depth." It was just what he needed, another kick in the balls.

One day, when they were alone in the apartment, he played his music for Becky. She came up behind him at the old piano, smiling.

"Drop the left hand—drop the schmaltzy arpeggio, sonny. You don't have to impress me. Just play for me that simple melody you wrote, the so-called awful melody the Juilliard mavens called 'the show tune.' The one I like. The one I can sing."

He did as he was told.

"Not bad. Not bad. Now take that melody and play it just for me two times in a row and then stop."

He did.

"Now play it in a different tempo, darlink, a *bissel frailech*— faster, happier."

He did.

"Now play me a little bridge for about forty-five seconds like 'Oh, My Papa,' then go back to the pretty theme one more time, so Katherine Murray would love to dance to it.

"Fine. Now play the theme, then the theme again, then the bridge, and then the theme, in that order, and do it all in about three or four minutes."

"Nana, that's an AABA structure!"

"No, it's a popular song. After listening to radio eight hours a day for ten years, I should know what I'm doing. So play already."

So he played. And under Becky's guidance he wrote his first "song." From then on it was fun and games because of his ear, his training, and his innate gifts. All he had to do was listen to the radio, study the elements of the crap he heard, and regurgitate a Richardized version. It was a cinch. He tried it over and over again.

He tested it on Joyce and David. They liked it.

He tested it on the girls at school. They loved it.

He tested it with the Juilliard crowd. They laughed.

He tested his songs against the radio. They were at least as good.

Still, he wasn't satisfied. He went back to the piano.

As if he were in composition class, he called on his musical training, writing unexpected chord changes and progressions into his songs. Slowly, a pattern developed, a style emerged. The themes were melodic and singable, even memorable. The chord changes were unique. The lyrics were warm and personal.

For the first time he visualized his name on a 45rpm and on sheet music. "Richard Feuerstein" was all wrong. He needed a name that sounded tall, rugged, manly, a name like Tyrone Power or Guy Madison or Buster Crabbe. He spent months agonizing over his new name, trying out different combinations on paper, in script and capital letters, imagining how each would look on a theater marquee.

"How about Dick Stone?" Joyce suggested, spreading her hands across the air with the imaginary name.

"Or, Dick Wad," David joked.

"Cut it out, guys. This is serious. I like the Stone idea, though. It's solid, like a famous name should be."

"Richard Stonehenge," David recommended.

"That's too heavy."

"Boy, I hope you never have children. Your kids will be grown up before they have names."

But the ribbing didn't deter Rick.

> Erik Strong
> Erik Stone
> Erik Viking
> Erick Derrick
> Erik Satie

"Shit, I'm coming full circle, all the way back to the classics." He kept at it.

When he found the right combination, he was ecstatic. No one could ever criticize him for changing his name—he'd merely Anglicized it. Now it was strong. It was hot. It was heavy. The connotations were formidable. Richard Feuerstein became Rick Firestone.

Rose's harsh voice broke the spell of his memory. "You wanna sing? You're *gonna* sing," Rose called out from the kitchen. "You're gonna sing. Mama will take care of it, Richard. *I* got you the publishing deal, now *I'll* get you a singing contract. Between your name, Joey's connections, and my chutzpah, we're gonna get you an audition."

"Aww, mom, please. Forget it."

But she wouldn't forget it. The next day, at Rose's insistence, he talked to Al Norman.

"You're gonna confuse them, Rick. They want either a singer or a songwriter, you can't be both."

"I *am* both, Al. Tell me why not."

"You wanna know why not, I'll tell you why not. But you're not gonna like it. Your voice is too high and too girlish. You're too short and you don't got sex appeal, kid. You're no performing artist. A songwriter, yes! You're super, you're great. A singer . . . no, never. Be happy with what you've got, kid."

Rick was devastated. He shouldn't have asked if he hadn't wanted to hear the truth. And he sure hadn't wanted to hear Al clearly and succinctly articulate his worst fears and insecurities.

When he left Al's office, he walked south on Broadway. He was dejected. Although he'd promised to drop by Hedy's new apartment in the Village, he just wasn't in the mood. Maybe Al was right, maybe he'd never be anything more than a songwriter and an accompanist.

Still, it just wasn't enough. He wanted more. When he saw the audiences stand up and applaud Hedy, his whole body tingled. He wasn't jealous of her success, he was happy for her, even though they no longer shared the old intimacy. Since she'd moved off the Brighton couch and into her new digs, and since she'd developed an avid cult following, their relationship had changed. Business had supplanted pleasure. Their once budding relationship had taken a back seat to their careers. They'd tried to keep the intimacy going, but the complications were too intense and conflicted with both their ambitions. So they'd made a conscious but passive decision to drift apart and let the relationship slide.

Seeing Hedy's success, Rick couldn't stop imagining himself out there on stage, singing his own songs, the crowds screaming for more. He had the talent, he just knew he did. All he needed was the chance to prove it. If Al wouldn't give it to him, he'd find somebody else who would.

He pounded his fist into his hand and raised his entwined hands up to his chin. He'd do it. He'd do anything. He'd go with

Rose and Joey. He'd show all those Al Normans who didn't believe in him that he *could* be a star!

* * *

When Rick slid into the back seat of Joey's new Olds 98, he felt infinitesimal. Rose and Joey were both bigger than life, sitting side by side in the front seat. Joey looked greasier than usual with his white tie and white shirt under his best iridescent black mohair suit—single-button, shawl collar lapels, Hollywood-style—and matching suede shoes. Rose, snuggled up next to Joey in the driver's seat, was equally dolled up. They looked to Rick more like actors on their way to audition for a summer-stock performance of *Born Yesterday* or *Guys and Dolls* than managers of a future rock-and-roll star.

Between Joey's cologne and Rose's heavy, sweet perfume, the smell in the car was overpowering. Al was right, Rick thought to himself, he shouldn't be doing this—the whole idea was ridiculous. He shouldn't be competing with the artists who bought his songs. He was just going to make a fool of himself.

A wave of nausea suddenly swept over him. "Joey, could you pull over? I feel sick."

"Richard, sweetheart, what's the matter?" his mother asked, turning to face her little darling.

"Just pull over, please hurry," Rick pleaded.

Joey screeched to a stop on the side of the Belt Parkway. The last thing he wanted was the kid puking on the pristine interior of his treasured new Olds.

Rick ran out of the car and, clutching his stomach, vomited onto the crabgrass. Straightening up, he looked out over the dark water toward Staten Island. The ferry was pulling into dock, cars were whizzing by. A tanker moved slowly into the Narrows from Gravesend Bay. All around him life was going on. He retched again. No one really gave a fuck about him, a short, skinny kid puking on the side of the road. There was no reason and every reason to be sick.

He tried his best to spit the foul taste from his mouth, then walked back to the car, his head hung low, and climbed into the rear seat.

"Feel better now, Richard?"

"Yes, ma."

"Must've been something you ate, poor boy."

"Can we get goin' now?" Joey said, aggravated. "After all the strings I pulled to arrange this audition, I'll be goddamned if we're gonna be late."

By the time they arrived at the midtown office of Black Jack Records, above a Chock Full O' Nuts on Fiftieth and Broadway, Rick was in a state. He looked around nervously at the walls of the anteroom, plastered with faded eight-by-ten glossies curling at the corners and turning a faded sepia tone. At Rose's insistence, he sat down on one of the cheap blond Scandinavian chairs. After a short wait, they were all ushered into a huge and tasteful Mediterranean-style office.

"Joey, baby, hey, glad to see you, man," Jack said in a deep, resonant voice as he emerged from behind the large desk to shake Joey's hand.

Rick immediately realized why the company was called Black Jack. Jack, last name Black, was a cool and imposing Negro, six-foot-three, with broad shoulders and wavy, processed black hair. The fingers of his left hand were wrapped around an ivory-handled walking stick. He wore a white silk suit and sported a pink camellia in his lapel. Dressed like a pimp, the record-company owner was a slick, tough-looking dude, with a rough edge to his smooth voice and the muscle of a blackjack in his arms.

He bowed slightly from the waist and took Rose's hand, enveloping her fingers in his huge grip and holding on a little too long and too tightly. "My dear, this is a real pleasure. You are a genuine knockout momma, let me tell you. I've seen you before, haven't I? On stage or in the pictures?"

Rose blushed with delight.

Jack turned to Rick. "So this is the little star. Glad you could come, son. Go to it, don't be shy. Do not wait, sit at the eighty-eight and play your stack for your uncle Jack."

Taking a seat behind his desk, Jack leaned back in his swivel chair and regarded the boy. Unfortunately, nothing would ever compensate for the kid's appearance, Jack decided. He was too short and skinny to be a star in anybody's eyes but his mother's. Even though he wouldn't find new talent here, he owed it to Joey Gold—who'd worked some financial deals with him and his boys—to hear the kid out.

Relaxed a touch by the big, black executive's cool manner, Rick took a seat at the piano. As he did so, the door to the office opened and two other men entered and took seats around the desk. It was just what Rick didn't need, but he cleared his mind and launched immediately into his repertoire.

Everyone was quiet.

Everyone was polite.

Everyone smiled.

Rick played four originals straight through and then stopped.

"Very impressive, baby, very impressive," Jack said, genuinely intrigued by Rick's writing. The boy definitely had talent, but not as a singer, not with that alto voice and that skinny-belinny body. Anyway, he wasn't right for Black Jack's R&B–oriented label.

"You have a unique voice," said one of the junior-executive flunkies.

"Lovely songs. Lovely and melodic."

"Gimme a week or so, Joey. Lemme mull it over, talk to my associates. I'll get back to you," Jack said, escorting the Feuersteins to the door. "I appreciate your comin' down here. And, honey, I'm genuinely glad I had the opportunity to hear your boy. Don't you worry, he'll be a star someday."

"Did you hear that, Richard?" Rose bubbled back in the car. "A star, he said. And he was no rinky-dink fellow, that Jack Black. A little big and scary, but nice, a real gentleman. He liked you, I could tell."

Rick knew better. The audition had been a disaster and he'd been given a polite brush-off. He'd seen the rejection and pity in Jack's eyes.

Al had been right. He was just a skinny shrimp with a girl's voice, and nothing he ever did would change that. He would never audition again. He would never delude himself like that again. But he wouldn't give up. He'd keep plugging his songs and working with Hedy. If he couldn't be a star through traditional avenues, at least he could make a name for himself. He wasn't going to sit in the background and let everyone else take the glory. He had to promote Rick Firestone, no matter what it cost—or at whose expense.

1958 - 59

"*H*EDY, SWEETHEART, IT'S SO NICE TO SEE YOU."

"Hello, Rose," Hedy said, leaning over to kiss Mrs. Feuerstein's cheek. She draped her winter coat over the back of the chair and sat down. "I'm so glad you picked Lindy's; it always reminds me of the day we met."

"Only this time, no cheesecake for me. Too fattening." Rose pointed to her stomach. "I prefer salads."

"Me too," Hedy said, smiling. No matter how hard she tried, Hedy couldn't manage to look svelte. The "boys" didn't seem to mind, though, so what the hell.

They ordered their salads and when they came, Rose quickly turned the conversation to business.

"I hear you're gonna do a big concert, honey."

"Yeah, some promoter who'd heard about the gay circuit and my boys—you know, my following—approached the Morris office. Figures I can fill two thousand seats on a Saturday night at Town Hall. Pretty schnazzy, huh?"

"Town Hall, that's great. Now you'll get big money, I suppose."

"Well, bigger than usual, Rose, but Rick's bringing in two girls to sing backup, and a drummer and a guitarist to fill out the sound, so I have to pay for all that plus rehearsal time. Rick and I will split whatever's left under our usual formula."

"Who would have thought Richard would end up playing a concert hall—Town Hall, no less—like this? So who knew?" Rose pushed her salad away and zeroed in on Hedy. "Sweetheart, will the concert have posters and programs, like a classical concert?"

Get to the point, Rose, Hedy said to herself. She hadn't wanted to come to this meeting, but Rick had begged and twisted her arm. "Please, Hedy, meet with her. She just wants to feel like she's helping my career. Come on, it won't hurt. Meet with her, please, for me."

"Rick, you know how much I care for you, how much we care about each other. But Rose isn't a part of our professional life together. I see no point in talking business with your mother."

"She worries about me, Hedy. Now that bookings are coming in regularly, she wants the best for me. You can't blame her, can you?"

So she got conned into this meeting with Rose, the erstwhile manager. "Rose, why are you here?" Hedy finally blurted out, cutting through the shit and the small talk.

"Hedy, dear, Richard and you make a magical team and I know how special your relationship is. Believe me, no one is complaining about the deal, but Richard has to think about himself sometime. He needs to promote his name and establish a reputation as a musician. As it is, when he works with you, he's practically anonymous."

"What do you want, Rose? You want me to bill the act as 'Hedy Harlowe and Rick Firestone in concert together at Town Hall'? Or do you want me to put his name before mine? Or maybe 'Rick Firestone allows Hedy Harlowe to join him in concert at Town Hall'?"

"Please, Hedy, don't be silly. I'm a reasonable woman."

Hedy began to lose her temper. "A reasonable woman? Bull!"

Rose ignored the insult. "Richard deserves some tiny credit. Whoever heard of a singer with a one-man band/chorus/orchestra/arranger/conductor supporting her every note, choosing her music, and not charging like Stan Applebaum for the charts?"

Rick had coached his mother well. He was all those things to Hedy, as well as her inspiration and support whenever she performed, and all he got for it was a quick nod, a little bow, and nothing else. He adored Hedy, but he had his own career to think about. He wanted "billing," but he didn't have the nerve to confront Hedy. Rose's hide was thick enough and she had the chutzpah to talk for him.

"Whew! I see a little bitterness has built up in Brighton Beach."

"Bitter, who's bitter? I'm just trying to be realistic."

This is foolish, Hedy thought to herself. I can give Rick credit in small print on the bottom of a poster and on the programs. If only he'd asked me himself, I would have been happy to do it. But Rose, she's such a—

Before Hedy could finish her thought, before she had a chance to make the next move and graciously accede, Rose made the mistake of going a little too far, too fast. Despite Rick's appeal for Rose to be subtle, tact wasn't her strong point. Anyway, she wasn't comfortable with Hedy, especially since Rick paid her so much attention. Once he hadn't needed anyone outside the family to support him. Now he was working and doing God knows what else with that girl.

Misinterpreting Hedy's momentary reflective silence as rejection, Rose suddenly came down hard. "And, Hedy," Rose said deliberately, "I don't think Richard can work the concert date under circumstances that aren't conducive to his being in a good frame of mind."

Hedy blew up. "Threats, extortion . . . where will it end, Rose?" Even as she spoke, she knew she couldn't walk out on that stage, or any stage, for that matter, without Rick Firestone beside her.

"Hedy, Hedy, we're all family."

"Family my ass, you mutha."

"Don't be crude."

"Listen, is that it, is that *the* demand, is that the whole deal, or is there more to this blackmail?"

"Darling, don't get so excited. All he wants is a little recognition."

All *she* wants is a little recognition, Hedy thought to herself. Rick is too naïve for this kind of *schtik*. "Done," she said, standing up and grabbing her coat. She didn't say goodbye, didn't offer to go dutch on the check, she just turned her back and stormed out of Lindy's.

Rose waited until three days before the big concert to make her next move.

Ticket sales were so phenomenal that the promoters added an additional show at midnight. Everyone worked feverishly on pacing, on lighting, on preparing new material. The posters were printed with a small box at the bottom reading, "Special Musical Arrangements and Accompaniment by Rick Firestone."

Even Rose couldn't face this one in person. She had to do it on the phone.

"Hedy, dear, this is Rose."

"I gave Rick all the complimentary tickets I could, Rose. Please don't ask for any more."

"No, darling, I'm not calling about tickets. I just wanted to suggest something to you."

Hedy stiffened. "Yes, what is it now?"

"You plan to make a big entrance after intermission, in a new outfit, don't you?"

"Yes."

"Well, the crowd will all be seated, anxiously awaiting you, no?"

Hedy didn't answer.

"You know, for the first five minutes, there are always stragglers in the aisles and people fidgeting in their seats, so I thought as a filler, just to build the tension and to give you a little more time for your makeup and change, that maybe Richard could do one of his original songs, with girl singers and a few instruments. Now wouldn't that be a nice way for him to be introduced to the public—a nice thing for a friend like you to do for him?"

Hedy couldn't respond. She was choked up, not with happiness at the idea of helping a friend, but because she wanted to scream and kill and rip the woman limb from limb! How dare she! How dare this woman try to piggyback her son on *her* career and *her* success, forcing *his* music and *his* voice down the throats of *her* loving audience! She suddenly realized that Rose couldn't and wouldn't be doing this without Rick's complicity. If that's how he wanted it, that's how he'd get it. She knew it really wouldn't hurt her. Her boys didn't care about anyone else. In fact, they'd probably want her all the more after Rick.

So she agreed, but not before she'd made a resolution. Despite the feeling between them, Rick had to go. Not right away, but sooner or later, at her convenience, when she'd covered her ass and could afford to dump him. Damned if she was going to let him and that bitch ride to stardom on her back.

After Hedy's smashing success at Town Hall, and Rick's politely received and quickly forgotten post-intermission song, Hedy received an offer to do "The Dick Clark Show," a new rock-and-roll program airing Saturday nights on ABC-TV and sponsored by Beech-Nut. Although they wanted her to lip-sync to a prerecorded tape, Hedy insisted on singing "live" and got the backing of the American Federation of Musicians. They finagled a full orchestra of twenty-two musicians for her number.

Rick spent weeks writing out the music for each of the instruments, relying on his years of classical training. For the first time, his arrangement would be amplified by all the violin strings and horns that he'd always heard in his head but had never been able to hear "live" because of their tight budget.

Despite the evident tension in their relationship, Hedy and Rick both looked forward to their trip to Hollywood. The day before they were scheduled to leave, however, Hedy got a call.

"Hello, Hedy, it's Rose."

Oh, no, she thought, not again. What does that bitch want now?

"You know, for the TV show in Hollywood, Hedy, I understand they give free plane tickets to artists' managers. So Joey and I were thinking, since you don't really have a manager, it would be no big thing if you asked for two more round-trip tickets—you know, first-class, like you've got. I mean, they'll pay, so it's no big thing."

"No big thing, huh, Rose? Well, it *is* a big thing, just like your mouth. For Rick's sake, I've let myself be bamboozled, conned, and bullied, but there's no way I'm gonna be intimidated for a social escapade of yours. This time you've gone too far. If Rick isn't at Idlewild Airport tomorrow morning at eleven sharp, I go without him!"

When eleven o'clock rolled around the next morning, Hedy stood at the Pan Am ticket counter, tears running down her cheeks. As boarding time grew closer and closer, she kept looking behind her despite herself, thinking she heard his voice calling out to her. She had his arrangements and charts packed away in her luggage and knew she could get through the show without him. After that, she had six free weeks to try to seduce him away from Rose or find a new accompanist. She'd find some guy on salary who would be fireable, whom she wouldn't have to give credit to, who wouldn't be a prima donna, whose name wouldn't be on posters, who wouldn't be singing in her act, and who wouldn't be saddled with Gypsy Rose Lee's mother!

Still, no one would ever replace Rick, at the piano or in her heart. She hoped he'd show up.

Meanwhile, Rick waited at home by the phone. "She'll call," Rose told him. "Don't worry, there'll be a last-minute reprieve. She needs you, Richard."

Hedy never called. The Feuerstein family watched "The Dick Clark Show" on television.

Hedy's network debut was staggering. Her singing, atop Rick's arrangement, was inspired. She sang her heart out, torn as it was between sadness and the giddy sensation of freedom and liberation. Rick had written such lucid, articulate instructions for the conductor and the twenty-two musicians that, ironically, his absence wasn't felt because his musical presence was.

He was with her by proxy, although his heart ached because he was in Brighton Beach while she—and his music—was in Hollywood. Rick wasn't sure what he was feeling, whether the painful choking sensation in his chest was jealousy or whether he was simply missing Hedy and missing being with her at her moment of triumph.

He knew Rose had gone too far, but he didn't blame her, not at first. She only wanted a piece of the action just like he did. He and Hedy had helped each other. She had used him and he had used her, and neither one had done it at the expense of the other. He hadn't done wrong by Hedy. She couldn't blame him for wanting to make it.

It wasn't his fault that the more he tasted her growing success and fame, the more intense his own drive became. If only he'd wanted to be a concert pianist as much as he now wanted to be a rock-and-roll star. He'd tasted the forbidden fruit vicariously and there was no way he could live without more of it, without having some for himself.

When Hedy's number was finished, the TV jangled with commercials and the oily voice of Dick Clark carried across the living room. The blaring television and the well-meaning but painful comments of his family made Rick cover his ears with his hands and suddenly jump up from the couch and reach for his coat.

"Richard, where are you going at this hour?" Rose asked.

"Out! To David's. Anywhere to get out of here!" he screamed, storming out of the house and slamming the door in frustration.

The months following the breach with Hedy were hell for Rick.

They talked by phone but couldn't break through the tension, and the calls became less and less frequent, just like Rick's gigs.

It wasn't long before he was out of high school, out of work, broke, unable to contribute even a dollar to the household. In fact, he was more than broke—he was broken. His spirit was devastated by the split with his friend. Hedy was the first girl he'd ever felt for (not counting Joyce, who was like a sister), the first girl he'd had sex with. The first girl to walk out on him.

He tried to blame his mother, but there was nothing he could do. He didn't have a way to fight back. He couldn't even yell or cry. Now, alone, he realized how much he needed Hedy. He no longer had anyone to experiment with, musically or otherwise. He had no audience, no concerts, no club dates.

The pain was made worse by the absence of David and Joyce. Although they weren't very far away, just in the city, they were too swamped with their freshman studies to spend much time in Brighton. With Joyce admitted early on a Merit Scholarship to Sarah Lawrence, and David at Columbia already immersed in countless extracurricular activities and thinking prelaw, the two other musketeers were sympathetic and understanding but not around enough to console Rick. He talked frequently on the phone with David and listened to his sound advice, but he was still living at home and it was Becky to whom he turned for real solace.

"Even though the crowd just tolerated me, at least I had an audience for my songs, for my voice, for me," Rick moaned, trying to explain his depression to Becky. "I can't go on without her, grandma. I can't go on. . . ."

"Darlink, remember the day you came home from music school and the world was crumbling? You feel like that now, don't you? You're angry with your mother—you think she made too big a *tzimmis,* asked too much. Don't be angry, Rickeleh. You and Hedy will be friends again, you'll see. There is nothing you can't do, nothing too good for you. Look at me. Have any of my predictions been wrong yet?"

"No, grandma, not yet. But I'm not going anywhere. I'm just one more struggling songwriter churning out sound-alike junk for other singers."

"You're better than that, Rickeleh. You're hurt, you're in pain, so go write about it. Put the pain on paper. Try a little Puccini, think a little Tchaikovsky—they always make you cry."

Becky was right—once again.

"How Can I Go On Without You?" was Rick's finest piece to date. Not a pop single but a showstopper in the tradition of "You'll Never Walk Alone." A song that only Rick's high alto range could really capture, it was filled with intricate piano arrangements, reminiscent of Bach's two-part inventions, set in counterpoint to the vocals. It was a sad song, a slow song, a torch song in a minor key, a man singing about a woman who had walked out on him, singing a poignant, desperate, plaintive plea: How could he go on without her?

As Grandma Becky listened, she began to cry. She knew. This was it. The music lessons, the false hopes, the disappointments, the pain, all the waiting had finally paid off. "I'm so happy, Rickeleh," she said through her tears.

It was the first and only time Rick had seen his Gypsy Grandma cry. As she sobbed, Rick suddenly saw her as she was, a little old lady, so much smaller than usual, so shrunken, so wrinkled and tired. He wrapped his arms around her and hugged her and held her tight.

When Rick first played it for Al, the publisher practically jumped out of his seat. They both knew it was the best thing Rick had ever done. With such a hot property on his hands, Al even invested a little extra dough to ensure a top-quality demo. When it was completed, Al distributed it to a number of key artists and record companies. Then he and Rick sat back and waited, keeping their fingers crossed.

Rick had swallowed his pride and restrained his burning desire to record the song himself. Even though he knew no one could sing it like he could, he resigned himself to selling the song to a first-rate talent.

A week later Al got a call from Jackie Wilson's manager. Jackie had a really sweet tenor voice and was a black man's Mario Lanza. And he was hot, with "Lonely Teardrops" climbing the charts. Like every artist, he needed a follow-up for his latest hit. His record company, his A&R man, his manager, all of them were on the lookout. But they'd found nothing, until Rick's demo arrived.

"Mr. Norman, this is Sammi Jo Parker calling for Jackie Wilson. Yeah, how ya doin', cookie. Listen, sweetheart, Jackie got your demo. He thinks it's super and wants to record it."

"That's great, Mr. Parker. I'm sure Rick will be very pleased," Al said, bubbling inside with delight.

"There's just one thing, sweetie. Jackie'll only record it if *we're* the publisher. He learned the hard way: got screwed too many times by all those white dudes. If you want Jackie to record your boy's song, we call the shots, like the big-band conductors did in the Forties."

The silence on the other end lasted only a few seconds. No way was Al going to capitulate to another Big Tony situation. "No deal, baby. You tell Mr. Wilson that's impossible. I found Rick, I invested in him, I stood by him and nurtured him. I'm in the publishing business—it's my only business—and I don't intend to get squeezed out."

The days following the phone call were torture as they waited to see whether Jackie and Sammi Jo would capitulate. Rick backed his publisher a hundred percent, but neither of them wanted to lose the Wilson deal. He was the hottest artist they could hope to get.

Rick was in Al's office when the next phone call came. But it wasn't from Sammi Jo Parker.

"Al, honey, baby, it's Bob Wills, A&R with Corale Records. Listen, darling, who's that kid, the one who sings on the demo you sent me?"

"That's the composer, Rick Firestone."

"Oh, yeah, the one who wrote the Rina Constance song. Who's playing the piano?"

"The composer."

"Can he write string charts?"

Al put his hand over the mouthpiece. "Can you write string charts?"

"Sure, why?"

"Yeah, but why?" Al asked into the phone.

"We think the song's so strong that it's worth a forty-five-rpm single shot, even as an unknown. If we just add some string sweetening—it won't cost much—we'll have a full-fledged master. No one'll know it's only a demo. Who owns it?"

"I do," Al answered.

"Okay, I'll give you a production deal. Corale will distribute your master of 'How Can I Go On Without You?' performed by what's his name. We'll pay an eight-percent royalty. You pay him from your end and we'll advance the recording costs and recoup them out of the eight percent. Is that fair?"

"Fair."

"A deal, cookie?"

"A deal."

"It's just a one-off deal, Al, but we'll have a written option for more product if this long shot pans out. I'll write it up right away."

The phone clicked and Al was left holding the black receiver numbly in his hand.

"Well?" Rick asked.

"Fuck Jackie Wilson, kid. Whatta ya say to recording the song yourself?"

* * *

Becky couldn't wait for the Fourth of July weekend at the Brighton Beach Baths. The '59 summer season was about to begin and she was ready to dance and to *kvell*. Her Rickeleh was a star and, in Brighton, so was she.

When she awoke that Saturday morning, the sun was already blazing. She dressed with great care, donning the special outfit she usually reserved for bar mitzvahs. She wore all her bangle bracelets and the shiny new hoop earrings that Rickeleh had bought her. She did herself up with rouge, lipstick, and perfume. Her hair was coiled high on top of her head like the Grand Duchess Anastasia, and on her feet she wore new wedgies that lifted her up but not so much that she couldn't dance. She took her time and dawdled over her appearance, thinking about her Rickeleh.

"How Can I Go On Without You?" had soared beyond anyone's wildest expectation. It topped the charts for over ten weeks and had already sold over a million copies. Al Norman had taken a new suite of offices, hired a secretary/receptionist, and even bought himself a new salt-and-pepper toupee. Rose got her new mink stole, Joey got to tell Jack Black "I told you so," and Rick got a new white Chevy Impala convertible, even though

Hedy, still strangely silent, wasn't there to sit beside him in the front seat.

Best of all, Becky at last felt fulfilled. Her dream had come true.

Rick had been the itsy-bitsy, teeny-weeny piece of her own flesh that had kept her young. He'd been her Tinker Bell, flashing about, dazzling everyone with his precocity and talent and proving that her genes lived on and that she would, after all, live through another. She had danced and sung and played with the boy until his ear was trained, until he could hear and distinguish different instruments and rhythms, until he could sing in harmony and imitate all the sounds on the radio. His life—and Hedy's—was the life she'd never had because of the hardships and poverty of her youth. But she'd stayed around long enough to see him succeed and she was happy. Now she would live forever through her grandson's music.

And Rick . . . Rick was just the same. He wasn't cute or gorgeous or sexy. He wasn't Frankie Avalon or Fabian or Bobby Rydell. There were no muscles, no jagged chin, no pompadour in his thin hair, no aquiline nose. What he was was sweet, and every girl in America between fourteen and seventeen knew it. His voice gave him away, telling the world that he was fragile, insecure, that he wanted to be mothered, that he was unthreatening, that he knew what it was like to be hurt, because *he* had been hurt—after all, he didn't know how he could go on without her. He was every girl's younger brother. He was a *mensch* and he couldn't hide it. Success couldn't make him inaccessible or difficult or petulant or reclusive or outrageous. He sat patiently for interviews, he showed up on time, he was thoroughly professional on stage and off, and—thanks to Hedy and Becky—he knew how to give a great show.

When she knew the Brighton Beach Baths would be full, long after the hour when she ordinarily began her sunbathing ritual, Becky started her stroll to the beach. In addition to her costume, her vibrant personality, and her "visions," Becky was known for having *the* best tan in Brighton. She worked on it all year round, going up to the roof with her foil reflector every sunny day, even in the winter, leaning against a large brick wall, and drinking up the sun. Her brown, leathery skin and Rumanian accent left no doubt in anyone's mind that she really was a Jewish gypsy.

She carefully planned her route to the Beach Club that day. On her way, she passed by all her old friends, receiving compliments and congratulations on her Rickeleh's sudden fame as if it were her own. And in some ways it was. At the Baths—the so-called private beach club where the locals gathered to avoid mixing with the visiting riffraff congregating on the other side of the boardwalk at the public beach—Becky was a local celebrity. Since everybody knew who she was, she no longer had to show her pass. The ultimate compliment.

The Baths had always been the center of summer social life in Brighton. Even the poorest managed to scrounge up the $30 a season to share a three-by-three locker with three other families, where they could change and store their bathing suits and the moldy towels they'd taken from Goldman's Hotel in New Jersey. Each member got a cardboard pass with his or her photograph stapled to it, the use of an overcrowded swimming pool, the use of handball and tennis courts, and the privilege of sitting at the bandstand and hearing third-rate imitations of Kay Kyser. The pass impressed many of the European Jews who had been desperate for visas and passports in the Forties and who still remembered the feeling of being asked to show their "papers" in the old country.

Becky would always oversee the family ritual, which began each time with Rose admonishing the children. "Now remember, girls, don't let Richard out of your sight, don't talk to strangers, and don't go in the ocean—it's polluted and you could end up with polio like Reva Shimkus," Rose, still known as Rosalind in 1948, ordered her daughters.

"Momma, we'll be fine."

"Sure, sure, 'cept it's the season and the dirty people use the beach 'cause they don't got bathtubs of their own."

"Momma, please!"

"*Oi gevalt,* these people pee in the ocean. I'm telling you, it's disgusting. You kids stay in the private baths where you belong, and wear your garlic so you shouldn't get polio, God forbid."

Becky used to pack a *peckala* with enough food to feed the Trapp family for a week, homemade sun lotion made from baby oil and iodine, tissues not for the nose but for the tushy because the caliber of toilet paper was not up to Feuerstein standards, and, of course, her foil reflector. That had been ten years ago.

Today, Becky was alone. No *peckala,* no kids, not even Rose. The sun was at its apex at 1:00 P.M., blazing on her silver-white hair, as she finally made her appearance at her little corner of the beach. The yentas and kibitzers stopped what they were doing. Slowly, as if on cue, everyone in the area stood and applauded, cheering and shouting out encouragement for the Jewish Gypsy Grandma. Then, like magic, an accordion appeared and the crowd began dancing the hora around Becky. She danced for them, inside the circle. And here, in the glory that she had waited for so patiently, in the sun that she worshiped, in the clothing that she created and adored, with her best dancing shoes slipping into the warm sand, Becky danced her last dance.

The crowd gasped as she fell, half-conscious, onto the white sand, her eighty-one-year-old heart starting to fail. When the medics lifted her onto the stretcher and into the ambulance—dancing skirt, wedgies, and all—she waved weakly but theatrically to her subjects, like the queen of England entering her Rolls-Royce.

Inside the ambulance, she looked up at the young, white-clad man bent over her and motioned him closer to her face.

"Yes, ma'am."

"So, you a doctor?" she asked in a whisper, her voice cracking.

"No, ma'am. But I'm well trained. You shouldn't try to talk."

"This is expensive, no?"

"Don't you worry. It's all covered."

"All paid for, yes?"

"Sure."

The ambulance began to pull away from the curb. The crowd outside was twenty and thirty deep.

"So how come I don't get the works?"

"Ma'am?"

"This looks like my last ride and I want I should go out in style, so all Brighton Beach knows I'm going. You know, sirens and red lights and all that *schtik*—the works. This is my finale. So, what are you waiting for?"

The young man patted her hand and whispered to the driver.

Becky smiled blissfully as the siren blared and the red light twirled above her, reflecting off the surrounding traffic on Coney Island Avenue. Her exit completed in grand style, Becky closed her eyes, still smiling, and felt her life on Earth slip painlessly away.

That night, amid the tears, Rick found a letter prominently displayed on top of the shoe box that held Becky's costume jewelry. It was undated, so no one knew when she'd written it, but she must have put it there that same day, somehow sensing that it would be her last. It contained her final requests. She wanted no somber music or speeches at her funeral; instead, she asked that the hora be played and that everyone dance in her memory, that she be laid out wearing a party dress like the one she was wearing when she died, and that she be made up glamorously with rouge and lipstick so everyone would see her in death as they had in life.

And she made one final request: that Rick sing "How Can I Go On Without You?" at her grave.

Although no one really had the heart to dance, the hora was played the next day at Wellwood Cemetery in Long Island. All of Brighton turned out for the funeral of their Gypsy Grandma.

When the ceremony was over, the rabbi turned to Rick. But Rick kept his head buried in Rose's shoulder, unable to stop the tears from streaming down his face. More than anyone, Becky had been his soul mate. She'd been his comfort, the one who had known who he was long before he'd known himself. It would never be the same, never, ever again.

Rose pulled him against her breast and shook her head at the rabbi. With a few short prayers, the service was completed and the crowd began drifting back to their cars. Suddenly, Rick realized it was over, and that all of Becky's wishes had been fulfilled except the last and most important. He pulled away from his mother and ran toward the grave, only to watch the workmen shoveling dirt over the coffin.

Rick's pain was unbearable. He'd failed her and couldn't forgive himself for letting her down. He went through the first day of *shivah* like a zombie, as if he were dead. He couldn't respond to all the words of sympathy and couldn't sleep.

Early the next morning, he got back into his Chevy convertible and drove the two hours back to Wellwood Cemetery. He had a debt to pay. It was drizzling and overcast, as was only fitting. It was her love of music, her teaching him the instruments, the rhythms, the dancing, that had made him a star. Now that little piece of magic in his life was gone. He loved her and he'd let her down. Now he had to make amends. So, on that morning, in a fine summer mist, with no one except his Gypsy Grandma in the audience, he sang, a cappella, "How Can I Go

On Without You?" And he meant it. He meant every word of it.

As he turned from the grave, he saw a familiar figure approaching. It was a young woman, sobbing and holding a hanky to her nose.

"Hedy? Is that you?" he asked, incredulous.

She nodded. "I hope you don't mind. I had to say goodbye to her, Rick."

"Mind? Oh, Hedy." They embraced.

"She was so good to me, you never knew how good. All those nights Becky and I shared the living room in Brighton, she encouraged me, she let me talk my heart out, she listened to all my silly dreams and fears. We talked girl-talk, shoptalk, anything. She let me be Lois Rabinowitz and yet she loved me for turning myself into Hedy Harlowe. She said she wished she could live her life again as me, that I was like her daughter. She was prouder of me than my own mother. Lois Rabinowitz is Rachel Rabinowitz's daughter, but it's Hedy Harlowe's mother who is buried in that grave."

"Becky would have wanted you here." But not as much as *he* wanted her. Secretly, he was glad she'd heard him sing for his grandma the song he'd really written for her. Even from the grave, Becky was prophetic. She'd said he would find Hedy again, and he had, thanks to her last request. When *he* went—whenever that would be—he would ask Hedy to sing "How Can I Go On Without You?" over *his* grave, just as he'd done over his Gypsy Grandma's.

"I didn't come yesterday because I was afraid you wouldn't want to share your Becky with me. But I had to come today, alone."

"Well, you're not alone now, Hedy. God, I've missed you," Rick whispered. Then they crushed each other in a tight embrace and cried, sharing their love for the Gypsy Grandma and, secretly, although they couldn't admit it, their love for each other.

BOOK

2

The Sixties

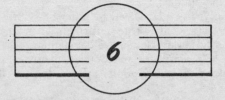

1962 - 63

WHEN JOYCE ENTERED THE COPACABANA, ON DAVID'S
arm, she felt overwhelmed and out of place. She looked around
at the vast room and shimmering lights with a mixture of awed
disbelief and disgust. The nightclub's decor was decadently
bourgeois, ultratacky, pseudo-rococo. The parade of fancy-
dressed adults all around her—women in sequined silk gowns
and expensive stoles—made her feel underdressed, self-
conscious, and defensive in her simple black jumper over a black
turtleneck and black tights, with patent leather pumps and her
distinctive black beret. And *she* thought she'd dressed up.

The Copa was a far cry from the artsy Sarah Lawrence campus or the smoky, downtown haunts, peopled with folk singers
and scruffy beatniks, that she frequented. Even if Rick *had* made
it big (had sold out?), she wasn't about to pretend to be someone
she wasn't. That was one thing Joyce Heller wouldn't do.

David at least looked respectable, even a touch pretentious,
in his usual tan tweed suit and vest, with his grandfather's watch

fob dangling from his pocket and a silver stickpin through his knit tie. Although he'd just begun law school (having graduated college in three years), he was already looking and acting the part. Joyce didn't seem to have nearly as much in common with him as in the old days.

Reluctantly, Joyce let David help her off with her coat and check their "wraps" like a true gentleman. Then they made their way hesitantly toward the maître d's station.

"May I help you?" the tuxedo-clad maître d' asked snobbishly, looking the young adults up and down as if they were chattel.

David spoke up. "Yes, we're with the Firestone party."

"Your names?"

"David Barry and Joyce Heller."

"Table one. Right this way, please."

As the maître d' led the way, gliding effortlessly through the maze of tables toward the front, Joyce steamed inwardly at the man's condescending attitude, then tightened her lips, closed her piercing green eyes, and stuck her nose in the air, in imitation of their snooty guide.

"Cut it out," David whispered, laughing and elbowing her in the ribs.

"Don't you dare tip him, David."

"Tip him! Where do you think we are, Yankee Stadium? He's not planning to wipe our seats off." Then he had second thoughts. What the hell did *he* know about nightclub etiquette? The only clubs he knew about were seedy jazz spots all the way uptown.

Before they knew it, they were down front at table one, on the same level with the stage/dance floor. Rose Firestone (neé Feuerstein) crushed each of them in a perfumed bear hug. "So glad you could come, kids," she said, beaming.

Joyce was shocked by the change. Rose's blond hair was now professionally dyed and teased, her wrists were dripping with jewelry, and a real fox stole was draped over her shoulders. A far cry from the old Rosalind Feuerstein of Brighton Beach.

"Joey, you remember Rick's old friends."

"Sure, sure. Honey, baby, how ya' doin'? Sit down. Have a drink, sweetheart," Joey Gold said, oozing oily charm and smelling of booze and expensive cologne.

Growing impatient at holding their chairs, the maître d' beckoned them to be seated. They took their seats and David finally found the elusive dollar swimming in his pants pocket, but only (thank God) after the maître d' was long gone. First crisis avoided.

They sat uncomfortably for several minutes, watching the collection of obnoxious adults at their large table drinking scotch, puffing on long cigars and cigarettes, and ignoring the existence of the two young people. Joey was in prime form, regaling the table with vulgar entertainment gossip and tales of his own role in "orchestrating" Rick's career. David leaned over and whispered in Joyce's ear. "That Joey guy gives me the creeps. I can't believe he's managing Rick. You think we should talk to Rick about it?"

"You're right, the guy's a number one slime. But it's not really our business, David." She said it with a twinge of sadness. Between schoolwork and Rick's career, neither she nor David saw much of their old friend anymore. If he wasn't touring, he was in the studio recording, doing hops, promotions, whatever pop singing sensations do. They still talked on the phone and she wrote him occasional letters, but mostly she devoured the "trades" to keep up with his career.

After his second single, "You're an Angel," shot to number one in 1960, everything Rick touched turned to gold. Since then, he'd had four more top-ten singles, a best-selling album, numerous TV appearances. Now he was headlining at the Copa and his star was still climbing. Just like his old friend Hedy Harlowe, who was making quite a name for herself as a singer and performer.

Of course, the press glamorized Rick's life, reporting that he was from "a fashionable oceanfront town" and that his mother was "an executive in a manufacturing company." He was also said to be five-seven and only eighteen years old. That gave him two extra inches and cropped almost four years off his life (which made Rick less threatening to the teenage girls and made Rose feel younger). Even though it seemed silly and unethical, Joyce realized that such stories were part and parcel of the whole media hype.

Because she loved Rick, Joyce loved his material. But other mellow white artists, like Ricky Nelson and Dion, weren't really her cup of tea. She liked it hard and raunchy, like Elvis, or relevant and political, like Joan Baez; Peter, Paul and Mary; or that new kid, Bob Dylan.

Finally, the houselights dimmed. The clatter of dishes and the buzz of voices gradually ebbed. The waiters, metal trays held high, flashed expertly between the tightly packed round tables, clearing half-finished plates and quickly refilling glasses. The smoky nightclub was jammed to the gills.

The loud twenty-five-piece band, dominated by the horn section, began to play and the Copa girls emerged in scanty outfits. The "girls" were all big, busty blondes and redheads—just the kind Rick swooned over. David wondered whether they were part of the teen idol's perks.

A pseudoballerina followed with fourteen minutes of turns *en pointe.* Then a stand-up comedian who'd been on the Sullivan show. After the dancing girls and the jokes, the headliner was due out. Rose grabbed Joey's hand and giggled in anticipation.

A rich-textured baritone voice announced over the loudspeaker, "Ladies and gentlemen, Jules Podell's world-famous Copacabana nightclub is proud to present the singing sensation of Corale Records, Mistuh Rick Firestone!"

Rick didn't emerge right away. He waited till the applause built to a crescendo and the band ran through the overture of his hits. Then, still offstage, he began singing "Pack up all my cares and woes . . . " finally emerging into the spotlight, mike in hand, to sing "Bye-Bye, Blackbird." He was smiling and waving as he sang, looking great in a beautiful steel-gray silk shantung tuxedo, his bronze face highlighted with dark pancake makeup, mascara, and eye liner. Under the intense lights, he looked handsome and un-made-up, a little taller and fuller than Joyce remembered (thanks to great tailoring and elevator shoes). A mammoth tourmaline ring graced his pinkie. The audience applauded enthusiastically.

For the first twenty minutes, Rick stayed out front, singing old classics, songs made popular by the likes of Eddie Fisher, Vic Damone, Dean Martin, Steve Lawrence and Perry Como. Every note, every gesture, every expression was professional and theatrical. He worked the crowd like a veteran, talking to them between songs, making them feel like he was there for them. By the time he took his seat at the black piano set under a spotlight in the middle of the stage, the crowd was eating out of his hand.

Joyce and David were in shock. They couldn't believe this was really their old friend, little nerdy Richard Feuerstein.

Only then, after he'd seduced the audience with their old favorites, did Rick sit down to sing his own songs. At one side of the stage, the backup singers, a trio of black girls, emerged to sing "doo-wop." At the piano, he was all original. All Rick Firestone. He was full of energy and enthusiasm, bouncing from one number to another until he had the audience singing along. He was wonderful and they loved him.

When he finished the set and walked into the wings, the audience stood on its feet clapping, shouting his name. After a few sips of tea and honey, he emerged for an encore. In a dark blue spotlight, he slowly and lovingly approached the front table and knelt down beside Rose. He smiled at Joyce and David but seemed to look through them. Then the band swung into action and Rick, taking his mother's hand in his, sang out his own, personalized version of "My Yiddisha Momma," singing to *his* mother and to every mother in the room.

Tears ran down Rose's face and the faces of many in the audience. When Rick sang his final note, they wouldn't let him go.

Feigning resignation and appreciation, and acting as though he hadn't planned it or rehearsed it all along, Rick finally quieted the audience with his hands and sat down once again at the piano. Then, very quietly, he began to play a Bach two-part invention, which evolved into his first and greatest hit, "How Can I Go On Without You?" Gradually, following Rick's exquisitely crafted piano arrangements, the band and then the string section joined in with a specially written Firestone obbligato.

At the second verse, Rick's voice cracked intentionally like a cantor's in the synagogue. He was thinking of his Gypsy Grandma and the day he visited her grave. He was thinking of Hedy. Tears dripped into his voice as he ended with a grand finale modulating up to a note so high that his range seemed operatic. Standing up from the piano while he held the final note, Rick tilted his neck all the way back and perched the microphone just an inch above his mouth as if it were a sword and he a sword swallower, as the light man narrowed the pink pinspot smaller and smaller and finally extinguished it.

The audience jumped to its feet again and applauded loudly, screaming, "More, more!" But there was no more.

Backstage, after the crowd had cleared and Rose had given the okay, Joyce and David pussyfooted into Rick's dressing room as if they were being granted a royal audience.

They saw the flowers and the telegrams and the bucket of chilled champagne. In the mirror, they could see Rick's face, so heavily made up that it looked eerie and unreal. Just as he was beginning to wipe away the ruddy No. 4 with cold cream, he noticed them and jumped energetically to his feet.

"Joyce! David! Wow, it's so great to see you! Did you like it? Did you like the show?" he asked, reaching out to hug them both. His voice raced, still high with the emotional charge from the performance. Like a true artist, his first thought was of himself, his first concern to satisfy his craving for approval.

David pulled back his hand and hugged his old friend. Joyce kissed him lightly on the cheek. The distance between the friends suddenly seemed immense.

"It was great, really great," David answered uncomfortably. Even though it had been a great performance, it had been very "adult," the kind of show David's parents would have better appreciated. He was more into jazz and soul.

"I couldn't believe it was you out there, Rick," Joyce said. "God, you're a regular professional!"

"Think so? Yeah, I guess I am." His eyes glazed over for a moment with a faraway look, as if he were contemplating his own achievement. Then the look faded and he returned to earth. "Cut the crap. You don't have to stand on ceremony with me. I know you think it's bullshit. But what the hell, it's a step up from the school shows, huh?"

Rick's self-mockery broke the ice and they all laughed, remembering old times.

"Come on, have some champagne." Rick poured the bubbly into glasses and handed them to his friends. "To old friends," he toasted.

"And new successes," David added.

After they'd clicked glasses and quaffed the champagne, Rick smiled impishly, like a little boy feeling his oats and delighting in all the attention. "So what's new? I want to hear all the news."

"Compared to you, nothin' much," David answered. "School, school, and more school. I can't wait till it's over."

"Same here," Joyce said.

"You graduate in a couple months, don't you?

Joyce nodded.

"So, what are you gonna do?"

She shrugged. "I've been working on my photography, but, seeing you, maybe I'll become a groupie," she teased. "Looks like it might be fun."

"You're welcome here, anytime."

"Hey, you don't need Joyce when you've got all those chorus girls," David said, shooting Rick a lascivious grin.

"Always room for one more. And what's with you, big shot? Decided what kind of lawyer you're gonna be? Besides a rich one, I mean."

"I'm not sure. Maybe entertainment. Then I could represent you, and you could get rid of that creep, Joey."

The smile suddenly disappeared from Rick's face. "What the hell's that supposed to mean?" he snapped. "I don't appreciate that at all, David. I know he's obnoxious, but Joey's doing a fine job. I've got no complaints." Rick lied. He was ashamed of Joey Gold and worried about Joey's business practices. Because of Rose, though, there was nothing he could do about it. David's comment had put him on the defensive.

"Yeah, but I'll bet you're getting big cash advances and guaranties when you should be getting higher royalties instead. With the royalties you make more money in the long run." David was feeling his law-school oats. "I just finished working on the Mantovani audit and I know—"

"Look, David, I don't need your advice. Go practice on somebody else. If you haven't noticed, I'm doing pretty well on my own. My life is in order. I'm really taking off. I'm well looked after. I've got my own corporation and Joey's building a nest egg. My future is secure."

"Sure it is, Rick. But you really should have someone from the outside check out the tax structure and the personal holding company and the Al Norman deal. It's a complicated business and Joey 'Gold Digger' might not know what the hell he's doing."

"David . . ." Joyce whispered impatiently, trying to get him to stop. But it was too late.

"Just can it, David. I don't want to hear your crap. All the time we were growing up, it was David this, David that, with little Rick tagging along. Well, the tables have turned. I make more in a month than your father makes in a year. And I've worked my butt off to make it. You don't have any idea what it's been like. The sleazy motels, the constant pressure, the million things I've had to do to keep my records selling. I write the songs, David. I sing the songs. I tour, I shlep, I save." Rick's face was turning red and his voice was squeaking in anger.

"This isn't school or the school show or amateur night. It's the real world. And I'm out here breaking my balls every night while you're sitting on your ass in some cushy library. So don't tell me about my legal problems. If I need advice, I'll buy it from the best fucking lawyer around, not some kid who's wet behind the ears."

Rick's voice was still and the room was deadly quiet. They all felt chagrined by the outburst.

"Jeez, Rick, I didn't mean to get you so pissed. I was just trying to be helpful. I'm real sorry."

Joyce put her arm around Rick and David's shoulders. "Come on, boys, what's all the fuss about? We're all on the same side, aren't we?"

Suddenly overcome with guilt, Rick reached his hand out for David's. "I guess I blew my stack," he said, hanging his head. "Friends?"

"Always, Rick," David answered, grabbing his hand warmly. "You can't take Barry seriously, Rick. You know he's always full of shit."

"I guess I forgot," Rick answered sheepishly.

"Forgot? That's something you can never forget," David joked. "Remember, everybody's full of shit. Except Joyce. Am I right?"

"For once, yes," Joyce said.

The tension was broken, but the three old friends still felt the heat of Rick's outburst and the chill in their relationship. All the questions Joyce had been dying to ask suddenly seemed unimportant. They chitchatted for several more minutes, then David and Joyce politely excused themselves when Rose and Joey burst in.

For the moment, each of them was happy to return to his own very different, very separate life.

* * *

Getting off the IRT at Sheridan Square, Joyce slung her trusty Kodak over her shoulder, walked the steep steps out onto Seventh Avenue, and headed east toward Washington Square. She was in a funk. Graduation was only weeks away, she didn't know what she wanted to do, her life was up in the air. Skipping class, she'd opted for her favorite pilgrimage down to the Village, where she could wield her camera—taking close-ups of bums, bag ladies, and beatniks for her collection—and then head to the Gaslight or the Figaro or the Night Owl for a long, introspective cappuccino.

She was into weird pictures, Diane Arbus stuff, and poetry like Ginsberg's "Howl." She'd had several exhibits at school— groups of photographs illustrating beat poems—but none of it seemed to be leading anywhere. Today she was thinking about putting together an album for Rick, a photographic illustration of his latest song—something to help them reconnect after the awkward scene last month at the Copa.

Entering Washington Square through the huge Napoleonic arch, Joyce weaved her way through the familiar hodgepodge of street musicians, tourists, NYU students, bums, protesters, and cops. The smell of marijuana wafted through the park. The early-morning rain had cleared and the day was steamy for May, with the sun playing hide-and-seek behind the rain clouds.

She paused near one of the benches, ran her hand through her long, straight black hair, and looked out over the crowd. Her eyes were drawn to a strange ray of light just across the grass. The whole park was bathed in shade except for one tiny spot, right around the fountain, where the sun broke through and top-lit a sandy-haired young man. Dressed in bleached dungarees, a red plaid shirt, and faded dungaree jacket, he was strumming an old guitar and talkin' the blues. His cheeks were scrubbed rosy; he had a peaches-and-cream complexion, an adorable cowlick, and he wore the cutest wire-rimmed glasses.

She felt an eerie chill, as if God had spotlighted him just for her. There was something genuine about him, something down-home and unpretentious that reinforced the feeling of fate or serendipity. She started snapping pictures, slowly moving closer and closer to him, all the while listening to his sweet-voiced, smooth-talkin' folk blues.

When she was only a few feet away, about to move in for a close-up and toss a quarter into his open guitar case, the young man suddenly stopped playing. There was a smattering of applause. Then he bent down, scooped up the change in the case, put away his guitar, and, without ever noticing her, began walking south out of the park.

For a moment she stood still, transfixed, watching the vision fade into the crowd. Then, impulsively, she took off after him, keeping a safe distance behind, and followed him several blocks until he descended the steps into the Café Bizarre. She waited outside a few minutes; then, without knowing what she was planning or why she was doing it, she walked into the club and took a seat at one of the tiny round tables near the front.

She casually turned her head to scope out the club, but the boy was nowhere to be seen. Mystified and a little crushed, she ordered a cappuccino, pushed aside the round candle, and reached down with resignation into her purse for the paperback collection of Emily Dickinson poems. Her vision gone, she was forced to come back down to earth and think about finals. When she raised her head, though, he was standing only a few feet away, guitar in hand, setting up a high stool on the tiny raised stage. She could feel the beat of her heart.

After he'd tuned up, he tapped the mike with his finger and cleared his throat. "Testing. Testing. Okay, Phil." He looked out over the six or so people in the dimly lit club, most of whom were reading or talking quietly. "Howdy, folks, welcome to Café Bizarre. My name's Derek Robertson and this here's a Bob Dylan song."

When he stared right at her with his baby-blue eyes and began strumming the guitar and singing "Blowin' in the Wind" in his midwestern accent, her flesh crawled with goose bumps and she became wet between her legs.

> How many roads must a man walk down
> Before you can call him a man?
> How many seas can a white dove sail
> Before she can rest in the sand?

He sang six folk songs, all covers, and received some weak applause from the distracted coffee drinkers and a hearty hand from Joyce. Then he packed up his guitar and walked right down to her table.

"How come you followed me here?" he asked, turning the chair beside her around and straddling it. Obviously he wasn't the kind of guy to wait for an invitation. She liked that.

She ignored his question. "I liked your singing," she said softly, her green eyes, like the eyes of a cat, penetrating through the darkness. "But you should do your own material. I liked your stuff in the park better." Like a true Sarah Lawrence co-ed, she had a definite opinion on everything.

"So you *did* follow me."

"Don't flatter yourself. I was just takin' a walk."

"You really liked that crap I was ad-libbing in the park?"

"Umm-hmm. You'll never get anywhere without your own

material. Unless, of course, this is just a lark and you're not serious about your music."

"Cool out, baby. Course I'm serious."

"Well . . . ?"

"Well, they won't let me sing my own material here. Anyway, it's no good. What's your name?"

"Joyce. Joyce Heller."

He looked at her soft black hair and heard the confident ring of her voice. She oozed strength and sensuality. He could definitely dig this kind of chick. "But I could use some help with my songs. You know, some inspiration."

"Well, what are we waiting for?" she said boldly. "Let's go get inspired."

He reached for her hand and they were off together, just like that, back to Derek's grotty little pad on St. Luke's Place, where they smoked a little grass and drank sweet white wine out of a jug. Derek burned sandalwood incense and turned the radio on softly so Shelley Fabares's velvet voice whispered her love of Johnny Angel.

Backs against the wall, sitting side by side on the thin mattress on the floor, Derek and Joyce sat awkwardly for several minutes, both with pounding hearts, both feeling high and self-conscious from the pot. Joyce felt the places where his arm touched hers; his flesh felt hot and sticky, like warm honey. She turned toward him suddenly, reached up, and slipped off his glasses.

He was beautiful. And, oh, so sexy with his blond hair falling down to his eyes.

In a moment, their arms were intertwined. He stroked her raven hair, then long and rich, pulling it back from her face, and began kissing her forehead, her eyelids, her tiny nose, and her parted lips. Their mutual need charged through their bodies like electricity. As he unbuttoned her blouse and she pulled the shirt off his muscular chest, the red shadows from the two hurricane lamps flickered over their smooth bodies.

It had never been this easy before. Everything flowed, everything was comfortable. Although neither was exactly a novice, this was something altogether new, this was spontaneous and electric, a thrilling desire that was carrying them both away. They reveled in their slippery sweat, laughing and exploring, and it was good—deliciously, wonderfully, memorably good.

After they had made love for nearly an hour, they lay side by side, naked on the wet sheets, and Derek lingered over her marvelous body, running his fingers up and down her leg, tracing the outline of her taut breasts, telling her the story of his life. He wasn't quite the American cowboy she'd imagined. The calluses on his hands were from guitar picking, not manure shoveling; his father was not a farmer but a well-to-do bank executive in Shaker Heights, Ohio, who'd bankrolled Derek to a stint at NYU, until he'd dropped out. But none of that mattered.

From that moment, they both knew it was no one-nighter. Unlike his usual high-school folk groupies, Joyce was bright and strong and pretty, a girl on the verge of womanhood, the kind of girl Derek could lean on. She wasn't clinging or too hung up. She was the kind of chick who'd ball you at a party and never ask, "Was I good?" She knew she was.

She started taking pictures of him that first night. He was raw and beautiful, always appearing luminous, as if lit from within, and bigger than life. Every time she looked at him, she felt wet with anticipation and her fingertip flicked the camera shutter with an erotic delight. He was her "Duke of Earl" and her "Good Luck Charm," and they twisted away that night and many more.

Two weeks later, when she graduated, Joyce decided she'd found a temporary vocation and his name was Derek Robertson. After saying her goodbyes to Rick, David, and her aunt and uncle, she pooled her funds with Derek and together they hopped an NYU charter to Europe and began bumming their way happily through Scandinavia, then south. They sang their way through Europe, with Derek working the streets and coffeehouses in Belgium, Holland, and France, singing American folk songs, while Joyce passed the hat, offered advice, and scrounged up gigs.

By the time they'd reached Paris and the Left Bank, Joyce had persuaded Derek to rough up his act a bit. It was early '63; the Beatles were just taking off in Europe, the Stones were about to be signed by Andrew Loog Oldham in London. She bought Derek his first electric guitar and they picked up a drummer and a bass guitarist. She kept badgering him to write his own material—remembering the lesson Rick learned from Grandma Becky—so he wouldn't be just a cover artist, copying other people's material. She began to mold an image for him, an image that suited the place and the times.

Looking at Derek one day, and remembering how Elvis shook

his fans into a frenzy, Joyce had a brainstorm. She talked him into letting his hair grow really long and persuaded him to take off his shirt under his denim jacket and to start moving around more on stage. He was reluctant at first, but he couldn't argue with the audience reaction. The girls ate it up.

When they reached London, the rock scene was hopping. The Beatles were just taking off, with a horde of groups kicking up a storm around them: the Shadows, Gerry and the Pacemakers, Billy J. Kramer and the Dakotas, the Searchers, Peter and Gordon, the Dave Clark Five. When Joyce checked out the scene, and used her balls and her brains to win a booking for Derek at a club on Jermyn Street, she knew what had to be done. She remembered Rick's performance at the Copa, how he had tailored his show perfectly to suit his audience. And she thought of the lusty Hedy Harlowe and the sexy, sensual performances she was famous for. She knew they hadn't gone far enough.

"You've got to trust me, Derek. If you want to make an impact, you've got to do it."

"But, Joycey, come on, don't ya think we're taking this image stuff too far? You're trying to turn me into a sex god or something."

"Well, aren't you?" she teased, snapping another picture of her new creation.

He stood six-foot-one in his old cowboy boots. His hair was now a little unkempt and shaggy, artfully lightened by Joyce in the sink of their cheap flat. The wire-rimmed glasses had been abandoned, as had the dungarees. Now he wore trendy bell-bottoms with no pockets, front or back, and no pleats. His usual size 30 had been exchanged for an extra-tight 28.

As he modeled for her, she said with a smile, "No, no, *mon cher. Maintenant, sans les* Jockeys."

"You've flipped, baby," Derek said, shaking his head but obliging her by removing his underpants and tugging his way back into the flares. The tight pants made him suck in his stomach and expand his chest. His genitals bunched together and appeared dramatically pronounced, just the way she wanted. He barely recognized himself in the mirror. He didn't know what to say or how to react. But Joyce knew.

She paced around him, giving him a thorough once-over. "Hmmm," she mused. "It's still not quite right. Too obvious." Then she had an idea. "Don't move. Wait right here."

"Yes, sir," Derek teased.

Joyce raced out the door and was back in a flash. "Put this on," she said, tossing him a black leather motorcycle jacket she'd borrowed from their next-door neighbor.

When he began to zip the jacket up over his bare chest, she grabbed his hand and stopped him. "Leave it half-open. . . . Yeah, like that. That's perfect, perfect! Wear it on stage like that until you're so hot and sweaty you can't stand it anymore, then whip it off and keep it off. Work stripped to the waist, but only when you're covered with perspiration."

He followed her coaching to a T and the word spread. The girls went wild, and soon the London music cognoscenti were wandering over to Jermyn Street to see the new American sensation.

Suddenly Joyce was so busy she didn't have time to think. She did everything. She arranged the lighting, seeing that he was lit from behind and above so he glowed the way she knew he could. She did the sound checks and made sure there was always cold beer and a warm terry-cloth bathrobe for him. She arranged a secret exit so they could avoid the screaming girls and so Derek would seem more mysterious and unattainable. She was his lover, his soul mate, his manager, his PR person—anything and everything to keep him happy, to keep things running smoothly, to ensure that he came across just right.

Somehow, without serious planning, Joyce and Derek were a team, with a gig and an income. For the first time, she felt she had someone and something to live for. Finally the nightmares—scenes of her father beating her mother, and her mother driving off—began to fade.

She was never jealous of the attention directed at Derek. She wasn't threatened or worried. Rather, she was happy just to stay in the background, knowing she was responsible for creating his image, happy to share that creation with the world. They were catching on, they were part of the scene. It was lovely and thrilling, and Joyce couldn't get enough of it.

One memorable night, after three hot sets at Jermyn Street, they stole out past the crowd, jumped into a taxi, and ended up alone at last at their East End flat. One bottle of wine later, her hands were wet and slippery with sweat and the juices of sex. It was July. Hot as hell outside but not as hot as inside of her. She was hooked on his body and could stop the craving only by feeling him deep within her.

The beads of perspiration on his face. The dozen candles

glowing, reflecting off his chest and highlighting the planes and angles of his face as it contorted in passion. She caught them all on the super-light-sensitive film in her new Hasselblad camera. As he began to breathe more heavily and his legs gripped her like a bareback rider gripping his horse, she pressed the automatic repeat shutter, capturing the convulsive, passionate experience of Derek Robertson's orgasm as he threw back his head, screamed in pleasure, and ejaculated into her.

That was the shot that became the photo sleeve for Derek's first hit single, "Looking at the Face of Love." Taken from below, the photo showed Derek's face and naked upper body bathed in sweat, with his muscular arms outstretched, his eyes closed, his mouth open, and his head thrown back in ecstasy. Thanks to her, girls all over England would soon be sleeping with that picture under their pillows, imagining Derek Robertson astride their *own* prone bodies, his face looking down at each of *them* with love.

It was only a matter of months before Derek was signed to a recording contract in London and the single broke. It was wilder than their wildest dreams. London was like a carnival, and Derek was the hottest new sideshow. The night life was fast and furious and in no time Joyce had to hire a bodyguard to keep the chicks from literally throwing themselves at Derek.

There was no high like the performance.

She taught him to jump out on stage and throw his head back theatrically, to emulate the now famous photograph. When he did it, the young girls in the audience practically wet their pants, driven to fanatic, almost religious, hysteria.

Derek never started slow. He came out hot and stayed hot and heavy, stroking and humping the long-necked red Fender Stratocaster until he worked the crowd to a frenzy. He slid up and down the shaft, treating the ax like a giant sexual tool, playing wild lead solos in the upper registers while he screamed out his passionate, lustful songs. It was music of the groin, explosively loud and distorted, shaking the floor and vibrating the ears of the audience until they were practically pained by the decibel level.

The more he gyrated and the louder he played, the more the fans loved him.

When Derek left the stage, placing his guitar on a Lucite stand, Joyce ordered the lights dimmed and an intense quartz pinspot zeroed in on the instrument. Left alone on the stage like a holy relic, outlined like a crucifix, the Stratocaster lay momentarily dormant and inert. Only the screaming crowd could bring it back to life.

Two thousand fans stood on their feet, holding lit matches, shouting, "More, more, more," stamping their feet in a rhythm that vibrated the steel girders of the club. They screamed frenetically when Derek returned, making him play encore after encore as if they couldn't bear life without him. When he finally did try to leave, the mob clawed at him like animals. As he and Joyce ran to the limo, raving fans pulled at his clothes and stripped the chrome from his car, clutching desperately for a piece of Derek Robertson.

From then on, for Joyce and Derek, there were no more secret exits and no more private moments.

1964

DEREK'S SINGLE SHOT TO THE TOP OF THE BRITISH charts in the winter of 1963–64. Then came an album, with the famous sleeve photo of the forty-five gracing the cover. Derek's passion-filled face plastered the walls of England, and suddenly they had money and notoriety.

It wasn't long before Joyce's photographic talents were in demand. Bands and record companies inundated her with freelance photographic assignments, and the rock community loved what they saw. Instead of the black-and-white, airbrushed glossies of the Fifties, which were posed, stilted, antiseptic, and uninspired, Joyce delivered a new kind of photo: musicians at work, with close-ups showing the stubble and the grimaces on their faces, the lines blurred in the frenzy of performance. She caught them at odd angles, blending in colored shadings and unorthodox contrasts.

The photographs looked like candid shots, even though some were carefully planned and deliberately posed, like Derek's whole act. Joyce satisfied the cravings of the young rock fans, providing them with intimate pictures they could moon over and clutch to their breasts.

When lightning struck, Joyce wasn't prepared.

Newly signed by an American record company, Apollo Records in New York, Derek had flown off alone to the States for a promotional tour in April of '64. Even if she'd wanted to accompany him—which she didn't, because of her work load— the record company wouldn't have picked up the tab. From the point of view of Thane Crawley, Apollo's president, Joyce was dispensable, if not downright burdensome. Without a management contract to wave in their faces, she was simply another groupie photographer, or Derek's "old lady," and there were always more than enough of those.

After a tearful, clutchy farewell at Heathrow, there followed a week of silence. Joyce placed a call to Derek at the Albert Hotel in New York.

"Hello? . . . Hello? . . . Derek, can you hear me?" The line clicked dead.

She redialed the operator. "Operator, I've been trying to call overseas to New York and I keep being disconnected. . . . Yes, that's right. The number is Turtle Bay 8-4500 and I'd like to place the call person-to-person for Derek Robertson. . . . That's right, Robertson. . . . No, not collect, operator, person-to-person . . . umm-hmmm. . . . It's a hotel, you'll have to ask for room four fifteen. . . . Yes."

Joyce waited impatiently as the operator reached the hotel, then rang Derek's room.

"Is this Derek Robertson?" the operator asked in a very nasal, very British accent.

"What?" came the disembodied, irritated voice across the ocean.

"Is this Mr. Derek Robertson?"

"I can't hear a fucking thing. Hey, turn down the radio, babe," he said, giving one of the little pixies a push out of bed. "Down, not up! Turn it down!" Derek shouted, and "Mrs. Brown's Lovely Daughter" finally faded into the background. "Yeah?" he said into the receiver.

"Mr. Robertson?"

"Yeah, I'm Robertson. What gives?"

"You've a person-to-person, sir, from Miss Heller in London. Go ahead, please."

"Derek darling, hi, how are you?"

"All right, I guess," he said coolly.

The crackle of static filled her ear. "God, it's good to hear your voice. I've been so worried, honey. The phones have been a mess and I hadn't heard from you. Is everything all right? You're not in any trouble, are you?"

"I'm fine, just fine. There's nothin' to worry about," he answered tensely and impatiently, sitting up higher in the bed and motioning for the sixteen-year-old redheaded nymphet to pass him the bottle of Jack Daniel's.

"I was crazy with worry. I didn't know what to think. It's not like you to drop out for a week without calling—that's not like my Derek—"

"*Your* Derek! *Your* Derek!" he shouted drunkenly into the receiver. "Hey, baby, let's get somethin' straight. I ain't nobody's man but my own and it's about time you realized it." He took a long swig from the bottle.

The pretty blond groupie, with the tattoo of a flower just above her pelvis, crawled back onto the bed, pulled the sheet off Derek's body, and, giggling, without preliminaries or subtlety, lowered her head down to his crotch.

"Derek, honey, it's me, Joyce. You don't have to cop an attitude with me, honey. We're in this together, aren't we?" she asked, grasping for contact across 4,000 miles. She heard the sound of muffled voices in the background.

But Derek was on the attack, his voice sharp as a razor. He was flying high from the booze and Librium, his inhibitions cut loose. "Cut the shit, Joyce. I'm tired of your running my life and trying to take credit for my career. You don't own me, you didn't make me, and your fucking awful photos don't sell my music. *I'm* the one who makes the music and sells the music, got that?" He reached over and cupped the perky readhead's breast in his hand. He tweaked her nipple cruelly, then slid his hand behind her head and pushed her roughly down beside the blonde, while she shifted her legs up toward his head.

There was silence on the other end of the phone.

"I'm hip to your tricks," he continued. "You've called the shots long enough. From now on we relate the way *I* want, on *my* terms, my way or not at all. I'm tired of being shadowed around by you, understand? If I want to talk to you, *I'll* call *you.* Hello? . . . Hello?"

The phone clicked dead. Derek dropped the receiver to the

floor, lay back, and let the two girls giggle and suck. When he couldn't get it up, though, thanks to the booze and drugs, he stumbled out of bed, pulled on his jeans, and, disgusted with himself, kicked the two teen queens out of the room.

He was flying high and his mind was a jumble. I oughta be proud of myself, he thought. After all, I did what Crawley dared me to do. No way was I gonna let a broad push me around and threaten my image or my career.

That was what Thane Crawley had told him last week at the headquarters of Apollo Records. The guy was cool and classy, real well bred, super-WASP, with a superposh office. Derek couldn't help but be intimidated. After a few minutes of small talk, Thane had walked up to the leather couch where Derek was seated and looked down at him with a commanding, almost paternalistic, expression. "Derek, this American tour will make you a star. You're going to be catapulted into the forefront of rock music. You're big-time now and I want to be sure that you're properly protected and properly represented. The first thing we have to do is obtain proper management for you and a top-notch booking agency. I've made some appointments for you this afternoon."

"But, Mr. Crawley, my girlfriend, Joyce, she's been managing most of my business," Derek said meekly.

"That won't do any longer, Derek," Thane said, cutting him off. "Look, I'm sure she's a very nice girl, but I'm equally sure that she doesn't know a thing about the record business. There are too many sharp characters out there just waiting to steal your money and take credit for your work. *You're* the artist, after all, and *you're* the one who has to look out for yourself. Besides, that association will only hurt your image. With your kind of act, you can't have a wife or a girlfriend in tow. It's girls who buy your records and they need to imagine you free and single. You can't disappoint them. Their fantasies mean money in your pocket."

"But—"

"No buts, young man. Remember, I'm the only one who knows how to look out for you and it's imperative that you trust me. If you want, call . . . what's her name again?"

"Joyce."

"Call Joyce your art director or your personal photographer or your executive secretary and put her on salary. But, Derek, you musn't be seen together in public as a couple. Everything you do is in the public eye now. If you want to make it big—and I know you do—your image has to be protected vigilantly. You don't want the press or your fans finding out that you have a girlfriend and that it's your girlfriend who runs your life. It could ruin your career."

Derek leaned back against the headboard and tried to blot out the memory of Thane Crawley. But when he reached down to the joint lying on the dirty yellow bedspread near his pillow, he couldn't help thinking of the record exec, since it was Crawley who'd provided the stash.

"Shit!" he hissed, squashing the flimsy joint between his thumb and forefinger. His head and heart ached. He picked up the phone and called London.

"Joyce, hi. I'm sorry, baby."

She was too groggy and confused to know how to react. The wound he'd opened was deep, and no glib apology was going to heal it. But she wanted everything to be all right.

"I'm sorry, too. I guess we're both a little edgy."

"Still love me?"

"You know I do."

And she did. But she wasn't sure any longer if *he* still did or if he ever really had. He'd needed her once, but now she'd served her purpose. Maybe she *had* been too clutchy, maybe she *had* emasculated him by always calling the shots. She'd tried to be sensitive to his ego, tactful and loving, but maybe she hadn't been empathetic enough, hadn't tried to see things from his point of view. She knew what was best for him and she had proved it. Maybe he hated her for it.

She knew damn well that wasn't the truth, though. Fans screaming his name; endless chicks spreading their teenage legs; cars, drugs, visions of big bucks. His ego was sky-high and he wanted to taste it all, literally and figuratively. Maybe little Joycey was obsolete. Maybe her presence reminded him too much of his mortality—and the lean days.

"I want us to be together, Joycey. We're good for each other. I miss you," Derek said, for the moment believing his own words.

"Me too."

"I met with the guy who runs Apollo. He got me a manager and a booking agent. He says I'm really gonna fly."

"That's great," she said, beginning to catch the drift.

"He thinks I should put you on salary, as my head honcho and photographer, for tax reasons, ya know?"

"Sure, sure, anything you want. Listen, it's the middle of the night here. I've got to get back to sleep, darling. I'm shooting a band from Liverpool tomorrow on location and have to catch the early train." She rushed through the farewells and clicked off quickly before he had a chance to object.

Then she cried herself to sleep.

When Derek returned to London, it was only a matter of weeks before their relationship turned sour and bitter.

The more dignified Joyce tried to be—the more she tried to play Mary Martyr and not stand in the way of his career—the more violent their arguments became. Every trifling matter from the past was rehashed and blown out of proportion. The little things that had once solidified them now tore them apart. Her very existence made him feel guilty and angry.

She wanted to be brave, self-reliant, self-assured. She wanted to tell him how much she loved him, that she'd always be there for him, that love was giving, not possessing. But his vitriol and the recriminations made it impossible.

The end came with a bang, not a whimper. He'd come back to the flat in Knightsbridge in the early morning after another all-nighter. She'd been sitting up half the night, sick with worry and burning with resentment. Why was he inflicting his selfish, childish behavior on her?

"You could have at least phoned, you know," she barked angrily, staring at the blond hair falling in his face, the hard lines in his forehead, and the newly acquired bags under his eyes. He was sloppy and drugged out yet again.

"Who the hell do you think you are, my mother? I'll do anything I damn please. If you don't like it, then get the hell out."

She couldn't take it anymore. Not the heartache, the abuse, or the erratic, druggy behavior.

"All right, Derek, if that's what you want," she said bitterly. She pulled her ratty suitcase out from under the bed and started packing. The suitcase brought back memories of the good times hitching around Europe. As she packed, she felt like crying but refused to let him see the tears that kept welling up in her eyes. If he wanted it rough-and-tumble, that's the way he'd get it.

Surly and silent, Derek sat rocking in the corner chair, watching her intently and pointedly, making no move to stop her.

"And I'll take this, too," she said, grabbing his Fender guitar by the neck and lifting it off its Lucite stand.

"Oh no you won't, baby."

"*I* paid for it. It's *mine.* Go buy your own, big shot."

Derek jumped up from his chair to grab at his guitar. Joyce pulled it as hard as she could, wrenching it from his grip, and backed away from him. With both hands laced around the neck, she lifted the Stratocaster up over her head. She held it like that for several seconds as their eyes met. He thought she was going to attack him. Then she slammed it down with all her might against the edge of a side table.

Derek jumped back, shielding his face. The wood split with a crack like the sound of a hardball off a bat. Joyce still held the neck in her hands, but the thin red sound box dangled limply, held by a wire string, like the strangled body of a dead animal.

Derek stared at her with shocked, wild eyes. Then he stepped forward and smacked her hard in the face with the back of his hand, like Bogey would have done. She stumbled back against the sink and fell to the floor, dropping the mangled guitar beside her. When she pressed the back of her hand against her lip, her knuckles smeared with blood.

He left. That was the last time Joyce was to see Derek Robertson for many years.

That afternoon she found a new flat. Then she walked to Kings Road and bought herself some Twenties glad rags, a moth-eaten brocade coat with a red fox collar, and some gaudy fun costume jewelry. She was all tanked up for a new life. For the next two months, she hung out at the Ad Lib on Leicester Square, drinking and sleeping her way around the London rock world—the center of the 1964 musical universe—trying to prove to herself that she didn't need Derek Robertson.

And she didn't. She would go on without him. The way Rick had gone on without Becky and without Hedy.

Her camera sat on the shelf, its leather case gathering dust. She didn't bother to answer her phone or follow up on photo-session requests. Instead, she danced, she drank, she screwed the nights away, until she woke up one morning with her mouth so dry she could barely swallow and her landlady pounding on the door, threatening to evict her if she didn't pay up on the rent.

Washed out and broke, Joyce took a hard look at herself in the mirror. She didn't like what she saw. She had been trying to prove something, to herself and to Derek, but she couldn't even remember what it was.

For the first time in weeks (except for an occasional sunrise), she went out into the daylight. There was nowhere to turn but into herself. She was going to make it on her own, or not at all. Just like her life before Derek came along.

Over a glass of tea, she sat scanning *Melody Maker,* the local music paper, her eyes stopping at the American record chart. "Looking at the Face of Love," was number ten with a bullet, and Derek's album, *The Eyes of Love,* was a hot pick. Under "Tour News" she read that promoter Sid Bernstein was planning a forty-two-city tour for Derek Robertson, commencing in the States and moving through Europe with a final set of concerts in the U.K.

Well, good for you, she thought to herself, her anger on the back burner. The waitress passed and Joyce impulsively flagged her down and traded her orange pekoe tea for a scotch and Coke—everyone she knew drank scotch and Coke—and lit up a Lark. It was an official ritual of British rock and roll.

Glass in one hand, cigarette in the other, she hesitated. What the hell was she doing, wishing that prick well? After all she'd done for him, she'd ended up with nothing but a hangover.

She put the glass down on the table without taking a sip and squashed the Lark into the drink, drowning it so it folded like an accordion and split open, gorged with brown scotch. She didn't like scotch and Coke and she couldn't stand Larks.

"Fuck him!" she said out loud. She paid her bill and walked resolutely out of the place, through the West End, down to Belgravia, and past Lions Head.

Slam, bam, alakazam, light bulbs!

When the idea finally dawned on her, she couldn't believe she hadn't thought of it sooner. It was so obvious, so perfect. An easy way to earn money *and,* better yet, get under Derek's skin.

She went to the Ad Lib that night as usual, but this time she had a mission. She talked to all the press people and PR folk she could find, picking their brains about souvenir books and rock paraphernalia. In bed at midnight and sober for a change, she awoke the next morning and headed for Levy's Lock and Loll Library, the best music bookshop in town, on the mews between

Brook and Oxford streets in Mayfair. Thumbing through some of the great Elvis picture books, with their super color reproductions, and the terrific album of Everly Brothers photographs, Joyce made note of the relevant publishing information.

When she spotted *The Rick Firestone Songbook,* a warm glow spread through her and she pulled it off the shelf hungrily. There were pictures, biographical notes, words and music. He'd really made it big, and she was glad. What with Derek and all, it had been almost two years since she'd talked to either of her old friends. High school flashed through her brain, but the old images wouldn't hold. The carefree days with Rick and David seemed like ancient history.

Derek always laughed at Rick Firestone, treating him like just another bubble-gum artist—as if *he* were something more—but Joyce had never stopped loving his songs and his musicianship. She knew he was just a young version of an old-fashioned crooner, but that didn't stop his songs from touching something deep in her.

She decided to buy the songbook with a few of her last shillings.

After hocking the Hasselblad to pay the rent, Joyce spent the entire next week closeted in her tiny flat preparing a photomontage mock-up of a book on Derek Robertson. From over a thousand pictures, she gleaned 200 that visually told the story of Derek's transformation from Ohio boy to rock sex symbol, from Greenwich Village to Paris to London.

These weren't just any photographs, though. These were most intimate, taken of Derek in various states of undress and arousal, unposed and alive, all taken in Joyce's unique style and revealing the photographer's special relationship with her subject. She had never dreamed of making these pictures public. Now the idea made her giddy with excitement. It was terribly daring, but daring was very "in" for London. The city was dedicated to "anything goes"—the newer and more far out, the better—and certainly there'd never been a music book quite like this one.

The British publishers, however, didn't see it that way. Through an A&R man at Apollo who knew someone at RCA who knew one of the editors at the house that published *The Elvis Photo Book,* Joyce arranged a meeting and made her pitch.

"I'm sorry, Miss Heller. It's not the photos or the layout—they're really quite nice, and we have no problem with the intimate nature of your selections. But this Robertson chap's just not a big enough star. One hit, even with that great photo of yours, doth not a superstar make. He's not nearly established enough to warrant the expense of a four-color reproduction on heavy stock, my dear. Save your photos and come back to us when he's had three big albums and six big singles."

"But by then it'll be too late," Joyce argued passionately. "License the book now to an American publisher and reserve the U.K. rights for yourself. When Derek tours the States next spring, the book will sell like hot cakes. Then he'll return to the U.K. and it'll be a gold mine for you, I guarantee it."

But the editor only shook his head and said, "I'm sorry."

Joyce was stunned and discouraged. She knew she was right, but she didn't know where to turn. Confused, she walked down Wardour Street toward Piccadilly Circus, contemplating a return to scotch and Coke, when she heard her name called out.

"Joyce . . . Joyce, hi there!"

When she turned around, she didn't recognize Brandon Levy in the daylight. He was from her fuzzy night world, one of the regulars with whom she'd caroused, gotten stoned, taken speed, and ended up forgetting more nights than she cared to remember. She stared at him blankly for a moment, then awakened from her daze.

"Oh, hi, Brandon. Sorry, I didn't recognize you for a moment. My mind was a million miles away."

"You look down-in-the-mouth, young lady. Come on, I'll buy you a spot of tea—unless you're up for starting a bender this early."

"Tea, please," she said, drawing out the words. "Booze is the *last* thing in the world I need."

She accompanied the always nattily clad Brandon into the nearest restaurant and watched him fill her cup. Wrapping her hands around the warm porcelain, she stared silently into the rising swirls of steam.

"Still fretting over Derek the Great, eh?" Brandon asked.

"No, not exactly. But I do think he's put a hex on me. I thought I had a super idea for a book about him, but I just got shot down by some hoity-toity publisher."

"Well, let's hear it."

She had nothing to lose. Brandon, after all, was a pretty influential fellow in the British rock-and-roll scene, even if he enjoyed "slumming" and tended toward drug binges and kinky sex. He was a rich Jewish boy from Leeds, whose father had staked him to a "literary venture" in London, as Brandon had so delicately phrased it one long night. That "venture" turned out to be the Levy Lock and Loll Library. With the success of that endeavor, Brandon had moved on to publish the music of some aspiring composers, had put out a few songbooks, and now was managing an avant-garde local group called the Silverfish.

Sharp, clever, fun, honest; raconteur, first-degree "poof," leader of the night pack, all-around druggie, Brandon Levy was clearly a pillar of the new society, the London rock scene.

Over tea, Joyce laid out the prototype of the photo album for Brandon. He studied the material carefully, his eyes lingering on Derek's muscular, nude body. After a long silence, he looked up at Joyce and smiled. "My dear girl, you're quite right. Publisher be damned, I'll give you a twenty-five-hundred-pound advance against a twelve-and-a-half-percent royalty in the U.S. and Canada, fifteen percent in the U.K., and ten percent for the rest of the world, for the right to publish *The Story of Derek Robertson*."

Joyce looked at him as though he were crazy. "You're kidding, Brandon."

"No, I'm not. I'm deadly serious. We're both going to make some money off your Mr. Robertson. Now, what about releases?"

Joyce pulled the release form from her bag. "Derek signed this for the 'Looking at the Face of Love' photo."

The release stated that "this photograph, and the entire photographic session, may be used for commercial purposes by the owner and photographer, Joyce Heller."

Brandon loved it. He could publish the book in England before Derek ever had a chance to enjoin it. But America was another story. "We're going to need more than this to bring out a legal edition in the States. Any ideas?"

She thought for a moment. "Well, I've got an old friend in New York who was studying law. He should be a lawyer by now. He's real smart, knows something about the business, and loves music. His name's David Barry. We were pretty close. I'm sure he'd represent me in some 'delicate' negotiations with Derek."

"Do it," Brandon said resolutely, "and don't worry about the money." He raised his glass and toasted: "To my new partner."

Joyce beamed with excitement. "To making money off Derek Robertson," she rejoined.

"I'll have a check and a contract for you this afternoon. Then we'll go out and paint the town."

They finished off their tea and prepared to leave.

"And, Joyce," Brandon said as an afterthought, resting his hand on her shoulder, "bring along your camera tonight. You never know where another book may emerge. There's a seamy side of London just dying to be captured on film."

1964 - 65

DAVID COULDN'T BELIEVE HIS EARS WHEN HE PICKED UP the phone and heard Joyce's muffled voice across the transatlantic line.

"Joyce! Is it really you?"

"It's me, all right. How ya been, hotshot?"

"I'm surviving. Just passed the bar and hooked up with a snooty firm in the city. I hate it already. I spend my few precious free moments hanging out with the brothers at the music joints uptown."

"Sounds like you're leading a typical schizo New York City life."

"You got it. But what the hell have *you* been up to?"

"You don't want to hear. It's too long and sad a story. Up until a few months ago, I was working with Derek Robertson."

"Derek Robertson? You mean that sexed-up rock star?" David asked, incredulous.

"The one and only. Actually, he's a real shit, but that's a whole other story."

"Sounds like interesting work," he teased.

"Yeah, a real ball. Any word from Rick?"

"Nothin'. Not a word. And I'm a little concerned."

"Well, if you do talk to him, be sure to send him my love. Listen, enough with the gossip. I'm calling on business."

"Business?"

"I'm planning to put out a book of intimate photographs of Derek."

"Intimate photographs! You really *do* know this Robertson character."

"Know him, I've had him! And I made him. He was a great lay from Ohio who I turned into the hottest bod in the biz."

"Joyce, are you the girl? The girl who took *the* picture— 'Looking at the Face of' you know who?"

"You got it."

"Shit. I always knew you were Margaret Bourke-White in disguise."

"Listen, David, I've got a partner on the project, a fellow named Brandon Levy who runs a bookshop in London. Brandon's prepared to publish the book in England, but we're looking for a U.S. publisher. No one will touch it in the States, however, without a release form executed by Derek, and he's recording in the States right now."

"And that's where I come in, right?"

"Right. You've got to help me. I really need the bread."

"Joyce, I'm just a beginner. I don't have any experience in these matters."

"I don't give a shit about experience. You're my friend and now you're my lawyer. You're the only one I can trust. You said you wanted to be an entertainment lawyer, didn't you? Well, here's your chance."

"Sure, but—"

"No buts allowed. We're gonna release the book in the U.K. anyway and it's bound to be bootlegged in the States. If we can get an authorized edition, maybe we can both see some dough."

"You know I can't refuse you anything. Okay, client, you got a lawyer. So tell me why Derek the shit would sign a consent?"

"Wait till you see some of the shots. I got some hot stuff on the boy. And he did sign a release for some of the shots, including the cover shot, which the record company stole."

"Where can I find him?"

"He hangs out at the Albert Hotel on University Place. He's signed with Apollo Records and his contact there is another shit, named Thane Crawley, who practically ordered Derek to can me. Let me give you Brandon's number in London. He'll help you in any way he can."

When Joyce clicked off, David went to work. After endless unsuccessful attempts to reach either Robertson or Crawley, David, frustrated, finally called Brandon Levy in London.

"Mr. Levy, David Barry here."

"Hello, Mr. Barry. Joyce has told me quite a bit about you. How are things going?"

"Not so well, I'm afraid. I need your help. I'm having some difficulty convincing Robertson and Apollo that they should take this matter seriously."

"Won't talk to you, eh? So how can I be of assistance?"

"Joyce mentioned some steamy contact sheets. Could you send me some to dangle in front of Robertson and get his goat? That might make him sit up and take notice so we can get on with negotiations."

A week later a package arrived at David's rent-controlled studio apartment. He could barely distinguish the photos on the eight-by-ten contact sheets, there were so many on each page. After several hours with a magnifying glass under a good light, he cut out two very intimate and unusual photos that he thought would produce a response and sent them to Derek Robertson, care of the Albert Hotel. Along with his business card he included a note that read: "I have called you unsuccessfully several times. You can call me at Klondike 5-8132 or you can ignore this note. If you do the latter, you will see a blowup of this photograph in the paper within the next 60 days."

Forty-eight hours later he was sitting across the desk from Thane Crawley, the recently appointed custodian of Apollo Records. After Apollo's take-over by Swisstone International, and the subsequent shake-up, Crawley had been plucked from the prestigious investment banking firm of Morton Collins to serve as "acting executive."

"All right, Mr. Barry, how much?" Crawley began, without civil preliminaries or even a handshake.

David instantly disliked the man's tone and appearance. He reminded David of the maître d' at the Copacabana. David screwed up all his courage and resolve. "How much what?" he answered.

"How much money does your client want?"

"She doesn't want money."

"Well then, what *is* it she wants?"

"She wants Derek Robertson to sign a release so she can put together a tasteful book of photographs. The book will be a fan's chronological picture of Derek's career and will contain a section of more-intimate photos of Derek as seen through a lover's eyes."

"Apollo is prepared to bring an action to enjoin release of this book."

"I doubt that. Take a look at Robertson's album cover. Joyce Heller owns that picture and I have a release signed by Derek to prove it. You never paid her for that photo and you never received a release from her."

"You're talking about an invasion of privacy, Mr. Barry."

"Not in the U.K. You can't stop the book coming out there."

"If that's the case, why do you want a release?"

"My client would like to have the book properly published in America. Without a release, though, no major publisher will touch it. Although she'd prefer not to, my client is prepared to go to one of the bootleg publishers. Whether or not we come to terms here, Mr. Crawley, the Robertson book *is* going to come out."

Crawley sat back in his chair and stared daggers at the young, pushy, obviously Jewish law novice who was trying to get tough with him.

"The photos you sent Derek—is that the caliber of tasteful material your client has in mind?"

"My client hasn't chosen that particular shooting session, at least at the moment. She does need money, however, and is anxious to sell her book. If she can't sell it, she just might sell some selected photos to the press."

"You're talking about blackmail, Mr. Barry."

"That's a rough word for pictures that Mr. Robertson posed for knowingly and willingly."

"Willingly? We both know he was probably stoned out of his mind."

"Were you there?"

"Were you?"

"Obviously, neither of us was. But are you going to defend

him by telling the world he's a druggie? Or would you rather have his fans think he's a transvestite? Why else would a grown man put on a woman's bra and panties and pose with his genitals hanging out?"

Crawley assumed his most haughty, rebuking tone. "Mr. Barry, the private intimacies of two young lovers under the influence of hallucinogens, or whatever they were on, should not be exploited commercially. It's a shocking betrayal of trust. Derek Robertson is a talented young man with a bright future ahead of him. I can't believe your client would be so cruel as to jeopardize Derek's future. And I'm appalled that a lawyer of your tender years would represent such a client. You, young man, should be ashamed of yourself. You're a discredit to your profession."

Instead of being intimidated, David rose confidently to his feet. He submerged the anger he felt toward the smug bastard and made sure his voice was even and his tone businesslike. "And I, Mr. Crawley, am appalled that you were the one responsible for breaking up this young couple. As I understand it, it was at *your* suggestion that Derek dropped Joyce and closed her out, even though she was the woman who shared his life and created his act. And you did it because you thought teenyboppers would prefer to imagine sleeping with an unattached Derek. That would encourage them to buy more records so you and Apollo could make more money.

"What right do you have to meddle in the lives of these young people and manipulate their vulnerable minds? You, Crawley, are the one who has behaved in a shocking, appalling, and morally reprehensible manner. Don't you dare lecture me."

David moved toward the door. "Good day, Mr. Crawley. The deterioration of our dialogue is not productive for my client. I now know how to advise Miss Heller."

"And just what does that mean?"

"My advice to my client is privileged information. The ultimate determination will be hers." David's hand reached for the doorknob.

Crawley spoke too suddenly and earnestly, afraid that Barry would actually carry through on his threat. "If Derek were amenable to a release," he said quickly, "could he see the proposed book? Could he have certain of those negatives and an agreement of ownership for some of the more unfortunate photos?"

David smiled to himself. He knew he had won. By staying calm and pretending to know what the hell he was doing, he'd played out the bluff and come out ahead. Maybe he'd make a pretty good entertainment lawyer after all.

An agreement was quickly reached. In the spring of '65, an expurgated American edition of *The Story of Derek Robertson* appeared, joining its previously published and more risqué British counterpart.

The book sold better than anticipated.

By now, the four young Silverfish were exploding onto the English rock scene and Brandon was flying high, with Joyce by his side as photographer, image consultant, and confidante. Thanks to Joyce, the Silverfish started taking home movies and distributing them as part of their publicity packages. She began to create little promo films of them in sync with their music. And it was at her insistence that Brandon began thinking seriously about a film deal for his boys.

By night, Joyce rode the merry-go-round with Brandon. And quite a ride it was. Brandon was *the* rock-and-roll man in London, and every door was held open for him. Joyce knew she was living on the edge again, but it was a way of exorcising the specter of Derek Robertson.

And for Brandon, well, it was just the perfect association of convenience and the best means of confounding the gossips. He trusted Joyce and felt comfortable with her around. She became his "beard" and clung to him conspicuously, snuggling next to him, hugging him, kissing him, doing everything she could publicly to quash the rumors that Brandon was a "poof." They went everywhere together. Not only was she perfect camouflage, she was bait as well, particularly for those chaps who wouldn't risk a "fag" but might "experiment" with another straight guy, or find it groovy if not kinky to go "three-way," a scene Joyce participated in on occasion.

For a while they were good for each other in a strange kind of way, each running interference for the other, protecting each other from the hurt and complication of a serious relationship, feeding each other's ego. Only Kevin Singh, Brandon's somewhat effete, overly social business associate and "companion," seemed at all put out by the relationship. In the end, though, the track proved too fast and too slippery for all of them.

The slide began on a chilly November night, damp as only

London could be, when the night air seemed to permeate your clothes and dampen your bones. Joyce paced excitedly around her new flat (courtesy of the Derek book), checking herself out in different mirrors, under different lights, to be sure she looked good enough for Brandon. "Look tough, look rough," that's what he'd told her earlier in the day. Although Brandon often escorted Joyce to exclusive clubs and discos, and made sure she was close at hand for official functions, he preferred the gay scene. And the rougher and more dangerous, the better. Tonight was going to be one of those nights.

Joyce kept staring at herself in the full-length mirror, fiddling with her hair, never quite satisfied. She couldn't fault her attire. Her black leather miniskirt, open black silk blouse (braless), and black patent leather spike heels were just right for the kind of evening Brandon had in mind. Her eyes looked enormous, like a Kewpie doll's, thanks to the false eyelashes on her upper lids, the so-called Twiggies on her lowers (each single lash glued on painstakingly, one at a time), and the green eye shadow that intensified her beautiful, oval green irises. As a final, almost garish, touch, she wrapped eight feet of bright red chiffon around her neck, aping the style and color scheme of a Piccadilly streetwalker.

At the sound of a car pulling to a stop out front, Joyce rushed to the window and stared down at the street. Drops of fog and humidity, like perspiration, covered the cobblestones and the bonnet of Brandon's shiny black Phantom V Rolls-Royce. As Brandon stepped out, Joyce saw his outfit: black leather motorcycle jacket over a black turtleneck, with jeans and black studded work boots. They'd look terrific together.

She had second thoughts, though, when Brandon appeared at her door and she saw him in the light. His pupils were dilated and his eyes had that silly, giddy look that she knew all too well. He had already started in on the booze and Valiums.

No matter how smashed, Brandon always managed to be suave. "Joyce, my dear, you look ravishing. Come along," he said, holding out his arm for her, "we're going to have a ball tonight. Just stay close to me and everything'll be fine."

In the back of the limo, Brandon downed glass after glass of champagne until he was slurring his words. He was slipping fast and nothing Joyce could do would stop him.

Despite the glitter, Joyce had come to dread nights like these. The sequence of Brandon's moods had become too predictable.

First the evil period, when he'd rant and rave and heap abuse
on everyone, including her. Then, in the middle of the night,
he'd become fearless and self-destructive, hitting on uniformed
bobbies or lorry drivers or, worse yet, scouring the docks for
Teddy boys or longshoremen, sometimes asking Joyce to act as
bait to lure his fancies to the car. Finally, at the end of the night,
in the early-morning light, she or Kevin would talk Brandon
through the depression and the maniacal suicidal ramblings,
until he fell into a troubled sleep in her arms as she rocked him
back and forth like a baby.

For a while she'd found the whole scene exciting. Until the
novelty wore off. Now it was only by drinking, smoking, or
"downing" herself into oblivion that she could numb the unattractive, creeping sensation that she was participating in one of
Brandon's lurid surrealistic fantasies.

She was finishing off her third glass of champagne when they
drove up a tree-lined, two-mile winding driveway and came to
a stop in front of a lovely red brick, white-trimmed Georgian
home near Wembley. Brandon stumbled on the first step and
Joyce had to support him up the rest of the front steps and into
the house.

The interior was exquisitely done, from the high sheen on the
checkered black and white marble inlaid floors to the Irish
crystal chandelier hanging high above the imposing entrance
hall. A double curved staircase of traditional Georgian design
elegantly dominated the anteroom. Fine antique wood furniture
and delicate *objets d'art* were arranged carefully throughout.

Against such elegance, the scene inside was incongruous. The
guests, both male and female, were decked out in a variety of
leather outfits, some with violent artifacts such as riding crops
or handcuffs dangling from their belts, others with vivid tattoos
displayed on their arms or buttocks. They looked and acted
more like street roughs or Hell's Angels than the well-educated
upper-class fops they were. The music, played at conversation-
stopping level, seemed to emerge from every room, beating out
the familiar tunes of the Silverfish, the Stones, and the Beatles.

The scene was much scarier than Joyce had expected and she
clung to Brandon for the first hour, making him promise not to
leave her alone, while he circulated, tossing back Drambuies.

On one of the tables, she noticed a crystal bowl filled with
little tabs of paper, each covered with tiny Mickey Mouse draw-
ings. When she reached her hand down into the bowl, Brandon

caught her wrist. "I'd be careful with those. It's blotter acid, a new kind of LSD, imported from San Francisco. Eat at your own risk."

Forgoing the acid, she stuck to booze and grass. When nothing too unusual happened in the first hour, she finally began to relax and got up the courage to excuse herself to the loo, singing along with the Strangeloves' "I Want Candy" as it blasted painfully through the speakers.

When she opened the door of the elegant downstairs powder room, she nearly screamed. She looked down at a mop-haired boy, syringe in hand and rubber tube wrapped around his arm, then slammed the door shut and hurried to another bathroom upstairs.

On her return, she looked all around for Brandon but couldn't find him anywhere. She wandered from room to room, arousing the interested stares of numerous dykes and rough-and-tumble characters, until finally, on the table beside the crystal bowl, she found a message scribbled on a strip of the blotter. It read, "I'm off to Buckingham Palace to see the changing of the guard," and was signed, "Love, Brandon."

It wasn't the first time she'd cursed him under her breath. And it wasn't the first time he'd left her stranded, a promise broken. This evening, though, Joyce was particularly upset. She told herself that at least she wouldn't have to play nursemaid to him or participate in another one of his wild nights. Despite her anger, she smiled to herself, imagining him actually going off to the Guards' dressing room to watch them change!

Finishing up her drink, she went off in search of the host. She'd have him call a local car service and she'd make a quick and graceful exit.

When she found the young host, he was surrounded by a group of real toughs. "Would you mind calling a taxi for me?" she asked nervously, watching the leather boys give her and her red scarf the once-over. "I've had a wonderful time but I really must be going."

"Already? What's the bird's hurry?" one of them called out. "Ain't ya havin' a good time?"

"Don't mind them," the host said reassuringly. "Here, have a drink while I go call a car for you."

She paced around the room uncomfortably, sipping at the punch and waiting for him to return. It seemed to take forever.

Little by little, she began to feel like the room was spinning.

She was overcome with a light-headed, dizzy sensation. Her hand began to shake and she spilled the ice cubes from her empty glass onto the blood-red Oriental carpet. When she reached down to pick them up, the floor seemed to move away from her and she jumped back in terror.

The punch had been spiked with acid. She was losing control.

She sank down onto the thick carpet for safety, crossing her legs and hugging herself, waiting for the rush to pass. Suddenly someone reached around from behind and popped something under her nose. Her brain exploded. Her heart pounded. The room turned light and dark and she thought she was going to die from the burst of amyl nitrite.

When the high passed, she relaxed for a little while, until she turned her head and noticed everyone looking at her. At first she thought it was simply drug paranoia and she tried to smile and stay calm. Then the calm turned to fear and she felt suddenly threatened and very vulnerable. She tried to stand up but slipped back down onto the carpet. Then she stood and began running, or trying to run, but someone was holding her.

She had no idea when or how they managed to undress her. The whole scene was muddy, like a poorly lit photograph. She saw herself lying on an Oriental rug and felt the panic. She heard herself screaming. All around her were guys in leather, laughing demonically.

Then it was black. They stuffed a ball gag in her mouth, blindfolded her, and tied her hands behind her back. She could feel the rope burning into her wrists and taste the rubber against her tongue. The more she gagged and choked and struggled, the more they laughed and shouted obscenities.

She blacked out for a few minutes. When she woke up, something or someone was tearing at her privates. There were hands all over her body, violating her, hurting her. Then someone ripped the gag and blindfold off.

There must have been ten people standing around her, men and women. One of them started whipping her and she could feel drops of blood trickling down her leg. She started screaming hysterically, trying to hide her face against the rug, but that only seemed to inflame them. Someone grabbed her hair tightly, close to the roots, and yanked it back. The pain shot through her whole head, but she managed to keep her mouth and eyes closed. She knew what was pressing against her closed lips.

She was dizzy and nauseous, her head spinning from the acid.

She tried to distance herself, pretend it was happening to someone else. But it was all too real.

They were talking dirty to her, asking her if it felt good, telling her how much they liked it. She felt warm semen dripping over her face and felt them whipping her again, harder and harder. They said she was being disciplined for being a bad girl. Dream images of her mother flashed through her semiconscious brain. She couldn't count all the bodies around her. They started taking her, one after another. She felt dirty, filthy, disgusting. Blood was seeping out from between her legs.

The room became darker and darker. She felt her mind slip. Then everything went black.

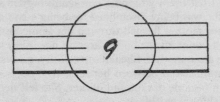

1965

*A*s David headed west on Forty-second Street en route to Black Jack Studio, he pulled on the fob that hung from his vest and checked his gold pocket watch. It was nearly midnight on the appointed Tuesday and the early September air was chilling.

He looked around at the unfamiliar turf. Unlike his firm's midtown east neighborhood or even 125th Street, where David was greeted with familiar nods and knew the right names to drop if accosted, Forty-second Street was a whole new ball game. This was a different and unknown set of hookers, hustlers, pimps, and pushers. He was going into a new scene and, as usual, remembered an old high-school lesson: Play it cool and confident.

Holding himself erect, avoiding any appearance of fear, he walked at a brisk but deliberate pace. He smiled at all the street people—a benevolent, enigmatic smile that put them off-guard. He imagined he heard their thoughts as they looked at him, wondering who the young dude with the fancy duds was. Was he a mob boss's son? The fuzz? A swell gone slumming? "Commodity unknown, stay away," was the unspoken message. He felt it . . . he knew it . . . he acted like he owned Forty-second Street and everyone was working the street for *him*.

He wasn't afraid. Instead, he felt embraced, as though he belonged, and elated at his walk on the wild side. After all, he was here at the invitation of Mr. Soul, the one and only Jackson James.

The invitation had come two weeks earlier, when he'd met the Man at the Baby Grand, a musicians' club on 125th Street and Lenox Avenue where David loved to hang out. The Baby Grand was remarkable for two things: a front window shaped like the top of a baby grand piano; and a young, white, almost foppish cool-cat lawyer who loved jazz and helped the "brothers" by conducting free counseling sessions as if he were a special division of the Legal Aid Society. David even sat in on the occasional session.

The night of Jackson's appearance, when Mr. Dynamite invited David to come to tonight's recording session, David had joined in four-hands at the piano with Bud Powell on "Foggy Day," seguing into "Don't Blame Me." He had been high on the thrill of improvising with a legend. And Jackson James had shaken his head in wonder at the white boy who was a kindred spirit.

David may have been overlooked and overworked at his law firm by day, but he was appreciated and sought after at night, whether he was at the Baby Grand or hanging out with the musical theater gypsies at Joe Allen on Forty-sixth Street and Eighth Avenue. By day, he did whatever Mr. Huntington wanted, but at night he inhabited another world; like a werewolf, straitlaced and boring by day, exciting and vibrant by night.

Because David loved the music and was growing more and more interested in the music business—thanks in part to Rick's influence and the work he performed for Joyce on the Derek Robertson case—he began doing freebie pro-bono work for indigent songwriters, starving musicians, and down-and-out record producers. He attended bar-association panels and seminars in music law and registered for all the Practicing Law Institute entertainment seminars. The argument at the Copa still lingered in David's memory; he hadn't talked to Rick since. But that unfortunate incident had actually intensified his interest in music law.

He never wore beads, bangles, long hair, lizard boots, rings, Indian turquoise, fringed suede, or any of the other required paraphernalia of "the music biz." He was unlike any lawyer the musicians had met. As a rule, lawyers were boring, supercilious, sanctimonious, and pompous, carrying attaché cases and wearing boxer shorts, Brooks Brothers suits, wing-tip cordovans, blue button-down Oxford shirts, Harvard Club ties, and steel Timexes. They wouldn't be caught dead or alive at the Baby Grand.

David was different. He was cool. He understood the street lingo and he understood the music. His attire was tastefully flamboyant—distinctive white vest; antique stickpin through his Windsor-knotted tie; pressed white handkerchief in his breast pocket, and a boutonniere in the lapel of his Savile Row suit. The brothers could dig it. More important, he came off as sincere and profoundly interested in the people he met. The combination of his charm, his keen memory, and his way with words made him shine in the world of the scuzzy "music biz." In no time at all, he was accepted as an insider, as "David the lawyer."

Even before he could see it, he could smell Tad's Steakhouse and the odor of seventy-nine-cent fat-and-gristle sandwiches. Then he saw the Pussy Theater and walked into the doorway of Number 126, the address of Black Jack Studio. He rang the bell and waited. After several interminable minutes, the elevator door opened and he squeezed into the smallest, smelliest elevator he'd ever encountered. He pushed the only button that worked, and after a groaning, agonizing two-minute climb to the third floor, the elevator discharged him—into the land of Oz.

When the steel door opened, he was looking up into the threatening faces of two Joe Louis look-alikes. "Mr. James is expecting me," David said nervously, holding out his fancy lawyer's card, engraved and embossed, "David Barry, Esq.," with the firm's name, Huntington & Richardson, in fancy script at the bottom.

The taller one, the one with the leather cap and the muscle-bulging T-shirt that read JACKSON JAMES, SOUL-MATE, studied the card for what seemed an eternity, feeling the raised letters between his huge fingers. When he looked down at the twenty-five-year-old David in his distinctive attire, he crinkled his left eye and scratched his head. The bouncer handed the card to his companion and tilted his head toward the back room. "Check it out, Leroy," he said in a voice as deep as Ronald Bright's on Johnny Cymbal's "Hey, Mr. Bassman."

David stood there uncomfortably, looking around. The room before him was cast in a muted, surrealistic glow. All the fluorescent light fixtures had been "neutered," stripped of most of their bulbs, with yellow, amber, and pink gels placed randomly over their grids. The carpet and ceilings were black, the walls stapled with odd lots of carpet scraps (for "sound baffling"). The air was thick with enough cigarette smoke to revolt even the most seasoned nicotine veteran. Opposite the elevator door was a Formica countertop marbleized pink and white with gold flecks (circa 1953). Colored metal ashtrays, pockmarked from years of accumulated ashes and overflowing with butts, were scattered along the counter.

David saw a group of pink- and amber-tinted people, some standing about, some lounging on beanbags in a makeshift "reception room." He watched as the elevator doors opened and two greasy young men delivered a small package into the hands of Mr. Bassman and received a bulging envelope in return. The scene was repeated several times in the space of ten minutes. David assumed he was witnessing a series of drug transactions.

Then Leroy reemerged. "Mr. Dynamite's man say it's cool. Follow me, brother," Leroy drawled. Running interference for David, Leroy led him down a narrow hall and up to a tall, portly, almost bald black man with a van dyke beard and thick glasses. He was stroking a cat that lounged in his arms.

"You the lawyer cat?"

"That's me," David answered.

"Right on time." It was just before midnight. "Come on in. I'm Reggie. I run the studio." Because of the half-inch space between his two front teeth, Reggie whistled every time he spoke.

"Pleased to meet you. I'm David."

"That's cool, man. Come on, I'll show you my layout."

"Well, I promised Mr. James . . . "

"No problem, man. He'll be right back. He went out for inspiration—you know what I mean?"

"Right." What *did* he mean? Booze? Ladies? Drugs? A walk? Who knew? Be cool, David, be cool.

Reggie opened a box on the wall that was filled with electrical wires and what looked like circuit breakers. He flipped one of the switches. "The elevator power is off now. It sort of secures the place, what with the fire doors bolted closed. Now the boys know they can turn on and do their thing without worrying about a bust. Jackson will call before coming back—that's how we do things around here. You dig?"

"I dig."

David followed Reggie through a maze of rooms. The place stank of stale cigarettes, rancid cat urine, and, above all, of pot. A lot of pot. Unabashed and uninhibited, they were smoking it all over the place. David had seen it, smelled it, encountered it before, but not like this. The place seemed less like a recording studio than a Chinese opium den in some Pearl Buck novel or the seedy digs of a Robert Mitchum–type private eye in a black-and-white movie.

Although it was a far cry from even David's accustomed haunts, he played it cool. He couldn't help imagining what was lurking in the dark corners: ashes, cat shit, cat urine, probably even human urine, booze, roaches, rats; it boggled the mind. He didn't dare remove his velvet-collared chesterfield coat. Where would he put it? He could picture himself taking off his coat at the office the next morning and a syringe or a roach (either kind) falling from his pocket at Mr. Huntington's feet! David laughed to himself. That was just what that stuffed shirt Huntington deserved.

"Give me your coat, I'll hang it up for you," Reggie said, ending David's dilemma as they approached a closet. After carefully hanging David's coat, Reggie led the way through a huge six-inch-thick steel door that looked like a submarine hatch. The lintel, jambs, and sill of the door were also of thick steel, and David had to step up and bend down to make his way through. What the hell was he getting himself into, going through watertight chambers three stories above Forty-second Street?

"Pretty bizarre, huh? Airtight. Used to be a fur vault," Reggie explained.

They passed through another, similar doorway and emerged in a glass-enclosed engineer's booth filled with exotic-looking mixing boards with red, green, blue, yellow, and orange buttons lit from within. Beyond the glass partition, David saw a huge room, at least two stories high, where a handful of older, white musicians, some with gray hair, others practically balding, were sitting around with their "fiddles," waiting.

David looked surprised.

"Not what you were expecting, eh, man?" Reggie said, picking up on David's vibes. "Well, these dudes may not look like they're hip, but, I'm telling you, they are *the* string men in the city. Listen up. Hear that hot soul beat? That's the rhythm, horn and guitar tracks we laid down earlier today and mixed on a master working tape. After Mr. Soul adds his voice-over, these cats 'sweeten' the track with strings, you dig? Believe it or not, they play on all the hot rock-and-roll and R&B tracks. They're a bunch of old Jewish refugees from Europe with classical training."

What Reggie didn't mention, although David was to find it out soon enough, was that these studio musicians were working off debts playing at Black Jack, debts incurred when they borrowed money from the studio, no questions asked, at exorbitant interest rates.

David took a seat in the control booth and sat quietly, drinking in the scene. At 12:30 A.M., Jackson and his entourage of attendants arrived and headed straight for the studio room. Mr. Soul was dressed in white, head to toe: wide-brimmed white hat banded with black; brilliant white three-piece raw silk suit; and white Italian loafers. Around his shoulders he wore a black velvet cape, just like the one that was draped over his shoulders at the conclusion of each performance, the one he kept tossing off as he returned, feigning reluctance, for encore after encore. A silver mezuzah dangled from his neck.

When he saw David in the booth, he flashed him his hundred-dollar smile and motioned for him with his hand.

David looked around to make sure he wasn't signaling someone else.

"Go ahead, mah man. He's wants *you*."

As David walked from the control booth into the studio, Jackson came up to him, grabbed his hand, and threw an arm around his shoulder. "Hey, bro', glad you could make it, glad you could make it. Aw right, you gonna be my good-luck charm, brother Dave. Like this." He clutched the mezuzah in his hand. "You see, I'm part Jewish. I don't take no chances!" He threw back his head and laughed like only Mr. Soul could. "You ready to see the King lay down tracks and make a hit record?"

"I'm ready."

Jackson lowered his voice and led David over toward a corner of the studio. "Listen, man, maybe you can help me. I have a problem with a friend who needs bread, I don't have to lay it out

for you—like could you . . . take whatever bread it takes to help
her and do it through your name—you know, your lawyer's
name—through your lawyer's account, those es-crow ac-
counts—you know, one of those jobs—so it's done without Mr.
Soul's name being involved? I don't want my friend to lose face."

So *that* was what he wanted. David didn't have to think twice.
It was a privilege. Jackson James would be either a paying
customer or indebted. "I'd be happy to take care of it, Mr.
James. Just give me the particulars."

David wondered whether he could pull off the delicate assignment. Then he relaxed. He always worried but always came
through.

"Aw right. You're mah *man* and mah friend. Now go sit
down and watch the King at work."

David hurried back into the control booth and watched Mr.
Soul take off his jacket, loosen his tie, and stick the bulky head-
phones over his ears. He was ready to go to work.

Two hours and twelve takes later, Jackson's voice was getting
husky and tension filled the air. He kept reaching for long drafts
of oxygen from a mask attached to a nearby full-size tank. But
every time the engineer played back the vocals superimposed on
the master mix, Jackson shook his head. "It still ain't right, man.
We got to do it again."

By this time the thrill had begun to wear even for David.
Although he was excited about witnessing a star's recording
session, and although he thought each of the takes sounded
great, the entire process was becoming tedious if not downright
uncomfortable and even embarrassing. Like everyone else in the
studio, he was feeling uptight.

When Jackson walked into the booth, David had a fit of
paranoia. Maybe it was him? Maybe he wasn't such a good-luck
charm after all. What if Jackson asked him to leave? He wasn't
sure whether he'd welcome the dismissal or be devastated by it.

"Let's take a half-hour break, fellas. Get me some hot tea with
lemon, some honey, and a bottle of Jack Daniel's," Jackson said
to one of the entourage. Then he shook his head, talking aloud
to himself. "I don't know, fellas. It's just not there tonight. The
music's hot, it's alive, I know it. And the song's a killer. But I'm
just not groovin' with it. Man, this never happened to me before.
I don't know what to do."

David could feel the intensity of the music. For the first time
he was beginning to understand the musical passions and emo-

tions, and not just the techniques. Tonight, though, he knew something was missing.

"Maybe an audience would help. You know, someone to perform for live, like you have at the Apollo," David suddenly said.

The room turned deadly silent and remained that way for what seemed to David like an eternity. This time he'd been too presumptuous or too naïve, he wasn't sure which. He'd made a complete fool of himself and blown the whole thing. Shit.

"I love it!" Jackson finally cried out. "Do it live, make 'em jive. Reggie, open up those folding chairs, line 'em up and down one side of the studio. Lonnie, Leroy, go out and hustle me up 'bout fifty bodies—brothers and sisters from the street."

By 3:00 A.M. the studio "bleachers" were filled with assorted shleppers, pimps, dealers, hookers, hustlers, and a few courageous late-night taxi drivers. It was a veritable Times Square convention.

Jackson drank hot tea and bourbon. His larynx loosened and so did he. When he went out this time, the speakers blasted full force into the studio and the string section played behind him live. Jackson faced the crowd, listened as the strings played the declining scale of the intro, then launched into the song.

He worked the audience, sang to them, performed for them. The studio became his stage. He screamed his heart out, tears rolling down his face. It was more than a recording; it was a gut wrenching, soul-searching social commentary that took every ounce of Mr. Soul's strength.

Three takes later it was all over.

Six weeks later it was ten with a bullet on the *Billboard* charts.

It was nearly dawn by the time David left the studio, exhausted but exhilarated, feeling high from the session and validated from knowing he'd contributed.

As the sun began to rise, a blue and pink tint haloed the Chrysler Building. Listening to the bumps and grinds of Manhattan awakening, David seemed to hear music everywhere. When he reached the public library on Forty-second Street and Fifth Avenue, he hailed a taxi and was whisked through the light traffic to his East Side apartment. He gulped down some coffee and breakfast, shaved, and showered. Changed back, like Cinderella, into his three-piece blue serge Brooks Brothers uniform, he made his way to the office. He was back in the real world, a world that suddenly seemed a little less tolerable than ever before.

When he hung up his coat in the front closet of Huntington & Richardson, no roaches dropped from his pocket onto the old man's shoes. David smiled to himself, remembering how uptight he'd been when he arrived at Black Jack. By the end of the session, he'd felt comfortable, as if he were in his own element. It was a feeling he'd never had, and never would have, at H & R.

Only minutes after he'd settled down behind his desk with a cup of coffee and a real-estate brief, Huntington's bossy, matronly secretary walked into his small office.

"Mr. Barry, Mr. Huntington would like to see you in his office. Immediately."

"Of course," David answered, the thumping of his heart belying his calm voice. An early, unscheduled meeting with the senior partner always boded ill. For a moment David felt like a teenager caught sneaking back into the house in the wee hours of the morning.

He slugged down his coffee and fastened the middle button of his suit jacket. Although inside he felt strung out, he'd never show it. After all, late hours were a lawyer's staple, and David worked at appearing crisp even when running on empty. Despite the wave of guilt, he knew Huntington's summons had nothing to do with the previous night. And what if it did? How he spent his few precious off-hours was none of the firm's goddamn business.

Already bristling, David was escorted into Mr. Huntington's huge office. He looked around at the ornate wood-paneled room with its brass fixtures and its walls hung with traditional prints of white-wigged English judges. When he inhaled, he smelled the pungent odor of thirty years of pipe tobacco emanating from the deep green carpet, the wooden English partners' desk, and the tufted leather English sofa. A far cry indeed from the look and smell of Black Jack Studio.

Without looking up from his papers, Huntington waved David into a seat. The senior partner was stately-looking, graying at the temples, with chiseled features and a slightly upturned nose. He was an overbearing and self-impressed man.

"David," he began, finally lifting his head and carefully replacing his pen in its holder, "I'm not one to beat about the bush. One of the partners showed me your latest proposal to take on one Ronnie Lee, formerly of the group Silverfish, as a client, and frankly I was shocked. I don't approve of the type of pro-bono clientele you have been bringing into this firm. I want to know why you are wasting the firm's time giving free legal counsel to music riffraff you pick up off the streets?"

David didn't bother to recapitulate his written argument: how Ronnie Lee was discharged without cause and never properly compensated; how he'd been instrumental in the founding of the group and partially responsible for its sound and image. What was the point? Hard as it was to believe, Huntington had never heard of the Silverfish and obviously didn't see the potential in a suit against the most popular rock-and-roll band in Europe. A band that was soon to invade America.

"Sir, I think you do the firm a disservice by not taking this client seriously."

"David, you're a fine young man," Huntington continued in his pompous and grandiloquent style. "Industrious, bright, sensitive, passionate about what you believe in . . . and that's fine. I tolerated your extracurricular work because you said it would result in clients profitable to the firm and guaranteed me that it would not interfere with the performance of your assigned duties. Although I can't complain about your overall performance, to date I have seen no money generated from your clients and I have a strong suspicion that your outside pursuits have monopolized your attention and done nothing to enhance the reputation of the firm."

Huntington stood up ominously from behind his desk. "I have had my fill, David. I demand that you cease working for these fly-by-night musicians and devote yourself one hundred percent to the business of Huntington and Richardson. Or else leave the firm."

David felt a chill run down his spine. He remembered his grandfather's advice about decision making, offered one high-school evening when David was thinking about college and a career. "You know how some classes are so painless they seem to end even before they begin? They're the classes you do well in because you enjoy them. Life's like that, David. Don't just listen to your brain, my boy. Listen to your heart as well. It will tell you what direction to take."

There was no doubt where his heart was taking him. Every day at H & R was growing longer, while every night seemed to breeze by, no matter how hard or how late he worked. Everything he did for his music clients, he loved. He loved being needed, being relied on, being important to people he could relate to. There was no woman in his life to fill that need for him; Rick and Joyce were off in their own worlds and he had no close friends; there was no one but himself to worry about supporting. He was on his own.

Still, he'd worked long and hard to make it this far as a lawyer, and a rash act after a sleepless night *could* jeopardize his future. But Ronnie Lee might be just the client to pave the way for putting his heart in tune with his career. Fuck it, David said to himself; he'd rather be happy and starve, if worse came to worst.

Following Huntington's lead, David stood up from his seat. He walked around the chair and placed his hands calmly on the seat back, facing his boss. "If that's the choice, then I resign."

For a moment, Huntington was taken aback. David caught it in the flicker of his eyes. But like the shrewd lawyer he was, the senior partner maintained his poker face.

"If I were you, David, I'd think carefully about this decision. Think how it will look on your résumé and how it will affect your career. Think also of the time, money, and energy this firm has invested in you, and of your moral obligation to us."

David didn't have to think. "Moral obligation!" David said, suddenly filled with righteous indignation. "I've been working my balls off for you, putting in sixty-hour weeks for the past two years. I've done a hell of a good job and I don't owe you a goddamn thing, Mr. Huntington. If your firm isn't willing to carry a few clients who can't pay now but who could bring in substantial money in the future . . . well then, I don't think I belong with this firm."

The moment was at hand. In a second there would be no turning back.

"Now, David, calm down," Huntington said in a conciliatory tone. "Let's not lose our heads. I'm sure we can come to a mutual understanding. I *am* concerned about your welfare and your future. I wouldn't want you to do anything foolish."

"That's too bad, Mr. Huntington, because I enjoy doing foolish things sometimes." David reached into his jacket pocket and pulled out a little windup, cymbal-clapping monkey that he'd bought on the street. Under Huntington's gaze, he wound the toy and set it loose on the old man's stately desk. The sound of the tiny cymbal echoed through the room.

"Goodbye, Mr. Huntington. I quit." And David spun around on the ball of his left foot and marched out of the office without ever looking back.

By late afternoon the euphoria had worn off and cold reality had begun to press in. Then David had an idea.

He walked across town to Times Square. In the bright light of day, it looked far less glamorous than it did in neon. The elevator at 126 West Forty-second Street stank of urine just as intensely as it had the night before.

Wending his own way through the labyrinth of empty rooms, David found Reggie in an office beside the studio, talking on the phone. When the conversation was over, the two men shook hands. Reggie didn't seem at all surprised to see him.

"Hey, mah man the lawyer, what's happenin'? Quite a night, huh?"

Quite a day, too, David thought to himself. "It sure was. I had a blast, Reggie. Thanks for the hospitality."

"Anytime, anytime, brother. So what can I do for you today?"

"Well, I'm in the market for some office space. Just a room, really—someplace I can work out of, have a phone, use during the days. I've decided to go out on my own."

"Congratulations, congratulations. No more boss man lookin' over your shoulder. I can dig it."

David smiled and nodded.

"And I bet you ain't gonna have any bread, at least not for a while, right?"

"Right."

"So you lookin' at all these rooms and wonderin', Hey, how about Black Jack?"

"You're too sharp for me, Reggie. You should be the lawyer."

"Well, you come to the right place, Dave. I'll make you a deal you can't refuse. Check out that back room, down the hall. It's big enough for you. You install your own phone, at your expense, and I'll charge you the mighty sum of one buck a month rent. In return, you do a little lawyer's work for the studio. See, I got all these guys that rent the studio, then stiff me on my fees. Now, if you could do a little collection work for me—ya know, using your legal clout—well, maybe I'll be able to get some of these dudes to pay their bills. What say, mah man?"

David didn't even bother to check out the back room. He

stuck out his hand. "You got yourself a deal." He wouldn't exactly be able to bring clients to his office, but it was a roof, a phone, and a mailing address, and the price was right.

David Barry, Esq., was in business.

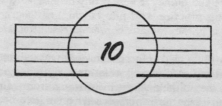

1966

HIT. I'M GETTING NOWHERE."

David pushed the chair back from his desk and started pacing the tiny "office" like one of the lions caged at the Central Park Zoo. His eyes scanned past his Columbia law degree on one wall and the signed picture of Jackson James on the other. Beside it hung an article, cut from *Billboard,* about Rick Firestone's string of hit songs. The sound of the horn section in the studio next door penetrated the thin walls and kept breaking his concentration.

At the edge of his cluttered desk, he stopped and picked up one of the tattered clippings from the *New Musical Express* that announced a 1962 Silverfish performance in Germany, with Ronnie Lee billed as the group's leader. The rest of the desk was hidden beneath stacks of law books and other clippings, photos, and paraphernalia of the old Silverfish, gladly provided by Ronnie Lee's dad in Manchester. David had gone through it all with a fine-tooth comb but hadn't been able to galvanize the material. He didn't have a case, and time was running out.

In the six months since his resignation from H & R, David had kept busy researching Ronnie Lee's case and handling numerous indigent clients. Busy but poor. Everyone had a problem. No one had money. Every penny he'd saved was going into his living, his practice, and into buying gristleburgers at Tad's for the struggling musicians he was representing. David was an easy touch.

The only thing he'd splurged on was fancy stationery: Crane's 100-percent-rag ecru paper, watermarked and engraved with a handmade die. If he'd learned anything from Huntington & Richardson, it was the importance of a great letterhead. Lawyers fingered other lawyers' stationery. The Crane's watermark, the tactile sensation of the heavy stock, the raised Tiffany embossing on the envelope flap, all made a strong subliminal impression on the recipient.

The Black Jack office had proved a godsend even though he couldn't invite anyone to his seedy digs and had to dance his way around lawyer meetings. Always claiming to be going to or coming from a meeting, he arranged his get-togethers in hotel lobbies or at the bar-association reading room or the Columbia Club. Collecting money for Reggie hadn't proved a problem either, especially after he learned that one Jack Black owned the studio and that the mere mention of the man's name put the fear of God into debtors. David suspected he was being used as an official, legal front for some sort of shady activities. But what he didn't know wouldn't hurt him.

At the moment he was climbing his own walls, desperate to find a way to help Ronnie Lee and himself. If only he could get a case going—he didn't care how weak as long as it was time-consuming and embarrassing to the Silverfish—the press would take care of the rest. There was no doubt in his mind that Ronnie Lee had gotten shafted. He'd called Joyce in London for confirmation. It was Ronnie who'd been the founder and the driving force of the Silverfish in the early Sixties. He'd formed them, written for them, housed them, road-managed them, and was responsible for getting them a manager, none other than Brandon Levy, and a recording contract. Then, immediately following their first recording date, in 1964, Brandon and the Silverfish told Ronnie to bug off. Six months later they were the biggest cult act to hit the music world since the Beatles—though they still lived in the shadow of the Fab Four.

Ronnie Lee had been left high and dry, four years of his life down the drain. He'd had no contract, no formal understanding, not even a handshake, no sheet music with his name on it, no copyrighted material, nothing but a tacit agreement that didn't count for shit in a court of law.

Ronnie was a broken chap, living on a broken dream. He'd let his bushy brown hair grow shaggy and unkempt, and he'd taken to drinking heavily, bitterness gnawing away at him. Every chance he got, he told his story to the press, recounting sordid details about the group. The fan mags were filled with Ronnie tales about the Silverfish and their personal "habits."

"I know why they did it," Ronnie had told David in his heavy Manchester accent. "They resented me. If it 'adn't been for me, they'd a never made a gig. But they didn't like me holdin' the money, wakin' 'em up to catch the trains, tellin' 'em when their playin' was rotten. If I 'adn't a doled out the cash, they wouldn't a 'ad any. If I 'adn't a kicked 'em in the arse and kept 'em off drugs, they woulda split up long ago. It was all my doin', and look what I got for it!"

Although Ronnie exaggerated some, the story rang true and David felt sorry for him. As soon as the dollar signs had appeared on the horizon, all the greed, resentment, and hostility had surfaced. The Silverfish decided to split four ways, with a manager, rather than five, so they cut Ronnie out without a cent. And now he wanted a piece of the action he'd never tasted.

David first tried negotiating with Brandon Levy. Despite their previous association over the Derek Robertson photo book, David didn't find Brandon at all cooperative. Levy was a tough cookie and knew that David didn't have a case, especially in the United States. Replacing a member of a band was common practice and legal under the terms of the contract with the record company; no contract had been violated; Ronnie'd received his share for what he'd done and wasn't owed anything. The Silverfish had no intention of settling out of court.

Now the band was in New York on the first leg of an American tour, practically creating riots, and David wasn't any closer to having a case. He stopped pacing long enough to switch on the radio. It was 7:30 P.M. and the Silverfish were due to sit in with Murray the K on his nightly "Swinging Soiree." David crossed his fingers: If they kept calling all through the show, one of the three girls he'd hired just might get through.

He listened with one ear to Silverfish tunes, played one after another . . . Murray the K's constant chatter about submarine race watching and Propa P.H. . . . the boys' playful mugging and the calls from ecstatic fans. Over the static, a young girl's question suddenly made David perk up. He leaned over to listen more closely.

"Please turn down your radio; we can't hear you, sweetheart," Murray the K told the caller.

"Can I talk to Colin."

"I'm right here."

"Well, I just wanted to tell Colin how much I love him. He's the most."

"Thank ya, luv," Colin answered.

David turned up the radio and turned on the tape recorder. She'd gotten through.

" . . . and I wanted to know what happened with Ronnie Lee and how come he wasn't with the band anymore."

"Oh, he was a nice lad, but he had a mess of problems." Just as David figured, this was a question Colin had been waiting for. He'd had his fill of Ronnie's bad-mouthing him and the group. "Forgetting lyrics, missing trains, not showing up for dates . . . Poor Ronnie, he just couldn't hack it. He messed up our first recording date so bad the record company insisted we do it again. I feel bad for him, but, ya know, we're professionals. Ronnie had some serious personal problems. We just couldn't rely on someone who was more into hard living—ya know, booze and drugs—than the music. . . ."

David snapped his fingers and grabbed the phone, a smile etched across his face. He dialed the Ace Limousine Service and asked for Tony. While he was waiting on the line, he began pecking out the summons on his Smith-Corona portable typewriter.

Forty-eight hours later, the Silverfish were cruising down Fifth Avenue in an Ace Cadillac limousine en route to their first appearance on "The Ed Sullivan Show." Barricades lined the streets near the CBS studio, barely containing the thousands of wild fans. High-pitched, almost deafening, female screams carried through the air. The Beatles . . . the Stones . . . now the Silverfish. The English invasion was in full swing.

When the limo finally came to a stop, police swarmed around the car, setting up a human barricade. As the black-clad chauffeur ran to open the rear door and let the Silverfish pile out, he handed envelopes to Colin and each of the other "lads." Colin shoved the envelope into his pocket absentmindedly, thinking it was another ticket request, or a groupie love letter, groupie phone number, charity request, or even a bizarre sexual proposition. That's what he usually got.

When the Silverfish, surrounded by policemen, finally made it into the building, the chauffeur drove over to Times Square, double-parked, and chugged up the elevator to Black Jack Studio.

"I'm lookin' for Mr. Barry," the uniformed driver told the black man in sunglasses and fur coat waiting at the elevator door.

In response, he got a thumb directing him back through the maze.

David stood up anxiously from behind his desk when he saw the tall Italian chauffeur approaching. "Well, Tony?"

"Well what?"

"Did you do it? Did you serve them?"

"Yeah, I did it. I gave 'em the papers, just like ya said. Where's my dough?"

"Just sign this affidavit of personal service on the members of the Silverfish and you've made yourself an easy two hundred."

The chauffeur signed, then counted out the bills that David placed in his hand. "Thanks, Mr. Barry. Glad ta be of service."

It was a hell of a lot of money for David, but it was money well spent, an investment in his own future. He immediately filed the case in the New York State Supreme Court. The court clerk, his palm greased with the usual twenty, placed a phone call to the local court reporter suggesting he check out case number 22031.

By that April afternoon, all the New York tabloids ran headlines like the two-incher that topped the front page of the *Tribune:*

SILVERFISH SUED FOR ONE MILLION DOLLARS
EX-MEMBER CLAIMS DEFAMATION OF CHARACTER

The legal jockeying began immediately. The counsel for the Silverfish moved that the court dismiss the case for lack of jurisdiction.

David filed a successful objection.

The attorney demanded the "complaint."

David, having done his homework, served the Silverfish with sixty pages of complaint and eight causes of action, written as much for the press as for the court, filled with irrelevant material about the history of the group and the victimization and malicious defamation of poor Ronnie Lee.

The Silverfish filed denials.

There were motions and preliminary hearings.

The case hung on the issue of jurisdiction. Could Ronnie Lee, a British citizen and resident, sue the four English members of the Silverfish in a New York court? If the jurisdictional issue had to be decided before the defamation suit, the case would drag on forever and probably be hopeless. David consequently gave every appearance of fighting for his life to avoid a pretrial hearing on the jurisdiction issue.

The press ate it up. Suddenly David Barry's name was plastered all over the pages of *Billboard* and England's *NME (New Musical Express).* Picked up by the Associated Press, UPI, and Reuters, the story of the suit ran in all the British and American tabloids, recounting the tale of poor Ronnie Lee and his American lawyer. Almost overnight David became a hero to all the downtrodden, disenfranchised, aspiring rock stars in New York.

That might have been enough for most lawyers. After all, David had garnered the publicity needed to give his business a shot in the arm. And, realistically, he didn't have a prayer of winning either case in court.

But it wasn't enough for David Barry. He was just getting started. Leaning back in his chair, he dialed the law office of Stevens, Erskine & Caldwell, the firm representing the Silverfish, and asked for Matthew Stevens.

"Mr. Stevens, this is David Barry. . . . Yes, I thought it was about time too. Listen, I've been giving the matter of this suit a great deal of thought and I don't think there's anything to be gained by our fighting over this jurisdictional question any longer. You're going to tie me up in court for months and there's nothing I can do about it. And you know as well as I that I won't see a penny till we get on to the defamation suit." David's tone was apologetic, almost self-effacing.

"So here's my suggestion." David sighed with resignation. "I'll make a motion for a special master to conduct a trial solely on the issue of jurisdiction. Only when that is settled will I ask the court to hear Ronnie's damage claims. I assume you find that agreeable?"

Although Stevens would have preferred that Ronnie Lee drop the suit entirely—and he tried to persuade David to do just that—he was delighted with David's capitulation. Brandon and the Silverfish would be delighted as well. Convinced that the defamation hearing would never be held, they would put the matter out of their minds, confident they had won and that the young upstart lawyer had gotten his.

David smiled to himself as he hung up the phone. He spent all night preparing the motion. In it, he argued that the testimony of the Silverfish was critical to deciding the issue of proper jurisdiction and that it was necessary for Colin and the other members of the group to testify in person.

The judge agreed and so ordered. David was on cloud nine. He knew the Silverfish wouldn't show for the December hearing. A meticulous orchestrator of the Silverfish image, Brandon would never allow his lads to taint that image with a court appearance.

When December rolled around, David sat anxiously in the judge's chamber of the New York State Supreme Court. Matthew Stevens, clad in his three-piece Brooks Brothers suit, sat opposite him. Reporters crammed the neighboring hall.

When the judge entered, Mr. Stevens informed the magistrate that his clients could not appear as a result of a previous concert commitment. He requested a postponement.

David immediately filed a second motion.

"Your honor, I move that a new date be set for the trial and that the Silverfish be held in default of one million dollars should they fail to appear a second time."

After strenuous objections from the shocked Mr. Stevens, the court agreed to David's motion and set a new date for the trial of jurisdiction.

That evening David received a call from Brandon Levy in London. Having finally forced the Silverfish hand, David felt smug and almost Machiavellian. His choreography had worked. The lawsuit was just show biz, and by playing "let's pretend" he had succeeded again.

"Let's talk, David," Brandon said. "I'll be in New York in

two weeks. Meet me on Saturday, December twenty-fourth at eleven P.M., 102 East Sixty-fifth Street."

* * *

The noise from the studio was so deafening that it took a good twenty seconds before the ring of the phone penetrated David's consciousness. Then he quickly grabbed the receiver.

"Hello, David Barry here," he shouted.

Between the loud live music in the background and the calling party's thick accent—he couldn't quite place it, but he liked its lyrical, musical lilt—David had to strain to make out the words.

"Mr. Barry, my name's Dwight Sharon. I read in *Mersey Beat* what you're doing for Ronnie Lee. I come all the way from Wales to meet you. I want to be a star, you know."

You and everyone else, David groaned to himself. At least this one's voice was melodious, and if he'd really come all the way from Wales, he got an "A" for motivation and three bonus stars for being British, in view of the current musical invasion.

No matter how tired or busy, David made a point of seeing all the struggling young artists who went to the trouble of looking him up. And there had been many since the publicity surrounding the Silverfish case. Poor kids, hitchhiking into New York from all over the country, charging windmills like Don Quixote, chasing dreams of rock stardom the way kids once beat down the gates of Hollywood hoping to become the next Gables or Grables.

David Barry was the one name they knew. "Barry, David, atty" was a listing they found in the Manhattan white pages. He was the lawyer who answered his own phone and didn't give them the brush-off.

"Come to Black Jack Studio tonight at eight, Dwight, and bring whatever you have to play."

For every ten cranks, crackpots, and self-deluded would-be stars, David was lucky to find one talented musician. But talent alone wasn't enough. The package had to include motivation, perseverance, and stability if they wanted to make it in the music biz. David wanted his artists to be strong, tough, and driven as well as talented. Only one out of a thousand had the right mix, and even then there were no guaranties.

Because he enjoyed the vicarious thrill of dealing with artists and potential future stars, David made a conscious decision to specialize in helping ambitious artists before they were devel-

oped enough to attract managers or agents. He not only listened
to their legal woes, he listened to their tapes and asked them to
play for him, establishing himself as a quasi agent/manager/
father/shrink to those singers/songwriters/producers who impressed him. If he couldn't be an artist like Rick, he'd go one
better: He'd be the man behind the artist—the go-between with
record companies; the man who secured, negotiated, and moni-
tored the record contracts; the man who bolstered and protected
the artist. He offered no bull, no jive lawyer palaver, no nonsense, just simple straight talk and simple logical agreements.
No "whereas" clauses, no "wherefore" clauses, no "parties of
the first part," no subparagraph 4AIII, no Huntington bullshit.

Of course, paying customers were few and far between. Although he was hoping for a monetary settlement of the Ronnie
Lee case when he met next week with Brandon Levy, money was
always a problem. Violating every rule of ethics and self-interest
drilled into him at Columbia and H & R, David didn't charge
fees—his clients didn't have the bread to pay anyway—but he
worked on contingent compensation, taking a percentage of his
clients' future earnings, hoping there would be earnings in the
future to take a percentage *of.*

When Dwight Sharon walked shyly into his office that evening, David let out a long, quiet breath. The kid couldn't have
been more than seventeen, was tall and gawky as an ostrich, and
was carrying a small guitar case. Worst of all, he was downright
homely, with a round face, a large bulbous nose, a space between
his crooked teeth, and kinky hair. A small silver hoop dangled
from his left earlobe.

"Come in, Dwight, come in," David said, getting up to shake
the boy's hand and directing him to a seat. "Can I get you
something? Coffee, a drink?"

Dwight shook his head and mumbled, "No, nothin', thanks."

David took a seat next to the young man rather than behind
the barrier of a desk. "So you want to be a star?"

"Yes, Mr. Barry. I come here all the way from Wales. I left
my family and sold everythin' I own to pay my way, and I won't
be goin' back till I make it. I love music, Mr. Barry, I really do,
you see. There's nothin' in the world more important." When
he mentioned music, his fat face seemed to radiate a special kind
of intensity.

"You've done a brave thing, Dwight. It took a lot of courage
to come over here all by yourself. You must be lonely."

Dwight hung his head. "I guess. But I don't care. I didn't have any friends back home anyway. I'm willin' to do anythin', Mr. Barry, anythin' I can to make myself into an artist."

"Tell me about yourself."

"Well, my real name's Herbert Sharon Waddington and I come from Aberystwyth in central Wales. I've four older sisters. My mom passed away last year and I never knew my dad. I play piano and guitar, and sing. I'm just startin' to write my own songs. . . ." His voice trailed off. "But I couldn't sing you my original songs yet."

Dwight didn't fill in the details. About how he'd been pampered and dressed up by his sisters until he felt like a Barbie doll. How he'd been beaten up so often by the local boys that he'd become reclusive, finding his only solace in the magic of music—its sounds, rhythms, and harmonies. How he'd been raped and abused as he grew older and ridiculed regularly as the local "poof" or faggot because he was so effeminate. His life was a lonely, torturous nightmare made tolerable only by his music.

"Why don't you play something for me. We can use the piano in the next room."

"That's all right, Mr. Barry. I got my own guitar." Dwight picked the beat-up black case up off the floor, plunked it into his lap, and lifted out the most pathetic, shabby-looking four-string guitar David had ever seen. It was barely larger than a ukulele.

He carefully tuned the guitar. "I'll play you somethin' by my very favorite singer and writer." Then he cleared his throat and began.

David didn't recognize it at first. Then, when he realized the Welshman was singing "How Can I Go On Without You?" he was amazed. Dwight was singing it soulfully, turning the song into a gospel piece. His voice was a tenor with a slightly nasal quality, but it was strong and melodic. The interpretation of Rick's classic was fresh and unusual.

David felt a shiver of joy. The kid wasn't sexy, he was even bizarre and more than a little faggy, but he had something special. David knew it in his gut and he knew it in his heart, because for the first time in years, even though he'd heard the song a million times before, this version made David remember the old days with Rick Feuerstein. And made him realize just how long it had been since he'd heard anything at all from or about his old friend.

When Dwight finished his song, David clapped heartily.

"Wonderful. That was beautiful. You've really got something special. So you're a Rick Firestone fan, are you?"

"Oh, he's my favorite. I've all his records and I've memorized all his songs. After my mom died, I played my old scratched recordin' of 'How Can I Go On Without You?' over and over again. It was listenin' to that song that made me decide that the only way I could go on without her was to leave home and come to America."

"What about your own material, Dwight? Can you play me just a little bit of something you've written yourself?"

"Well, I don't know if I can, Mr. Barry. I'm not real happy with anythin' yet."

"Just play a little something for me on the piano so I can get an idea of your style. Come on, we can use the studio next door."

Reluctantly, Dwight followed David into the empty studio and sat down at the upright. He practically attacked the piano, playing a short bluesy tune without words and then a faster, more upbeat piece with a few scattered lyrics. Then he turned meekly to David. "I'm sorry, sir, but I've not much more original material that I'm comfortable playin'."

Although it wasn't much, David liked what he'd heard, especially the boy's distinctive, self-taught piano style and his strong voice. "Listen, Dwight, I think you've got tremendous potential. I want to take you on as a client."

"You do? For real, Mr. Barry? That's super!"

"But it's going to take a lot of time and a lot of hard work on your part."

"Anythin'. Anythin' at all."

"First off, you've got to develop a writing style that's as unique as your singing style. It's not the Fifties anymore. The trend now is for singer/songwriters. Doing other people's hits works only for middle-of-the-road artists like Steve Lawrence. You can be more than that. You've got to concentrate all your musical energy on digging deep into yourself and coming up with your own material."

"Aw, Mr. Barry, I don't know if I can do it. I mean, I'm a singer, I've not written that much. . . ."

"Come on, Dwight, I know you can. You had enough balls to cross the ocean and come here to meet me. You want to be a star, don't you? Well, dammit, you can do it. You just have to focus all your energy and attention on your writing. With the right material, your style, and a little work on your image, I know you can make it. What do you say?"

"I'll give it my all. If you think I can do it, then I guess I can."

"How much money do you have?" David asked, looking at Dwight's ratty, fading blue jeans and work shirt.

"I didn't have even six dollars this mornin', but now I've thirty-five more, so that makes almost forty U.S. dollars."

"Well, congratulations. Did you find yourself a job already?"

"No, not exactly. I sold my blood this mornin' at the Ninth Avenue Blood Bank."

"For God's sake, don't ever do that again!" David scolded. "If I can get you a job as a gopher, a band boy on the road with a group touring the country, will you take it?"

"If you think I should, I will."

"All right, let me see what I can do. You won't get any chance to perform, you understand, and the band's just an opening act, but it'll pay about fifty a week, plus meals, hotel, and travel, so you can save every dollar and sock it away."

"Sounds fine."

"The most important thing is not to get discouraged. I could go out right now and try to cut a record deal for you, but it's premature and we might end up with the doors shut in our faces and nowhere to turn later. While you're out on the road— working every chance you get on your writing, right?—"

"Right."

"—I'll be making calls here, laying the groundwork. I'm going to send personal notes to the big record-company execs— like Thane Crawley at Apollo, Clive Davis at CBS, and Ahmet Ertegun of Atlantic—telling them about a remarkable new talent emerging in Wales. I'll tweak their interest, get your name tossed around, tell them you're developing musically but that you're not quite ready. Then, when the time is right, I'll arrange the proper introductions. How's that sound?"

"Super, Mr. Barry. I don't know how to thank you. You know . . . I don't have any money to pay you now, but I'll give you all the money I make on the road, if that'll help."

"Don't be silly. You hold on to your money. I want a piece of a big star, and that's what you're going to be. As big as Rick Firestone. Now, come on, I'll treat you to an all-American steak dinner downstairs at Tad's."

* * *

"Mr. Barry to see Mr. Levy," David informed the doorman.

Directed through the elegant lobby to the first-floor apartment, David was admitted by a butler into a posh, sprawling living room. He was as surprised by the setting for this meeting as by its date (Christmas Eve) and late hour.

Brandon Levy was lounging on the couch, a glass of brandy in one hand, a joint in the other. He was wearing a black turtleneck and blue jeans. His black work boots were propped against the upholstered arm of the light green couch. His pale complexion, short but styled brown hair, and high forehead served only to heighten the impact of his penetrating brown eyes.

"Sit down, David," Brandon said, without bothering to get up.

David took a seat in the uncomfortable Victorian chair beside the mahogany coffee table. He refused Brandon's offer of a drink.

"Tell me if I've got this right," Brandon began immediately, lying back on the couch and staring up at the ceiling. "You never intended to bring the defamation case to trial, did you? No, don't bother to speak, I already know the answer. You knew bloody well you couldn't win. Even if you could prove Lee was defamed, you didn't have a prayer of showing damages. The bloke was unemployed at the time Colin made an ass of himself on the radio and you couldn't possibly prove we'd done any more harm to the poor bastard than he'd already done to himself." Brandon took a long drag on the joint, held the smoke in his lungs, then exhaled.

"So you concocted a little trap, didn't you, and my fucking solicitors fell right into it. You set us up. You bluffed them into leaving my lads open to jeopardy. And while they were being lulled into complacency, you were planning to have your cake and eat it too. Not only would you emerge as the knight in shining armor, glamorous defender of the poor, victimized Ronnie Lee, but you'd get your settlement as well. Quite clever, Mr. Barry, quite clever indeed. So how much is this little fiasco going to cost the Silverfish?"

Before David and Brandon had a chance to get down to the nitty-gritty of financial negotiation, there was a knock on the door and a muscular young man in a black motorcycle jacket was admitted into the room. His hair was slicked back and black leather gloves and a red neckerchief jutted out of the rear pockets of his jeans. The back of his jacket was painted with a white skull and crossbones.

Brandon immediately got up from the couch and walked several circles around the stud, eyeing him lasciviously. He looked at the young man as intently as a horse bidder examining a thoroughbred at an auction.

"Yes, you'll do quite fine," Brandon said, more to himself than to the young man. "Go wait in the back room. I won't be more than an hour." Having directed the young man into the rear bedroom, Brandon returned nonchalantly to business, acting as if nothing unusual had transpired. He smiled pleasantly at David, revealing two distinct dimples, and got right down to the business of negotiation.

David remembered a conversation he'd had with Joyce over a year before, when he'd picked her brain about Ronnie Lee and Brandon Levy. She had mentioned something about Brandon's more peculiar habits and peccadilloes, but David hadn't expected him to mix business and pleasure so intimately. From what Joyce had told him and from his own contact with the man, Brandon still impressed him as sharp and demanding, a man who knew what he wanted and who expected a lot from others.

By 1:00 A.M. they had reached a financial understanding and formulated a mutually agreeable press statement. The Silverfish would appear generous, Ronnie Lee would end up with enough to stake him to the purchase of a respectable country inn and the wherewithal to regain some of his lost self-esteem, and David Barry would retain his shining image.

It was more than David had ever expected. But he'd played it cool and it had paid off handsomely.

"Enough business for one night, David. There's another reason I called you here tonight. Something else I wanted to discuss with you." Brandon rose from the couch, poured himself another drink, and began to pace.

David couldn't imagine what it was.

"It has to do with Joyce Heller."

David sat forward in his chair, his exhaustion suddenly forgotten. "What about Joyce? I haven't heard from her in nearly a year. Is something wrong?"

Brandon closed his eyes and took a sip from his scotch. "Yes," he answered. "She's been in the Stanmore Clinic for the past twelve months."

"Clinic? What happened?"

"I probably should have told you sooner. She had an unfortunate accident last fall."

"What kind of accident?"

"She was raped. Rather badly, I'm afraid. It was all rather brutal and traumatic." Brandon felt the wave of guilt wash over him yet again. He still remembered that night as if it was yesterday.

The note left for Joyce had been accurate. When he left the party, so stoned and drunk that he could barely stand, his driver had taken him to Buckingham Palace and followed behind him at a prudent distance as Brandon went ahead on foot to survey the tall, beautiful guards. In his state, they looked like Greek gods in uniform, standing not six but seven feet tall, towering over him as they looked imperiously straight ahead.

Just before the midnight changing of the guard, he slipped a note into the tunic of one of the guards, knowing full well that the man could not react or move from his formal position of attention. The note read: "Meet me outside the duty gate. I'll be waiting for you in the dark burgundy and black Phantom V Rolls limousine." Brandon staggered back to his car and poured another Drambuie. He ordered the driver to pull up to the duty gate. Then he waited.

The windows of the limousine were one-way, so passengers could see out but no one could see in. Just like the royal family, Brandon thought. How appropriate—I'm a queen too!

Brandon was thrilled by the danger. If he was beaten up occasionally, so what? He deserved it. As long as the bruises stayed with him, he could relive the delicious pain of the evening. If he was robbed, so what? He could afford it, and he deserved to be robbed. If his body was abused . . . well, that was the best.

Just after midnight, Brandon saw the guards leaving the gate. Three chaps approached. Between the double Drambuies, the two framboises, the champagne, and twenty milligrams of Valium, Brandon wasn't sure whether or not he was seeing triple. All of them seemed to be in their early twenties and as beautiful as gods, but what did he know or care? He just opened the door and beckoned whomever or whatever was walking toward him. Three young men got into the limousine. It was too, too delicious.

Until the next morning, when he returned to Wembley to find

Joyce bleeding and practically catatonic. He rushed her off to the exclusive Stanmore Clinic, some 100 miles outside of London. Catering to the rich and famous, Stanmore was the favored retreat of those seeking discreet professional treatment; the place to dry out, go cold turkey, or nurse a nervous breakdown. As Brandon knew only too well.

At the insistence of his dark-skinned "companion"/aide-de-camp, Kevin Singh, Brandon had checked into the clinic on a number of occasions: to ease off a drinking binge, to hide the facial wounds inflicted by an overzealous rough, and once again, several weeks after Joyce had been admitted, to have his stomach pumped of twenty-six blue Valium. That halfhearted suicide attempt had been prompted by his feelings of guilt and remorse at having abandoned Joyce on that fateful night. And by the other horrible, unexpected news about her.

"Oh, my God, poor Joyce," David said, overcome with shock at Brandon's revelation. The thought of Joyce being victimized tore at his heart. He felt angry at himself and at her attackers.

"Unfortunately, there's more. That isn't the worst of it."

"More?" David said incredulously. "What more could there be?"

"When the doctors examined her at Stanmore, they discovered a tumor. Joyce has uterine cancer, David."

"Cancer! Oh, Joyce." David sank back into his chair. His fingertips tingled. His stomach flip-flopped. "I'll make a plane reservation tomorrow. I can be there in a few days."

Brandon shook his head. "No, please, David, don't do that. She refuses to see anyone yet. She's absolutely adamant. She didn't even tell *me*—I had to bribe one of the doctors to find out. She's in rather bad straits, physically and emotionally."

"How bad?"

"Physically—they had to operate. Hysterectomy. She's on chemotherapy and seems to be responding. But they don't know anything for sure. Emotionally—I can't say. She's been very distraught, nearly suicidal."

"There must be something I can do."

"I'm afraid not. Not now. She's just about to be released from Stanmore. Give her a couple of months to get settled back in London. I'll let you know when the time is right, when she's ready. I think she's going to need moral support and a lot of time. By the way, she thinks the royalties from the book have been paying for the treatment, so when you do talk to her . . . "

"I understand. I won't say a thing."

David's head was swimming. Just at the moment of his greatest professional success, he felt totally empty. Joyce in the hospital with cancer. He'd tried to reach her a few times, but he'd been so wrapped up in himself. . . . And Rick . . . he'd made some inquiries and the word on the street was bad. Rick's career was taking a nose-dive. No hits, no publicity, no nothing. David's two best friends were falling apart. They needed him. He had to do something.

1967

AS RICK DRAGGED HIS FEET DESPONDENTLY THROUGH the February slush, he pulled his worn cotton coat tighter around his now corpulent frame and lowered his head against the harsh New York City wind. It was only another block to the Brill Building. Al would have work for him. He had to.

In the old days, Rose and Joey would have been there with him. They would have been traveling by limo. If Rose wasn't holding his hand, there was always another tall, big-breasted chorus girl to keep him company.

Now it was 1967 and, at twenty-seven years old, Rick was all alone, walking the New York streets like any other nebbish. No Rose, no entourage, no nothin'. The gin and tonic he'd downed at lunch wasn't having its desired effect; instead of making him less anxious, it was only making him more depressed and maudlin.

It was fear as much as anything that had kept him going through all of 1966. And hope. He'd kept imagining that the next song would break out and put him back on top. But it hadn't.

Suddenly nauseous, Rick flashed back to the roadside along the Belt Parkway, to the nausea and despair, to the audition and the rasping voice of Joey Gold. He'd come a long way since that humiliating audition in front of Jack Black. Twelve top-ten records, five chart-topping singles in a row; four best-selling albums; nightclubs in Vegas, Reno, Tahoe, Miami, Bermuda, New York, even Tokyo and Paris. He'd been the top bill, a headline act everywhere, and a staple on TV talk and variety shows. *His* glossy graced the window of Lindy's. Rina Constance, working Club Elite on Ocean Parkway in Brooklyn, was a nobody compared to Rick Firestone. Even temperamental Hedy Harlowe hadn't come close to boasting Rick's national cross-demographic following.

He'd been on top of the world, and then suddenly, or maybe slowly, perhaps inevitably—Rick never knew which, or understood why—it was all over.

Joey gave him the first kick in 1964. He'd felt that one right in his gut. But it was the Beatles and the British invasion that really did him in. Like a stone rolling down a rocky mountainside, his career seemed to career downward with increasing momentum and there was nothing anyone—not Rose, Joyce, David, or even he himself—could do to stop it.

It began in January '64, even before the Beatles did the Sullivan show, when Rick was headlining at the Fontainebleau in Miami Beach. The evening of his last show after New Year's, he was sitting at the square glass table in Rose and Joey's opulent and tacky adjoining suite. He'd just come in from their balcony overlooking the dark beach and the white-crested Atlantic. His damp elbows stuck to the "Welcome to Florida" paper placemat on the table. At twenty-four, his hair was thinning and beginning to recede prematurely, but he hadn't lost any of his boyish charm. He still looked as young and fresh-faced as he had in high-school.

The sitting room was done in vivid Florida colors, mostly aqua, with a pattern of oranges on the wallpaper and florid yellow slipcovers on the love seats. The room was filled with baskets of fruit and flowers sent by well-wishers. Rick never liked such gifts and would have thrown them all out, but Rose loved them.

"Hey, shut that door, will ya. Yer ruinin' the air conditioning.

It's gettin' humid in here," Joey shouted impatiently toward the bedroom, pointing to the sliding glass door that opened out onto the balcony. He was fixing himself another glass of twenty-five-year-old Chivas from the fully stocked bar. Joey was hitting the booze even better than usual that night.

"Sure, honey, sure," Rose said, hurrying in from the next room. Her dress was unzipped in the back and she was trying unsuccessfully to fasten her new diamond watch while shuffling across the carpet in her stocking feet. She'd aged noticeably in the past few years, no matter how much she overdressed or how much extra makeup she wore to hide it. Her hair was still a bright, teased gold, but coarser and stiffer. The bags beneath her eyes and the distension around her stomach were noticeably pronounced. With the money rolling in, and no more Becky to sound the voice of reason, Rose had puffed up literally and figuratively with her newfound status. Although her Richard was the star, it was her Joey whom she worshiped.

She stopped to pat Richard affectionately on the shoulder before she shut the glass door.

"Can we get on with this, please?" Rick said quietly but impatiently. "I have to get ready for the show, you know."

"Of course, of course, Richard," Joey said without moving an inch. "Hey, Rose, you want another?"

"Why not?" Rose said flamboyantly, going over to Joey and turning her back to him. "Zip me up, will you darling. You don't think my watch is too much for tonight, do you? I'll wear the matching earrings and necklace, too. I thought I'd wear the ermine stole to go with the ensemble."

"Anything you want, sweetheart," Joey answered tolerantly, pulling up on her zipper. But when he couldn't manage to fasten the top clasp, he pushed her away roughly and shouted in frustration, "Jesus Christ, who the fuck am I, your maid?" His hands were damp and shaky.

Rose meekly reached around and fixed the clasp herself. Then Joey handed her a Tanqueray and tonic, and sidled over to the table. He placed his drink on a shiny red Hialeah coaster and sat down in front of a leatherette-bound financial report.

Rick thought Joey looked foolish and overdressed in his black tux, white silk shirt, and alligator shoes, with his permanently tanned and shadowed jowls. He couldn't stand the man or his tough-guy act and abrasive manner. Joey was playing at being Colonel Parker to Rick's Elvis. Rick had never trusted him, despite what he'd said to David at the Copa, but all efforts to extract himself and his money from Joey's control always ran smack-dab into Rose. The last time he'd brought up the subject, she had practically gone berserk. "My own son is going to kill me." Rose poured on the guilt. "This is the thanks I get. After all Joey and I did for you—traveled with you, supported you, gave up everything for you. Where would you be without Joey? You'd have thrown your money away. Now you want to ruin my life."

"Cut it out, mom, please," Rick pleaded. "After all, it *is* my money."

"Cut it out? I'll cut it out, sure. I'll cut out my heart—a mother's heart. I'll pack my bags and leave, if that's what you want. If Joey goes, I go too, Richard." She walked away, an invisible knife protruding from her back. She gave him the silent treatment for the next month, as only a mother, and long-suffering martyr, could.

So Rick had closed his eyes to Joey's shenanigans, even though he suspected Joey was skimming from him and taking cash payments under the table.

Still and all, Rick couldn't complain. Rose was living in style, he'd bought houses for his sisters and paid for their children's orthodontia. He had everything he desired. His life was full, if not fulfilling. It was busy and exciting. There were songwriting sessions, new fittings, new arrangements, new tours. There were speedboats and the dog track in Miami and the tables in Vegas and a few drugs. There was an endless array of fantasy bed-mates—blond Jayne Mansfields and Jane Russell brunettes with giant jugs, whom Joey thoughtfully provided. There were two Mormon companions/bodyguards who reported to Joey and went everywhere with Rick. He missed his old friends, especially Hedy and David and Joyce, but he was never left alone long enough to feel too lonely.

There was no denying that Joey took care of everything. All the arrangements, all the bookings, all the money. Every performing date was booked through him, every letter and phone call screened by him. It was Joey who set up the corporation, Firestone Limited, which would save Rick millions in taxes. It was Joey who found the office-building tax shelter in Monticello. Joey who found the oil leases, the cattle deal, the airplane lease-back. According to Joey, Rick was a millionaire with "diver-sified assets, all with projected income and extra cash flow generated by leveraged financing structure," whatever that meant.

"Richard, here's your financial report for the last quarter of 1963," Joey said, opening the thick, expensively prepared report with funny tissue paper between the sections. He turned it around so Rick could peruse the gibberish of neat numbers. "I think you'll be happy. You better be." He laughed.

Rose came up beside Rick and looked over the figures.

"Now, as you know, Richard, we've got you set up as a corporation. This is smart business because you'll end up givin' the government less of your dough and that's what we all want, right?" Joey didn't wait for an answer. "It's all legit, mind you, but to keep it legit you can't personally control the money. I know you want to, but legally, technically, Rick, we gotta keep you on allowance—a salary—and let the corporation pay the bills. But you're not complainin', are ya? You got more than enough dough, right?" Joey leaned over the table and chucked Rick lightly on the jaw with his fist in a fatherly way.

Rick flinched. He couldn't stand it when Joey got playful and manhandled him.

"Of course, Joey," Rose answered for Rick. "We've got everything we need."

"Okay. Now take a look at that big number over there in the right-hand column," Joey said proudly, pointing his index finger to the ledger sheet. "That's one and a half million dollars. That's what we got from Apollo Records when *I* renegotiated your contract and signed you up with that classy Thane Crawley's new outfit. And see that other one million dollars? That's what *I* got you for re-signing with Al Norman. Of course, my twenty-five-percent management fee comes out of that, but it's like they're paying my fee instead of you paying it."

"Oh, my God!" Rose exclaimed. "Two and a half million dollars! I can't believe it, Joey. You're a genius!"

Rick could hardly believe it himself. He had trouble imagining a thousand dollars, let alone a million. And all for doing what he loved more than anything in the world: writing songs and singing. Somehow it didn't seem fair that others hated their lives and their work while he earned millions doing what he'd gladly do for free.

If only Becky could see him now. Rick hoped that she could, somehow, somewhere.

"The current assets for the corporation are over four million clams," Joey continued. "The other investments are all doin' pretty well, as it says over there, where it's marked 'Real Estate Investments.' " If you want, I can go into each one separate like and we can read the footnotes and special provisions."

"Oh, don't be silly. Richard doesn't want to be bothered, do you? Anyway, he doesn't have time. Go on now, Richard. You'd better get down to your dressing room. I can't wait for the show!" Rose beamed.

Rick dutifully got up from the table, pecked Rose's cheek, and walked into his adjoining suite.

"Break a leg, kid!" Joey called after him.

After the show, Rose came backstage to congratulate her boy. Rick was sitting before the dressing-table mirror in a terrycloth robe, sipping from a can of Coke. The neck of his robe was discolored by the ruddy No. 4 pancake. As he rubbed cold cream into his face to remove the last traces of makeup, he was still feeling the postperformance high. His insides glowed and he felt that spent satisfaction that came only after singing his heart out and soaking in the applause of a loud, adoring audience. There was nothing like it. Every other sensation, sex included, paled in comparison.

"What a performance!" Rose said, coming up behind Rick and kissing him on the head. "My boy is the greatest."

"Thanks, ma," Rick said, opening his eyes and looking around. "So where's your better half?"

"Joey? I don't know," she answered with a touch of concern. "He left for the men's room just before your first encore. How long can it take to piss?" she joked. "He's probably up at the room. Too much to drink. So what else is new?" she said philosophically.

It wasn't till early the next morning, when Joey still hadn't appeared, that Rose began to panic.

"Something's happened to him, I just know it. God forbid, he's lying in the gutter somewhere, beat up by thugs. All that drinking and smoking cigars, he had a heart attack. What am I going to do? I'm calling the police." Tears rolled down Rose's still heavily powdered cheeks. She'd been up all night waiting and had neglected to remove her makeup.

"Take it easy, ma. Take it easy," Rick said, taking the phone from her hand and replacing the receiver. "You know perfectly well that Joey's probably out gambling again. But if it'll make you feel better, I'll go talk to hotel security, okay?"

With the help of the house detective, a few well-greased palms, and a few phone calls, Rick had the story pieced together in a matter of hours.

He was angry, but not really surprised. He wanted to scream and yell, imagined his hands tightening around Joey's neck. He felt betrayed and victimized, as if he'd been raped. All the years of success suddenly felt unclean. He should have been more careful. He shouldn't have let it happen!

As he rode the elevator back up to the room, he knew he couldn't feel sorry for himself. Not now. Not when the worst was still to come: how to tell his mother.

Rose jumped off the couch when Rick entered the sunlit Fontainebleau suite. "Have you found him, Richard? He's dead, isn't he? Oh, my God!"

"He's not dead, ma. Far from it. I think you'd better sit down, though."

"Sit? Who needs to sit? So tell me, what could be so bad if my Joey is still alive?" she shouted, lapsing, in her angst, into her old Yiddish intonation.

There was no kind way. In any event, Rick was torn: Although he loved Rose and wanted to spare her the pain, he couldn't help blaming her. "He's flown the coop, ma. Split. Taken off."

"Coop? . . . Split? . . . What are you talking? Tell me in English, Richard."

"He left the hotel last night and boarded a plane for Rio de Janeiro. He was carrying a briefcase that had all our money in it."

"You're talking like a *meshugeneh*. If you think this is a joke, it's not funny."

"It's no joke, ma!" he said, raising his voice. "Over the past month, *your* Joey withdrew all the liquid assets of Firestone Limited. All the cash—every red cent. I talked to the banks this morning. All the shares of the corporation were in his name and he had checkbook signatory power. That's why he set up the corporation, so he could control the money. If he was saving on my taxes, mom, it was so he could rob us blind. And he has. Wiped us clean. God only knows what else he's done all these years."

Rick wrapped his arms around his mother and tried to hold back his own tears. "He's gone, ma. You'll have to forget him," Rick said as he let his head drop against his mother's shoulder.

"We've still got each other, and that's what counts. We did it before and we can do it again, right? Fire and stone, remember? We're indestructible. We can bounce back."

For once, Rose had nothing to say.

Afterward, however, Rick's resilience was gone. Not only had Joey Gold embezzled all Rick's cash, he'd mortgaged Rick's future to do it. The new auditors and investigators informed him that Joey *had* sold him short, just as he'd suspected, not only skimming off the top but booking Rick into extra, unpaid shows at the casinos to pay off his gambling debts.

And that wasn't the worst.

The worst was the record contract and the publishing contract. Joey cleverly had overadvanced the new deals, sacrificing long-term gain for up-front cash. He hadn't negotiated for higher record royalties or for Rick's right to own his master recordings or for the reversion of those masters at the end of the contract. He hadn't obtained publishing or even co-publishing rights for Rick's own music. No. He'd cross-collateralized the deals so that all the money Rick had earned or would earn in the future from past work or future work had already been paid out. From here on, Rick would be working to pay off a mortgage on his life.

When Joey flew the coop, he literally left Rick with nothing from his past and nothing to look forward to in the future. It was just as David had warned back at the Copa. Although Rick thought long and hard about turning to his old friend, he just couldn't bring himself to call him, not when David had been so right.

In the weeks following Joey's disappearance, Rose was hysterical. When she finally calmed down, she was too humiliated to face Rick or the world. The chutzpah, like her man, was gone out of Rose's life. Instead of a flashy gun moll, Rose now looked and acted the part of a broken, beaten-down, aging lady.

Rick, however—despite the financial fiasco and his feelings of frustration and helplessness—felt a sense of relief. He'd been taken and taken badly, thanks in no small way to his own mother. Instead of being consumed with resentment, though, he felt free and in control of his own life for the first time. He had his health, he had his talent, he had his career. He was determined to take charge. He tried to.

But everywhere Rick turned, there were Beatles. Their music, their haircuts, their clothing, their lyrics. You couldn't buy their love, they wanted to hold your hand, you loved them do. When he turned on the radio, instead of his old favorites, he heard loud British bands like the Animals, the Kinks, the Stones. The kids were going crazy, growing their hair, wearing Nehru jackets, buying British. He couldn't find his classical roots anywhere in the new music.

He didn't understand it. What he did understand, though, was that his life was suddenly a hard day's night. The next two albums he recorded for Apollo—two of the many he'd already been paid for—never made the charts. And his singles didn't make the top hundred, let alone the top ten. He was nowhere, man. No matter how much he listened, he never heard his songs played on the radio. He called Murray the K, the self-proclaimed "fifth Beatle" and New York DJ, in an effort to plug his new record.

"Rick Firestone! Hey, sweetie, baby, cookie, honey, so glad to hear from ya. Tell furry Murray, whatta ya been up to?"

"Keeping busy. I've got a new album out, you know. There's some great cuts on it, Murray. It's mellow, but it's got some real hooks."

"Ra-hight," Murray said, drawing out the word and pulling it apart like a bar of Bonomo's Turkish taffy.

"You got a copy from Apollo, didn't you?"

"Yeah, yeah. I got it here somewhere."

"So how come you don't play it on the air?" Rick asked, trying to restrain his frustration. "All I hear is English stuff, but the kids out there still love me, Murray. I know it."

"Sure they do, honey, baby, sure they do. It's just, you know, the Be-a-zeatles are what's happenin', baby. But for you, Rick, after all the hops you did for me, I'll see what I can do."

That night Murray did spin one of Rick's songs on the "Swinging Soiree." But it wasn't the single off the new album, or any other cut off the new album. It was one of Rick's early top-ten hits from 1962, which Murray sent out to the kids in Brooklyn as an "oldie-but-goody."

Almost overnight the world seemed to turn against Rick Firestone. The phone stopped ringing. He began hustling for gigs. Vegas and Tahoe dried up when he wouldn't accept anything less than top billing, and they weren't offering anything more than their small lounges. His appearance on ABC-TV's "Shindig!" in April of '65—along with Millie Small ("My Boy Lollipop"), Freddie and the Dreamers ("I'm Telling You Now"), Neil Sedaka ("Breaking Up Is Hard To Do"), and Derek Robertson ("Would You Do Me?")—only confirmed his fade-away. The audience didn't want to hear his new material. They wanted only his classic old hits—like "How Can I Go On Without You?"—over and over and over.

Then the record company began hemming and hawing about his next album. Even Al Norman started putting pressure on him. "Take your time, sweetheart," Al told him. "Work on new material. Try to change your image. You're behind the times, baby."

And he was. He was becoming passé right before his own eyes. He tried to let his hair grow long, but it was receding and too thin to look anything but ridiculous. It made him look like Benjamin Franklin. He tried smoking dope for inspiration, but it only made him so drowsy that he giggled and fell asleep at the piano. He tried wearing Nehru jackets and then tie-dyed shirts. When he wore beads and amulets, they made him look and feel silly instead of hip.

The one thing that didn't change was his music, and that was the problem. This time, though, there was no Becky to help him. Rose, a broken woman, was no substitute for the Gypsy Grandma, and Rick was too proud to lay the burden of his problems on his old friends. Besides, Joyce was off in England, and David was busy with his law practice.

As humiliation followed humiliation, Rick grew more and more depressed. He couldn't bring himself to get out of bed in the mornings. When he did get up, he ate compulsively until he gained so much weight that he resembled a pudgy buddha more than a boyish rock-and-roller. Finally, he stopped writing. He stopped feeling inspiration. The only vitality he ever felt was on stage. And ultimately he lost that, too.

Nobody wanted him as a headliner anymore. The best tour he could book in 1965 was as the opening act for Herb Alpert and the Tijuana Brass on the heels of "A Taste of Honey." He was allowed to sing for fourteen minutes to a fidgeting, coughing audience that barely tolerated his presence. The "Summer Spectacular" of 1966 at the Hollywood Bowl wasn't interested in Rick Firestone; instead, they signed on the Spoonful, Chad and Jeremy, the Byrds, Percy Sledge, and something called Captain Beefheart and His Magic Band.

Forced to return to Vegas as a lounge act, he sat at the piano on top of the bar in his ruffled shirt and played "Strangers in the Night" to a drunken crowd. They didn't even want to hear his old hits.

Like an addict suddenly deprived of his fix, Rick went cold turkey, unable to score, cut off from the high of his once adulatory audience. Although he kept going through the motions, like the shooter pumping weak smack into his veins, the kick was gone.

No matter how low he went, there always seemed to be another rung lower down on the ladder, until he ended up in the summer of '66 playing at Finkelfein's Château d'Or, a bungalow colony (known locally as a *kuch-alein*) just outside of Monticello. No one in the audience was under sixty. Rick wanted to die.

"Ladies and gentleman," the old Yiddish *tummler* (emcee) began, "he was born Richard Feuerstein. You all knew him as Rick Firestone, the *boychik* from Brighton Beach, Brooklyn. Tonight we have a real *somebody,* a real 'yenta-tainer,' who was once a *star.* Let's hear a big welcome for our very own . . . Rick Firestone!"

As the "band" of four nineteen-year-olds began to butcher his overture—music that Rick had originally scored and arranged for a thirty-piece orchestra—the crowd applauded. Standing in the wings beside the faded green velvet curtain, Rick felt overcome with fatigue and nausea.

He could have tolerated the quality borscht-circuit hotels like Kutcher's or Grossinger's, but instead he'd ended up at Finkelfein's Château d'Or, a grade D hotel advertised in the *Daily Forward* as "located conveniently only five miles from the Triangle Diner near Grossinger's in Upper Ferndale, halfway between Monticello and Liberty, in elegant Sullivan County, New York. European or American plan, dietary laws strictly observed; your host and hostess, Leon and Serena Finkelfein." The employees called the place the "Shadow Door" and referred to the Finkelfeins as the Cranstons (after "The Shadow," Lamont Cranston). Leon and Serena knew "what evil lurked in the hearts of men" because they personified it: They were cheap, mean, tasteless, and pathetic. There were "Finkelfeins" lurking all over the mountains, and Rick had worked for them all.

The show was in the "rec" hall, which served as the square dance and social hall, children's day camp, and indoor basketball court. For weekday movies and Saturday night entertainment, the room was transformed into a nightclub, with wooden folding chairs (purchased from a defunct funeral home) set up auditorium-style for all the "landsmen." The odor of mold and mildew that permeated the walls and the ancient upholstered furniture was exceeded in pungency only by the ever-present odor of chicken fat used for frying.

The place was the pits. The Finkelfeins were the pits. The performers were the pits.

At nine o'clock Yussel announced the start of the show. He introduced Leon, who made a dramatic entrance wearing a double-breasted, off-white, shawl-collared evening jacket, like a boy at a high-school prom. His toupee was slicked down with Brylcream, he reeked of Old Spice, his fly was open.

Leon was followed by Sasha Leonoff with his "singing accordion." An old-timer in the mountains, Sasha had just come from the Esther Manor down the road, where he'd been the opening act. After the Château, he would hurry to the Swan Lake Lodge to be the third act.

Sasha played the favorites. His specialty was "Lady of Spain" and his finale was a twelve-minute version of "Ochi cherniye" played as an accordion solo. His pièce de résistance, though, was his vibrato, obtained by shaking his accordion violently to the wild applause of the geriatric Russian-Jewish audience, who stamped their old feet in rhythm.

After another Yussel interlude, the second act, Sally Moskowitz, "the Sullivan County Nightingale," made her entrance. Sally was a bleached blonde with a bad nose job that made her look like a thin Porky Pig. Her arrangements dated back to 1944, when she'd gone out on a USO tour. Her performance ended with "If I Loved You," segueing into "You'll Never Walk Alone" and then "With a Song in My Heart," which she called her special tribute to "my dear, dear friend, the brave and courageous Jane Froman."

Standing in the wings, exhausted, Rick heard the sound of Jane Froman rolling over in her grave and heard Yussel give him the big, humiliating intro. He wanted to run away and cry and bury his head in his mother's chest. Anything to avoid facing the ancient audience of sunken eyes awaiting him out front. Instead, he gritted his teeth, took a deep breath, and resolved not to run away. He performed his songs in a daze. When he was finished, he kissed dry-mouthed old ladies and signed autographs on eight-by-ten black-and-white, airbrushed glossies from 1961, which showed him smiling in a black mohair suit and string tie, courtesy of Joey Gold.

When the performance was over, Rick shuffled back to the shabby dressing room and quickly collected his belongings. He still had one more show to do. All so he could keep supporting himself and help Rose out a little.

He didn't recognize himself anymore. Once he'd thought he was different and special—Becky had been so sure of it. Why then did he feel like a talentless good-for-nothing who'd flashed and burned out like so many other supernovas?

He looked down at the stack of his photographs on the floor. Like his photo, he was out-of-date, a dime-a-dozen collector's item. At twenty-six, he was over the hill, still breathing, but buried alive. Just two and a half years since the Fontainebleau . . . now he was a has-been.

He couldn't bear to look at himself anymore. Tears streaming down his face, he raised his foot and squashed it down hard against the thin, lifeless photograph. Lines of dirt—the imprint of his scuffed elevator shoe—slashed his glossy face and obliterated his expensively capped, fixed smile.

With the latest Catskill gig still fresh in his memory, Rick made his way out of the cold into the Brill Building and up to Al Norman's plush office. He was kept waiting nearly an hour before he was led into the office of one of Al's associates.

"Sweetie, baby, I'm Al's associate, Herb. Glad to meet you." Rick didn't accept his outstretched hand. "Where's Al?"

"Tied up, cookie. Business. You understand."

"No, I don't understand at all. What the hell's going on here? Al called. He said he wanted to see me."

"He did. That's right."

"So, has he got work for me?"

"Jeez, not exactly, sweetie. But we're workin' on it. Any time now, something's bound to turn up."

If he didn't have work to offer, why the hell had he called? Rick became suspicious. "Then what gives? Did he hear from that snot Thane Crawley at the record company?"

"Funny you should ask. That's why he wanted you to come by." Herb pursed his lips and squirmed in his chair. "I don't know how to say this, kid, so I'll just tell it to ya straight. They dropped you. Crawley's canceled your record contract."

For a moment, Rick stared straight at Herb in disbelief. Then he dropped his head into his hands.

"Apollo lost so much on the last album, they weren't willing to bankroll another. Al tried to talk Crawley out of it. He did everything he could. I'm sorry, cookie, really I am."

Suddenly it all came clear. Al didn't have the nerve to face him, the coward. He knew this was the coup de grace. Without a record contract, Rick was officially finished. He could read about himself on the obit page of *Variety*.

In a daze, Rick shuffled out of the plush office into the bare hallway and pushed the down button for the elevator. The sight of his old haunt only depressed him. The Brill Building was now filled with unfamiliar faces, long hair, English flags, weird Carnaby Street costumes. He felt out of it and out of place, like a washed-up ballplayer walking unrecognized through his old clubhouse.

When the crowded, old-fashioned elevator stopped at the fifteenth floor, the black operator, Joe, a Tin Pan Alley legend in his own right, wearing white gloves and a blue uniform, cranked the door back by its handle and croaked impatiently, "Goin' down!" The moment he spotted Rick, though, his whole manner changed. "Well, tan my hide!" he shouted, smiling to reveal a set of crooked, nicotine-stained teeth. "How-de-do, sir. Been a mighty long time. Everythin' all right?"

Why did they ask? Everyone knew. "Terrific, Joe, just terrific. Been writing a new Broadway show," he lied. "Got any room in there for me?"

"There's always room for *you*, sir," Joe said, turning to the packed crowd in the elevator. "Make way, folks, make way. Step back. There's plenty room in here."

As Rick squeezed in, he caught the resentful expressions on the faces of the young passengers. They all looked alike: stringy long hair; beads; malnourished bodies with twenty-six-inch hipless waists; imitation-leather high-heeled boots. Behind their arrogant attitude, Rick saw their fear, innocence, and naïveté. He'd been like them once. Even though the clothes had changed, he knew the script hadn't. They were going from publisher to publisher, being ripped off and ripped up, just as he had once. Now those days seemed so far off, he could barely recall their flavor.

Suddenly, the tall young man beside him, the one with the red bandana and the ponytail, tapped him on the shoulder and

looked him square in the eyes. "Hey, man, weren't you somebody once? I mean, weren't you Paul Anka or somebody like
that? I seen you on TV with Dick Clark, ain't I? Come on." He
smiled.

The tone was matter-of-fact and genuinely inquisitive. But
this was the unkindest cut and it stabbed Rick to the heart.
He felt himself start to blush. If only there were a hole to crawl
into . . .

Joe saved him from utter humiliation. He'd seen them all
come and go—some mean as rabid coons and a few, like "Mr.
Rick," real fine gentlemen. No matter who they were, how
famous or rich they were, they were all human. Up one time,
down another, just like the elevator. Nobody, but nobody, deserved to have his face *rubbed* in shit.

So Joe did the kindest thing he could. He stopped the elevator
on the next floor and said, "*Your* floor, Mr. Firestone. I hope
your many companies continue to flourish, sir."

"Thank you, Joe," Rick mumbled, getting off on the strange
floor. He headed immediately for the fire stairs and descended
the dark stairwell as fast as he could until he emerged out the
side door.

He wandered through the streets of New York aimlessly, for
hours, fighting the shame. "I don't have to run. I don't have to
hide," he repeated to himself. "I haven't done anything wrong.
I'm not a flash in the pan, a manufactured pompadour, or an
airbrush creation. I'm me. I'm a singer and a writer. I'm a
survivor."

No matter how loud or how often he repeated the words,
though, he couldn't make himself believe them. The past three
years seemed like 300. He felt like a relic from another age, a
walking time capsule. His hard-earned money was in Brazil with
creepy Joey. His talent was in doubt. His psyche was tattered
and fragile and he felt on the verge of complete collapse.

When he finally awakened from his trance, he was standing
on Fifty-third Street just east of Fifth Avenue in front of a group
of turn-of-the century brick town houses. Two of the brown-
stones were boarded up and a large sign, tacked to the plywood
over one of the glassless windows, read: MAJOR OFFICE BUILD-
ING TO BE ERECTED ON THIS SITE. FOR INFORMATION . . .

Instinctively, Rick walked through the open front door of the
building on the right, stepped into the French-style wrought-
iron elevator, and pushed the button for the third floor. The

inspection certificate above the controls said, "Maximum 3 passengers." He noticed that the elevator hadn't been inspected in over three years. Maybe the threes were a good sign.

When he reached the floor, he opened the door to the office and looked around. There was no one behind the reception desk and the office seemed to be in the midst of a major redecoration. He heard the sounds of voices down the hall and saw a brass plaque with the engraved words, The Law Offices of David Barry and Associates.

He took a deep breath and walked down the hall. He was running on empty. He couldn't go on without someone to talk to, someone to trust, someone to guide him. He had nowhere to turn but to his old friend, David Barry.

1967

"WHEW," DAVID SAID TO HIMSELF AS HE HUNG UP the phone after a series of long-drawn-out conversations with the legal department of Apollo. When he heard the faint rap on the door behind him, he spun slowly around in his chair. "Yes?" he asked.

But he didn't need an answer. His eyes told it all, though he could hardly believe them. Like a ghost appearing out of nowhere, just when David had been summoning his spirit, Rick Firestone was standing in the doorway of his office, shifting from foot to foot shyly, embarrassed, more like the old Richard Feuerstein than the great Rick Firestone. He'd been huddled outside the door for nearly ten minutes, trying to look inconspicuous, waiting for David to end his phone call.

"Rick!"

"I'm sorry about what happened at the Copa," Rick blurted out. "You were right. Everything you said was right. I should have listened to you." He hung his head and tears began to roll down his cheeks. He jammed his hands protectively into his pants pockets. He couldn't stop now. "Listen, I know it's been a long time, but I have nowhere else to turn. I don't know what's happened to me. Everything's gone sour. Nothing's like it used to be. I don't know where I went wrong." He raised his head and stared across at David with his tired, bloodshot eyes. "You've *got* to help me, David. Please. I need you."

David sat still, stunned, for several seconds. Then he stood up from his desk and rushed to his old friend. "Take it easy, Rick, take it easy. Come on, sit down."

His knees wobbling, Rick leaned on David's arm and stumbled over to the brown couch. He wiped the tears from his face but couldn't wipe away the expression of grief and defeat. "I know I should have come sooner. I . . . I just couldn't bring myself to. I've been isolated for so long, cut off from my friends and my roots. I thought I was different or better just because I was a star. Now all that's changed. Now you're a hotshot lawyer, a star, like in the old days, and what am I?"

"Please, Rick, forget the past."

"Don't be angry with me, David. I'm just so low. My career's hit bottom and I don't know how to get it back up. You'll help me, won't you?"

Poor Rick. Why did he have to ask? "Of course I'll help you. I'd do anything in the world for you."

When they embraced, the old friendship seemed to well up and wipe away the barriers that had built up over the years. Regaining his composure, piece by piece, Rick confessed to David the gory story of his decline, the tale of Joey and Rose, the Catskills, Apollo. Rick felt like a prodigal child returning home. After the problems with Joey and even when everything else had started turning rotten, he'd been too proud to turn to his old friend. Somehow the childhood rivalry and the Copa scene had seemed too strong and forbidding. Now the fear had passed and he wondered why he had waited so long.

"Listen, Rick, I've also got some bad news."

"More?"

David nodded. "It's Joyce. She's very ill."

"My God! Our Joyce! Sick?"

"Very. She was just released from the hospital in London." David suddenly realized what had to be done and the role he could play. "She needs us, Rick. I want you to come to London with me. Spend time with her. Help her out." That was the plan:

to reunite his two old friends in their time of need so they could help each other.

Rick wanted to. More than anything in the world. But how could he help poor Joyce when he couldn't even help himself? He hung his head. "Gee, I don't know if I can, David. . . ."

"Of course you can. Look, there's no point in your staying here any longer. You need a change of scenery. Come with me. Try your luck in England for a while. They still remember Rick Firestone. You might find the audiences more receptive."

"You think so?"

"I *know* so. I've got some contacts over there. I can set you up with some people. Plus Joyce knows the music scene."

Maybe David was right. Maybe England *would* hold something for him. A new environment, new audiences, a new life. When Joyce recovered, she could show him the ropes and help him get acclimated, even get back on his feet again—if that was still possible. Shit, he had nothing to lose. And nothing to hold him in the States.

"Okay. When do we leave?"

"As soon as I hear from Brandon. Maybe a week or so. Can you manage that? How long will it take you to fulfill your commitments and wrap up your affairs?"

"Oh, about half an hour."

"Go to it, then. We have to get to Joyce as soon as we can. She needs us."

When they arrived in London, David set Rick up in a small flat on the East End. They were about to pay their first visit to Joyce when David caught his friend by surprise.

"You'll have to go alone, Rick. I've got to see Brandon on business. It can't wait. I'll join you when I can."

"Well, maybe I should wait—you know, till you get back, so we can go together."

David shook his head. "Nope. Go to her now. Don't worry, I'll meet you there shortly."

Rick was perplexed but dutifully taxied to Joyce's neighborhood and, address in hand, made his way up the steep steps and knocked on an old wood-and-glass door.

"Excuse me," Rick said as the door opened to his knock and he gazed at an emaciated young woman in a tattered housecoat. Her eyes were dark, ringed with sadness. Her short black hair was dull and bedraggled. She wore no makeup to hide her pallor.

"I'm sorry to bother you. I must have the wrong apartment. I was looking for Joyce Heller."

He was about to turn and walk back down the stairs when she spoke. The voice sounded tired.

"What do you want with her?"

"I'm an old friend. David Barry gave me this address. Do you know where I can find her?"

She laughed without smiling. "Sort of. So who are you?"

Rick removed his sunglasses. "I'm Rick Firestone."

The woman put her hand to her mouth and gasped. Instinctively, she moved around behind the door to hide herself from his gaze.

Rick made an effort at a smile, then cocked his head to one side to watch her peeking around the door. The green eyes gave her away.

"I've missed you, Joyce," he said softly.

She closed her eyes.

"Want me to come back another time?"

"No!" she said immediately. She opened the door a few more inches. "Please. Don't go."

Rick took several steps forward into the small flat. Joyce closed the door behind him and stood still, her back against the door, hugging herself tightly, her fingers clutched into her armpits. When Rick turned around, the sight of her cringing against the door, biting her lip, overwhelmed him. She had the sad, frightened look of a child left alone too long in the dark. He reached out for her, slowly, and wrapped his arms around her bony body.

"You shouldn't have come," she said into his shoulder, without meaning it.

He hugged her tightly, then released his grip.

"Let me put on some clothes." She kissed his cheek, their hands lingered, then she went off into the bedroom.

Rick walked around the apartment. It was sparsely but lovingly furnished, with a green corduroy couch, a rolltop desk in the corner scattered with papers, and tons of books and records in various piles on the floor, the bookshelf, and beside the hi-fi. A little room off to one side was overflowing with photographic equipment and looked like a makeshift darkroom. There were plants everywhere, but many were dry and dying.

The air inside was cold and damp. All the signs were there. The flat, like Joyce herself, was in a state of neglect and disarray.

He moved to the bookcase and scanned the shelves. An over-size red binding caught his eye and he bent sideways to read the perpendicular title. A warm feeling swept through him. It was his songbook. His hand slid down instinctively to his bloated stomach and up to his thin hair. God, he must look like a monster; she hadn't even recognized him!

He squatted down and thumbed through the albums that were propped against the wall along the floor. She had all the latest stuff: Jefferson Airplane's *Surrealistic Pillow,* the Door's debut album, the Monkees' hot new LP, the Beatles' *Revolver* . . . the new sounds he couldn't relate to. Farther back in the pile, he found his own albums. All of them, including the last several flops. He felt a chill of remorse.

He stood up and moved into the kitchen. Numerous bottles of pills were lined up on the counter. He read the labels:

Heller, Joyce. One tablet every 4 hours or as needed for pain. Percodan, 50 tab. Compazine, 50 tab. Dr. Powell.

Heller, Joyce. Take one capsule daily, with food. Medroxyprogesterone acetate. Dr. Powell.

It went on and on. Rick didn't have to read all the labels to know how sick Joyce was. Looking at her had told him that.

When she returned from the bedroom wearing jeans and a black button-down shirt, Rick tried to put on his best face, even though he felt about as low as he could.

"How long has it been?" he asked, taking a seat at the table.

"A long, long time. Since the Copa. Almost five years."

"Wow. And you've been here all that time?"

Joyce nodded.

"Long time away from home."

"This *is* my home. There's nothing for me in the States." She turned and looked at him. Then she brought a teapot and glasses over to the table.

Rick felt an overwhelming need to open up to her and draw her out to him. It was a feeling he hadn't experienced in many, many years. Not since Hedy. Not until he'd gone to David. Anyway, he had to talk if he wanted her to talk to him. "I felt that way too, when my career hit the skids. After my manager ran off and my albums stopped selling, I was too proud to turn to anyone for help. It was more self-pity than anything else. I can see that now. When I finally went to David, I was really glad. He was so anxious to help, he made me feel silly for not coming to him sooner. After all, that's what friends are for."

Joyce didn't answer. She poured the tea into two glasses and sat down facing Rick. His face was puffy and there were small circles of hurt under his eyes, but Joyce saw only the warm, vulnerable expression. His rosy skin and thin strands of hair were like a baby's. But his baggy pants and wrinkled Oxford shirt atop his short, fat frame made him look old and worn, like a piece of secondhand clothing. Her heart went out to him.

"What are you doing here, Rick?" Joyce finally asked.

"David brought me. He thought it was a good idea. A change of scene, a new audience. Something to rejuvenate me. Any longer in the States and I would have ended up singing on street corners for nickels. Or worse."

"That bad, huh?"

Rick propped his elbows on the table, cupped one hand in the other, and rested his mouth against the backs of his hands. "Yeah, it got pretty bad," he said dejectedly. "After all that work . . . I gave them everything I had, Joyce, my heart and my soul, and then they turned on me."

"I know what you mean," Joyce said, thinking back to her time with Derek and the way she had been used.

"I didn't mind the grueling schedule, the anxieties of performing every night, getting psyched for every show, writing songs in motel rooms between gigs, driving all night, sucking up to all the local DJs. As long as they loved me, I loved it all.

"I worked for it, I really did. You can't imagine how many hours I put in writing, arranging, working on my act. And that's not counting the day-in, day-out job of self-promotion. God, I remember how my whole family used to spend hours on the phone, calling radio stations all over the country, using phony names and phony voices to get my songs on the air. Running to Forty-third Street every Sunday night to get the trades at the newsstand opposite Toffinetti's to see if I made the charts." He looked off blankly at the wall behind her.

"It got pretty sleazy sometimes, with the help of the record company. You know what I had to do? You won't believe this. Mom and my sisters and I, we'd drive to some small city and buy up a hundred of my own forty-fives from the local record store for ninety-eight cents each. Then we'd give that pile of brand-new records as a 'gift' to the local DJ, who'd sell them all back to the record store for fifty cents apiece, cash. In return, the DJ plugs my song over and over on the radio till the kids go out and buy it. So the DJ makes fifty bucks, and the record store makes a hundred and fifty—fifty on their sale and repurchase, and another hundred when the kids buy. Even though I'm out a hundred, my record gets hot and I make it all back, and more, in the long run. That's how it's supposed to work, at least. Sort of primes the pump. Pretty shady, huh?"

"You still had to have the will and the talent, Rick. You know that."

"I wonder," he said sadly as he looked down at the copy of *Melody Maker* lying beside his elbow on the table. "Now I don't even understand the rules. It's a whole new ball game and there's no place for me anymore. How am I supposed to compete with this?" he said angrily, pointing to the headline story.

It was datelined March 1967, from Finsbury Park, London: JIMI HENDRIX SETS GUITAR AFIRE ON STAGE!

Rick brought his hands up to cover his moist eyes. He hadn't meant to appear so weak and vindictive, but he just couldn't help himself. "I'm sorry, Joyce. You don't want to hear any of this. You've got your own problems," he said, shaking his head.

She reached out and wrapped her thin fingers gently around his wrist. The touch was intimate without being sexual, sending emotional electricity between them.

Rick raised his head and looked into Joyce's deep green eyes. He slid his hand down and covered hers. "Talk to me, Joyce," he pleaded.

She let her hand drop to the table. She wanted to run and hide, but instead she stood up slowly. She'd been alone so long, so long without human contact, that she was terribly frightened. If she shut Rick out, the way she'd shut everyone else out . . .

Taking several hesitant steps into the darkroom, she reached to one of the shelves, took a manila folder and a bulky envelope into her arms, and cradled them like a baby as she came back to the table. She laid them down gently before Rick, then remained standing quietly behind her chair. He looked at her questioningly, but she simply lowered her eyes.

He flipped open the folder. It was filled with black-and-white photographs, taken in odd lights and unusual angles, every one a picture of Joyce. Each shot was placed and dated on the back. As Rick slowly turned over picture after picture, he realized that Joyce *was* talking to him, in the only way she could, by showing him her most intimate diary, a photographic journal of the last twelve months of her life.

The pictures were harrowing. Starting in Stanmore, they

graphically recounted the deterioration in Joyce's physical and mental state. In some she was crying; in others she looked spent and lifeless, as the disease progressively ravaged her body.

The pictures were sharp and clear, but the year in Stanmore was a blur in Joyce's mind. Although she'd once visited Brandon at the swanky retreat a couple of years back, she'd never dreamed of ending up there herself. She'd always thought she was too stable and hard-nosed for such a place.

After the night at Wembley, though, she had been so crazed and catatonic that Brandon had driven her directly to the Stanmore Clinic outside of Bath. It was weeks before she could bring herself to get out of bed. She felt helpless and scared, like a child. She wanted to blame Brandon or Derek for what had happened, but she ended up reviling only herself. Instead of anger, she felt gnawing self-doubt.

The therapy sessions with the psychiatrist were pure hell. The guilt and humiliation were overwhelming. She couldn't escape the feeling that she'd been bad; that God, just like her parents, had punished and abandoned her. She felt as if the entire preceding year—everything from her meeting with Derek to the night in Wembley—had been fated, punishment meted out to her for sins of the flesh and of the heart. The feeling of desolation suffocated her, like a gag tied over her mouth.

When she learned she had cancer, she felt almost relieved at first. As if the physical disease dispersed the cloud of mental anguish. It wasn't long, though, before the deterioration of her cells started eating away at her. In her sleep, she imagined the cells multiplying and metastasizing, taking control of her body, sapping the last drops of her strength. She felt like she was dying. And she was, in a way.

After the hysterectomy, she felt even weaker. The chemicals they pumped into her veins to fight the cancer drained her will and made her nauseous. She felt as if the blood were being sucked from her body.

She hated the silence of the hospital. Like sleep, it filled her head with haunting memories that she had to block out. To avoid that silence, she filled her hours, waking and sleeping, with music from the radio. She imagined little vignettes, little films, images in her mind to accompany each song. Her fantasies soothed the flaming pains that ate away at her, inside and out.

Dozing in bed with an IV dangling from her arm, she wavered back and forth between consciousness and unconsciousness.

Barely able to distinguish sleep from waking, she slid impercep- tibly from nightmares to pain to a stupor induced by the Bromp- ton's mixture of morphine, cocaine, and Compazine. A bell kept ringing in her head and she imagined herself in the operating theater again. Faceless, masked, green-clad figures stood over her, probed and violated her. All around her, machines buzzed and hummed menacingly, as if preparing an attack. She tried to move, but her arms were tied down. She tried to scream, but no sound emerged.

As the months rolled on, she felt more alone than she'd ever thought possible. When she looked in the mirror, she barely recognized herself. Her once stylish short black hair was still cropped mannishly close, but her straight bangs hung limply over her forehead. Her face was pale gray and washed out, devoid of even a trace of natural color, her cheeks hollow and sunken.

The hysterectomy brought home the emptiness with a ven- geance. Although she'd never seriously contemplated children, and memories of her own childhood made the prospect of child- rearing terrifying, she had never faced the idea, much less the reality, of childlessness. When she reached down between her legs, she was dry and empty. There was no feeling inside her. She would never be a woman again; she would never be a mother; she didn't even remember what it was like to be a daughter!

She had nowhere to turn and no one she wanted to turn to. The more help Brandon offered, the less she wanted from him. She didn't want to be a burden. She refused to let Brandon tell anyone, including David and Rick.

With her skin shriveling, her hair thinning, her mouth dry as the desert, Joyce saw her present and her future dying before her eyes. It was fitting irony that her mother might be to blame. One of the doctors suspected she was a DES baby, but of course Joyce had no way of finding out for sure.

Now her old friend was here with her, and her whole perspec- tive seemed jumbled. She sat down at the table. "I also have eight-millimeter films I took," she said. "But I don't think you want to see those."

Rick picked up the album of Joyce's photographs again. There were notes of helplessness and despair written across some of the pictures, and the word *cancer* appeared frequently. Rick went through the pile a second time, then a third. When he came to the end, there were tears in his eyes.

"Why, Joyce? Why?" he asked plaintively.

"Why the pictures? I don't know. Therapy, I guess. It was my way of making it unreal. A way of distancing myself."

"What about these, Joyce?" Rick pointed to the photographs of her holding a gun to her head and a knife to her throat.

"I thought about it all the time. Once I even did try to kill myself in the hospital. But I couldn't do it. Something kept holding me back, a tiny voice that kept whispering that I wasn't ready to die yet, that I hadn't suffered enough, that something in my life was unfulfilled."

Rick listened carefully. He heard the pain in her voice, but he saw something else as well, maybe in the glow of her eyes or the nervous tap of her fingers. He felt a spark of determination smoldering beneath her fear. It made him feel ashamed of himself.

"You made it this far. That's something to be proud of."

"Is it? I wonder. I *am* supposed to be in remission, although I don't look or feel it. And I haven't stopped taking pictures, although I can't bear to photograph anything or anyone but myself."

Suddenly she jumped up from the table and ran into the darkroom. When she emerged, she was holding her old Hasselblad and focusing in on Rick's face. Instinctively he raised his hand up in front of his eyes. "Please, Joyce . . . " Then he caught himself. He was about to say no until he realized what was happening. Her face was bathed in concentration and she was taking pictures. Of *him*. He lowered his hand and turned on his best, bloated, baby-faced smile.

Just as Joyce snapped the picture, they heard the rap of knuckles on the door. Joyce's face and body flashed instinctively with fear.

"It's okay. Go on."

She moved to the door and opened it hesitantly. David stood there, smiling, looking tall and handsome. Joyce instantly threw herself into his arms. She cried, but for once the tears were mixed with joy and relief. The musketeers were together again.

Joyce pulled away, bent down on one knee, and held the camera up to her face.

"Smile, hot dog!" Rick called from across the room.

David's mouth curled into a broad smile. He held his hands out toward Joyce, trying not to show the anguish he felt at the sight of her wan, emaciated body. He could feel it. His plan was working. They *would* be good for each other.

Rick looked on with a new resolve. At last, he'd been reunited with his old friends. Even though David would be going back to the States, he would still have Joyce. Maybe England wouldn't be so bad. After all, he wouldn't be alone anymore.

* * *

The cigarette smoke in the pub was so thick that the spotlight barely cut through the haze. No matter how many adjustments she made, Joyce couldn't get enough illumination on the scruffy piano.

"Bugger it," she said softly to herself. The Golden Garter, in Manchester, was a workingman's pub and the thirty patrons wouldn't look up from their ales and stouts and Rothman's anyway. She moved away from the lights and slithered and bumped her way past the rowdy drinkers, around the dart shooters counting down from 501, and came up beside Rick at the semicircular wooden bar. The room was stiflingly hot and his hands were sweaty and shaking. She kissed him on the cheek and pursed her lips in the semblance of a smile. "Ready?" she asked, tipping her head slightly and raising her dark eyebrows.

"Yeah, I'm ready," Rick said sarcastically as he finished off the last of his Guinness. "Ready to pack it in. I've had it, Joyce. I can't face another rejection. They don't *want* me. They don't give a damn about me or my music. I can't do it again, really. Please, get me out of here."

"Come on, Rick," she pleaded. "You're just having a go at me. You're no quitter."

"Yes I am. I can't face them anymore. It's been too hard."

Joyce couldn't deny that. The past few months had been hellish for Rick. He'd worked the blue-collar pubs and clubs all over Britain, playing the Wooky Hollow in Liverpool, where you had to walk over a bridge to reach the stage; the Bag o' Nails off Carnaby Street; and driving his Mini-Morris six hours up and back in the same day to play Stockton near Sheffield. He'd sat quietly as they shouted for him to sing "How Can I Go On Without You?" and tossed worthless coppers at his feet. He'd suffered the humiliation of opening for Frankie Howerd at Talk of the Town, and still he couldn't make ends meet.

So he'd worked the streets. Even if Joyce had money to give him—which she didn't—he never would have taken it and she knew better than to offer. He put on crazy outfits so no one would recognize him and started playing the parks, going from Green Park to Charing Cross to Marble Arch to South Kensington and even down into the underground. Calling himself the Yankee Busker, an old term for a wandering minstrel, Rick dressed himself in Revolutionary War attire and sang old American songs for the farthings tossed him by strolling passersby.

All they had was each other.

They'd become inseparable over the past months, as soul mates but never as lovers. Sex was an idea that terrified Joyce, and the prospect left Rick flat. She showed him London, taught him photography, built up his self-confidence; he taught her piano and rekindled her will to live. It was really more for Joyce's benefit than for his own that Rick screwed up the courage to hit the pubs. He'd worked up an act, but only on condition that Joyce do the lights, that Joyce work the board, that Joyce help him pick out and rehearse the songs. And on no condition would he play any of his own songs.

They were like two inadequate sticks leaning against each other for support, made whole by their togetherness. Each one held up the other, and if one fell, down they'd tumble.

"You can't give up now, goddammit," Joyce pleaded, raising her voice. "It wouldn't be fair to me. *You* were the one who kept telling me to hold on, that things would get better, that life was worth living. You can't bugger out on me now. I need you to be Rick Firestone so I can be Joyce Heller."

She surprised herself with her vehemence. The past months had been harrowing for her as well. Although for the first time she felt a glimmer of hope, the uncertainty was always there and she could never be sure the worst was behind her. Every sensation was magnified out of proportion, every pain resonant with fear, every trip to the doctor turned her into a quivering mass.

Some of the fear, however, had turned to fight. Some of the self-hatred had turned to anger and determination. Now she wanted to get back at all the fuckers like Derek who'd raped her one way or another. There was too much she still wanted to do, too much she hadn't yet done, to give it all up. She wasn't ready to die. And neither was Rick.

Rick hung his head in shame and assumed his pouty little-boy expression. "I guess I'm feeling sorry for myself again. Don't worry, I won't let you down."

She ruffled the strands of his hair with her bony fingers.

"Don't mess the hair," he said in mock seriousness. "Not before the big show."

"What hair?" she teased.

His mouth dropped open and he propped his hands on his hips. Then he wound his way to the piano at the front of the bar.

There was no introduction. Joyce merely flashed the lights on and off several times. Then Rick adjusted the swivel chair, sat down at the piano, and began playing his repertoire of old British bar classics.

Through the first few songs, the noise in the bar practically drowned out the music. When Rick began "It's a Long Way to Tipperary," singing impishly and spiritedly over the cacophony of the crowd, heads turned slowly and voices lowered. The bar was filled with poor, honest folk out for a good time, and this was their kind of music. They didn't know a rock from a roll, a Stone from an Animal. They didn't know that *Sgt. Pepper's Lonely Hearts Club Band* had been released in June and was turning the rock world on its head. They didn't know about the battle of the bands—the Who versus the Jimi Hendrix Experience—that was taking place at Brian Epstein's chic Savile Theatre. They didn't know about the Monterey Pop Festival in California. For their few hard-earned bob, all they wanted was something catchy and familiar.

And that was what Rick gave them, thanks to Joyce's coaching.

Dressed in a Fifties-style band jacket, Rick remembered Hedy at the Baths and pretended to himself that he was playing before thousands of adoring fans. "Come on, you blokes, I can't hear you!" he shouted, coaxing them to join him in the refrain of "Tipperary." Although the songs weren't exactly Rick's glass of tea, they were stirring and melodious, a far cry from the noisy electric-guitar anthems that were deafening British youth.

At first, only a few joined in. Then, little by little, the singing grew louder, until the entire bar stood up, arm in arm, their mugs swinging back and forth in time to the music, and sang the refrain at the top of their lungs. Warm stout from an enthusiastic singer's mug sprayed onto Rick's arm. But he didn't mind. Like a shot of speed, the thrill of performance was seeping into his veins. He felt like he was taking his first steps after a paralyzing injury. All the elements he'd once honed to perfection—phrasing, styling, audience manipulation—he was now relearning from scratch, on old material, in a new country, in a different era. He knew it was just a beginning. After all, practically anyone could rouse a drunken bar crowd with the right material. But they weren't booing him, and at least he didn't feel he was betraying himself completely.

When he finished up with "Roll Out the Barrel," the applause swirled around him and he heard shouts of encouragement. "Good show, mate!" someone called out, slapping him on the back so hard that he practically fell to the floor.

Joyce came up beside him and hugged him. It was only a tiny skirmish, but they'd come out flush.

"Thanks, Joyce," he whispered into her ear. There were tears in his eyes, but he wasn't sure whether they were from joy or sadness. He had someone who cared, who helped, who listened. He needed her.

Joyce felt good again. She needed to be needed—and Rick really needed her. It felt so good.

"Hey, that's what friends are for," she said, smiling, as she handed him a warm stout.

13

1967

THE DRESSING ROOM BACKSTAGE AT THE PANTAGES THE-
ater was strewn with clothes. The entire Frederick's of Hollywood catalog of undies, sequined pants, boas, and tall flowered
hats lay draped over the chairs and scattered across the carpeted
floor. With the overhead light off, the bright bulbs framing the
dressing-table mirror cast eerie shadows over the room, painting
the white marabou-trimmed kimono and the cheap flower arrangement atop the bureau—courtesy of Abe Sanders—in chia-
roscuro on the far wall.

In the swivel chair before the mirror, Hedy sat tensely, staring
at herself, dressed only in a black lace teddy, black silk stockings, and high stiletto heels. She reached down for the iridescent
metallic-blue eye shadow and brushed it on heavily. Then she
shook another two Percodans from the plastic bottle and swilled
them down with a tequila sunrise. No way was she going on
without a first-rate buzz.

Hedy ignored the knocking at the door. When the banging

persisted, she screeched, "Fuck off!" Bette Davis–style. But the door opened anyway, very hesitantly, and in her mirror Hedy saw the beautiful, animated face of a young black woman peek around the corner of the door.

"It's show time, Miss Harlowe," Nadine said in a whisper. As the youngest, fattest, and newest of Hedy's backup singers, she'd been nominated to urge Hedy out. It wasn't a job anyone relished. Hedy'd already run through dozens of assistants and roadies on the tour, until she'd ended up alone.

When Nadine saw the mess of costumes on the floor and Hedy sitting half-naked before the mirror, she whistled in amazement. "Lawdy, Miss Harlowe, you not nearly ready! You got to move your white ass or we *never* gonna go on." In mock animation, Nadine started collecting the clothes and hanging them up. "You should see that crowd out there, Miss Hedy. They jes' dyin' for ya. They chantin' 'Harlowe, Harlowe, Harlowe,' like they at a gospel meetin'. You jes' can't keep 'em waitin' too long or they gonna up and riot. Now come on, whatcha gonna wear?"

Nadine's Butterfly McQueen routine always lightened Hedy's mood and she smiled at the mention of the crowd. The gay men and raunchy girls in the Los Angeles audience were her worshipers. Followers who chanted their mantra to the goddess of smut. After all, hadn't she put out for them for the past seven years? Concerts at every godforsaken spot in the country, albums, TV appearances; she'd given them everything they wanted and then some. But where had it gotten her? The same cult following, a couple hundred thousand in record sales, a reputation as the lurid darling of the press. Was this really all there was? Didn't she deserve much, much more?

"Maybe I'll just wear this. Whatta ya think?" Hedy stood up from the chair and spun in a circle, her hands propped under her huge breasts. "Plump and juicy like a Butterball turkey. Hold the mayo!"

"Miss Harlowe—"

"Can it, Nadine. You worry too much. That crowd ain't goin' nowhere without their heavenly Hedy. Hell, they wouldn't know what to do if I came out on time. They expect it. It's part of the act. Just go fix me another drink. In fact, make it a double and fasten your seat belt, it's gonna be a rough night!"

Nadine shook her head in dismay as she lifted the tall frosted glass from the dressing table and left the room, saying, "Honey, I don't even look like Anne Baxter!"

Reaching to the floor, Hedy picked up the February *Playboy* and thumbed through it until she reached her pages. Then she began reading, again.

PLAYBOY: What do you think about sex today?

HARLOWE: Okay, honey, I'm ready.

PLAYBOY: Let me rephrase the question. What do you see as the role of sex in today's society, in 1967, as opposed to five years ago?

HARLOWE: There's more *of* it and I'm all for it. All you need is sex, sweetie, that's my anthem.

PLAYBOY: Do you see yourself as a leader in the free-love movement?

HARLOWE: Listen, honey, I'm an entertainer, not a politician. I lead by example. Every time I go on stage I blow as sweet as I can with my voice and the audience comes all over me. I'd call that free love, wouldn't you? Free *after* you pay admission, I mean.

PLAYBOY: You're known for your outrageous behavior on stage and off. You've even been quoted as saying that you achieve orgasm while performing. Do you?

HARLOWE: Performing is a totally sensual experience for me and I try to impart that eroticism to the audience. Every song I perform is a climax, for me *and* the audience. Everybody knows that Hedy Harlowe gives good concert.

PLAYBOY: Is it true that you were strip-searched for drugs on your way out of Canada last month?

HARLOWE: It's true. The Royal Canadian Mounted Police manhandled me, and I loved every minute of it. I won't tell you the lurid details, but I did learn firsthand why they're called Mounties.

PLAYBOY: You've been called the Princess of Evil and the Body Snatcher. A number of groups in middle America have vilified your performances as devil worship and as a corrupting influence on today's youth. How do you react to such criticism?

HARLOWE: Just bring me those good ole boys. I'll show 'em some body snatch. They're all bisexuals anyway. They buy it whenever they can get it—get it?

PLAYBOY: Is the real Hedy Harlowe as outrageous as her public persona?

HARLOWE: Try me, cookie!
PLAYBOY: Is there someone special with whom you're
romantically involved right now? . . .

She thought of Nadine and stopped reading. She couldn't take
any more. The notoriety and the pose took her only so far. In
the end, no matter where she turned, the loneliness caught up
with her and seeped through into her soul. She frantically flipped
from the interview to the photos.

There she was, straddling a chair in black thigh-high boots,
black bra and panties, with a riding crop dangling from her
hand. And again, lying on her side on a shag rug, her chin
propped in one hand, her tongue licking her upper lip, and one
huge rosy nipple peeking out from the thin negligee. Her eyes
were closed and the soft, filtered light showed the ecstasy on her
face as her hand crept down between her thighs. Then, more
explicitly, Hedy standing in chaps and cowboy hat, lasso in
hand, with both breasts exposed and a tantalizing hint of fire-
engine-red hair sneaking out from inside her bikini shorts.

She wasn't the typical Playboy model, there was no denying
that. Her face wasn't perfectly shaped, her nose was too big, her
thighs and stomach were far from flat. But her tits were all-pro
and she oozed a sensuality that the photographer captured and
the readers drooled over. Hedy's attorney/manager, Abe Sanders, had thrown a fit when he'd seen the pictures and the controversial interview. As had Thane Crawley at Apollo Records. But
Hedy didn't give a shit. She'd made enough money for both of
them and they'd done diddly-squat for her. She'd do whatever
she goddamned pleased, even if that meant heaving a music
stand through the sound-booth window and walking out of her
recording session, both of which she'd done last week. Hell, it
was expected of her—she was Hedy Harlowe, after all.

After rave notices and five moderately successful albums,
nothing on vinyl sounded right to her anymore. The first album,
with Rick's charts, was still the best. In fact, he was still the best.
Lately she'd been singing a little bit of jazz, a touch of blues,
some show tunes, a few Beatles songs, but none of it seemed to
take off. She felt stagnant. She wasn't growing. She wasn't sure
where she was coming from or where she was going. The routine
had become boring.

Thank God her cult audience still adored her.

She looked down again at the lewd photos. Who'd have

dreamed that Lois Rabinowitz, fat slob from Brooklyn, would end up spreading her cheeks in *Playboy* for all to see? When nobody in particular cares to look, though, you might as well show it to everyone. For a fleeting moment Hedy wondered whether "everyone" included Rick. Why weren't they together?

By the time Nadine delivered her double, Hedy was finished making up and had settled, for a starter, into a gold lamé sheath dress with a long side slit as revealing as a full-length mirror. She slid her hands down over her hips and posed. The pills were kicking in and she could feel herself floating. The pump was primed and her engines were starting to rev.

As she opened the dressing-room door, Hedy heard the stamping, screaming, clapping audience, and the chants of "Harlowe" echoing through the theater. She pranced to the wings, blowing kisses at the stagehands and drinking in their best wishes. The stage manager practically swooned with relief when he spotted her. He touched her hand to his lips and immediately cued the lights and the intro.

Standing in the wings, glass in hand, Hedy swirled the drink with an orange plastic swizzle stick shaped like a naked woman. The grenadine blended with the tequila and the triple sec, the colors twisting and turning in the glass. One more swallow and she was ready.

When she heard the rousing introduction, she studied the colors in her glass before gulping the liquor down in one long swig. As she swaggered onto the stage, her last thought was of the tequila. Funny, she thought to herself, how it looked more like a sunset than a sunrise.

On stage, Hedy was transformed. Her cheeks glowed, her tits bounced, her body was bathed in sweat. The energy was contagious. Back and forth across the stage she prowled, like a cat in heat, alternately purring and yowling, her lips and hands cradling the microphone as if she were sucking it dry. When she mounted that stage, she was like a rodeo cowboy mounting a bull. The ride was fast and furious, crazy, chaotic, insane.

She started slow and easy, gliding into her own unique versions of "Fly Me to the Moon," "Yesterday," and "I Can't Give You Anything but Love." Changing into an outlandish Carmen Miranda costume, she clipped out "The Lady in the Tutti-Frutti Hat." She donned a skimpy soldier's outfit for her filthy dirty renditions of "Over There" and "Yankee Doodle Dandy."

Back in black velvet and long white gloves, she started heating up and the clothes started coming off à la Gypsy Rose Lee. She belted out "blue" material from black artists of the Fifties, such as Hank Ballard and the Midnighters, singing "Roll with me, Henry" and "Annie, please don't cheat, give me all my meat" from "Work with Me, Annie."

Finger by finger, she eased out of her elbow-length gloves until they came off in her hands. Then she twirled them one at a time above her head and tossed them into the frenzied crowd. She kicked off her shoes, propped her leg on a chair, and rolled down her stockings to the beat of a snare.

"Listen up, loosen up, lay down, get ready, people, 'cause I'm gonna fuck you with my voice!" she drawled as she segued into "Love for Sale."

"If you want to try my wares/ follow me and climb the stairs/ Love, sweet love, for sale./ If you want to pay the price/ for a trip to paradise/ try my love for sale," she crooned.

For the next half-hour, she was raunchy and vulgar, sensuous and sexual, as only heavenly Hedy Harlowe could be. Her act was a cross between Judy Garland, Belle Barth, Dinah Washington, and a triple-X-rated live sex show. She oozed decadence, re-creating the hot, steamy environment of the Baths, where raw lust had filled the air. She straddled the fence between vulgarity and sensuality, but, bottom line, what she gave her audience was great show business. Fabulous, dynamic, unadulterated entertainment.

As usual, Hedy asked for the houselights so she could get a glimpse of her adoring fans. While most of the crowd screeched with delight, she unzipped her black velvet dress, let it drop to the floor, and gave a sneak preview of her translucent white undergarments before quickly wrapping herself in a creamy fifteen-foot fox stole. A few in the audience, however—a middle-aged couple and a group of tourists who loved Hedy's records but hadn't been prepared for her show—had had enough and began to walk out.

From the front of the stage where she was singing, smiling, and grabbing hands with her front-row fans, Hedy noticed the movement in the orchestra seats. Suddenly her whole expression changed. She leaned back, away from the grasping hands, and straightened up. Her eyes shot daggers toward the crowd. Her nostrils flared and in the middle of a phrase she stopped singing. Angry and hurt, she turned toward the wings and marched off the stage!

The crowd whispered and fidgeted, unsure of what was happening. The band, accustomed to Hedy's fits, kept up the music and prayed she would return. The stage manager wisely lowered the houselights.

Hedy stalked to the wings, screaming for Abe Sanders, and demanded the band stop playing. Nobody listened. For several minutes, as the band played on, she ranted and raved.

"They're walking out on me!" she screamed. "I'm a star, they can't walk out on *me!* I won't take it. I give 'em the best goddamned show they've ever seen and what do I get in return? Shit—they treat me like shit! I don't have to take this crap. Hell's gonna freeze over before I go back out there—let 'em beg all they want!" Then she slumped cross-legged onto the cold floor beside a pile of ropes and wires, wrapped only in her long, luxurious fox, and started crying quietly. No one dared come near her.

Nadine sneaked off stage, came up and put her arm around Hedy's shoulder. She handed Hedy a drink and two blue Valiums and watched her swill them down without missing a beat.

"I won't go back on, Nadine. I refuse to go back on," she said softly but adamantly. The undercurrent of desperation bubbled to the surface, washing over Hedy the performer and reducing her to a heap of vulnerability and insecurity.

"Come on, sweet pea. You the queen. You got to go back on. It's your job. They all waitin' on you."

"Did you see them? They walked out on me. They hate me. They all hate me."

"Hell they do, Miss Harlowe. They worship you, they do. That was just a couple old fuddy-duddies you seen. Give 'em their money's worth, darlin', they gonna love you. You the best. Ain't nobody better. Now, you take a deep breath. . . ."

Hedy breathed in and out deeply as Nadine patted the tears from her eyes and called for a makeup girl. Then she helped the singer to her feet.

"Come on, honey, we countin' on you. You all right now?" Hedy nodded. "I've still got it, don't I, Nadine?"

"Course you do. There's nobody as hot as Hedy Harlowe."

Hedy's face suddenly became animated. "I'll show 'em, Toto. They ain't seen nothin' till they seen my cyclone. So, are we in Kansas yet?"

"We there. That's the spirit, Dorothy. Stick it to 'em."

When Hedy finally reemerged, she was ready and raring to go.

"Now let's get down and make some *real* love, baby," she said, smiling broadly and dancing her way into a steamy version of Percy Sledge's "When a Man Loves a Woman," as if nothing had happened.

It was only a matter of minutes before she overwhelmed the crowd with her talent and had them eating out of her hand once again.

"Baby, I'm gonna rope you and make you mine!" she twanged from center stage as she whirled the microphone around her head like a cowboy ready to rope a heifer. The mike smashed against the stage, sending a wave of distorted feedback through the speakers.

Hedy was cooking now.

She picked up another mike and threw off her fox stole. Her body was damp with sweat and her diaphanous slip clung to her loins and her breasts, revealing more than a little of her hot, naked flesh. When she started singing this time, she was melody and she was heartache, and she didn't stop for nearly an hour. All stops were let out. She bumped and ground, strutted and posed—but most of all, she sang. And, oh, how she sang, with a range and feeling that burrowed deep into everyone's heart, that made spines tingle and hands sweat, that carried from the first row of the orchestra to the last tier of the balcony. She sang new hits and old, finishing with Rick's "How Can I Go On Without You?"

There were encores and more encores until, finally, the show was over and Hedy returned to her dressing room. She was bathed in sweat and high as Mount Everest, her adrenaline pumping at full speed. She couldn't sit still or concentrate long enough to remove her makeup. Her eyes were blinded from the glare of stage lights and her ears rang with the chant of her adoring fans, crying "Harlowe, Harlowe, Harlowe. . . . "

Long after the music had stopped and the theater had cleared, Hedy sat alone in the dressing room, reliving every precious moment. Then the lights dimmed, the stage manager knocked on the door, and Hedy had no choice but to go "home."

Tonight the hotel suite seemed even lonelier than usual.

Wrapped in her white terry-cloth robe, Hedy pulled aside the curtain of the Château Marmont bungalow and looked out. She saw only shadows. Why hadn't Abe booked her into the Continental Hyatt where at least she could gaze out at the hookers and lights on Sunset Strip? Why was everyone conspiring against her?

Now was the worst time. When her body felt drained and exhausted but her mind raced like a dragster. Inside her head she could still hear the fans shouting her name, begging for a look, a wave, an autograph, worshiping at her feet. She could see the paparazzi's flashbulbs popping, the reporters buzzing, the security guards leering and secretly whispering requests for her signature. She was all alone, and alone seemed so much emptier, quieter, hornier after all that energy, love, and adoration lavished on her only hours before.

All she wanted was someone she could touch and feel, someone warm and close. Anyone, if only he'd hug her and stroke her, hold her and snuggle her. Forget "the act," it wasn't the sex she craved as much as the companionship. But everyone was afraid of her. The band members, her gay hairdresser, her fans, all shied away from her as if she were untouchable. They couldn't separate the public from the private Hedy. Any more than she could.

She'd called too many "dial-a-dick" male escort services to go that route again. That was too demeaning even for Hedy Harlowe. She'd tried coming on to her lead guitarist, and they'd done it once, but he'd run away from intimacy a second time, claiming bad vibes and potential disaster for the tour. Now that the tour was over, she *could* try him again, but she knew she wouldn't. She could try Nadine again, but that experience had left her unfulfilled and feeling strangely, puritanically guilty.

Nothing was turning out the way she'd planned. All around her, people were finding bedmates, going dancing, having fun. She was a prisoner of her name and her face. She could create a furor at any street corner, but she couldn't find anyone to care for or anyone to care for her. She was twenty-seven but felt like seventy-seven. Anywhere, even the cooler, would be better than here, where there was nothing and no one to cool her down.

Even though she had the money now, there wasn't anything she wanted to buy. She'd blown $125 on a Beverly Hills Hotel pool towel just so she could rub it across her face and feel like a queen. But it hadn't worked. She was hooked on delusions and illusions, trying her best to feel and act like an outrageous, extraordinary, inaccessible superstar so she could forget that she was only plain Lois Rabinowitz, ornery and on the edge.

She didn't even get off on her own music anymore. She

thought she sounded a little bit like Diana Ross, a little like Aretha Franklin and Millie Small, all rolled into one, but never like herself. No matter how hard she looked, she couldn't seem to find herself, musically or otherwise. She was facing the abyss: no more tour; an album she couldn't finish; the threat of suspension by Apollo; no place to go.

She walked to the TV set, switched on the radio at the bottom panel, then turned back to the window. The local L.A. station played one pop hit after another: the Troggs' "Wild Thing," the Mamas and the Papas' "Monday, Monday," the Monkees' "I'm a Believer," the Stones' "Paint It Black," Tommy James and the Shondells' "I Think We're Alone Now." With the exception of Mick Jagger, none of the new sounds or artists hit home for Hedy.

Actually, there *was* one, but he was already out of fashion. And it wasn't his music Hedy was interested in. When she'd caught "Shindig!" on TV over a year and a half ago—sitting alone in her room at the Howard Johnson Motel Lodge in Camden, New Jersey—she'd seen a hunk of a guy with blond hair falling in his face singing a suggestive, bluesy, ballsy, hot, electrified number entitled "Would You Do Me?" He played his guitar like he was playing with himself. His name was Derek Robertson, and Hedy couldn't take her eyes off him or his picture on the album cover. He was hot, all right, even if his music wasn't anything to write home about.

On that same show she'd seen Rick, looking sad and overweight, singing the same old songs with the same old backbeat. Even then it was obvious, his career was on the skids. He'd stopped growing musically. Across the airwaves she'd felt his despair. Now no one seemed to know where he was or what he was doing.

The last time she'd seen him in person was back in '63 when they'd both worked Jerry Lewis's muscular-dystrophy telethon. That was when her star was still rising and she was practically a regular on "The Tonight Show," and when Rick was still recording hits. For those few moments they'd dropped their guard and re-created the magic. They kissed and hugged with a spontaneous passion that neither of them had felt in years. In each other's arms, they shed the affectations, pretensions, self-delusions, and inflated egos—the trappings of their musical success—like snakes shedding their skins.

Although they'd both lip-synced to their own recordings earlier in the evening, Rick sat down at the piano and, live, accompanied Hedy in her smoldering original version of "I Can't Give You Anything but Love," to the delight of the studio audience and the millions watching at home. Hedy sang it just the way she had the first time, practically seven years earlier in Al Norman's tiny new office. It was a great moment of live television.

Between singing and answering phones, Rick and Hedy raised over $100,000 that night for Jerry's kids. Then, empty-handed and filled with longing, unable to either identify their feelings or react to them, and locked into months and years of empty obligations, they went their separate ways once again—alone and apart.

The thought of Rick turned Hedy from the window and back to the bottle of Cuervo Gold standing upright on the edge of the bar. Forgoing the salt and lime, Hedy poured herself another shot and tossed it back quickly. Then she reached for the phone book on the night table, sat down on the edge of the bed, and thumbed through the yellow pages.

She was hungry. Not for food, but food would have to do. Letting her fingers do the walking, she settled on Sal's Pizzeria, just down the road on Hollywood Boulevard. She dialed the number.

"Sal's," the gruff voice answered.

"Hey, baby," Hedy said in her most sultry southern accent. "This here's bungalow five at the Château. Would you be a darlin' and deliver me a really big, juicy pie. One with a very large sausage. Umm-hmm, that's right, a *large* sausage pizza. Sooner the better, honey. I'm just famished." She hung up the phone, lay back on the bed, and closed her eyes.

When the buzzer sounded, Hedy jumped. She'd nodded off. The buzzer sounded again.

"Hold your horses, pisan, hold your horses, I'm comin'."

She opened the door to a young, muscular, dark-haired Italian stallion with a perfect aquiline nose and a sweaty, sleeveless T-shirt that read SAL'S. Her appetite was suddenly whetted.

"Well, my-oh-my," she said. "What have we here?"

"Pizza, lady? You order a large sausage pizza? Says here, 'Bungalow Five.' "

"Come in, come in, young man," she said, gesturing for him to enter. "And what do they call you down at Sal's?"

"Anthony, lady. But my friends call me Tony. Where you want this?"

"Right there on the table. That's perfect. You look like you could use a drink, Anthony."

Tony stood awkwardly beside Hedy, looking around the suite. "Nice digs, lady. Yeah, I could use a drink. That parlor's so fuckin' hot all the time—oh, sorry, no offense."

"None taken." She poured them both shots of tequila and handed him a can of Olympia from the half-refrigerator in a corner of the room. "Here's mud in your eye."

"Likewise," Tony answered, downing his shot and taking a long draft from the beer. "I don't know if this is gonna cool me down, but it sure hits the spot. That'll be six-fifty, lady."

"What's the rush, Tony? You don't have to be back right away, do you?"

He hesitated and gave Hedy a closer look. She was wearing little or no makeup and her hair was a mess, but she wasn't hiding the mounds under her robe or the smolder in her eyes.

"Well, I . . . I guess I don't hafta go *right* back," he stammered.

She refilled Tony's glass and came up beside him. He smelled deliciously sweaty and masculine and good. "I have to warn you, though, Tony. It may be hotter here than at Sal's. Want me to turn on the air conditioning?" she said, letting her robe brush against his arm as she turned and switched off the overhead light.

"Naw, I can take it, lady," Tony answered.

"I sure hope so." She reached her hand out and ran it across the bulge in Tony's jeans. "You weren't kidding about the large sausage, were you!"

He stood still for only a moment. Then he grabbed her roughly and pulled her to him. His lips came against hers and she felt his tongue inside her mouth. She could feel her breasts crushed against his heart and his strong arms twined around her. Her toes were barely touching the ground.

"Whew, it *is* hot in here, cowboy," Hedy said when she came back down to earth. "Why don't you make yourself at home."

"Ah . . . I don't know. They're expectin' me back at work. . . ."

Hedy pointed to the phone. "You've been delayed. Your car broke down. You had to take me to the hospital. I'll bet you can think of something. Unless, of course, you'd rather deliver pizzas . . . " She was playing it cool, but her own heart was pounding.

Tony sat on the edge of the bed and made the phone call. Hedy sat down next to him, ran her hands through his hair and down over the muscular ripples on his upper arms and chest. As he stammered out his excuse, she unzipped his fly and gasped, while he practically choked on his words.

He wasn't wearing underpants. It was big and growing.

"I ain't never done this before," Tony said nervously when he hung up and looked down at Hedy twining her fingers in his pubic hair. "I'm a little embarrassed, lady. This is pretty crazy."

"You're doin' fine, kid. Just don't tell me you're gay. Or that you're an aspiring actor delivering pizza till you get your big break."

"Get outta here. My uncle Sal owns the pizza place. I'm takin' accountin' classes at Pepperdine so I can learn the business."

"I'm not looking at your books—only at your rolling pin. Can you accommodate me?"

"I can sure try."

She stood him up and slid his jeans down to the floor. Then she pushed him down onto the bed and took his throbbing, engorged cock into her mouth. She worked him slow and smooth until the saliva was dripping down the side of her face. She felt his hands caressing her hair.

Suddenly, he pulled out of her mouth and stood up. Hedy looked up at him in surprise. He grabbed her by the hand and lifted her up beside him. Undoing the knot of her robe, he slid the terry cloth off her shoulders and let it fall to the floor. He took her in his arms and kissed her tenderly, his tongue exploring the recesses of her mouth. She could feel him hard against her stomach. He held her so close that she melted against him. Her knees began to give way.

His hands wandered over her naked flesh, lingering on her nipples, then slipping down to caress the softness inside her thighs. Hedy heard herself moaning at the feel of his fingers in her hair and his lips sucking at her nipples.

"Turn around," Tony said. She complied, willingly.

He bent her over the bed so her feet were planted on the carpet but her face fell against the bedspread. She could feel his hands running along her back and caressing her wet insides.

When he started rubbing the head of his cock against her, teasing her, entering little by little and then pulling out, Hedy finally screamed out in frustration. "Please, Tony, all the way in!" she pleaded as she thrust her pelvis out to meet his.

"Okay, baby, you got it," he said, pushing himself all the way inside her until she was filled with his hard flesh.

"Yeah, that's it, Tony, do me, yeah, like that," Hedy moaned. She felt him deep inside her and it was hot and delicious, filling the emptiness that she'd felt for so long. Finally, she had a real man.

He moved slowly at first, round and round, back and forth, building the heat between them. She raised up on her arms and rotated her hips to meet his thrusts. His hands wrapped around her and squeezed her breasts, first gently and then roughly. The pain mixed with the pleasure, turning Hedy even hotter.

Then, slowly, he pulled out again and Hedy whimpered. But he merely turned her around and lifted her up in his arms. With her legs wrapped around his middle and his strong arms holding her up, he entered deep into her. As he carried her, and she rode him, she felt him sliding in and out of her, in and out, until they fell back on the bed together and she felt the full weight of his beautiful body on top of her.

When the wave came, she saw colors inside her eyes and felt the wave breaking all the way up in her throat. But Tony didn't stop. He kept on, for what seemed an eternity, rolling and tumbling until she screamed out again and again, and felt his warm liquid shoot into her. She felt him throbbing, the salty sweat dripping from his face onto hers, his warm garlic breath in her ear. It was sweet, so sticky sweet to Hedy that she prayed it would never end.

They lay there, hearts pounding.

When he finally stirred, Hedy held on tight. "Don't go," she whispered. "Stay with me, please."

He remained still, resting inside her, for a few minutes. Then he propped himself up on his elbow and kissed her sweetly on the lips. "I'd better be going," he said softly.

As he started to pull out, she grabbed on to his buttocks for dear life, then locked her hands behind his back and thrust her hips forward. "I won't let you go," she said forcefully.

"Sorry, I got to go," Tony said, pulling out and easily breaking the lock of her hands.

She groaned in anguish.

He stood up beside the bed and reached down for his pants. "That was great," he said sincerely as he pulled on his pants, buckled his belt, and went to the mirror to comb his hair.

The vision of the empty room made her jump up from the bed.

"Don't go, Tony!" she said desperately. "Stay the night, please. I'll make it worth your while."

"Sorry, doll, I gotta get back to work. Another time, maybe," he said, slicking back his hair and watching her in the mirror out of the corner of his eye.

When she held the hundred-dollar bill out to him, he turned from the mirror and looked down at her hand, then up at her face. There were tears in the corners of her eyes. The lines of his face deepened and his eyes narrowed in contempt. "What the hell is that?"

"For you, baby. Stay with me. There's more where that came from." She reached out and grabbed his hand. She pushed his palm against her pussy.

He yanked his hand away and slapped her hard, across the face. "What the fuck do you think I am, lady, a goddamned whore? You think you can buy me like a piece of fuckin' meat? Jesus, and I was gonna come back, too. I'm sorry for you, lady, you sick broad. Just gimme my six-fifty and I'll get the hell outta here."

Hedy, humiliated, reached back into her purse. She came out with a wad of bills and change and threw them furiously at Tony's feet. Mumbling under his breath, he picked out the six and a half bucks from the carpet and raced out of the Château Marmont, slamming the door behind him.

Alone again, Hedy lay face down on the carpet and felt the yellow shag bristle against her naked skin. Her cheek stung from the blow. The odor of cold pizza pervaded the room. It wasn't just her imagination; she wasn't just paranoid; everyone here *was* against her. She had to get the hell away. From everybody and everything.

The sound of the radio slipped back into her consciousness. The wailing guitar riff faded into a deep, sexy, hypnotic female voice, chanting out a familiar theme to a new, raucous beat. Hedy couldn't help but listen:

> Don't you *want* somebody to love?
> Don't you *need* somebody to love?
> Wouldn't you *love* somebody to love?
> You better *find* somebody to lo-o-ove.

When the song ended, Hedy picked herself up off the floor and raced to turn up the radio. This one *had* hit home.

The band was called Jefferson Airplane and the singer, Grace Slick. Hedy heard the DJ rap about the scene in San Francisco, about Ken Kesey and his Merry Pranksters, about Grace and a hot new Texas-born singer named Janis Joplin and her band, Big Brother and the Holding Company. Up there, man, the street people ruled the city. Everybody did their own thing and, "like wow," the more outrageous the better.

It sounded like paradise.

As he jabbered on about the beautiful scene at the first Human Be-In last month in Golden Gate Park, Hedy listened up. Ten thousand tripping, flowered kids tuned in, turned on, and dropped out to hear Ken Kesey, Allen Ginsberg, Timothy Leary, and Jerry Rubin talk poetry, acid, politics, mysticism, peace, and love; 10,000 fans reveling in the mind-expanding music of the Grateful Dead, Jefferson Airplane, and Quicksilver Messenger Service. There was talk of an upcoming pop festival in Monterey.

Suddenly, Hedy knew what she wanted. To go north, to San Francisco, where it was happening. Everything would be different there. Staying in L.A. was staying in nowhereland, looking for a nowhere man, and becoming a real nobody, but in San Francisco she'd find somebody to love.

1967

*W*HEN HEDY ENTERED THE AVALON BALLROOM, SHE was bombarded with sensation. A psychedelic kaleidoscope of sensation.

The music filling the dark theater was mind-shatteringly loud, emerging from racks of humongous speakers piled one atop another at either side of the raised stage. Amorphous colored shapes floated like drops of liquid across the screened backdrop and along the ceiling, where the words *Jerry Abrams' Head Lights* shimmered as if part of the firmament. On the walls, pictures of flowers and mountains alternated with old movie clips. A blinding white strobe pulsing from one of the corners cut every gesture in half, alternately revealing and concealing the wild young crowd. The dancing was nonstop as kids grooved on the rambling instrumentals and exotic lyrics of the Grateful Dead, whose long, free-form set was just coming to an end.

The way Hedy felt, she might have been grateful to be dead. She couldn't get her bearings; she was being bumped and jostled by long-haired kids with bare feet and painted faces, wearing flowers and feathers in their hair; the strobe was making her dizzy and nauseous. Wandering aimlessly in the huge hall, she finally worked her way up the stairs to the lounge, where there were tables and chairs, a bar with fruit and egg rolls and punch, and a puppet show.

It was almost harder than walking up the steep San Francisco streets.

In the far corner, a bank of black lights illuminated a series of Day-Glo posters that announced, in psychedelic print, past and upcoming concerts at the Avalon and the Fillmore. Hedy stared at a bearded swami with a third eye in his forehead and a brown pyramid overshadowing his face. The poster, several months old, advertised the January '67 Gathering of the Tribe for a Human Be-In. The tiny print at the bottom read, "Bring food to share, bring flowers, beads, costumes, feathers, bells, cymbals, flags."

The next poster was dripping red with an ominous yellow spidery creature in its middle. No matter how hard she tried, Hedy couldn't fathom the psychedelic script. Obviously, the electric Kool-Aid in the nearby punchbowl held the key, if she wanted to read the posters, understand their significance, and become one with the infinite mystery of life.

Even though practically everyone in San Francisco was on acid—LSD-25, Owsley, blotter, windowpane, purple micro-dot—Hedy had yet to unlock the door. When she first arrived, she thought she'd landed on another planet. The entire city was a psychedelic experience, from the vertical streets to the puffs of fog mystically rolling in from the sea, to the frilly Victorian houses that reminded Hedy of Grandma Becky's eyelet kitchen curtains. Even the colors of the city—the deep, rich yellows and blues and greens—seemed painted in Day-Glo and chemically induced.

All around her, people were expanding their minds, altering and distorting their perceptions, raising or lowering their consciousness. They were spaced out and stoned, ready and willing to imbibe anything and everything, begging for "spare change." They were "tripping," and to Hedy it seemed they were falling flat on their faces more often than not.

Still and all, she loved it, even though she didn't yet feel a part of it. She loved the laid-back energy, the wandering minstrels, the outrageous freedom, the spaced-out camaraderie, the spirit of adventure. She, too, was a lost soul in search of a new self. She, too, wanted to be transported and transcendental. But she was afraid.

She was here alone, on her own, and only Abe knew where she was. She'd told him she was researching material for her next album. Which was true, in a way. With a pad on Pine Street, her own light machine, and a new set of old gypsy clothes, Hedy was doing her best to fit in. She didn't much go for the grungy, paisley, Indian-beaded-leather look. Or the shabby crushed-velvet, Renaissance Maid Marian look. Or the painted, feathered, cowboy-and-Indian look. But she blended in well enough in colorful peasant skirts, Polish dirndls with tightened strings that accentuated her enormous breasts, blouses off her shoulders, necklaces, bracelets, and, of course, sandals, Becky-style.

Musically, she was still floating, though. She'd sung with a pickup band a few times at the Coffee Gallery in North Beach but couldn't get into it. She was on a different wavelength and couldn't relate to the obscure, pretentious lyrics and the open-ended improvisational style.

More than anything, she wanted to make a name for herself here. But she couldn't bring herself to sing spiritual, sociopolitical drivel—she was too steeped in her own sexual brand of show biz to do that. If she wanted to make it here—where Hedy Harlowe was hardly a household name and the street people hardly had households—she had to find a way to superimpose her own *schtik* onto the scene.

"Quicksilver," a voice screamed into her ear from behind.

Hedy practically jumped out of her skin. She turned around and looked up at the tall blond figure beside her.

"It says 'Quicksilver,' for Quicksilver Messenger Service. You know, the group," the voice said, pointing to the Rick Griffin poster. "And if you look at the black part of these letters, you'll see the name Charley Musselwhite."

For an instant Hedy thought her eyes were playing tricks on her. She wondered if that was how it felt to drop acid. Then the strobe caught his face and she saw his rosy cheeks and his blue eyes. Even though his eyelids were heavy and his eyes glazed over, there was no mistaking him.

"It looked like you were having trouble reading the poster," he said, leaning over and shouting into her ear so she could hear him over the din. As he stumbled slightly against her, she felt his warm breath in her ear.

"I was," Hedy answered. "Thanks."

"Can you see it now?"

She gave him a puzzled look.

"The name, I mean." He pointed to the mush of red shapes near the bottom of the poster.

"Yeah, I can see it," Hedy lied.

He swayed his head away from her and gave her a quizzical once-over. "Hey, I know you. You're Hedy Harlowe, aren't you?"

She smiled. "Only if you're Derek Robertson."

"And if I'm not?"

"Then I must be somebody else." See? She could play the game.

"But you're not, so I guess we're all who we think we are." He handed her a joint. "I've heard a lot about you."

"Nothing good, I hope. When I'm good, I'm good; but when I'm bad, I'm better," she said, without crediting Mae West.

"Only that you're one hot mama. And that your shows really smoke. I was into that kind of stuff, too, once."

I'll bet you were, she thought to herself. "Guess that makes us soul mates, huh?" She took a toke on the joint and handed it back to Derek. She noticed his eyes were glued to her breasts.

"Guess so."

"I saw you on 'Shindig!' a couple years back."

"Gimme a break," he said, smiling. "That was in another lifetime, man. I don't need that shit anymore." He put his hand on her shoulder, pointed toward the bar, and let her lead the way.

Hedy wasn't sure what he meant. Or—judging by the shape he was in—that he knew himself. It made no difference, though. Every move he made was so fucking sexy that she got hot just looking at him.

From the punch bowl on the corner table, he poured out two cups of the red, electric Kool-Aid and offered her one.

"No thanks," Hedy said.

"What gives?"

"Not my drug of preference. I always preferred fizzies."

"Baby, you don't know what you're missing. This stuff's dynamite. Come on, try it."

Hedy shook her head.

Derek would have hassled her more if she hadn't been saved by the bell. The silence was unmistakable. The recorded music stopped and the stage lights dimmed. Fans suddenly thronged forward toward the stage, shouting and stamping their feet in frenzied anticipation.

"Come on, let's get up front," Derek said, putting his arm around her waist and running interference for them. Thanks to Derek's pushing his way aggressively through the throng, they bolted down the stairs and secured a spot reasonably close to the raised stage. Bodies crushed against them on all sides. Derek kept his arm protectively around her shoulder.

"I used to play with these guys," he whispered to her.

"Really? What happened?"

He shrugged. "Chemistry wasn't right."

As if out of nowhere, the band materialized on stage and the music started. When the singing began, Hedy was instantly mesmerized.

Go on, go on, go on, go on . . .
Didn't I make you *fe-eel,*
     like *you* were the only man?
Didn't I give you *every*thing
     that a woman possibly can?
But with all the love I give you,
     it's never enough.
But, I'm gonna show you, baby,
     that a woman can be tough.
I want you to go on, go on, go on, go on . . .
Take it, take another little piece of my heart now, baby.
Break it! Break another little piece of my heart now, baby.
Have a! Have another little piece of my heart now, baby.
You know you got it, if it makes you feel good.

It was Janis Joplin. The Avalon Ballroom was going wild.

The music was San Francisco psychedelic, but the vocals were pure, unadulterated, shit-kicker country blues. Every note Janis sang, she wrenched up from the depths of her soul. The anguish was so real that the audience could feel the strain on their own vocal cords. Clearly, Janis didn't give a damn about her voice. She sang it all out, the only way she knew how.

In a world steeped in fantasy and smoky illusion, she was the real thing. You could hear it in her crackling, raspy voice and see it in her passionate gestures, all washed down with a desperate swill from her nearby bottle of Southern Comfort. Joplin wasn't performing for the Avalon Ballroom. She was living her life on stage, flashing her naked soul for all to see.

Hedy was drawn forward with Derek. Her two hands clutched his arm. Her stomach twisted into knots. She was overwhelmed with jealousy, and hatred. Janis was everything Hedy wanted to be. And never could be. Both of them were loaded with talent, both racked by despair and loneliness, but only Janis was living the pain out on stage. Where Hedy was show-business, Janis was gut-wrenching emotion. Where Hedy was sensuous life, Janis was living death, burning her candle at both ends for all to see. Where Hedy was a consummate performer, dazzling and flashing for effect, manipulating her audience, Janis wasn't acting at all. There was no Joplin persona. The Joplin on stage—stripped of inhibitions, weird, passionate, unhappy, battered, ugly—that was the only Joplin there was.

Hedy raged within. She imagined herself picking up the beer bottle lying beside her foot and tossing it at the stage. Somehow Janis had betrayed her, had torn the heart and soul right out of her breast. There was no doubt in Hedy's mind that Janis was stealing her act, her pain, even her lurid passion. It wasn't fair.

The rage was only a cover, though. A way to cope with the feeling, trembling deep within her breast, that compared to Janis, Hedy Harlowe was a fake.

After watching for forty-five minutes, Hedy'd had enough. She wrapped her arm around Derek's waist and said into his ear, "Let's split outta here. How's about taking me home, partner?"

When he snapped out of his trance, Derek looked down into Hedy's sensuous eyes. This was one invitation he wouldn't turn down. "Why not? Let's blow this joint."

When Hedy emerged on the street, her ears were ringing, the speakers still blasting inside her head. The image of Janis, on her knees, screaming the blues, was burned into her brain. She felt threatened and disoriented.

Derek led the way up the block to an all-night deli. "Let's get some beer," he said. "Got any dough?"

Hedy paid for a six-pack, then followed Derek out to the street, where he suddenly grabbed her hand and started running. "Come on!" he yelled, hopping onto the back of the cable car and pulling her up beside him.

"Hey, where're we going? My pad's the other way."

"You'll see."

After a short ride on the cable car, Derek jumped off and directed Hedy through a winding trail in Golden Gate Park, past the renowned "Hippy Hill," to a deserted mound of grass.

"This is it. Bitchin' spot, isn't it?"

They lay back on the damp grass, alternated hits of grass and beer, and looked up at the stars. The cool breeze off the bay sent a chill through Hedy's bones and she snuggled close to Derek for warmth. She was desperately glad he was there. For the past month or so, she'd done her best to deny the loneliness, pretending it was only natural, filling her days with endless activities. Now she felt it crashing down around her. Despite the new surroundings, she'd been feeling as empty as ever. If not more so.

Until tonight.

They lay together, body to body, silently, for a long time. No words were necessary. Not when their bodies spoke the same language. Even before their flesh touched, sparks arced between them. For once, the energy was there, for both of them, and they both felt it.

Derek let his hand run down her blouse, over her breasts, and down between her legs. His touch was light and spacey. When he leaned over and curved his tongue along her lips and into her mouth, she shivered and opened up to him. Her tongue played against his and she felt his hands working at the buttons on her blouse.

"Let's go to my place," she whispered hoarsely.

Derek went on kissing and unbuttoning. Then he shook his head. "No way. I want you here and now, outside, under the stars."

She didn't want to be square, but the Lois Rabinowitz in her wasn't used to an audience, even if Hedy Harlowe was.

"I don't know, Derek. What if somebody comes?"

"Fuck 'em. Who gives a shit? Come on, baby, mellow out, loosen up. You're too uptight."

She laughed. No one had ever told her *that* before!

"Let me show you how," Derek said. He reached into his pocket and slipped something into his mouth. Then he leaned over Hedy and kissed her passionately, his tongue darting inside her mouth. Before she knew what had happened, he'd transferred the tiny paper into her mouth and it had slid down her throat.

"Hey, what the—"

He kissed her again and she felt a bitter, papery taste linger in her throat. "Trust me, baby. You wanna see the aurora borealis, don'tcha?"

At first she was frightened, but in a half-hour the northern lights were dancing in her head, and their bodies were generating enough electricity to light up Golden Gate Park.

She rode alternate waves of joy and terror as he undressed her and she felt his hands glide over her naked body. The damp grass caressed her back and thighs while Derek's fingers roamed in and out of her moist insides. When she burst out crying, he rocked her in his arms until the fear passed, then he laid her back down on the soft, enveloping grass. For a moment she shivered uncontrollably, imagining that she was an electrical wire and that Derek was unraveling her insulation. She felt naked and charged.

"Just lie back and relax, baby. It's gonna be all right," Derek said soothingly. "You've got nothin' to be afraid of. Just spread those legs for me. That's a girl."

She felt the damp trail of his tongue and the wet flick between her legs. She cried out. Circles of light whirled before her eyes when he drew warm circles on her labia. His tongue slithered, like a serpent, inside and around all the openings of her body.

He tasted her insides and bit into the flesh on her thighs. He was flying now and his breathing became more staccato and his touch rougher and more frantic. His passion charged, he seemed to change, like a werewolf under the bad moon rising. He ripped off his pants and moved over her. His hands gripped her wrists and pinned her back against the ground. His eyes, reflecting moonlight, looked wild and threatening. His head shook back and forth and his blond mane whipped against her face. Suddenly, Hedy was terrified.

"Derek, stop, please. I'm frightened," she pleaded.

He ignored her pleas and pushed his knees between her thighs.

"Let me go. Let me go!" she screamed, panicking at the touch of his cold, hard cock against her. "You'll kill me!"

"Shut up, bitch!" Derek hissed. "I'm gonna fuck your brains out, baby, whether you like it or not."

Like a stallion, he mounted her fiercely, penetrating her thrust by thrust until she thought she would split.

"Oh, my God, Derek. Oh, my God," she whimpered.

The animal was alive, inside her, and she bucked and kicked to get him out. But with each thrust, she went farther under. His scent filled her senses. She could smell her own musky odor on his face. She heard his heavy, rapid breathing. Instantly she, too, was an animal and she was moaning wildly, her insides burning with sensation. He was riding her, frenetically, and they were climbing and descending the San Francisco hills.

Hedy dug her nails deep into his back and used her muscles to suck him deeper. He was firm and hard and rigid and powerful. He kept up the rhythm, on and on, never stopping, never missing a beat. She never wanted to lose it, she never wanted the music to stop.

Longer and harder, longer and harder, he moved inside her until she could barely endure the intensity. She had to be dying, the pain and pleasure were so inseparable, indescribable, interminable. The tempo increased. She imagined herself a guitar, a red Stratocaster, being played higher and higher on the register, the pick in Derek's hand moving faster and faster, making her body screech out an endless psychedelic solo. He was radiating up from her toes, down from the tip of her head, right into her center and then out again. The hairs on her body were so sensitive that every brush of his skin shocked her system.

When she hit the high note, she cried out at the top of her lungs, screaming and moaning, sobbing and laughing, as orgasm after orgasm picked her up and let her down, picked her up and let her down, until she was totally out of control.

"Please, stop! Please, stop!" she begged. "I'm freaking out!"

He thrust one final time and let out a bloodcurdling moan. Hedy felt like her insides were drowning. Finally, he slowed the tempo until he was only gently sliding in and out. Then he collapsed on top of her. It was the first time he'd come in over a year.

When the sun came up, they were wandering the streets like two lost puppies. Past Far-Fetched Foods, the I-Thou Coffee Shop, Tracy's Donuts, the Panhandle. Everything looked hazy, and Hedy's body felt strange and clammy. She was wired, from her fingers to her toes, and she couldn't control the roller coaster of emotions.

By some miracle, they made their way back to her pad. She

was shaking badly. "Take this," Derek said, handing her a blue capsule. "It'll help you come down."

"I'm frightened."

"Just take it, baby. Really," Derek said.

"Are you gonna take one?"

"I got my own way of comin' down," he said, disappearing into the bathroom.

When he didn't come out for what seemed to Hedy an eternity, she started knocking on the door in a panic. "Derek, are you all right? Derek, answer me!"

She put her ear to the door but didn't hear a sound. Slowly turning the handle, she pushed open the door and looked in nervously.

When she finally uttered a sound, the scream was guttural and wildly hysterical.

Derek was sitting on the toilet, a syringe dangling from his hand, his head nodded to one side. His eyes were rolled up toward the ceiling and his body seemed lifeless. A trail of blood trickled down his forearm.

When Hedy awoke, she was slumped on the cold tiles, huddled against the bathroom floor. She opened her eyes and looked around. The bathroom was empty.

Her body ached all over and the light over the sink was painfully bright. But the haze had cleared and she felt in control again. She pulled herself up off the floor, leaned against the porcelain sink, and stumbled into the bedroom. Derek was lying on the bed. Crawling up beside him, she laid her head on his bare chest. She could feel the rise and fall of his rib cage and hear his soft breath. The tension broke inside her. "I thought you were dead," she whispered, tears choking her words. "God, I really thought you were dead."

His hand stirred and rested on her head. She felt his tender stroke along her scalp.

If that was "tripping," Hedy never wanted to leave the house again.

* * *

The huge second-floor loft near the corners of Haight and Ashbury was bare except for a couple of ratty mattresses on the floor, an old International Harvester refrigerator in the corner (with a Grateful Dead skull painted on its door), and strings of red and green beads hanging from the high ceiling. The moldings were Victorian, an old fireplace graced the corner, and one of the windows was stained glass. Handbills, covered with footprints and announcing events at the Radha-Krishna Temple and the free medical clinic at Happening House, were scattered about the floor.

Derek led the caravan up the stairs, carrying his own two guitars. Behind him, four scraggly band members and a couple of their lackey friends struggled up the stairs lugging instruments, amps, soundboard, mikes, wires—the technological trappings of acid rock.

Derek didn't deign to help them set up. Instead, he ambled over to the corner, grabbed a can of Coors from the fridge, and settled down on one of the mattresses. He lit a Camel and blew smoke rings into the air. From across the street he could hear Tom ("Big Daddy") Donohue on radio KMPX playing "Light My Fire," the first single of a new group called the Doors, then Scott MacKenzie's new pop hit, "San Francisco (Be Sure to Wear Flowers in Your Hair)."

What a dive, Derek thought to himself. After years of slick rehearsal halls and fancy recording studios, this was the pits. A fucking concrete reminder of just how far and how fast he'd fallen.

Looking back, he realized Joyce had been the turning point. For better and for worse. Sure, he was flying high for the year after she left. Endless tours, countless broads, more drugs than he could ever consume, all thanks to Apollo. But by the end of '65, the fans and Thane Crawley were singing a different tune. Tired of Derek Robertson, they'd left him behind for another, hotter flash in the pan.

Suddenly, his creative juices had stopped flowing. With no Joyce to encourage him, direct him, support him, baby him, nurture him, light him and dress him, with no one he could trust, he was left high and dry, without strength, self-confidence, or self-esteem. When the second album bombed, Crawley reneged on all his fancy promises. Apollo refused to pick up its option for a third album and Derek found himself without a recording contract. He felt betrayed and used. Chewed up, sucked dry, and spit out, like a wad of old tobacco.

Feeling down-and-out, he returned to London, the scene of his greatest fame. He imagined himself rekindling his old fans, but when he arrived, all he could think about was Joyce and rekindling the old flame. Like a man obsessed, he looked every-where—checked old addresses, frequented familiar pubs, hung out at old haunts. But Joyce was nowhere to be found. No one had seen her in months.

Alone, really alone, for the first time, Derek became despondent. He didn't write, he didn't play, he didn't sing. His fragile ego began to crumble. He couldn't bear to face the bitter reality: that Derek Robertson had been a mere figment of Joyce Heller's imagination. That he was a one-hit artist. That he was merely a name and never had been, or would be, a star. If it was true, where did that leave him?

When he returned to the States and San Francisco in early '66, the scene was popping and Derek felt rejuvenated by the energy. He let his hair grow down to his shoulders, became a regular with the acid-dropping Merry Pranksters and the Family Dog, attended Ken Kesey's three-day "trips festivals," grooved on Eastern mysticism, hung out at the Psychedelic Shop in Haight-Ashbury. At one time or another he played around with all the local groups—the Charlatans, the Great Society, even Big Brother—but he never lasted. Everyone knew he was too burnt, too spaced out and unreliable. He wasn't into music anymore. He was into drugs.

They'd become his alpha and omega, his crutch, his wake-up call, his bedtime companion. After running the gamut of illegal substances—black beauties and crystal meth, sopors and ludes, acid, peyote, and STP—Derek still found himself too conscious, and too empty.

When he found smack, his quest was over. Nothing else could compare. It was like finding God. Nothing and no one else mattered, including women and sex. In the land of Kool-Aid and flower power, Derek started shooting up. And making bread off supplying junk to fellow travelers in the rock scene.

When Hendrix had called him last month, his ego had soared. Jimi Hendrix, man, far-fuckin'-outta-sight. For two days he'd actually believed Jimi would ask him to join the Experience. But all Jimi had wanted was a connection.

"Hey, where the fuck is she, man?" Rodney, the bass player, called out across the room. "Are we gonna have to wait another fuckin' hour for her again. We only got this dive from seven to nine. Jesus Christ."

"Cool out, man. She'll be here. Don't hassle or you'll blow your big shot. Guys like you are a dime a dozen around here.

I can replace you like that," Derek said, clicking his thumb and middle finger. "And don't you forget it."

He stood up on the mattress and sucked down the final drops of his brew. Then he cruised over to his ax and plugged in. For the first time in years, he felt like playing music. Things were gonna change now. Already they were lined up for a big gig at Mount Tamalpais in early June. The mix was unbeatable. They couldn't miss. In no time at all, his career would be back on track. His whole life would turn around. He'd be famous again. And rich.

Hedy Harlowe would see to that.

* * *

The crowd was 15,000 strong for the two-day Mount Tamalpais Fantasy Faire and Magic Mountain Music Fest in Marin County.

Camping out on the mountain grass under the bright June sun and into the crisp nights, smoking pot and dropping acid, the fans lay back and grooved. Mimes and magic, gurus and organic goods, prayers and pulsing beats, the fest offered good vibes and beautiful head music. The setting was mystical and the music nonstop, echoed across the mountains by such heavyweight bands as Jefferson Airplane, the Doors, the Byrds, Country Joe and the Fish, Smokey Robinson, Dionne Warwick, and the hot new duo of Hedy Harlowe and Derek Robertson.

As Sgt. Pepper promised in the just released Beatles album, "a splendid time is guaranteed for all."

Hedy paced back and forth in the tiny trailer, waiting for their cue. Her nerves were on edge. She worried about the band, about Derek, about the material, about herself. She knew damn well she was taking a risk. If they hated her . . . Jesus.

When she'd called Abe last week, he'd practically had a conniption. "Hedy, baby, cookie, Derek Robertson is a *shlemiel.* He's a washed-up nobody, grabbing on to your skirt tails for all he's worth. Everybody knows he's looking for a free ride. He'll bring you down with him, darling; he'll drown you. Please, listen to your uncle Abe. Don't sing with him, don't go on stage at some *fakokteh* festival with him. If you do, I won't be held responsible. I wash my hands of the whole matter."

Abe might have been right. Derek *was* a freeloader and a head case. And he was into drugs in a big way. She should know, she was living with the guy. But he was hot and she liked his sound. Anyway, she'd gone way too far to turn back now.

"Listen, Abe, do me a favor. Shut up. I don't need your piss-poor advice anymore. There's only one thing I want you to do for me. Go to that shit Thane Crawley and get me a new advance and a new contract. I need cash. And tell him my next album's gonna be hard rock, with Derek Robertson on guitar. Got that?"

"Sweetie, honey, Hedy, have you lost your mind? Thane Crawley. You don't mess with him. You're already overadvanced and on suspension. Remember the little incident of the music stand? The one you tossed through the glass and tried to shove up your producer's *tukhas.* And your last album, it didn't sell so hot, remember? Darling, he'll kick me out of his office. He'll tear up your contract. Please, tell me you're joking with Uncle Abe. Some joke, to give me such *tsuris.* "

"It's no joke, Abe."

"But, darling, Crawley already wiped his hands of that dreck. You still owe him one album and you can't force Derek down his throat."

"Fuck the album requirements, Abe. If he won't accept this and demands another album, I'll give him a fucking vinyl ashtray with a hole in it. I'll deliver the top ten singles of Israel on one side and the showstoppers of the 1940s on the other. Look, Abe, you're supposed to be my lawyer. Just do what I say or I'll find somebody else who will."

"Okay, okay, Hedy, whatever you want. But it's your head."

"Just do it. Crawley may even be in San Francisco now, checking out the new acts. Just get to him, soon, all right?"

For all she knew, Crawley was out in the audience right now.

When the knock on the door came, Hedy almost pissed in the skimpy pants under her long skirt. Before she could say "Come in," Derek burst through the door, bubbling with drugged-up energy. He was wearing a flowered shirt open all the way to his waist, his perennial supertight jeans, and bare feet.

"We're next, baby. The crowd's flyin'. Wow, it's gonna be beautiful, just beautiful!"

He tried to kiss her, but she shied away. The past month with Derek had been anything but calm and they were just coming down off another of their knock-down, drag-out fights. This time she'd shattered all the dishes in the cupboard. With Hedy's temperament, Derek's drug-dependent manic-depressive mood swings, and their tumultuous rehearsal sessions, it was a miracle they'd ever made it to Mount Tamalpais.

At least she wasn't lonely. Between the drugs and the music and the parties, she'd been on an emotional high for weeks. And there was no denying the sex smoldered, when he wasn't too high to get it up. Working together had been Derek's idea. With her chutzpah, his guitar, and their bodies, they just might have something going.

When they burst on to the stage together, the Mount Tamalpais crowd gave them a hearty but not overly enthusiastic welcome. It didn't take long, however, for Hedy and Derek to turn them on. The combination was raw and sexual, the way rock-and-roll was meant to be. The music was driving and contemporary, mixing new Derek material with acid-rock versions of his and her old hits. Hedy had a new urgency in her singing. The smooth, polished sound now had a rough edge.

It wasn't the music, though, that rocked the house. It was the sexual energy between Hedy and Derek, the turn-'em-on, let-your-hair-down, spread-your-legs sensuality that emanated from Hedy Harlowe and her tight-jeaned beau.

They sang a new song, entitled "What I Wouldn't Do for You," with Hedy falling to her knees before Derek and unzipping his fly. She whipped off her long skirt and crooned to Derek and the crowd in her see-through short-shorts. With Derek lying on the stage picking away furiously at his guitar, she straddled him and sang the blues. Then she lay in his lap, cradling the mike, and made him play her like a guitar while she sang "When a Man Loves a Woman."

Their performance was hot and bluesy and campy and it brought down the house on the side of the mountain. When they finished their fourth encore and finally called it quits, Derek was higher than a kite.

"Hedy, you were fabulous," he said back in the trailer, one hand hugging her, the other wrapped around a bottle of Cuervo. "They loved us, baby. Didn't I tell you? I can see it now. It's a whole new ball game. Big-buck record contracts, world tours, the works. The promoter says slews of big record execs were out in the audience. I just hope that fuckin' asshole Thane Crawley's out there. 'Cause I wanna see him come crawlin' to us. This time around, we're really gonna make it big."

"You think so?"

"I know so. You and me, we're a team. We're as hot as you get. In no time at all, we're gonna be the talk of the town. The whole country's gonna be eatin' out of our hand."

She'd been right to come to San Francisco after all. Maybe she'd even found the one she wanted to love. She was ready. Go ahead. Take another little piece of my heart now, baby.

15

1967

THE CROWD OF 50,000 WAS STILL ON ITS FEET WHEN Thane motioned to the marshal to escort him to his waiting helicopter.

"Move aside! Move aside, folks!" the hefty marshal ordered as he pushed his way through each row, like a boat making waves, leaving a narrow wake for Thane to follow.

Their progress through the boisterous throng was slow. All around them, exuberant fans clapped, whistled, and stamped their feet against the cushion of what had once been green grass. Holding lit matches up above their heads, they shouted for more. The sweet smell of marijuana smoke from the audience and burning plastic from the stage wafted through the open field and settled on it like a ground fog.

A clammy hand suddenly grabbed his shoulder. "Congratulations, Thane," a voice said.

When he turned around, Thane found himself looking down at one of the countless young A&R men who were swarming over Monterey like bees around honey. They were indistinguishable but unmistakable, decked out in the *de rigueur* uniform of the "with-it" record exec: newly grown long hair a little too neat; beads; bleached army-navy surplus jeans (custom tailored in Beverly Hills); tie-dyed shirts; sandals; and the ever-present hand-tooled, very expensive but funky-looking crude leather pouch slung preciously over the shoulder.

Thane was the only one who never dressed up or down for his work. Unlike the others, he never bothered to remove his Cartier tank watch and replace it with a white steel Timex (so as not to appear too "establishment"). He had neither the need nor the desire to ape the slovenly fashion of the musicians—he knew such meaningless displays of "solidarity" inspired more contempt than confidence among the artists. Anyway, Thane thought the attire grotesque and unbecoming.

Instead, he stood tall and handsome, a Viking in a cream-colored linen jacket over pale blue slacks. His hair was blond, traditionally cut, and never out of place. His eyes were a deep, penetrating gray, always nervous and alive, as if charged with electric power. Standing in his white yachting shoes, Thane Crawley was every inch a gentleman.

"Wow, man, you pulled some coup if you really signed that act to Apollo. That's outta sight. Oh, wow . . . groovy . . . heavy. He's one hot talent."

Hot was the word, all right. Even though the sun had already set over Monterey and a cool breeze was coming in off the ocean, everyone and everyplace around the huge open stage was hot. Even Thane himself—usually so cool and aloof that he willed his pores not to sweat—felt the heat. The music got through to Thane—Jimi Hendrix forced the perspiration out.

Thane smiled condescendingly at the flunky and moved on without responding. He wasn't sure who was more worthy of his contempt: his pushy, crass, so-called colleagues in the record business; the idiot-savant artists who, as if possessed by the devil, produced throbbing, entrancing sounds they couldn't explain, sounds that stirred even his own soul; or the rowdy, drugged-up fans who reveled in orgiastic frenzy, hypnotized en masse.

Only the music, the power, and the perks made it worthwhile.

Finally emerging through the crowd at the side of the stage, Thane asked the marshal to tell his pilot to prepare for takeoff. Then he strode toward the long white trailer parked in the restricted area behind the stage. *He* didn't need to show a backstage pass; the guard waved him through immediately. Just as he reached the trailer/dressing room, the door burst open. Hendrix and his entourage appeared, en route to the stage for another encore. Dressed in skintight black pants with a frilly Victorian shirt and a cowboy hat, Jimi moved toward the stage unsteadily. His eyes had a wild, half-crazed look and his whole body shimmered with sweat and intensity.

Thane watched the emerging star waver as he tried to mount the stairs. Thanks to Swisstone and his access to the British scene, he'd known about Hendrix for some time. All London had been buzzing for months, ever since Jimi's performance at the Bag o' Nails last November. When he'd poured lighter fluid over his guitar and set it aflame on stage at Finsbury Park—just as he'd done only moments earlier here at Monterey—the London fans and the London rock luminaries had gone wild. Confident of Hendrix's commercial appeal, Thane had approached him last month in an effort to sign him to his first American recording contract.

Unfortunately, the young A&R sycophant had sucked up to the wrong party. If Swisstone had only given him the financial rope, Thane could have pulled Hendrix into the Apollo coral. With the lid they'd placed on his budget, however, they had tied his hands. Instead of signing the big act he so desperately wanted, he'd watched from the sidelines, frustrated, while Hendrix slipped through his fingers to Warners'.

Thane needed to sign a big English act, and he needed to do it soon. The feelers from England were more than promising. They were tantalizing. But it would all be for naught if he couldn't persuade Swisstone to open its deep pocketbooks. In no time at all, the whole American market would dry up. Apollo would be left parched and empty with no original talent to distribute, with nothing to feed the giant worldwide machine they had built.

It was all coming clear in Thane's mind. San Francisco and London tastes were merging. The success of the Monterey Pop Festival was about to push rock music and its purveyors into the forefront of American culture. Strange as it seemed, acid-rock stars were emerging as the heroes and gurus, the political and spiritual leaders of the teenage population. The economic force of that record-hungry mass would push the new music, showcased here, into the arms of big business. Thane and the other record company hotshots—Joe Smith from Warner Brothers,

Clive Davis from CBS, Ahmet Ertegun from Atlantic, even Artie-the-Ripp of Kama Sutra—were all here to jump on the bandwagon and cash in.

Thane hadn't bothered with the Mount Tamalpais Festival the week before. Nobody very important from the business had. It just set the stage—and compared to Monterey, everything that came before was only small potatoes. Monterey introduced Hendrix, Joplin, the Who, Otis Redding, and even George Harrison's sitar instructor, Ravi Shankar.

The rest of the lineup read like a Who's Who of new stars in the rock firmament: the Byrds, the Dead, the Association, the Electric Flag, Canned Heat, the Mamas and the Papas, the Blues Project, Jefferson Airplane, Country Joe, Quicksilver Messenger Service, the Paul Butterfield Blues Band, Laura Nyro and Buffalo Springfield.

It was to see, seduce, and sign acts that Thane had flown in and out of Monterey numerous times over the past three days. By now, he'd had his fill. He was ready to return to L.A. But he hadn't signed any important acts. Clive snatched the best of them away for CBS.

With his arm up and his head down to shield himself from the thrust of the wind, Thane approached the waiting helicopter and climbed into the cramped compartment. When the pilot gave the thumbs-up sign and the chopper lifted into the air, Thane could still hear the roar of the crowd over the loud chop of the blades. As they sailed up and over the stage, he looked down, like a god from Mount Olympus, on the assembled mass of humanity.

He knew he was observing a cultural phenomenon. He was savvy enough to appreciate that, in the minds of the fans, Monterey was much more than a concert. It was a spiritual and metaphysical happening. For the first time, thousands of young potheads were discovering thousands of kindred spirits, and a feeling of love, power, and commonality embraced the crowd. It was a new kind of outdoor event, one meant to herald a new age of gentle, loving vibes, of flower people and flower power, of oneness and religious understanding, of music over money, all led by the philosophers, poets, and statesmen who played the music and inspired their minions.

From Thane's perspective, it seemed a form of mass hysteria, pure and simple, and one he had every intention of exploiting. Although he picked the music that made their souls dance, and although he, too, loved the sound, he wouldn't dream of associating with the rock audience. They bought the records he commissioned and the artists he chose to nurture, but actually rubbing elbows with them went far beyond the call of duty. He preferred looking down at them from above.

Thane liked this particular taste of the music business. Strangely enough, even though it had taken him a few years to really appreciate it, the music business seemed to suit his lifestyle. If you'd told him ten or even five years earlier that at the age of thirty-two he'd be custodian of a record company, he would have scoffed in contempt. His family, the Crawleys, had all the right credentials. Mommy was a McDonald of *the* McDonalds. She did only two unforgivable things in her life: She was born a Catholic and married an Episcopalian; and she was born poor and married poor.

Not that anyone thought they were poor. When the original trust had been established, Mary Ann had ended up with a fixed income in 1928 of $100,000 a year. At the time, that must have seemed like an awful lot, but it certainly didn't run a household in the Forties and Fifties. Not with three sons, all of whom had to be properly clothed and schooled, and not when your properly inbred husband had no income of his own.

Nathaniel Crawley III's lineage traced back to the Windsors themselves. The Crawleys were terribly impressive—they knew everyone, they went everywhere, and although they had some land and wealth "on paper," two generations had survived without cash.

When Thane (short for Nathaniel, IV) was growing up, he didn't feel poor, at first, and was unaware of any real deprivation. Mommy discreetly sold the Samuel Pepys clock one year, a Georgian silver service the next, and each year something else. The flat on Park Avenue became "less cluttered," and when the Southampton house, too, started to look a little bare, she explained, "We're going into a more contemporary look. The boys need a little more room."

They felt the pinch badly in the late Fifties when inflation, the cost-of-living rise, and three prep-school tuitions all hit at the same time. It was then that Mary Ann McDonald Crawley and Nathaniel Gideon Crawley III decided, for the protection and the preservation of their class, that they would have to make new and special arrangements of convenience, which required their both doing things they did not enjoy doing.

In both instances, it meant dealing intimately and regularly with *those* people—the people who did not play lawn tennis at the Hampton's Green Grass Club or golf at Arbor Rock or ride at Chance Hill or shoot pheasant at the Champlain Hunt Club. It meant dealing with Jews.

Mary Ann worked out a terribly clever plot.

From her committee to "Save Bowling Green," she knew Sarah Loeb Frehmann. The Frehmanns, at least, were German Jews, cultured and refined. And they controlled Frehmann & Company, a small but fast-moving investment bank on Wall Street. The Frehmanns could do just about everything except break into the Crawleys' social world. That was reserved for the Morgans and the Mellons and the other establishment WASP banking families.

Breaking convention, and with her eye on the future of her family, Mary Ann invited the Frehmanns for the Fourth of July weekend in Southampton. To be a houseguest that weekend was especially flattering. Although the Southampton season started a month earlier, the month of June was a mere preliminary to the gala weekend that launched the season.

Mary Ann worked hard to prepare the family's Victorian white-elephant beach "cottage." Although the upkeep was impossible, the plumbing archaic, the heat nonexistent, for three crucial months each year they made do. The faded look was "in," she claimed, and the boys worked the gardens and lawns to "build their character," she told her friends, never mentioning that it saved the family several thousand a season.

The cottage had been built by a McDonald in 1880 next to the Parrish House. The beachfront had become "smart" by the Fifties, but giant dinosaurs were unfashionable, and the mammoth Victorian clapboard classic was just that. It was 68 feet high and 185 feet long, with twelve bedrooms, 22,000 square feet, and 160 windows, all with shutters, all latticed, all warped, with rusty hardware. The house was a symbol of a bygone era, with imposing, creaking staircases, reading room, trophy room, billiards room, music room, parlor, and furnishings from vastly different periods. It was moldy, smelly, wonderful. A wonderful house for Thane and his brothers to summer in and grow up in, but a devil of a house to run and pay for.

Into this world, like foreigners entering a strange land, came the very first of the Hebrew persuasion, the chosen people, chosen by Mary Ann Crawley: the Frehmanns of Riverside Drive, New York City, and Temple Emanu-El.

The Crawleys were gracious. They actually gave a reception for the Frehmanns, with fireworks, and invited all the "right" people, the ones Sarah Frehmann read about in the society columns, people who frequented El Morocco and the Stork Club. (All evening long, Sarah kept jabbing poor Zachariah in the ribs every time she spotted another "society" face.)

Zach Frehmann sensed something was up but wasn't quite sure what. In appreciation for their hospitality, Zach felt obliged to invite Crawley to lunch at the Frehmann firm. From that lunch, Nathaniel Crawley emerged with the promise of an engraved card announcing he was "with" Frehmann & Company. He would have an office, a driver, a secretary, an expense account, and a percentage of the fees generated by the clients and deals he brought into the firm.

The marriage of convenience suited both parties. Zach received credible entry into the WASP world of big business, and Nathaniel received personal business credibility, a way to earn easy money and enough perks to make a dent in his family's overhead and keep up appearances—which was what really counted.

Not surprisingly, the Crawley family managed to spend everything that Nathaniel made—and more. After all, they were expected to live properly. No longer genteel old money with a good name, Nathaniel was now a "Wall Street Banker." The right charities couldn't be slighted and the Crawleys couldn't be embarrassed by making only token contributions.

Mary Ann did try to make do with sprucing up what they had. Southampton got a new roof, a fresh coat of paint, window boxes, geraniums, a swimming pool, cabanas, and new decking. The dunes were planted with flowering wild roses, and a two-story Victorian conservatory was purchased in England, dismantled, and rebuilt facing the ocean. A formal English rose and herb garden was laid out. That was sufficient for now, but certainly not enough. Not enough to suffer jokes about yarmulkes and about mezuzahs hanging in their newly painted doorway.

In this atmosphere of love and hate—loving the material rewards and hating the Jews for being their source—Thane grew up. A touch anti-Semitic, snobby, defensive about his family, accustomed to living on credit far above his means, and committed to making it big, at any price.

Until 1963, his life had seemed quite set. Raised as a young WASP prince, he had sailed through all the right schools—Saint

Paul's Academy, Princeton, Harvard Business School—ending up with a lucrative position in the prestigious investment-banking firm of Morton Collins. Though he might have preferred the life of a country gentleman, whiling away his days on the Crawley Southampton estate, the realities of his family's finances demanded he work for a living.

And so he had, quite respectably, quite predictably, for a number of years. Then his life took a strange twist, one that jibed remarkably well with his one secret passion: music.

A Swiss record company, called Swisstone, jointly owned by pharmaceutical magnate Philippe Phochet and insurance magnate Wolfgang Hermann, had, in the early Sixties, bought up the finest small, independent record companies and the most prestigious music publishers in critical areas of high sophistication and high population density around the world. By 1962 they owned thirty-five record companies in thirty-five territories and controlled nearly eight percent of recorded music outside the United Kingdom and the United States.

When the Beatles took the entire world by storm, the record industry was suddenly transformed. The world no longer wanted to hear local, regional, indigenous product exclusively—everyone wanted the new sounds emanating from the U.K. and the U.S.

Swisstone was in all the right places at the right time. The American and British record companies, anxious to peddle their wares worldwide but without means to do so, had to turn to Swisstone for distribution. Suddenly the Swiss company found itself competing with EMI and Polygram at the forefront of the worldwide record business. When Swisstone decided they wanted their own sources of original U.K./U.S.A. product as well as a wholly owned U.S. outlet for their own worldwide artists, they purchased Apollo Records, a small but prestigious American record company. Morton Collins was called on to arrange the financing.

Not long after the deal was consummated, an internal audit of Apollo revealed massive corruption. Swisstone promptly dismissed Apollo's management and took control of the company. The entire record industry buzzed about the "foreign" owners; Apollo stock plummeted; Apollo artists became jittery and threatened to jump ship.

Swisstone knew what had to be done. They needed to establish credibility with the Americans. They needed to silence the hysterical rumors that threatened to ruin Apollo's reputation. They needed to calm the artists, managers, auditors, and the industry, and impart to Apollo an aura of stability and security.

As an interim measure, the Dutch controllers, spearheaded by their chief operating officer, Dr. Hans van der Rogdt, turned to Morton Collins and asked them to locate a temporary custodian, an "acting" boss. It had to be someone above reproach, someone so proper and patrician that his very presence at the head of Apollo would allay industry fears and defuse the situation. It also had to be someone they could trust and feel comfortable with.

Thane Crawley was that man. He was everything the Dutchman wanted. In an industry where most of the executives worked their way up from the streets, starting as promo men or marketing men or A&R men or personal managers, wearing gold chains and speaking Yiddish, Italian, or street language, Thane was well bred and well spoken. No gold chains ever touched his body. No four-letter words and no "baby" or "cookie" escaped his narrow, unsensual lips. He belonged to the right clubs, had crewed for Princeton, played squash and polo, and dressed elegantly.

The selection proved serendipitous. In the three and a half years since his appointment, Thane had displayed an uncanny knack for the ins and outs of the record business. Part of it was luck and good timing: He not only had European resources and know-how at his disposal—including Swisstone's honest, straightforward accounting and payment procedures (a novelty to many artists)—but he had early access to British product at a time when the British were invading the American music scene and were highly sought-after commodities.

The rest was Thane's savvy: an unerring business sense and an incredible instinct for commercial music. He was open to new sounds, acquisition-minded, and understood the roles of independent record producers, new labels, and new talent. Besides, he loved music in any format, from Jerry Lee Lewis to Béla Bartók, Charlie Parker to Hank Williams; it was his one human weakness, his one common bond with the plebeians. Music made his heart beat faster and pumped energy through his veins. Music made his soul come to life in the same way that power, money, and sex (of a certain sort) did. Although he never played an instrument other than his stereo, music—good, gutsy music—was something he understood and appreciated instinctively.

Most important, however, was his platinum ear. For whatever reason—possibly because he'd been raised to be discriminating and had always displayed perspicacity in his musical taste; possibly because he was strangely in tune with the musical tastes of the masses—Thane Crawley could hear commercial potential in any form and at any decibel. Where others heard noise or nothing at all, he heard a sound that could translate onto vinyl and start toes tapping.

Time was running out, though. Derek Robertson had come and gone; Rick Firestone had come and gone; Hedy Harlowe was over the hill. If Apollo was to compete with the other big-time companies, Thane *had* to sign one or two of the emerging superstars, and he had to do it soon. If he didn't, Apollo would be mired in passé mediocrity and his position as custodian would be in jeopardy. More important, his ever-growing and blinding ambition—to become *the* leader of the music industry—would be dealt a crushing blow.

The dull sound of the chopper's descent grated on Thane's ear and vibrated his body unpleasantly as they approached the private strip at the east side of San Francisco International Airport. Even without any further delays, he wouldn't be back in L.A. until after 10:00 P.M., too late and too early to place those crucial calls to Geneva and London. If everything went according to schedule, he'd be in London next month, with the prospect of closing the deal of a lifetime. If he could pull that one off . . .

He walked across the dark tarmac to the private plane parked on the runway.

"Good evening, Mr. Crawley. We've been expecting you," the perky young stewardess said as Thane sank back into the plush seat. "May I get you some champagne, sir?"

"Please," Thane answered.

While he sipped the Taittingers and the plane taxied down the runway, Thane opened his briefcase and removed his leather appointment book. With all those calls to make and pressing business to transact in the morning, why had he agreed to a breakfast meeting with Hedy Harlowe's obnoxious lawyer, Abe Sanders? Considering his plans for London, Thane had more important things on his mind than a vulgar bitch like Hedy Harlowe. All along she'd been more trouble than she was worth.

As far as he was concerned, she was as worn out and useless to Apollo as her old accompanist, Rick Firestone. They were both yesterday's news—oldies but baddies.

Thane's L.A. office was East Coast elegant and understated by L.A. standards. The carpeting was a rich red Sarouk, the writing table eighteenth-century French, the tapestry on the wall an authentic Gobelin. Except for the audio equipment shelved unobtrusively behind the doors of the Flemish armoire, there was no indication the office was that of a record-company executive.

In the adjoining private dining room, a square Chippendale table covered with a blue silk damask tablecloth was laid out with grapefruit, orange juice, cream cheese, pink-grapefruit marmalade, kiwi jam, and fresh hot croissants, all served on Minton bone china. Matching napkins were carefully folded under the Georgian silver flatware. A simple, shallow Steuben vase of fresh peonies served as the centerpiece.

When Thane hung up the phone, having completed five calls to London and the one crucial call to Dr. van der Rogdt in Geneva, the intercom on his desk buzzed.

"Yes, Wilma?"

"Mr. Sanders is still waiting, sir."

"All right, send him in." Thane looked down at his Cartier. It was 7:45 A.M. Fifteen minutes was just long enough to make Sanders wait.

When the attractive redheaded secretary opened the door and showed Abe Sanders into the office, Thane stood up from behind his desk. "Abe, good to see you," he said, leaning across to shake the diminutive man's hand.

With thin hair, wire-rimmed glasses, bulbous nose, and protruding gut, Abe was definitely not a sight for sore eyes. In fact, he looked more like a Lower East Side tailor than the cutthroat lawyer he was. By reputation, Abe was a hired gun—a killer like Paladin with a calling card that read: HAVE BRIEFS, WILL SUE.

"Likewise, Thane baby, likewise," Abe said, pumping Crawley's hand enthusiastically. His thick hide made him so impervious to slights that he seemed unfazed and unoffended by the wait.

"Come, let's have some breakfast. You must be starved." Thane rested a hand on Abe's shoulder and indicated the way into the dining room. He knew food was one of Abe's weaknesses—a potential distraction to Abe's concentration—and that "taking a breakfast" was Abe's shorthand for "renegotiating." "Tell me, how's the family?"

As soon as the words left his mouth, Thane wished he hadn't asked. He'd straight-manned his way right into Abe's vaudeville routine, a nonstop patter intended to disarm his adversary and make himself appear more the fool than he really was.

"The family? Always the same, sweetie, baby, always the same," Abe said as he approached the table, gesticulating wildly with his hands and eyeing the breakfast spread. "I think my wife's been unfaithful—to the tennis pro, that is. Now she's trying to jump the kid who takes care of our tropical fish. And my daughter—uggh! Fifteen and already she's on the pill *and* has a diaphragm. She hates me so much she has to see a shrink three times a week to learn why I'm such a lousy father and why she needs to *shtup* the entire UCLA Marching Band just to get back at me. Can you believe it?"

Thane did his best to smile. At his suggestion, they both took seats at the elegantly set table. Maybe if Abe started eating, he'd stop talking.

No such luck. Abe spread one of the croissants with cream cheese and kiwi jam, shoved practically the entire thing into his mouth, chewed a few times, and started again, like Demosthenes, to talk and chew at the same time. Crumbs and jam scattered down his chin.

"She takes after her mother, no doubt about it. When Delores first became pregnant, they didn't inject the rabbit, they injected her instead, with the rabbit's blood. Now she screws like a bunny. With my luck, my son'll turn out the same way. As soon as he discovers his peepee, *he'll* want to fuck the UCLA Marching Band as well!"

"Abe, please, I can't laugh in the morning. Have another croissant." Thane held up the plate. Then he scooped delicately at his own precut half-grapefruit while he watched the lawyer molest the second pastry and brutally deflower his once pristine napkin. Thane couldn't help but loathe the man's vulgar, pushy Jewishness. The sooner they got down to business, the better.

Abe finally finished eating, sipped at his coffee, and lit a cigar. He was trying his best to get Thane's goat, perfectly aware that Crawley abhorred cigarette and cigar smoke. It was all part of the battle. The breakfast performance was his retaliation for being kept waiting by this rude fucker WASP.

Exhaling aggressively, Abe began. "I suppose you're wondering why I asked for this meeting."

"No," Thane said, speaking so softly that Abe had to lean forward to hear him. "I thought you simply wanted to try out your new routine on me."

"Well, I've been talking to Hedy recently."

"How *is* the heavenly Hedy?" Thane asked in mock seriousness.

Abe rocked his palm in the air. "Between you and me, baby, I'm worried about her. Your putting her on suspension didn't help things. You know how precarious her ego is. She's a fragile creature."

"Creature, yes—fragile, no."

"Thane, cookie, please, no sarcasm. What our dear Hedy needs now is your support and your confidence. She needs to know that you still believe in her."

"What does she want, Abe?" Thane lifted the cup of steaming black coffee to his lips. He blew on the edge, sipped, and swallowed. It burned for a moment, then left a residue of warmth.

Abe searched in vain for an ashtray, then flicked the ashes of his cigar onto the translucent fine china. "She's in San Francisco, working on new material. It's very exciting stuff, Thane. It's today, new, with-it. It's just what the kids these days want."

"Are you telling me Hedy's into acid rock?"

"Sort of, sort of. She's organized a hot new band. With a name guitarist." Abe wasn't looking forward to springing this surprise. Crawley—the pompous, sanctimonious prick—was already in the driver's seat. This wasn't going to be easy. How the hell had he let that stupid slut talk him into approaching Crawley when he didn't have a leg to stand on?

"And what name would that be, Abe?"

"The guy's totally cleaned up his act. He's got new material and a whole new image."

Thane waited patiently.

"Derek Robertson."

Thane's aloof, uninterested expression didn't change. When he'd heard about Hedy and Derek playing together at Mount Tamalpais, he'd laughed to himself. Sure, Hedy could work any crowd, but the idea of the druggie and the bitch staying together and recording . . . Well, no one in the industry with any brains would touch them with a ten-foot pole. They were a sideshow attraction, at best.

"They've been working together for months. They've got a new sound."

Thane opened his palms. "I'm curious to hear it. What have you got for me?"

"Nothing yet, nothing yet, but soon, real soon. They taped the show at Mount Tamalpais, but you wouldn't want to hear it. Quality's no good. You know they stopped the show there, don't you?"

"Nobody even remembers Tamalpais, Abe. Everybody who's anybody was at Monterey. Where were *they?*"

That was a good question and one Abe chose to ignore. They *had* been invited. As far as he could determine, though, they'd been too stoned to make it out of the Bay Area. "What does it matter, cookie? They'll make the next festival. You're not telling me you've lost faith in Hedy, have you?"

"Of course not," Thane lied.

" 'Cause if you have, you know there're other record companies out there just dying for a piece of Miss Hedy Harlowe. If she were a free agent now—which I grant you she is not—I could go to any number of your colleagues and negotiate a fat new contract and a hefty advance. Hedy's seen the figures; she knows Capitol just signed the Steve Miller Band for a fifty-thousand advance, a hundred-thousand bonus, and options that could net him seven hundred and fifty thousand over four years. And God knows how much Warner paid to sign Hendrix."

Thane responded quietly and precisely. His patience was wearing thin, and when angry, he became more controlled and deliberate. "You know as well as I that those artists are in a new league. Hedy's track record indicates limited sales and a very predictable, very narrow audience. Besides, if I'm not mistaken, she's still under contract to Apollo. She owes me."

"That's just the point, Thane, baby. She's gonna expand her appeal *and* her audience. She's gonna reach the young kids now. If only you give her that vote of confidence that she needs, she'll be back in the studio within the month." Abe hesitated, scouting the table for something more to eat. "If you don't . . . well, you know how messy things can get. We could litigate or, worse yet, Hedy could deliver you one last piece-of-crap album to fulfill her contractual commitments—you know, like the ten top singles of Israel or the most famous Easter hymns. But we wouldn't want that to happen, would we?"

Thane ignored the veiled extortion. "How big a vote of confidence?"

"Let's say a hundred thousand to start. As a bonus. And a brand-new, renegotiated contract with an appropriate advance." Abe dabbed his damp forehead and upper lip with his now sticky, stained napkin.

"A hundred thousand as a bonus buys me the privilege of renegotiating," Thane repeated sarcastically.

"Look what it would accomplish. You'd reaffirm your belief in Hedy; you'd prove your commitment to her, her music, and her fans; and in return you'd get six more albums, with Hedy's new sound, under contemporary terms."

Thane knew that was a euphemism for higher royalties. "And what about the money she owes Apollo? Do you realize how *over*advanced she is now? Even if her next album went platinum, it still wouldn't get her out of the red." Thane spoke softly but indignantly. "Do you have any idea how much her little temper tantrum at the last recording session cost the company?"

"Thane, Thane," Abe said in his warmest, for-old-times'-sake, Bronx/Beverly Hills accent. "After what you've done for our Hedy, considering our special relationship, I don't want to screw you. I want you to have a special deal. You think I *wanna* go to another record company?" His fingers pointed to his own chest for emphasis and left a slight jelly imprint on his tie. "Just put up an appropriate amount of advance money, sign a new contract, and recoup the money she owes from her existing catalog. Then we'll all be happy."

Thane got up from the table and walked to the picture window that looked out over L.A. from the height of the Strip. That Sanders had *some* cheek, thinking he could bluff him into believing that other record companies were beating down the door for Hedy. They both knew it was bullshit. Thane held all the cards. All he wanted was to recoup his losses and cut Hedy loose. But now wasn't the time to tell that to Abe.

Recoup from her existing catalog, that's what Abe had proposed, wasn't it? Yes, that *was* an excellent idea. It planted a seed he would cultivate. He could cover his losses and ruin Hedy's marketability in one fell swoop. When Apollo was through with exploiting Hedy Harlowe, even Black Jack Records wouldn't touch her.

Thane walked back to the table. He was smiling. Towering over the seated Abe, he reached out to shake his hand, indicating clearly that the meeting was concluded. "Abe, let me mull over your proposal, talk it over with my business-affairs people. You've stimulated my thinking. I'm sure we can work out something that's fair to all parties involved. I'll be back in touch."

Sanders stood up, wiped the last remnants of jam from his hand and the crumbs from his shirt, and grasped Thane's hand. "I'll wait for your call, sweetheart. But, please, don't keep Hedy waiting too long. You know how impatient she becomes."

Thane kept a straight face and a fixed smile.

As soon as Abe closed the office door behind him, Thane pressed his intercom.

"Yes, Mr. Crawley?"

"Wilma, get me Arnie Schultz in Marketing, then Walter Serling in Legal."

When the call came through, Thane picked up immediately. His mind was racing. "Arnie, I've got a project for you—call it 'Operation Hedy.' I want you to work out how many permutations and recombinations of her previously recorded tracks would work for new LPs repackaged at discount for over-the-counter sales. Then see if we have sufficient material for a quadruple album, *The Best of*, with, say, forty of her most popular tracks. That's right. For a possible television package. And make an estimate of how many units you think we could unload during the Christmas season and the profit margin on the units. As soon as possible."

He hung up and was immediately on the line with Walt Serling. "Listen, Walt, can you do a quick précis of Hedy Harlowe's contract regarding our flexibility in pricing and packaging? Check our right to mix her cuts with other artists. Uh-huh. That's right. I want to do a K-Tel-type mixed-bag album. . . . Terrific."

"Wilma, get me Arnie again." He was on a phone roll.

"Arnie, you know the *Greatest Hits of the Sixties* package? When's it due out? . . . Easter, perfect. Pencil in any two of Hedy's biggies for inclusion. I know, I know. It's disastrous for her image, dilutes her impact, cheapens her. That's just what I want. Thanks."

When he replaced the receiver, Thane leaned back in his chair. He felt a warm glow of satisfaction. Abe Sanders and Hedy Harlowe were about to discover that Thane Crawley was more than a stuffed shirt.

He reached for the intercom button again. "Wilma, find Hedy

Harlowe for me. Somewhere in San Francisco, I think. . . . No, no phone call. Just send her three dozen long-stemmed roses boxed with ribbons and a note that says, 'Everything just rosy. Hope the next LP is as wonderful as you. Warmly, Thane.' "

* * *

The Pine Street apartment looked as if the great quake had struck again. Clothes and papers were strewn haphazardly on the floor, dirty dishes were piled high in and around the sink, the corner mattress was a rumpled mess. The only hint of brightness in the dingy flat was the milk bottle full of wilting roses on the kitchen table. Dark red petals lay scattered on the table and floated lifelessly in the cup of moldy coffee, as though heralding Fall in the Harlowe flat.

Hedy dragged herself out of bed and walked naked to the sink. Restacking a pile of dishes, she filled the kettle with tap water and placed it on the stove. Then she opened the cabinet above the sink and pushed her way through various cans and bottles in search of instant coffee. If she didn't have some soon, she'd never wake up.

Her head ached something fierce and her body felt completely drained. Whatever new drug combo Derek had given her the other day had knocked her for a real loop. The whole trip was a total blur—like the whole week before and the week before that. The only thing she remembered was that Derek was supposed to have returned last night and never had.

"Fuck him," she said out loud.

For the few weeks since Mount Tamalpais, she'd been on an emotional roller coaster that wouldn't slow down. The first week, they'd basked in glory and partied their brains out. But after Monterey, everything changed. Suddenly the whole country was talking about Janis and Jimi and *the* festival. She'd never forgive Derek for making them miss it. Frustrated, confused, and, most of all, bitter, she felt like Tantalus: the prize ripped from her hand just as her fingers were closing around it.

Not surprisingly, her relationship with Derek had turned sour. There was no more denying how little they had in common. Or how serious a junkie Derek really was. The only bright spot had been the flowers from Thane. If Abe could actually swing a new deal, then maybe—just maybe—everything could still work out.

The teapot whistled and the phone rang, at the same time, of course. For a moment, Hedy stood stock-still, confused. Then she hurried to the stove, turned down the burner, and went searching the cluttered floor for the phone. Grabbing the black wire, she followed it into a pile of Derek's clothes and emerged with the receiver.

"Yeah?" she said brusquely.

"Hedy, honey, baby, sweetie, it's Abe. How's my favorite singer?"

"Like shit, as usual. So, what's the news?"

"The family's the same, baby. My wife—"

"Cut the act, I'm not in the mood, Abe. What happened with Crawley?"

"That's what I was calling about, darling. I went to see him, just like you said. We had a friendly chat. I told him you wanted a new advance and that you were willing to sign a new contract and that we'd sue the hell out of him if he didn't come through."

"Yeah, yeah, I know all that," she said, looking across the room at the dying flowers. "So what happened?"

"He said he'd get back to me. So I wait and I wait. Today I hear from his lawyer. I'm afraid the news ain't so hot." He hesitated. "They're not interested in renewing your contract."

Hedy practically dropped the phone. She couldn't speak.

"In fact, they don't seem to give a shit about the final album. Instead, they're planning to reissue a bunch of cheapo collections of your best hits, doing a K-Tel TV package, selling the hell out of your old stuff to make back the dough you owe them."

When she heard that, Hedy regained her voice. "Why, that *swine!* That double-dealing piece of *shit!* He can't do that to me!" she screamed into the phone.

"Hedy, honey, sweetie, calm down," Abe said, holding the phone away from his ear. "I'll sue him for all he's worth. When he's through with Abe Sanders, he'll be sorry he didn't sign you to a fat new contract."

"He can't do it, Abe, can he? Legally, I mean? Doesn't my contract say he can't issue those crappy compilations?"

Abe cleared his throat. "Sweetheart, cookie, don't you worry your pretty little head about it. Abe will look into it. It's complicated. Maybe he can, maybe he can't, I don't know. Whatever happens, I can tie him up in court. I can—"

"Abe. Abe! Shut up and listen carefully. There's something I want you to do for me."

"Anything, darling, anything."

"Get my contract, honey. I'll hold on. Just go find my contract." She waited until Abe returned. "You got it? Good. Okay, take the contract, roll it up into a nice long cone. Good. Now shove it up your ass. You're fired, shmuck!" she yelled, slamming down the receiver. She was beside herself with rage. In her whole life, she'd never felt so humiliated and double-crossed.

Marching over to the table, she grabbed the wilting roses and yanked them out of the bottle, spilling the remnants of the dank water and spreading dead petals all over the floor. Then, still stark naked, she walked to the door and opened it, intending to throw two-faced Thane Crawley's rotten roses out into the street.

Only, when she opened the door, she was face-to-face with the band's long-haired, ratty-jeaned bass player, Rodney.

"What the hell do *you* want?" Hedy demanded, one hand on her bare hip, the other holding the roses.

Rodney's mouth dropped open.

"What'sa matter, boy, ain't you never seen naked pussy? Can't talk, huh? Cunt got your tongue?"

It took Rodney a few seconds to regain control of his vocal cords. "It's Derek."

"Yeah, what about him?"

"You gotta bail him out," Rodney said.

"What are you talking about?"

"He got busted last night. Selling smack to some narc. Word on the street says someone fingered him."

"Jesus bloody Christ!" Hedy exclaimed. She couldn't believe it. If there'd been any life left in their match-up, Derek had just snuffed it out. No record company would talk to them now. All around her, the walls were tumbling down.

"He's at the precinct. He told me to tell you to come get him. Bail might be pretty high, so he said to bring your checkbook."

Hedy reared back and shoved the dead roses into Rodney's stomach. "Take him these, Rodney. They'll brighten up his cell. I'll wait for him—I'll count the days. I'll even pray he doesn't get poked too badly by his fellow inmates at Alcatraz," she said melodramatically, playing the gangster's moll in a Jimmy Cagney movie. "Just be sure and tell him one thing for me. When he gets out, I don't want to see his filthy fucking face around here ever again. As far as I'm concerned, he can rot in the pokey for the rest of his life. You got that?"

Rodney stood still for a moment. Then, when Hedy turned

around and started tossing Derek's clothes, item by item, out onto the sidewalk, he shrugged and turned away. About halfway down the block, he spotted a garbage can and dropped the roses face down into the trash.

She didn't know where to turn. Slipping into an old peasant skirt and blouse, she rushed out of the apartment and down the almost vertical street to Madame Love's, her local reader/astrologer. Tears were streaming down her cheeks.

The storefront had stars and planets painted on opaque glass and a small half-moon sign hanging over the sidewalk, announcing MADAME LOVE'S. Hedy opened the front door, heard the bell jingle, and walked into the tiny room. In a corner were two wooden chairs and a small round table topped with a frilly cloth, a pack of tarot cards, and an ashtray. A low bookcase, filled with books on the occult and statuettes of Christ, rested precariously against one wall. A "Peace and Love" poster was tacked on the wall, slightly askew. Behind the table, a grimy curtain and gold wind chimes separated madame's office from her living quarters.

"Sit down, my child," Madame Love said, emerging around the musty red curtain and setting off the cacophony of chimes. Like the salon itself, Madame Love was a maze of contradictions. Dressed in gypsy garb, with a bandana in her dark brown hair, she looked to be anywhere between forty and seventy years old. But the braid in her hair, the sandals on her feet, the round black and white peace button with the upside-down Y, and the painted flower on her cheek made her look more like a San Francisco flower child than an aging seer. She always reminded Hedy of Grandma Becky.

When the madame took a seat, a pudgy calico cat jumped into her lap and made herself at home. Madame Love stroked the cat, adjusted her seat, and quietly turned her attention to the deck of tarot cards lying before her on the table. After shuffling them gingerly in her fragile hands, she began the reading, turning each card over and placing it in the mystical pattern: The Emperor on the left. The Lovers on the right. The Hanged Man on top. The Hermit on the bottom. And upside down, in the center of the cross pattern, the Wheel of Fortune.

Madame Love pondered the configuration silently for a long time. Then she began to speak, softly, in an eerie, accented, trancelike voice. "The cards tell of many changes." She pointed to the picture of the Lovers in the descendant position. "A lover passes out of your life. You are choked with unhappiness. You are not sure which way to turn."

Hovering over the cards, Madame Love's hand moved almost imperceptibly over to the Hanged Man in the upper, midheaven, position. Then she looked up into Hedy's red eyes. "But fear not, my child. Like the seasons, fortune changes in the blink of an eye. The Emperor is ascendant. See how he smiles upon you. Look to one who calls to you from the past. An old friend. Or an old friend's friend. A prince. *He* will help you. Turn away from the old and embrace the new. For now, the Wheel of Fortune turns your way. After, I cannot say," Madame Love mumbled, looking down at the nadir, occupied by the lonely Hermit.

Hedy sat mesmerized. An old friend. Or an old friend's friend. Her mind began clicking through the possibilities. "Can you tell me something more about this Prince or Emperor, Madame Love? His sign, for instance?"

The madame looked up from the cards and down at Hedy's hands. "Look to the fourth sign of the zodiac, to Cancer, the crab," she answered, her finger coming to rest on the center card. Suddenly, the cat jumped from her lap and scampered to the back, setting off the chimes.

"I can say no more," Madame Love whispered.

Hedy squeezed a ten-dollar bill into the gypsy's hand. "Thank you. Thank you," she said sincerely, standing up and rushing out of the office. The cards never lied. Maybe there *was* someone she could turn to.

Two days later, Hedy stepped into the tiny wrought-iron elevator of the condemned town house on Fifty-third off Fifth Avenue and rode up to the third floor. Even though she was exhausted—she hadn't slept a wink on the red-eye flight from the Coast—she had a determined bounce to her step.

The office had been spruced up considerably in the past year. Music posters now covered the walls. A secondhand dark brown couch, covered with odd pillows, and a glass coffee table filled out the reception area, indications that David Barry and his newly hired associates were slowly but surely building a client roster of commercially viable artists.

"I have an appointment with Mr. Barry," Hedy said, looking down at the young receptionist whose braless upper body was covered by a casual T-shirt emblazoned with THE SILVERFISH.

"And your name, please?"

"Shit, has it been that long? Hedy Harlowe."

"Oh, yes. Mr. Barry's expecting you. You can go right in." She pointed the way.

When Hedy entered the modest office, David stood up from behind his round desk and came out to greet her. He stood broad and handsome, wearing his natty British attire. "Hedy. This is a *real* pleasure," he said, taking her hand and leading her to one of the leather chairs. "It's been a long time." He was amazed at how buxom and sexy she now looked. "This may sound fake, but I really am one of your biggest fans. I've followed your career avidly. And, of course, any old friend of Rick's is an old friend of mine."

That was how she'd made the connection. The "old friend" had to be Rick. And the "old friend's friend" had to be David. Not only did she remember David from the old days in Brighton, but she'd heard his name popping up in professional music circles. He was known as one of the new breed of hip, young, honest music lawyers. The pieces fit perfectly, so she'd called David's office for an appointment and hopped the first available plane to New York. She needed only one more piece to complete the puzzle.

"What do you hear from Rick?" Hedy asked.

"Not much, I'm afraid. I took him to England. I thought a change in scenery might give his career a shot in the arm. He's still singing and playing, but . . . you know . . . it's been pretty rough. I'm hoping to see him in London next month."

"Send him my love, will you? Tell him I'm thinking of him," Hedy said in the soft, vacant voice of reminiscence.

"I'd be happy to." David sat on the edge of his desk and leaned forward toward Hedy. "What can I do for you, Hedy?"

"I need your help, David. I fired my lawyer, my record company's trying to screw me, my recording contract's about to expire. I don't know what to do."

David wasn't surprised. The word on the street was that she was trouble, and that her career was flagging. The recent scuttlebutt from San Francisco didn't paint a pretty picture of Hedy Harlowe or her career. None of that bothered David, though. He knew she was loaded with talent and that representing her could prove to be a feather in his cap. Even if it wasn't, he knew how much she meant to Rick.

"Tell me the whole story. If you don't mind."

She told him everything she could. About Los Angeles, about Derek, about Mount Tamalpais. About her resentfulness and her loneliness. David listened so carefully and sympathetically—interrupting only occasionally with direct and insightful questions—that Hedy found it easy to open up to him.

When she finished, her head hung low. David walked over to her. "I know you're discouraged, but you've got to believe in yourself. You're overflowing with talent; we just have to find the right way to present it."

"There's no right way. I just can't keep up with the new music scene," she said dejectedly. "I'll never sell enough records to be more than a two-bit entertainer."

"Then don't try. No matter what you put down on vinyl, it's never going to capture the real Hedy Harlowe, the one that goes out on stage and knocks the audience dead. Your whole act is visual. No matter what musical style you choose, you're never going to squeeze Hedy Harlowe onto an audio track."

"So what am I supposed to do, give up? Quit the business?" she asked, shocked at David's true but depressing statement.

"Not exactly. If you want my advice, forget your recording contract. Let it lapse. Forget the recording business entirely, at least for a while. Lie low."

"And do what?"

"Make movies. Rick told me you were also a fine actress. You're tailor-made for Hollywood."

Hedy's eyes lit up. "Do you really think I could be a film star?"

"Yes, I do, Hedy. I know you've got the talent."

"Could you help me? To get parts, I mean?"

He nodded. "I think so. I could try, at least. You'd have to start small, of course. With nonsinging parts. But in time . . . who knows? As a matter of fact, I've got a friend casting a new movie right now. If you're interested, I can arrange a screen test for you. For a supporting role, remember. Nothing starring. No guaranties."

Hedy stood up from the chair and went over to David. "That's a great idea. The best I've heard in years," she said excitedly. "Fuck Thane Crawley and the music business. I don't need them and their double-dealing crap."

"That's the spirit."

Hedy felt liberated, for the first time in years. "How's about you and I go have a few drinks to consummate our new relationship? That is, if you're interested in representing me," she said, batting her eyelashes.

David smiled. "I'd be delighted to represent you. But as for the drink, I'm afraid I'll have to pass on that for now. You know how it is. Business calls."

"Honey, business can always wait when you've got pleasure staring you in the face," she said provocatively, pushing her shoulders back and forcing David's eyes to wander toward her chest. She moved her face to within inches of his and rested her hand on the back of his head. "I need to work *very* closely with my lawyer. Intimately, in fact. You know, so I can learn the ins and the outs of the business. You'd do that for me, wouldn't you, David?"

David felt the heat from her body. Other clients had come on to him before, but none quite as steamy as Hedy Harlowe. He knew he was treading on thin ice. No matter how he played it now, no matter what he did or said, he was in jeopardy. She was tempting, all right. And it wasn't as if he had other irons in the fire. Still, no matter how often it happened, business and pleasure mixed about as well as oil and water, and the last thing he wanted was to blow this opportunity. With Hedy "under his belt," so to speak, and his professional relationship with Brandon continuing to develop, things were beginning to look promising.

He chose his words carefully. "Yes, it's essential that we work together closely if we're to have a good working relationship. And that we trust and respect each other. Unfortunately, a drink just now might cloud my mind and muddle my objectivity, and you wouldn't want my counseling abilities impaired. I've got to keep my head on straight. Perhaps another time, another place."

Hedy scowled, pulled her hand back, and stepped away. She felt like she'd been slapped; but the sting lasted only a few seconds. Although she despised rejection, she had to compliment David on his style and aplomb. If he'd fallen over her, or if he hadn't been able to handle her approach with finesse, she probably wouldn't have trusted him. He'd passed the test.

Her scowl turned to a smile. "You're right, David. Keep your head on straight. But remember, it's not what's *in* your head that counts, but how you give it!"

He breathed a sigh of relief.

There was only one more test. "One final question," Hedy said.

"Shoot."

"What's your sign?"

"My sign?" he asked.

"When were you born, David?"

"In July. Oh, my *sign*. Cancer."

She smiled. "You're a prince. Now make me a movie star."

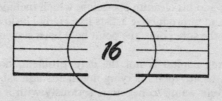

16

1967

I T WASN'T TILL SEPTEMBER OF '67 THAT THE PIECES started coming together and Thane set out on his long-awaited trip to London.

Throughout the summer, he'd tried in vain to arrange a meeting in Geneva with the Swisstone board of directors. The pattern soon became monotonous, and predictable: A date was set; a crisis flared somewhere in the Swisstone world; the board was most apologetic but the meeting had to be postponed. Thane was beginning to lose his confidence, and his patience, when Dr. Hans van der Rogdt, chief operating officer and workhorse of the Swisstone empire, paid a surprise visit to the Crawley Southampton estate over the Labor Day weekend.

After Thane had escorted the Dutchman on a grand tour of the vast Victorian mansion—gaining the upper hand by rubbing Hans's face ever so slightly in the trappings of his social and ostensibly financial superiority—the two gentlemen sat down to business in the elegant parlor. Over coffee, Thane made a precise and thoroughly documented case for a vastly expanded budget, clicking off the names and the contract terms of potential superstars recently signed by other labels, and recounting the details of his loss of Jimi Hendrix to Joe Smith. He outlined his plans for Apollo, and his cleanup operation, which included releasing expensive and unproductive artists like Hedy Harlowe. Then he went on to the sore point, the point he'd been stewing about for months.

"Operating capital is not the *only* problem, however. My interim status at Apollo is tying my hands and sabotaging my plans. No one wants to negotiate seriously with a mere 'caretaker' or 'acting president,'" Thane said, sarcastically emphasizing the final two words. "If you wish me to pilot Apollo to the forefront of the American record industry, Dr. van der Rogdt, I *must* be appointed president," he said adamantly, trying to restrain his hostility. He resented Swisstone and their staid, tightfisted Dutch representative for compelling him to demean himself and beg for what he deserved.

The Dutchman listened carefully. Short and bulky, with a trim reddish beard and deep-set eyes, van der Rogdt was a fierce Sephardic Jew, intense and humorless. Whatever softness he may have had as a child, the Nazis had ripped from him when they'd slaughtered his parents and sister, after taking them from their home in Amsterdam while Hans was off studying at the London Conservatory of Music. When he spoke, the words emerged in precise, heavily accented English. "If we were to expand your budget, Mr. Crawley, what major British or American acts could you promise to deliver to Apollo?" he inquired, ignoring Thane's demand.

Crawley answered firmly, aware that the Dutchman was trying to force his hand. "Until contracts are signed, there are no guaranties in our business. Artistic personalities, especially temperamental adolescent ones, are highly unpredictable, as you well know. I *can* guarantee you this, however. If Swisstone *doesn't* loosen its purse strings and remove the 'acting/caretaker' stigma hanging over my head, Apollo records will never become a major force in the U.S. market."

"Yes, yes, you've made your point," Hans said impatiently. "But I require names. If you wish to persuade Swisstone to increase your operating budget and appoint you president of Apollo Records, it is mandatory that you sign a major talent immediately and chart out for me projected results."

That was Catch 22 and van der Rogdt knew it. He was testing Crawley's mettle, egging him on, trying to frustrate him. It was this ability to manipulate employees that had helped propel Hans upward in Swisstone management. That, along with his war-bred ruthless energy, his sound grasp of music, and his marriage to Ariane Phochet, niece of Philippe Phochet, the founder of Swisstone.

Thane's back was to the wall. Unless he dangled the deal in front of the Dutchman, he hadn't a prayer of receiving carte blanche. But if he dangled and didn't deliver . . .

"I *had* been on the verge of signing a major British act earlier in the summer," Thane lied coolly. "That was why I was anxious for an early meeting with the board. Whether now, after all this time, I can reopen negotiations . . . well, I can't say for sure."

"The name, Mr. Crawley."

Thane paused dramatically, then answered, going against his better judgment. "The Silverfish."

"Ahh, the Silverfish. Indeed, that *would* be a feather in Swisstone's cap," van der Rogdt said contemplatively, sipping his coffee and stroking his short red beard. "I trust you *will* be able to reopen negotiations?"

Thane backed down a step. "Let's hope so. Their two-album American contract with Capitol is due to expire this month, and to my knowledge the U.S. rights have yet to be sold. I understand Joe has been pursuing them actively, however."

"And, after the Hendrix debacle, you wouldn't want Mr. Smith to outduel you again, would you?"

"It *would* be a shame for Swisstone to come up empty-handed yet again," Thane answered, turning the dig back against van der Rogdt. He resented the Jew's snide insinuation.

For the next fifteen minutes, van der Rogdt pumped Thane with questions about the Silverfish and the parameters of a potential deal. When he was finally convinced of Crawley's grasp of the situation and of the potential benefit to Swisstone, and to himself, Hans sat back in his chair, puffed on his thin cigar, and let his eyes wander around the elegant room. Although he would never admit it publicly, he was impressed with Crawley's guts and panache, and secretly jealous of his social status and comfortable American life-style. Obviously, Crawley was the kind of man who could afford to have integrity. Yes, Thane Crawley might prove even more useful than he'd anticipated.

"Mr. Crawley, I have made my decision," Hans said, breaking the long silence. "When I return to Geneva tomorrow, I will recommend that the board expand Apollo's budget."

"How encouraging. And the presidency?" Thane queried boldly.

"I'm afraid that will have to wait until after the signing. But rest assured, you have *my* complete support."

Thane imagined himself wringing the wily Dutchman's neck. Instead, he said politely, "Thank you, Dr. van der Rogdt. I trust I will live up to your confidence."

"See that you do," Hans said pointedly as he rose from his chair and prepared to make his exit. "I intend to inform the board that you have all but finalized a deal with the Silverfish. If this deal, and others like it, are not consummated in the near future, I assure you that the board will ignore my support of you and demonstrate their disappointment."

Thane breathed deeply, trying to control the swell of contempt. The bastard was threatening him. Instead of reacting, he escorted van der Rogdt to the door, smiled amiably, and shook the man's hand in farewell. Although van der Rogdt had probably expected an invitation for lunch, the Jew bastard wasn't going to get one. Thane might report to the man but he didn't have to socialize with him. And he liked the distance he could keep when he had the upper hand.

Closing the door, Thane's smile faded and feelings of rage and foreboding surfaced. He'd gotten most of what he wanted—but at a very high price. He was finally free to deal, with the enormous finances of Swisstone behind him. But it was clear that the ruthless Dutchman was giving him just enough rope to hang himself. Now he had to put up, or shut up and dangle in the wind.

* * *

As the limo wound through the streets of London en route to Brandon Levy's Curzon Street town house, Thane fought back his nerves. Reaching for the Courvoisier on the back-seat bar, he poured himself a snifter and swirled the brandy as he rolled over in his mind the permutations of the current London rock-and-roll scene.

When he had arrived in London, he'd made his usual round of the rock clubs, checking out the Bag o' Nails off Carnaby Street, the Cromwellian, the Scotch of Saint James, the Marquee, the Speakeasy, Central Polytechnic, the new Day-Glo Flamingo, and the Savile. It didn't take him long to draw a bead on the music scene. Psychedelia seemed to be peaking there, as it was in San Francisco.

Of course, everyone was still high on the first and ultimate art-rock concept album, *Sgt. Pepper,* released in June of '67 by the Beatles. No one was quite sure how to take it. Was it simply good, wholesome fun—a whimsical, fanciful, campy, circus, like life itself? Or a profound, mystical, esoteric bible, filled with double entendre, surreal symbolism, and hidden subtexts? Even the cover was a novelty, with frivolous, nostalgic cutouts of figures like Mae West, W. C. Fields, and Laurel and Hardy.

Some compared the album to Lewis Carroll's *Through the Looking Glass.* Others searched for apocalyptic significance in the endless final note, played by a forty-piece orchestra and reaching a frequency of 20,000 hertz (audible only to a dog), that completed "A Day in the Life." Everyone, however, agreed that the album was innovative and musically brilliant.

He'd read the news today—oh, boy. But where could the Beatles go from there? he wondered. There was no way they could produce another album with half the impact. And with Epstein out of the picture, all signs pointed downward. Already the "fab four" were sitting at the feet of some half-baked swami, the Maharishi Swami, and setting out by bus across the English countryside on a "Magical Mystery Tour." By his reckoning, the Beatles, too, might have peaked. They were in for some backbiting, internal squabbles, and instability now that their referee and manager was dead. That *could* leave a crucial chink for the Silverfish.

Despite all the psychedelic heat, Thane could feel the edges of a thaw. Maybe it had begun when Brian Epstein O.D.'d at the end of August. Or with George Harrison's revulsion during his walking tour of the burned-out, spaced-out, freaked-out San Francisco streets. Or with the violent murder/dismemberments of Shob and Bill Thomas, the infamous Bay Area dealers. Or with the media hype and the commercialization, exploitation, and establishment embracing of the whole scene. Whatever it was, Thane felt the winds of change. Everything was happening fast—too fast for anyone to keep up. If acid rock was cresting and a new style lurking on the horizon, discovering a new talent was essential. And with Epstein gone, the Beatles vulnerable, and Brandon Levy anxious, there was more pressure than ever to nail down the Silverfish. They had been bubbling under, cult-followed, and outrageously innovative. He was sure their time had come.

It was early evening when Thane stepped out of his limo in front of Levy's office. He took a quick survey of the elegant surroundings: embassies, consulates, private clubs, multinational corporate headquarters. Evidently Brandon Levy either harbored delusions of grandeur or knew how to surround himself with a style and class far above the Piccadilly tawdriness usually associated with London's music scene.

Thane mounted marble stairs into a beautifully appointed drawing room filled with Italian designer furniture, Dali etchings, a *faux marbre* desk, and a massive rectangular wire-glass and metal table. He was surprised at Brandon's somewhat foppish appearance and at the presence of the other man seated beside him at the table.

"Mr. Crawley, so pleased to meet you. Glad you could make it," Brandon said, rising from the table, retying his black silk smoking jacket, adjusting his red silk ascot, and stepping forward to shake Thane's hand. "I believe you know my solicitor, David Barry."

"Yes, we've met," Thane said absently, nodding toward David. He remembered Barry well enough. Their encounter several years back over Derek Robertson's embarrassing photos had left Thane with a foul taste in his mouth. This time he'd put the young upstart in his place. Between the swish Brit and his inexperienced lawyer, Thane didn't anticipate any trouble. Clearly, they were overmatched.

"Well now, Mr. Barry, this *is* a surprise. Who could have anticipated such a precipitous rise in the legal world? My congratulations," Thane said, with a tinge of sarcasm. "How long have you been representing the Silverfish?"

"Oh, over a year now," Brandon piped in. "He's my *consigliere*. I don't do anything without consulting him."

David smiled at Brandon's tactful and strategic positioning. Thank God Levy was in top shape tonight; only a smidgen of brandy and a joint to relax. If David had any hope of negotiating a deal tonight—a deal both he and Brandon wanted desperately—that was just what he needed: Brandon's unconditional support and the man in good shape.

It had taken a long time to earn that support. He'd first been called in by Levy back in '66 to consult on merchandising rights.

The opportunity to represent the Silverfish, in any capacity, was a young lawyer's dream, but unfortunately the meeting hadn't gone quite as planned. Summoned to Levy's palatial duplex penthouse on the Fifty-eighth Street side of the Plaza Hotel, David sat silently, observing the expensive English decor and the bustle of assistants, waiting until Brandon finished talking on the phone, sipping port, and nibbling on Stilton and crackers.

Finally, Brandon turned to David, introduced a few of his "aides," and then, like a caliph, clapped his hands for silence. He recited the terms of the proposed Silverfish U.S. merchandising agreement and asked David to prepare a contract immediately. When David started asking pointed questions in his usual way about the licensing agreement—suggesting that Brandon demand approval of samples and prototypes and that he monitor quality control of all Silverfish products—he got himself into trouble. Without warning, Brandon cut the meeting short and dismissed David.

Thinking he'd blown the chance of a lifetime, David had wallowed in self-doubt and self-analysis. Only when Brandon summoned him again the next day did he discover the nature of his mistake.

Alone this time, Brandon berated David for his lack of tact and prudence, although agreeing in substance with his warning. In England, lawyers were mere scriveners, he asserted. He demanded that David explain his presumption.

"Brandon, I'm a pushy New York lawyer whose clients are generally young, immature, and unsophisticated. They look to me for counsel. I level with them, tell them the truth. When their heads are swelled, when they begin believing their own reviews and the screams of their fans start going to their heads, I set them straight. I respect them and they trust me to guide and insulate them. Yesterday, I guess I was just instinctively doing that. Looking out for your best interest. Believe me, I had no intention of embarrassing you in front of your staff. If I did, please accept my apology. Not for what I said, but for how I said it and the circumstances in which I said it."

Brandon eyed him intently, giving him the once-over. "What'll it cost me to buy you, David Barry?"

"Not a cent. You don't want to buy me. If you owned me, I'd be afraid to tell you the truth. And from what I gather, you've got enough sycophants in your operation."

Brandon knew he was right. "I never wanted an empire. I

never planned all this; it just happened. I'm moving too fast in a world I know too little about. I need someone I can trust. I'm surrounded by fawning yes-men who tell me what they think I want to hear. I'm the emperor all right, but no one has enough balls to tell me whether I'm wearing new clothes or walking around stark naked. That's why I need you."

And so they'd struck a deal. David became the unofficial Silverfish lawyer and Brandon's confidant. Now he was moving into an even bigger role, negotiating with Thane Crawley. And this time he'd be sure not to let Brandon lose face.

"Shall we get down to business, gentlemen?" David suggested, motioning Thane toward the table.

"A drink, Mr. Crawley?" Brandon asked as he poured himself a stiff brandy.

"Just coffee, please." Thane took a seat opposite the two men at the bargaining table.

The first hour was spent talking general terms. Both sides danced cautiously but to the same tune. Brandon was encouraged. Then the session toughened.

"The Silverfish drug bust . . ." Thane said casually, letting the phrase dangle unfinished in the air. "The boys were arrested for possession of cannabis last month in Scotland, were they not?"

Before Brandon or David could answer, Thane held up his hand and continued. "Look, I don't care what drugs anybody does. What I don't know won't hurt me. I *am* concerned about U.S. Immigration, however. They've started cracking down on visa authorizations, especially for performers with drug convictions. Obviously, an American contract will require the Silverfish to tour the States again. What assurance can you give me that their H-1 visas will be renewed?"

Even though the question was reasonable, David didn't like Thane's tone or his timing. "It's not a problem," David answered, thanking God for Jack Black. "If you insist, we can make their visa approval a contract condition. I can guarantee their H-1s will be renewed for a U.S. tour."

"Excellent," Thane said, wondering how Barry could manage that.

Thane had tried to put them on the defensive, but two could play rough, David thought to himself. There was no point in keeping the gloves on with a bastard like Crawley. After all, it was Thane who had dropped Rick and Hedy from his label. He wished he could see Thane's face when he found out who was representing Hedy now. But that surprise would have to wait until after they'd struck a deal.

"Since we're clearing the air, there *is* one thing bothering me that I'd like to bring out into the open," David began. "We both know that a certain amount of goodwill is essential in these negotiations, and that personal trust is an important element in any agreement we might reach. The Silverfish need to feel your confidence in them. Since you are only *acting* president of Apollo, what assurance do we have that the eventual *permanent* president will live up to the spirit and the letter of any agreement?"

Brandon's heart sank. What the hell was David trying to do, sabotage the whole deal? Brandon rose from his seat a little too abruptly and quickly poured himself another glass of brandy. He was trying not to show it, but he was afraid. After what had happened to Joyce, and the terrible guilt, he'd become frightened of assuming responsibility for anyone or anything. He was terribly afraid that his Silverfish, his surrogate family, his "boys," might actually turn against him if he didn't secure an important and lucrative American deal.

But even more, he was afraid of falling behind the times, of falling out of sync with the new music, the new values and life-styles. Once *he'd* been the guru, the mover and the shaker; now he kept busy with drug deals and details while the boys seemed off in another world. Fortunately he was expanding the other sides of his business. With the help of his constant companion, Kevin Singh, he was branching out into film and other musical areas, trying to build something called L.O.L., Levy Organization Limited. Then, at least, all his eggs wouldn't be in one basket.

Across the table, Thane sipped his coffee and hid a scowl, damning van der Rogdt, David Barry, and Brandon Levy under his breath. He was experiencing the "Jewish conspiracy." All of them could go back to their hill, Kike's Pike, or wherever the chosen people came from. He'd show them. If he signed the Silverfish—and that was still a big *if*—he was confident he could force van der Rogdt's hand and win a permanent place as president of Apollo.

"Have no fear, gentlemen," Thane responded. "I can assure you, in the strictest confidence, that Swisstone shareholders plan to announce my appointment as permanent president of Apollo in the near future, probably at the December Swisstone convention in San Francisco."

"And can we make *that* a condition of the contract?" David asked pointedly.

Thane's mouth dropped. Barry was a worm. "Well . . ."

Brandon jumped in. "Now, now, gentlemen, that isn't necessary. We can take Thane at his word."

The thrust and parry completed for the moment, the talk turned to the nitty-gritty of terms and conditions. Three hours and countless cups of coffee and brandy later, negotiations bogged down. Although both parties agreed on a signing fee of $250,000, plus $250,000 per LP for five LPs delivered over sixty months, David was insisting on a number of additional points—such as funds for tour support that weren't recoupable from Silverfish royalties, plus a guaranteed minimum number of album pressings, no discount on mechanical publishing rates on copyrights, and the Silverfish right to retain coupling rights—all of which Thane resisted.

"Look, David, I might agree to some elements of your first three conditions, but when it comes to coupling rights, I need to have the right to use the Silverfish masters any way I see fit."

"I'm sorry, Thane. That's unacceptable and a deal breaker. What's to prevent you from sticking Silverfish cuts into package compilations of other artists just to induce sales, as I believe you've done with some of your other artists? I can't risk your cheapening the Silverfish impact by diluting the market." Although he wanted it to appear so, it wasn't Hedy's experience that made David insist on retaining the coupling rights.

Brandon was beside himself. He kept seeing and feeling the $1.5-million deal slipping through his fingers. "Excuse me, gentlemen. David, can I speak with you privately for a moment?" Brandon said, leading the way into the rear sitting room.

The moment the door to the lushly carpeted back room was closed, Brandon turned to David. "What the hell are you doing out there?" Brandon exclaimed, pacing around the room. "The guy's agreed to the money. Who cares about bloody crap like coupling rights?"

"Brandon, please, you've got to trust me. Thane wants this deal as much as we do, if not more. Some of the points I'm insisting on are essential; others are mere psychological ploys. As to coupling rights, you know damn well about our deal with Jack."

"Jack Black? The Mr. Fixit character?"

"Right, the one saving our ass by taking care of the H-1 visas. We *can't* give away exclusive coupling rights to Apollo."

"But you're endangering the whole deal. You know no one else has made a serious offer yet. If we lose Thane—"

"Calm down. We're not going to lose Apollo. Look, you've been great tonight but I'm afraid your patience has worn thin. Please, for your own sake and for the sake of the Silverfish, do me a favor. Take a pill, go rest, go out, anything. But leave the rest of the negotiations to me. Just let me play out this scenario and I promise you we'll make the deal."

Brandon was secretly glad to relinquish his role to David. He couldn't bear the tension. "All right, David, I can take a hint. If you're really sure you know what you're doing . . ." He shook a Mandrex out of his pill case and washed it down with the brandy.

"Want a good idea? Why don't you and Kevin go see Rick and Joyce?" David suggested. "Rick's playing at that little fish-and-chips place down on the East End, the place where they play bingo during the entire show. Go on down there. He needs a lift. Cheer 'em both up. I'll join you later."

"All right. Anything to take my mind off these bloody negotiations. I'll head out the back way. Good luck, old man."

When David reemerged from the rear room, he emerged alone.

"Thane, I think we've had enough for one night," David said, looking down at Crawley from across the table. With Brandon out of the picture, he could start playing head poker. "We appear to be at an impasse. I'm not really convinced you're as committed to the Silverfish as you say. Let's call it quits temporarily and talk again next week."

Thane stared into David's eyes, trying to penetrate his psyche. The prospect of leaving the table at this point, without a tentative agreement to show van der Rogdt, terrified him.

"Come now, David, you know how much I believe in the Silverfish. We're so close. Why don't we give it one more shot and try to reach a tentative agreement?"

David shook his head. "No, I really don't think that would be productive. Look, we're both tired. Better to step away from the table and think things over at our leisure. Brandon is mulling it over, and the decision will ultimately be his."

Thane didn't have the leisure. But he couldn't simply capitu-

late, without even a show. If he did, he'd be left without a shred
of self-respect and no leverage over Barry and the Silverfish. He
had no choice. "All right. Let's talk again in a couple of days,"
he said. "I'm confident we can iron out our differences."

"I hope so, Thane. I sincerely hope so," David said, showing
the Apollo executive to the door.

"Please say my goodbyes to Brandon. I hope we'll be working
together in the near future."

"Of course. By the way," David added nonchalantly, "if
you're in San Francisco for your convention in December,
there's an act you might want to catch. A gifted young Welsh
singer by the name of Dwight Sharon." David didn't mention
the note he'd sent Thane over a year ago.

"Oh?" Thane said noncommittally. "Where will he be playing?"

"He's been working the Red Cock. Check it out if you have
the chance. He's quite unusual—extraordinary, in fact."

The Red Cock! Barry had to be kidding. All Thane could
think about was flying to Amsterdam tomorrow, at Swisstone
expense. If he wasn't going to finalize the Silverfish deal tonight,
he needed Amsterdam's special medicine, desperately, to keep
himself from falling to pieces.

Thane waited two days before calling. By then he was so
bruised from the whip that he could barely sit down. Although
his cock was limp from hours of continuous sex, each new pain
reminded him of the exquisite excitement he had experienced.
Exhausted, he placed the call to David Barry in London.

Amsterdam was just what the doctor ordered. A city where
sin was organized as an industry, and cleanliness and anonymity
guaranteed by the government. There, Thane lived out the wild
fantasies that he craved, even needed, to make him into a rock-
hard man.

Unlike some men, who turned to drugs or gambling as an
outlet, Thane Crawley sought out the sound of the whip and the
voice of a big black whore standing over him ordering him to
do her bidding. After the encounter with Brandon and David
had started his competitive juices flowing, he clamored for the
titillation of a wild, mindless encounter to unleash his own juices
and his screaming, pent-up frustration.

He loved the game and all its filth, including the costumes and
the paraphernalia. Playing slave to a Nubian goddess, he wel-

comed the sting of the cat-o'-nine-tails and the grip of the cock ring tightened around his swelling member. When the dominatrix screamed out her filthy, abusive tirade and ordered, "Eat me, scum!" he grew harder and her juices tasted even sweeter. He thrilled at the orchestrated subjugation and humiliation. As long as it was a game that he controlled, paid for, and arranged, he reveled in the degradation. To the world, he played for power and control. But secretly, when the world wasn't looking, he lusted after punishment and release.

The call to London was short and sweet. He knew he was capitulating, but it really didn't matter. Although he would have liked to stand his ground against Barry on some of the minor points, like the coupling rights, none of them was essential. Especially since he was really risking only $500,000. If the first LP didn't fly, he'd drop the Silverfish flat. They could sue all they wanted, but he'd simply prove breach of contract. All he had to do was follow his standard operating procedure: keep tabs on their drug buys and then claim violation of the morals clause.

Fortunately, David didn't play coy this time. The fact that Thane called, and so soon after the last meeting, told the whole story. It took only a few minutes for them to agree to terms.

Bathed in relief, Thane took off for Geneva to visit old "van der Rot," the Flying Dutchman, and shove the Silverfish contract down his throat.

After a night of celebration with the Silverfish, Joyce, Rick and an ecstatic Brandon, David put through his own call to Jack Black in New York.

"Jack, it's David Barry."

"Hey, kid, what's happenin'?" Jack asked in his distinctive basso-profundo voice.

"I'm in London. We just signed the Silverfish to Apollo."

"Congratulations. I always knew you were a smooth operator. Even before you did."

David laughed. Jack was right. When they'd first met, David was just starting out, with his office at Black Jack Studio. Brashly, David had come to Jack's office in an effort to obtain royalty statements for two pothead producers who'd claimed Jack was cheating them. Even though there were half a dozen people waiting in the reception area of the Black Jack office, above the Chock Full O' Nuts, David was shown right in.

Jack's office was huge, three times as long as it was wide, and decorated handsomely in tasteful Mediterranean style with natural terra-cotta floors, Spanish throw rugs, Spanish oak chests, wrought-iron tables and chairs, and scattered glazed clay figurines and desert plants.

The man behind the desk was handsome and commanding, if not downright ominous. His height, his jet-black hair and skin, his huge square shoulders and slick attire (black cashmere jacket, white vest, fresh camellia in his lapel) made him one imposing figure.

Knowing something of his reputation and seeing the man in person, David had second thoughts.

"Come in, come in, kid," Jack said, waving toward David. "Sit."

David did as he was told.

"I got your letter. Nice stationery. Nicely done. Very impressive. Reggie tells me good things about you. So why the hell are you representing a couple of scumbags?"

For the next hour, Jack interviewed David, probing into his background, asking pointed questions, feeling him out. All the while, people kept coming in and out, and Jack carried on business as usual, as if David weren't present.

One of the exchanges made David practically shit in his pants. A distraught man, looking like a loan shark in an iridescent sharkskin suit, rushed into the office. "Jack, I gotta talk to you," the man said, looking over at David.

"So talk, sweetheart. I'm all ears."

"You know Uncle Ernie, the DJ at WQBC?"

"He's a putz."

"Well, the putz is trying to fuck us."

"Yeah?"

"We gotta get QBC to break Philly. Without Philly we can't break Washington. Without Washington, we can't break—"

"Shut up, Carmine. I don't need a lesson in record promotion. I gave you bread to take care of Ernie. So what's the problem? You're not holding out on me, baby, are you?"

"He turned down the two hundred bucks. Says he wants seven hundred."

"Seven hundred, huh?" Jack leaned back in his chair and thought for a moment. "You know, it's almost cheaper to have the motherfucker killed," Jack said, patting the head of his cane into his palm and smiling all the while at David. "I'll handle him, Carmine. You just take care of the other jocks."

Jack picked up the phone. "Get me Ernie." The call came through. "Ernie, Jack. Just stay cool. Don't be no fool. Take the bread. Or you'll be dead." Then he hung up.

"Excuse me, kid. Sorry for the interruption. Where were we?" Jack said nonchalantly.

That was how David learned of Jack's network of independent promotion men. The record companies took care of Jack, and he in turn took care of the radio stations to ensure air play for selected artists. None of the record companies was sure if the money they paid helped break records, but they were too paranoid *not* to pay. Jack and his compatriots had become a force to reckon with in the record business.

Jack told David the story behind his producer clients: how they'd gotten busted and into Jack's debt, and then tried peddling stolen Black Jack tracks under their own names. Even though David soon realized that he didn't have a legal leg to stand on, Jack surprised him.

"Your clients are shits, kid. But you, I like. And you done me a few favors, though you might not know it. So I'm gonna settle, even though you ain't got a case. Take your fee, pay off the assholes, and spread the word on the street that you got money out of Jack Black. It'll help, believe me. Just don't forget Jack. We can be good friends, you and me."

And he was right. Jack had helped David out on a number of occasions. Now David was pleased to return the favor.

"Jack, I'm paying off my marker for the H-1 visas," David said exuberantly over the phone.

"About time, sweetie. Whatta ya got?"

"We've got coupling rights. Whenever you want, you have your pick of the Silverfish cuts for your compilation, *Best Artists of* . . . series. Crawley will shit, but who cares?"

"That's cool. I'll pick a couple after the American release. But I'll hold the album a while so it doesn't hurt your client. Keep me hip, gotta trip. Ciao, baby."

David hung up the phone and sighed. So he wasn't pure as the driven snow. So what? It was part of the business. It was one of the ways he helped his artists. What was he supposed to do, turn his back on an angel?

* * *

The line of stretch limos outside the stately Fairmont Hotel wound up the steep side streets for as far as the eye could see. The combination of the colored Christmas lights strung brightly from lamppost to lamppost, the shiny headlights of the Lincolns and Cadillacs, and the reflection of the full moon overhead seemed to illumine San Francisco in a psychedelic glow.

The bounty of colors only mirrored the glow Thane Crawley felt inside as he left the appropriately titled Presidential Suite and pushed his way through the lobby's revolving door. Everything at the Swisstone convention was going according to plan. Not only had Hans van der Rogdt just announced Thane's official appointment as the new president of Apollo Records, but the critical word out of London on the Christmas television premiere of the Beatles' *Magical Mystery Tour* was overwhelmingly negative. Their first creative setback. The Silverfish were perfectly positioned for an American invasion.

Thane had been right. Things *were* changing. The Beatles weren't invulnerable after all. Progressive FM radio was sliding into AM-format programming, Murray the K had been fired from WOR-FM in New York, and troubles at San Francisco's own KMPX had begun to surface. More and more rock stars seemed bent on a collision course with the law: The Grateful Dead and the Stones' Brian Jones had been busted for drugs, and Jim Morrison had been arrested on stage for disturbing the peace. Woody Guthrie and Otis Redding were dead, and the new music rag *Rolling Stone* was running an exposé of the financial mishandling of the Monterey Festival profits.

In his speech at the convention, however, Thane painted a rosy picture of Apollo's future. With Americans spending over a billion dollars on records in 1967, and album sales outstripping singles for the first time, the new Apollo president forecast increased revenue and dramatic changes in musical taste. He promised that Apollo would hover on the musical cutting edge.

"Come on, Thane—we're all waiting!" the promo man yelled loudly from the back of one of the limos.

Thane waved politely, forced a smile, buttoned his black cashmere coat, and headed past the doorman, out through the brisk northern California ocean breeze toward the car. Ordinarily he would have preferred other companionship, but tonight it was *noblesse oblige.* As president, he was expected to accompany the employee riffraff, the troops, the "farkals," as he called them, for a night out on the town, San Francisco–style. Being one of the boys, one of the common folk, was not an easy role for Thane.

When they arrived at the Red Cock Club, the twelve Swisstone record execs were practically peeing in their pants at the prospect of seeing a fag drag show that featured a Diana Ross/Supremes look-alike contest.

The maître d'—in a slinky black leatherette dress and elegant black beehive wig—escorted the group to three small, round ringside tables marked "Reserved" along the perimeter of the slightly raised stage. Each of the Formica tables was covered with a cheap white lace tablecloth and graced with a vase holding a single red rose. After two quick rounds of watered-down drinks and seemingly endless boring executive chitchat, Thane was feeling irritable and impatient. Wondering how soon he could politely leave, he let his mind wander to alternate, preferable rites of celebration.

Suddenly the houselights dimmed and a butch-looking announcer, dressed in Hell's Angel chic leather, appeared on stage under the spotlight.

"Ladies and gentlemen, the Red Cock is pleased to present a very gifted young man from Wales—Dwight Sharon!"

The applause for the warm-up act was polite. For a minute, Thane couldn't place the name. Then he remembered David Barry's parting words in London. Jeez, if he'd remembered that earlier, he would *never* have come.

Dwight made his entrance, looking outrageous. The skinny, gawky kid who had strummed a small, beat-up guitar in David Barry's office had been transformed by a four-month stint with the Cockettes into a wild camp queen. His hair and newly grown beard were dyed shocking orange, teased to a frizz, and sprinkled with fairy-dust sequins. Draped in a purple cape with imitation ermine collar, wearing feathered pants, rhinestone earrings, lots of bangles, and multicolored rings, he pranced across the stage in platform shoes that made him look like a combination praying mantis and transsexual version of Lucille Ball.

The audience was floored!

When he sat down at the piano and started to sing, though, the audience was even more shocked. Playing like a cross between Liberace and Jerry Lee Lewis, and singing like Johnny Ray, Dwight attacked the piano keys with a vengeance, belting out soulful renditions of six recent pop hits, including Lennon and McCartney's "Hello Goodbye," Gladys Knight and the Pips' "I Heard It Through the Grapevine," and the Strawberry

Alarm Clock's "Incense and Peppermints." Incredibly, his versions sounded better than the originals.

Thane couldn't help but be impressed. The kid was unique, all right. He was loaded with style *and* talent. But without his own material, he was no better than a Vegas lounge act.

As though reading Crawley's thoughts, Dwight completed his final cover version and instead of leaving the stage to the Motown girls' lip-sync festival, he remained at the piano. For the first time ever in public, he prepared to sing one of his original compositions, entitled "I'm a Sad, Lonely Man." Alerted to the presence of Swisstone executives in the audience, he seized the opportunity, knowing he was about to offend his co-performers and jeopardize his job.

In less than a minute, the audience was mesmerized. Crying his heart out through song, Dwight Sharon wrenched his voice and his soul in telling the poignant autobiographical story of a freak, rejected by man and woman alike, whose grotesque physical appearance hid from the world the beauty that was inside him.

He didn't stop there. He couldn't stop.

This buffoon-turned-Pagliacci segued into song after moving song, turning from the piano to the guitar, alternately shouting and whispering and wailing until the audience was choked with emotion. Even the four Diana Ross look-alikes standing in the wings stopped bitching about Dwight's stealing their spotlight and cried unabashedly, dabbing their eyes over and over, their makeup spoiled.

The crowd stood and demanded three encores before they allowed Dwight off stage. When the show was over and the Diana Rosses finally began their parade across the stage, Thane excused himself from the table and walked over to the slinky maître d'. The sound of "Baby Love, My Baby Love" was muffled by Thane's racing thoughts.

"Excuse me . . ." He didn't know whether to say "sir" or "madam." "I wonder if you would give Mr. Sharon my card and ask him if I might have a word with him."

The maître d' batted his long eyelashes at Thane and took the card from his hand, letting his fingertips brush against Thane's. When he read the card, he raised his penciled eyebrows. "Of course, honey. If you'll just wait a moment . . ."

Something about Dwight had touched Thane and his golden ear. Not only wasn't he put off by the outrageousness of the garb and the act, he was actually attracted by it. And he had observed how the hardened, jaded band of brigands who accompanied him all melted into adoring fans. In his mind's eye, he could see Dwight's antics on stage and hear his strong voice over the airwaves, ringing the cash registers for Apollo. This was the new look and the new sound America was waiting for.

In no time at all, Thane Crawley was backstage in a cramped little closet of a dressing room shaking hands with the bizarre-looking string bean named Dwight Sharon, who was still dressed in his wild costume.

"I don't believe it. Are you really from Apollo Records, sir? You're not pullin' my leg now, are you?" Dwight asked with a sincerity worthy of Bette Davis in *Jezebel*.

Thane smiled. "It's no joke, Dwight. I'm really the president of Apollo."

"Well, I'll be. I wish I could offer you some tea or somethin', but I don't have anythin'. . . . I still can't believe that you were really in the audience!"

"Listen, I thought your show was tremendous, especially your original stuff. I think you've got outstanding potential as a performer *and* as a recording artist. If you're interested, I'd like to fly you down to Los Angeles so we can talk terms for a recording contract with Apollo Records."

Dwight's mouth dropped. "That's wonderful, sir. Only . . . only . . . I'm afraid I couldn't do it."

"What? What do you mean you can't do it? Are you already signed?"

"No, but I couldn't go alone, without talking to my lawyer."

"Your lawyer? You have a lawyer already?"

"Yes, sir. He made me promise never to talk to anyone about a contract without him."

"Well, tell me who it is and I'll get in touch with him, Dwight," Thane said, laughing to himself. What was the world coming to? Even Dwight Sharon had some San Francisco queen acting as his "lawyer"!

"His name's David Barry, sir. I believe he's in London now."

David Barry! Christ, he was haunted by that shit. Of course, he should have expected it. Even so, he wasn't going to pass up the chance of Dwight Sharon.

"Well, that's most fortunate, Dwight. Mr. Barry and I are good friends. I'll speak to him in London and make arrangements. As far as I'm concerned, the sooner we can have you in the recording studio, the better. I hope you're ready, young man, because I have every intention of turning you into a star."

And he did, of course. That evening became a historic one, another music-industry legend. And Thane became an indelibly etched part of music history as the man with the golden ear, the man with the courage to try something new, the man whose career was so closely linked to the signing and subsequent astounding success of Dwight Sharon. Five albums, all double platinum; sold-out concerts; pandemonium perfectly executed to create hysteria. A shooting star, burning a little too brightly.

BOOK

3

The
Immaculate Conception

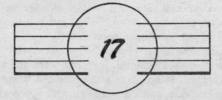

1972

*A*FTER NEARLY SIXTEEN WEEKS IN THE ISRAELI DES-
ert, the heat and dust had become unbearable, even for the crew.

Worst off were the apostles, covered in authentic hand-
loomed robes wrapped loosely with hemp; the elaborately
hooded Pharisees; and the heavily robed extras. Despite the
large fans blowing dust off the cameras and rustling the palm
fronds in the hands of the 600 extras, the actors were dropping
like flies. What with the endless, boring repetition, the heat
prostration, and the dysentery, the casualty list for the shoot was
reaching epidemic proportions.

Just arrived on location in his thinnest polo shirt and slacks,
David was wet with sweat and caked with grime. He could feel
the sand in his shoes and taste it between his teeth. All around
him, technicians in sun visors, T-shirts, and chic imitation satin
baseball jackets—many embossed with the logo IMMACULATE
CONCEPTION, but others with previous film logos—roamed the
set talking into their expensive walkie-talkies.

"Watch the wires!" someone shouted. "Don't walk there, mister. Keep off those cables, please," one of the electricians scolded David as he tried to pussyfoot his way toward the trailers. With so many assistants, and assistants' assistants, and union-dictated specialization, it was a wonder the entire set wasn't utter chaos. And it would have been, if it weren't for the strong hand of the assistant producer.

Joyce Heller was in her element. She was vibrant, energized, and in control. Like Toscanini, she conducted the entire crew, handling everyone with a firm and dexterous wand. Everyone had a role, a function, a job, and an ego, and Joyce was sensitive and wise enough to extract the best from each. Even though the shoot had long passed the point of sanity, Joyce, miraculously, was still cool and in charge. After what *she'd* lived through, this nightmare wasn't at all frightening. In fact, she'd come to love it.

"All right, Joe. Get back to the lights and *I'll* talk to him. . . .

"No. No more extras. You'll have to go with what we've got. Get the next take started so we don't lose any more. She'll do it right this time, I promise you. . . .

"Chip, check the sound on the right speaker.

"Makeup, makeup!" She pointed toward the apostles. "They need help."

She looked up at one of the cameramen perched on a crane. "Snuff the joint, Hal. Yeah, you, pothead!" she shouted. "Don't gimme that innocent look. You know the rules on this set. Pot—hobby, not habit, remember? Try not to fall, will ya?"

The whole crew laughed as Hal sheepishly put out the joint.

Unfortunately, but not unexpectedly, Brandon Levy, the titular producer of this multimillion-dollar musical extravaganza written and conceived by the world-renowned Silverfish, was nowhere in sight. That was why it hadn't been easy for Joyce. Even though she was one of the boys, had paid nearly four years of dues in the British movie industry, and had helped Brandon handpick a core of the most skilled, stable, dependable technicians available, she'd still had to earn her stripes on the set. Only when she'd shown a firm hand and a bottoms-up grasp of moviemaking had she earned the crew's respect and made them forget that she was a woman producing her first feature film.

Brandon and the Silverfish were well aware of Joyce's assets. It was Brandon, after all, who'd helped her get started in the movie business. They trusted her as a friend and as a professional. She was one of the few people who knew the music *and* the movie businesses inside out. For those reasons—and because of Brandon's current "state"—she'd become indispensable to this project, the film version of the Silverfish's great religious rock opera *The Immaculate Conception.*

It was a new Joyce David was seeing. Even though she still looked as thin and manly as ever, her body consciously hidden beneath a loose blue denim work shirt and army fatigues, her face devoid of makeup, her hair pulled back severely and bobby-pinned into an almost dykish washerwoman's bun, she now radiated an inner strength and natural beauty that caught David by surprise. Despite the severity of her appearance and the sorry state of the project, he was happy for her. Clearly, the period of weakness and vulnerability had passed. Out of the flames, like a phoenix, was rising a new woman, fire-tested into maturity and confidence.

And none too soon. Because Joyce needed every ounce of strength to keep this ill-conceived project rolling, in the face of mounting costs and tensions and the temper tantrums of its spoiled star. Any further delays on the set could provoke a wholesale mutiny by cast and crew.

"Take sixteen, the virgin-emerging scene!" the assistant director shouted, snapping the black and white slate board and walking away from the small, biblical-looking village in the midst of the desert.

"Quiet on the set! Okay, background movement!"

The fully orchestrated Silverfish music swelled over the speakers. The large wind machines increased their velocity. The lighting director cued a shimmering, almost holy white light to radiate out of a small, unassuming clay hut. The three makeup men, hidden in the hut, dabbed on the final touches of powder and pancake.

"Action!" the director shouted.

Suddenly, ineffably, a white-clad figure stepped forward out of the shack, backlit by the blinding, iridescent white light. The camera slid slowly forward a hundred feet on its narrow, custom-built railroad tracks until the cinematographer focused solely on the star's pure, angelic face peeking out from a white muslin shawl. Her expression was simple, beatific, even mystical. The crew, dead silent, was awed. She *was* the Virgin Mary, Mary Immaculate, Mother of God, about to sing to her newborn child.

When she opened her mouth to sing, one of the countless flying insects attracted by the intense, artificial light flew into her mouth and got caught in her throat. The Virgin Mary choked, then spoke:

"Can't you DDT these fuckers? Jesus Christ! I can't sing with fucking gnats in my mouth! My contract says no goddamned bugs!" she screamed, spitting into the sand.

The director shook his head, folded his hands, and continued to let the cameras roll. At least he'd have another "out-take" to send to his friends back in Beverly Hills for their "screaming" rooms.

"Why the hell aren't we shooting in L.A.? I'm sick of this place—I'm sick of having the fuckin' runs! Who's gonna believe this stupid *schlock* opera, anyway? Hedy Harlowe as a virgin *and* a mother—that's a special effect worthy of Charlton Heston and *The Ten Commandments!* You can't tell me this broad got pregnant without getting laid! Gimme a break! What fun is that? Maybe she gave Joseph a blow job and it went down the wrong pipe!"

The crew didn't laugh. Not anymore. Not after all these weeks.

"Okay, cut. Cut! Cut! Cut! She's at it again."

"I am not, asshole!" Hedy screeched. "I'm sick. Sick of your bullshit ineptitude, sick of this hot, stinking desert."

Yet again, Hedy huffed off the set and stormed into her huge trailer, slamming the metal door behind her.

David moved beside Joyce and rested his hand on her shoulder. She looked up at him, smiling slightly at Hedy's antics, then simply shook her head and sighed. It was happening again.

David didn't smile. He blamed himself for bringing Hedy and the Silverfish together, and he blamed Hedy for what she was doing to Joyce, to the budget, and ultimately to herself. At twenty million and still mounting, the picture was bound for financial overruns unparalleled since Liz Taylor's *Cleopatra*. And all because of one star, his client, the ever-lovely Hedy Harlowe, whom he'd helped build from a flagging recording artist into a multimillion-dollar film star and nightclub entertainer. After four record-breaking, nonsinging film roles, this was to be Hedy's screen singing debut as well as the Silverfish's chance to cash in on their own rock opera, aping the theatrical successes of the Who's *Tommy* and Andrew Lloyd Webber and Tim Rice's *Jesus Christ Superstar*.

True to character, however, Hedy was pulling every stunt in her book of prick-tricks to ensure that no one forgot who she was and what she meant to the box-office potential of this otherwise unfinancable, unproducible, garbage opera. With each success, Hedy had become more difficult, more spoiled and more ornery, until she'd been labeled the scourge of directors and the bitchiest actress in Hollywood.

Joyce turned to the director. "How's the time?"

"Forget it. The day's shot. If we don't complete the scene within the hour, the sun'll be casting all the wrong shadows and we'll never match our earlier shots. No way that cunt'll ever come back out. I'm telling you, baby, I want off this picture."

"Take it easy, Brad. I'll take care of it." Touching David's arm lightly, she whispered, "Wish me luck. I'm off to the lion's den."

She heard him say "Good luck" as she turned and walked across the sand to the huge cream-colored Winnebago. Climbing the stairs and knocking firmly, Joyce entered the largest trailer on the set without hesitating or waiting for permission. Inside, she was met by a welcome blast of cold air generated by the supplemental air-conditioning unit that Hedy had demanded.

The trailer was white and spacious, with several large dressers, an unkempt bed, a kitchenette, and in one corner an upright piano. Hedy was seated at the dressing table surrounded by her hair stylist, the makeup man, and the dresser. Her lips were pursed petulantly, like a defiant child's.

"Excuse us," Joyce said quietly, motioning the three out of the trailer and taking a seat at the table just behind Hedy.

As soon as the door closed, Hedy started in, scowling at Joyce's reflection in the mirror. "Don't lecture me, Joyce. I don't want to hear bullshit about all the jobs on the line. About your career or Rick's career or David or the fucking Silverfish. Fuck all that shit! No lectures, honey, okay?"

"Okay, Hedy, no lectures. Just tell me what's bothering you."

Hedy buried her face in her hands. Out there, under the sun and the lights, with the crew and the director scowling at her, she felt she had to live up to her image, had to play Supercunt just to survive. She'd gotten worse recently, and even *she* wasn't sure why. Whatever it was, she felt the burning loneliness welling up inside her again. Thank God she had Joyce to talk to.

"I'm frightened, Joyce," she confided.

"Frightened? You? What have you got to be scared of?"

"Everything, honey, every fucking thing." She got up from the dressing table and started pacing around the trailer, looking beautiful but incongruous in her virginal white outfit. Hidden beneath the makeup, there were lines in her forehead and bags under her eyes. If anything, though, her body was firmer and tauter than ever before.

"You know I've been mouthin' off all along, sayin' I don't give a shit about the film or the budget. I'm Hedy Harlowe, right? Surefire box-office smash. You put up with all my shenanigans because I'm the one that's gonna sell the tickets. . . . Well, it's all bullshit, Joyce. I've got everything to lose. If this film goes down, I go down with it. It's not your neck or Brandon's that's at stake, it's mine. They're all gunnin' for me out there: the director, the crew, the critics. They wanna see me fall flat on my tits. And this time I'm afraid it's gonna happen."

Joyce wasn't sure how to respond. From the beginning, she'd known the material was weak and the casting unsound. Even so, she hadn't been fool enough to pass up the producing opportunity of a lifetime. The experience was invaluable and, really, she had nothing to lose.

Hedy was another matter, however. Hollywood would tolerate her petulant act only as long as she continued attracting the fans. As soon as she stopped clicking the turnstiles, they'd swoop down on Hedy like vultures over a decaying corpse. Joyce decided to lay it on the line.

"You're absolutely right, Hedy. It *is* your neck on the block. So why the fuck make matters worse? Why slow down the film, add to costs, alienate more people, and generally do your best to live up to your reputation? If you wanna commit professional suicide, you could have picked a cooler spot. For God's sake, Hedy, either walk off the movie now and save us the money and the agony, or finish it like a pro. I can't bear to watch you self-destruct like this. I care about you too much."

Hedy stopped in her tracks opposite Joyce. Tears gathered in her eyes and started rolling down her cheeks. She fell to her knees and buried her head in Joyce's lap. "Oh, Joyce. I can't tell you how hard it's been. You don't hate me, do you?"

"Of course not," Joyce said, running her hand gently through Hedy's hair.

"I don't know what's gotten into me. The movie sucks, Joyce, you and I both know it. It was ill-conceived and ill-cast, but I don't blame you or David or Brandon. We were all sucked in, swept up by the excitement."

Hedy was right again.

"Maybe it's Rick," Hedy said softly.

"Rick?"

"Yeah, seeing him again. Working with him again. I'm all churned up inside. Like I'm eighteen."

"Do you want him off the set, Hedy?"

"No, God forbid. I want him here, with me. That's why I requested he do the charts and the arrangements for the movie. I can't get him out of my head, Joyce. I can't forget Brighton Beach, when I was too young and ambitious and naïve to know anything about my feelings. I drove him away then, and now it's too late. Now he's as scared of me as the rest. . . ."

Joyce raised Hedy up by the elbows and walked her over to the edge of the bed. Then she went to the kitchen and fixed her a cup of tea laced with a shot of bourbon.

"Here, drink this. It'll warm you up inside."

Hedy sipped at the tea and smiled. Joyce was so calm and unthreatening, and treated her like a real friend. On the surface they were night and day, but deep down they had more than a little in common. One shared intimacy in particular drew them together.

"I can't tell you how many there've been since Rick. All of them faceless, except for one. The one with the body and no soul. I was a fool to get involved with him. He hurt me more than I care to admit. But I guess you know all about that. . . ."

Joyce knew, all right. And the bitterness still lingered. "Anyone who gets involved with Derek is a fool and a masochist. He's a learning experience, though. After Derek, you don't make the same mistake again, do you?"

"That bad for you, too, huh?"

Joyce nodded.

"I hear he's in Europe. Traveling dope dealer to the stars."

"I don't want to know about it, Hedy. I've had enough angst where Derek's concerned. Now I know how Dr. Frankenstein must have felt. Jesus, I created a fucking monster!"

Partners in experience, both women burst into conspiratorial giggles.

"I'll tell you what, Hedy. Let's finish this scene now while the sun's still up, and afterwards I'll tell Rick that I want him to rehearse the next two musical numbers with you. Alone. In depth. How's that sound?"

"You're one fucking doll, Joyce."

"I'll send your entourage back in?"

"Send 'em in. If anybody can turn me into a virgin, they can. You think Rick would be more attracted to me if he thought I was a virgin?"

"I'll ask him."

"Don't you dare, Joyce! Joyce . . . !"

Waiting outside in the shimmering 100-degree heat, David wandered over to Brandon's trailer. The generator was noisy and vibrated the entire Winnebago.

"How is he?" David asked the tanned, muscular security guard who was sitting on the steps reading a cheap paperback.

"Asleep."

"How long's it been?"

"About sixteen hours."

"What was it this time?"

The boy shrugged. David knew damn well what it was. One of Brandon's usual cocktails of Nembutal and Mandrex washed down with a bottle of scotch.

"Where'd he get it? You were supposed to keep him clean."

"Beats me, Mr. Barry. I don't know *where* the hell he gets the stuff."

Yeah, sure. "I'll just check on him."

David climbed the stairs and entered the chilly trailer. Brandon was out cold on the bed, still dressed in his French twill pants and silk shirt. He had a slight yellow pallor, from his deteriorated liver, and his sleep seemed unnaturally deep.

David didn't bother trying to wake him. What was the point? He knew what he'd find. Shaking hands, a dull glaze over the eyes, slurred speech. Then Brandon would order coffee, pop a Ritalin, start talking a blue streak, pupils dilated, eyes darting, pop a couple more Dexies until he finally switched to downers and collapsed for another sixteen hours. The pattern had become too predictable.

He missed the old Brandon. The one with the vision, the acute intellect, and the razor-sharp sarcasm. The one who'd steered L.O.L. into a multimillion-dollar company. Now the mishaps were frequent, the misjudgments commonplace. He still functioned, of course, but he was flawed, drowned in a sea of booze and pills. The saddest part was his inability to perceive his own deterioration. Just yesterday, over the phone, he'd told David, "Don't worry, I know when to stop—I won't let it get out of control. Don't treat me like some junkie, David! I can take care of myself."

The time to stop had passed years ago. Still, David couldn't help but feel guilty. Brandon was his friend, his client, his mentor. More than anything, he wanted to put an end to Brandon's self-destruction. Wasn't that what he was famous for, counseling and advising, running other people's lives, living vicariously through his clients to make up for the coldness and emptiness of his own life? At least that's what he used to do. Now David wasn't sure *what* he wanted anymore. Brandon was out of control, and no one, not even Kevin, seemed able to stop him. The money and the fame were obstacles to any cure, rather than assets. Whether at his home or at the Stanmore Clinic, he simply bought or intimidated everyone around him: doctors, nurses, bodyguards, servants. Given the proper incentive, everyone did his bidding and led him closer, step by step, to the abyss.

David covered Brandon with a blanket, then quietly closed the trailer door and stepped back out into the searing heat. The blazing sun quickly dried the few tears that dared congregate in the corners of his eyes. It was a cardinal rule, a rule to live by: David Barry never showed emotion.

"David!" a high voice shouted from across the desert.

He looked around. Then he saw the familiar short, stocky, balding figure trotting across the sand toward him.

The two men embraced. "Rick, old buddy. I didn't realize you were here."

"Yeah, I've been here for a couple weeks. I wish I weren't, though."

"Had enough?"

"Why does she do it, David? What is she trying to accomplish? Jeez, I haven't been that embarrassed since Rose. She had me practically crawling under the trailer."

David laughed. When everything and everyone around him seemed in flux, himself included, Rick was the only one who was still the same caring *mensch,* still the same old friend. Even though he'd had hardly a break in five years, he was still plugging away, head down and eyes closed. At least he was finally writing his own music again, even though he hadn't screwed up the courage to play anything for David. There was no doubt about it: Beneath all that fat, there still beat a washed-up heart of gold.

The two old friends wandered over toward one of the large umbrellas, picking up a couple of iced teas on the way, and settled down in the promised land.

"I don't understand her any more than you do," David said, reclining beside Rick in one of the lounge chairs. "I'll tell you, though, if I'd known then what I know now, I'd never have taken her on as a client."

Rick was surprised. "That's not like you, David. I thought your door was open to everyone."

"Not anymore. The world has changed and I've changed with it, Rick. Monterey and Woodstock are long gone. Jimi and Janis are dead. Jim Morrison's dead. The Beatles are kaput. It may be February '72 and only five years since you left the States, but 1967 is light-years away. Now it's Charles Manson and Kent State, money and bubble-gum pop. The thrill is gone."

"I can't believe I'm hearing this from you. What happened?"

"What happened? I got fed up with the greed and the self-indulgence. I got sick of wiping the asses of a bunch of petulant little kids who do nothing but piss and moan about their careers, their image, and their income."

Rick had to lean forward to hear David's soft but intense words. His voice was lower and quieter now than it used to be. After the doctor discovered polyps and nodules on his vocal cords, David hired a voice coach and learned to speak from his diaphram. On the phone he sometimes sounded like an obscene caller. In an industry where yelling and screaming were the norm, David Barry's quietly modulated voice became his calling card. A powerful, seductive, readily identifiable symbol of his internal strength and composure.

"It used to be my clients were in it for the music, pure and simple. Money was a bonus, an afterthought. I believed in them and their music, and they trusted me.

"Now it's all different. Now all they care about is box-office gross, record sales, chart performance, and all they know about is drugs and how a Ferrari handles over a Porsche or a Maserati over an Aston Martin. They think everyone's out to get them. All the managers are leeches, taking percentages and sucking them dry. The agents are flesh peddlers who don't give a shit about the music and care only about the bucks. Everyone's out to exploit them, undermine them, use them for their own gain. . . ."

"Well, it's the truth, isn't it?"

"Yeah, it is. But what am I supposed to do about it? I'm tired of the middle-of-the-night phone calls invading my privacy. Tired of mediating the lives of grown kids who can't take care of themselves."

David turned in the lounge chair to face Rick. "The music isn't there anymore, Rick. It's not natural and spontaneous like it used to be. Now it's contrived, it's bullshit. It's all business and no feeling. It's Harry Nilsson, and America, and Donny Osmond singing 'Go Away, Little Girl,' and Paul and Linda chirping about 'Uncle Albert/Admiral Halsey.' There's no more fire, no more rebellion, no more humanity. Today's rock stars are just as superficial and shallow as the world they bitch about."

"Come on, David, it's not all *that* bad. There are still some real artists out there. What about Dwight Sharon or the Stones, Roberta Flack, Creedence . . ."

"Sure, there're exceptions. But you wouldn't pay them any mind if you'd seen what I've seen, and done what I've done, these past years. Ran interference between the stars and their bands, between them and their old ladies, their managers, their agents, their mothers and fathers. Met with shrinks and drug counselors and astrologers. Bargained with judges to keep them out of jail and with reporters to keep their names out of the gossip columns. Anything and everything to insulate them and perpetuate their self-deluded lives.

"I can't tell you how many times I've seen a mother shove her fourteen-year-old daughter into a dressing room in hopes of having the band fuck the little girl's brains out."

"Why would a mother do that?"

"Why do you think? So the parents can extort money from the band. You know, scandal, statutory rape . . ."

"Jeez, David . . ."

"I used to love it, the biz back when. But then it was a novelty. Now I resent my own clients. They're weighing me down, Rick. I can't stand this dirty, filthy, fucking business anymore. I'm sick of parents exploiting their kids; of groupies sucking and fucking their way through rock bands; of girls getting their rocks off by collecting plaster casts of rock stars' cocks—"

"Plaster casts! You're kidding! Gee, nobody ever did that to me!" Rick said with a touch of remorse.

David started laughing and it broke the spell of his fury.

"I'm sorry, Rick. I guess I got carried away. What do you want to hear about my problems for? You got more than enough of your own."

"Don't be sorry. That's what friends are for."

"What, to complain to?"

Rick nodded.

"Well, it's your turn. Complain."

"Me? What have I got to complain about? Five years of blood, sweat, and tears on an island and nothing to show for it? What more could there be in life? Still the same fat little roly-poly, balding oldie-but-goody that I always was. I'm yesterday's news and I'll always be yesterday's news. At least I can live vicariously now, through Joyce—and Hedy."

"Stop feeling sorry for yourself, Rick. If it weren't for the movies, Hedy wouldn't be any better off than you."

"Maybe I should become a film star too. What do you think? You're a star maker. Can you turn me into another Gable?" Rick asked, flexing his flabby nonmuscles and throwing his head back in the Firestone version of a sexy pose, but looking like Fatty Arbuckle.

"Cut it out."

"Thanks for getting me this job, by the way. I could sure use the exposure and the dough."

"Don't thank me, thank Hedy. She made it a contractual condition that you had to do the charts. No Rick, no Hedy. That was the deal."

"Really?"

"I wouldn't lie to you, pal."

"Wow! She always used to depend on my arrangements. We made a pretty good team back in the old days."

"You make it sound like you're ancient. For God's sake, you're only thirty-two."

"Thirty-two going on fifty. Look at Hedy—she still looks like she's eighteen. So what if she's cranky? She can carry it off, she's a star. She's got presence, just like she had when I first met her in Al Norman's office. And that voice! Nobody sings like her, David. She turns notes on paper into pure honey. God, I love working with her. . . ."

David picked up on the tone of Rick's voice. "You sure that's all you love, Rick? All strictly professional, right?"

"Heck, David, I'm not sure of anything. You know how I feel about her. It's never changed."

"Well, why don't you do something about it?"

Rick was saved from answering by the sudden commotion in the distance.

"Okay, set it up, boys!" the director yelled. "Miss Harlowe will be out in five."

Rick and David stood up and hastened back toward the set, watching as Joyce and the crew jumped back into action.

"She pulled it off again," Rick said, shaking his head in wonder. "I don't believe it. Is there anything our Joyce can't do?"

"She's one miracle worker, that's for sure."

It was only a matter of minutes before Hedy made her entrance, calmly and radiantly, down the steps of her trailer. Voices hushed and all eyes turned her way as she nodded to the director and took her place once again in the tiny hut.

"Take seventeen, virgin-emerging scene."

"Background movement. Action!"

The bright light shone, Hedy stepped forward, the music swelled. Everyone held their breath.

Then she started singing, mournfully, plaintively, telling the mysterious story of the virgin birth and her child in the manger. Hedy's brilliant voice cut through the heat and seemed to carry across the entire desert, the notes floating in the air like leaves caught in a warm breeze. When she reached the final chords, she dropped dramatically onto the sand, cupped the hot granules in her palms, then let them slip, little by little like the sands of time, through her fingers. Finally, weary, she lay down in the sand and her voice, with the music, faded into sleep.

"Cut. It's a wrap," the director said quietly, as if afraid to break the mood.

For a moment the entire set was still. Then, spontaneously and in unison, everyone burst into applause.

Hedy raised her head up and smiled joyously. Then she held her hands out and Joyce came running into the sand to embrace her.

The beautiful music emanating from Hedy's trailer carried over the desert and filled the moonlit night.

They'd been playing for hours, first rehearsing the remaining two songs in the script as Joyce had urged, then effortlessly sliding into a selection of their old songs. For both of them, it was manna from heaven, the chance to recapture a touch of the old magic.

"Rick?" she said quietly, coming up behind him.

"Yes, Hedy?" His fingers still floating over the keys, he kept his head down, embarrassed to look her in the eye.

"Play me one of your new compositions."

Rick's fingers suddenly stopped dead on the keys. He froze with fear. "Oh, I couldn't. Really. They're no good. You wouldn't want to hear them."

"Once, you used to write songs just for me. Remember?"

"Of course, Hedy. How could I forget." Once? It seemed like all his songs, then and now, were written for her, or about her. She'd never stopped being his inspiration and his fantasy.

"Well, if you won't play for me, then take me for a walk out in the desert."

His heart started to pound. "Sure thing. How about we bring a drink?"

"Yeah! Champagne! Get the bottle out of the fridge."

Rick jumped up from the piano and pulled the bottle of Dom Perignon out of the icebox. Hedy grabbed two glasses, threw a blanket over her head and shoulders, and, like a Moslem woman of the Casbah, tied a white kerchief into a veil over her mouth and nose. "Lead the way, master," she mumbled, bowing her head.

"Call me Lawrence," Rick said, covering his head with a shawl, raising his fist, and bursting out of the trailer door like Peter O'Toole. He tripped on the first step and went flying headfirst into the sand, cradling the bottle in his arms.

Hedy came running to him. "Are you all right?" she asked, trying to keep from laughing. She bent over him and brushed the sand from his cheek. Her touch was soft and loving. It made Rick shiver.

"It was the filthy Turks. Shooting at me again. They may get me, but they'll never get the treasure, ha, ha!" He held up the still-intact bottle of champagne.

"My hero," Hedy sighed.

Then, hand in hand, they trudged across the desert until they found a perfect spot under a lone palm. The brilliant moonlight reflected off the sand and turned it into an endless sea and their blanket into a tiny desert island.

Rick popped the cork and poured. "To you, Hedy. You're the greatest."

The greatest. The greatest what? Hedy wondered. The greatest clown?

They clicked glasses and sipped the cold champagne. A few granules of sand mixed with the bubbly, and Rick flashed back to the sandy Nathan's hot dog they'd shared on Brighton Beach.

For a long time they lay back on the blanket, side by side, motionless and silent.

Hedy waited, aching for his touch, but it never came.

"I guess you don't find me attractive anymore, huh?" Hedy whispered. "After all those show girls . . ."

Rick propped himself up on one elbow. "How can you say such a thing, Hedy? You're gorgeous."

"Yeah, for a virgin mother."

"Cut it out. You're beautiful."

"Well then . . ."

Rick plopped back down and spoke to the stars. "I'm afraid. I've lost so much already. First there was Grandma Becky. Then the split with Rose. I lost my youth, my innocence, my career. I even lost you once. I don't think I can take any more."

"You don't have to," she whispered as she reached for his hand and squeezed it tight.

He could feel her pulse and their hearts beating in sync. He raised her hand to his lips and kissed the backs of her fingers tenderly. Then, screwing up his courage, he turned on his side and they fell into each other's arms.

They lay like that for a long time, hugging and nuzzling, almost afraid to let go. Softly, Rick rolled Hedy back onto the sand, leaned over her, and sweetly kissed her eyelids, her cheeks, her neck. When their lips met, the touch was slow and lingering, their tongues meeting comfortably like old friends.

This time he undid the buttons, opening her up like a desert flower until the moon shone off her petals. He slipped off his own clothes and, like children, they caressed and explored each other's naked body as if discovering the joy for the first time.

She ran her fingers through his pubic hair and wound her tongue around his cock so softly, so gently, her lips curling around and under his head, that he moaned aloud in exquisite pleasure and felt himself levitate off the sand.

When he leaned over and moved between her legs, Hedy, finally feeling like a star, stared up at her moon until the sensation became so intense that she had to close her eyes. First it was his soft, wet tongue, running smaller and smaller circles around her open lips. Then he moved inside her and, oh, it was sweeter than any opening night.

Together, they rocked and rolled on the sandy sea for an eternity. She met each of his slow, rhythmic thrusts with a melody of her own, until they were singing together once again, a siren's song, cresting like a ship on the rising surf.

Their sweat mingled, and Rick, rolling off to one side, ran his finger lovingly around her beautiful breasts. She slid her head into the crook of his arm and sighed. It was a miracle. For the first time ever, she actually felt like a virgin.

For Rick, the serenity lasted only a few minutes. Suddenly his touch became more tentative and his fingers turned cold. His mind started churning and the fear returned with a vengeance. Like quicksand, the dread sucked him deeper and deeper. Suddenly he jumped to his feet and started dressing.

"What's the matter, darling?"

"It won't work, that's what's the matter."

She sat up and covered her breasts with her arms. "Don't say that, please. It has to work. We'll make it work. I need you too much."

"It can't happen. You're a star and I'm a has-been. It's guaranteed to fail. I couldn't stand the rejection." He was afraid. Afraid of failing, afraid of loving, afraid of being hurt. But most of all, he was afraid of being overwhelmed.

"Rick, come back here. Sit down. You're talking nonsense. Nobody's gonna hurt you." She reached out and clutched his hand.

"No. I'm telling it like it is. I'm not gonna play Norman Maine to your Vicki Lester. I don't want pity. I couldn't live with myself. You'd be tired of me in no time. I'd only drag you down. I couldn't bear it, Hedy. I couldn't. Please, let me go. I'm sorry."

"Rick . . . Rick!" she called out as his hand slipped from her grasp like the sand through her palms.

But it was too late. Just like that, he was gone. Off, through the sand, back to his music, leaving her naked, alone, and lonely once again.

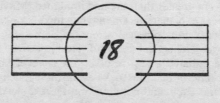

1972

*A*FTER, MIRACLE OF MIRACLES, THEY'D FINISHED
Immaculate Conception early in the year, Joyce knew it was
time for a change. When David offered her the opportunity to
join a hotshot production company in the Big Apple, she jumped
at the chance. The States represented a fabulous career opportunity. If only she hadn't had to leave Rick.

The past four years in London, until the Silverfish movie had
come along, had been rougher than she cared to admit. She'd
tiptoed her way through the years, living in fear of dying, emotionally and physically scarred from the cancer. Embarrassed
and revolted by her secret—that she wasn't a whole woman; that
she was defective and deficient—she'd avoided practically everyone's company other than Rick's.

Cell by cell her body had deteriorated. Any single cell of
billions could have metastasized and brought the hateful,
dreaded disease back to her. For five years now she had lived
with excruciating uncertainty. She magnified each pain and bod-

ily sensation out of proportion, as if they represented terrible hurdles that had to be overcome.

Up till now, Joyce couldn't presume the worst was behind her. What she did know, however, was that her own inner strength and drive were greater than she had imagined. Maybe there was some medical explanation. Or maybe she'd simply turned her psychic energy into physical strength. Somehow, some way, though, Joyce Heller had survived. Had endured.

Now she radiated a new resolve. She'd never had it safe or secure. She'd never had the Rock of Gibraltar to lean on. Except for David and Rick, and not counting Derek, she'd been alone for as long as she could remember. Yet her fierce determination and independence hadn't left her, even if they were sometimes hidden. Miraculously, the physical and mental devastation of the cancer had never overwhelmed her.

Sure, she'd been frightened. But she'd turned inside herself for strength. Others had family to turn to, or religion, drink, or drugs, or they hid in a cloudy world where they anesthetized their brains so as not to confront the horrible reality. But not Joyce. Stoically, without complaint, she made it on her own, against the cancer. Out of her fragile, tortured body rose a new, strong being, with a raw momentum of intense self-belief that sustained her. With independence and strength of character, Joyce Heller willed herself to fight, willed herself to overcome, willed herself to win. Death would have meant capitulation, losing, and she wouldn't tolerate that. Her five-year ordeal was coming to an end and she was emerging as a stronger person. She could bear anything now. She had faced death and she had beaten it. Now it would take even more courage for her to face life.

The movies had saved her, in a way. They'd given her an outlet and a release. Of course, she'd had to slave away for years, fetching and groveling for coolie's wages, running errands, grinning and bearing the occasional pinch on the ass, all in the hope of earning the title "production assistant."

She did everything and loved it all: working with extras, in makeup, in wardrobe; watching the continuity lady match the shooting scenes to the script. She typed, she gophered, she noted who was on schedule, how much footage was shot, how many setups, what went to the development lab. She learned a new vocabulary of double systems and composite prints, picture reels and working tracks, looping and dubbing.

Filmmaking was a complicated and expensive process, and Joyce was eager to learn. The lazier the production team, the more she got to do. Arriving early and leaving late, she was the one who always knew what scene was being shot where, and who had to be called at what time.

She had her friend Myrna to thank for teaching her the most important lesson.

"Honey, we're only going to the Bull and Bear for drinks. Come on, let's go," Myrna urged at the end of a long day on the British set back in '69.

"No, I don't think so, Myrna. I'm committed," Joyce answered.

"You *should* be committed. You've ducked every social opportunity since you started on this movie. We're a family, honey, you can't do that. If you do, you're not going to get work again."

"As long as I do my job, I can get work."

"Sweetheart, wise up. Anyone could do your job. A lot of people out there would give anything for the opportunity to be even the lowest man on the movie totem pole. Honey, you're not building relationships. You don't have to fuck 'em, you know. Just be one of the boys. They all think you're a dyke anyway."

Joyce was confused. "Lay it on the line for me. I know I'm being a little dense. . . ."

"If you're standoffish, the crew's uncomfortable. If they're uncomfortable, they won't trust you. If they don't trust you, they don't have fun with you. And if they don't have fun with you, you're not hired the next time around."

"So that's the way it is, huh?"

"Sure. Why, if you traced the genealogy, the family tree, of every guy in this movie, you'd find that somewhere along the line they'd all worked together before. They all know each other and it's a 'bring a buddy' system. We've got eight weeks of shoot left, Joyce, and you've got to make friends, get buddies, otherwise you'll be left out in the cold.

"Christ, cronyism is practically a religion with these guys. They worship at the Church of the Cronies. You scratch my back, I'll scratch yours; you cover my ass, I'll cover yours—that's the name of the game. Turn a blind eye, take what you can get, no one'll snitch. Make some friends and you'll keep working as a member in good standing."

It was a lesson Joyce never forgot. "Okay, Myrna, the Bull and Bear it is."

That night, Joyce laughed at the bawdy humor, never blushed, slapped backs with the boys. She came off cool and the guys liked her. She learned a lot by staying up late and playing poker with the boys. About innocent corruption and cost overruns, about poker debts covered by "blind mistakes," about the cover-your-ass filmmaking buddy system. She stored it all away for future reference.

When Myrna came down with hepatitis several weeks later, Joyce was asked to cover for her. She didn't get a raise, of course, but she did get the title, "production assistant." A great title that meant garbage lady, do-it-all lady, for fifty pounds a week.

It was no surprise that she still gravitated to the music end of the business. With Brandon's help, she wheedled jobs on two musicals in the late Sixties. In her free time, she attended the initial laying down of the music tracks and their final rerecording and sweetening. She watched with fascination as every single frame of tens of thousands of feet of film was balanced with the audio—the mix—so that special effects, background sounds, music, and dialogue were all present and realistically balanced, sometimes artificially superimposed, sometimes artificially heightened or suppressed. The lessons proved invaluable when it came time for the making of *Immaculate Conception.*

Now, here she was in New York in 1972, five years after the nightmare had begun. The medically imposed statute of limitations had finally passed. After all the treatments and checkups, the chemo and the radiation, the years of meditation and alternate therapies, the discovery and unleashing of her internal energy, Joyce finally believed it was over. At least she hoped so.

Her body had changed, inside and out, but at last she believed in a tomorrow. She was still wearing her drab army-navy ensemble, without makeup or jewelry, trying her best to appear untouchable and nonthreatening to men and women alike, successfully dissuading any sexual overtures. But her hair was now a little looser and a little straighter, and her body much more shapely and curvaceous (thanks in part to the hormone treatments) under the intentionally floppy garb. No matter what she wore, though, she couldn't hide her white, translucent skin, as soft as fresh peonies, or her intense green eyes, as deeply colored as blue spruce.

As the ferry chugged its way across the waters of Great South Bay toward Fire Island, Joyce leaned against the front railing and looked out at the endless strip of sand that stretched across the horizon. She breathed in the fresh salty air, felt the warm Long Island breeze against her face, watched the orange rays of the late-afternoon summer sun dance off the water. After another sweltering August week in the city, she finally understood what they meant by TGIF. She thanked God it was Friday, that she was out of the city and that her current picture would probably "wrap" within the week. Then she'd give David a piece of her mind. New York City my ass! Not in the summertime, anyway. Not without air conditioning, thank you.

Resting her arm lightly on Guy's shoulder, Joyce looked around at the other forty or so passengers crowded around the ferry. They were all men, most in their thirties or early forties, looking very Madison Avenue in light blue cords or khaki-colored Paul Stuartish suits, carrying small, smart cases of canvas and leather with the occasional yappy little dog. A few were dressed quite casually, like Guy, in jeans and faded blue denim work shirts, scruffy boots and, in Guy's case, a cowboy neckerchief.

As they approached the Pines Boatel slip, the passengers buzzed with renewed energy and excitement. Some, like prisoners smelling freedom, stripped off their conservative shackles and emerged free in bikini bathing suits and sun shirts, bright scarves and rhinestone sunglasses.

When the ferry docked, men who had stridden manfully onto the ferry now sashayed off and rushed to the nearby bicycle racks to unlock little red children's wagons. Piling them high with their groceries and luggage, they pulled the wagons along the noisy, rickety wooden walkway through a maze of connecting paths.

Guy and Joyce headed to one of the bars on the dock to wait for their host. They ordered blue whales and listened to snippets of conversation from the passing boys.

"I'm telling you, the size of his meat is not to be believed! And his cum! It's fucking Ponce de Leon's fountain of youth!"

"Don't give me that. He's just another vegetable—a brain like a pea and a cock like a cucumber! Just pass me a popper."

Joyce was riveted. She was a visitor to their homeland, their motherland. A guest on their turf. The pent-up, cover-up, bite-your-lip, keep-your-wrist-firm, butch-it-up week in the city and in the office—with uptight, upright, closet-case co-workers—was over once again and now it was let's play queen for a weekend! Anything goes. Anybody goes! Rules and regulations were lifted—they had arrived at the Pines. So this was the mystical island filled, like Bali Ha'i, with decadent delights.

Even though she spent most of her free time with homosexuals, she'd never seen anything quite like this. Unlike straights, men like Guy were sweet, beautiful, *and* unthreatening. So what if she was sometimes called a "fag hag" or a "fruit fly"? She had the companionship without the complication, and that was all she cared about.

When she turned away from the scene on the boardwalk, she noticed Guy staring at her.

"What?" she asked smiling back at the hunk of Marlboro man seated next to her. At six-foot-two, with black hair, chiseled jaw, and body of steel, twenty-nine-year-old Guy Jamison of Butte, Montana, was every woman's—and every man's—dream. An extra on Joyce's current shoot, he was recognizable on the streets as the most striking and memorable of the Marlboro men, a regular walking American dream. After beating her at poker one long night, he'd broken through her defenses, her "I vant to be alone" pose, and they'd become fast friends and "constant companions." Well, not exactly "constant"—particularly not after eleven or twelve o'clock. Often she went home alone. But they both liked it that way.

Guy was hard-drinking and hard-talking. A backslapping, joke-telling, sports-loving cowboy whom only a practiced eye would recognize as anything other than a he-man. He liked them butch and he liked them straight, but he didn't go in for rough trade, which Joyce found a welcome change after Brandon and his "poof" life-style. By hanging together, she could be Guy's date—even playing Jane to his Dick last Memorial Day when his parents came to town—and he could help keep her creepy, horny fellow workers at bay.

The only thing she couldn't stand was his hitting on guys in her presence. Like just last week, when they were at a restaurant and Guy picked up a blond flight attendant from Texas. She threw a fit when he tried to sail off with Abilene and leave her high, dry, and alone.

"Don't you *ever* do that to me again," she threatened. "I won't be used by you and I won't play second fiddle to your sex life! Look, Guy, I don't care *what* you do when we're not together. You can fuck and suck anybody your heart desires, from that flight attendant to one of the bums on the Bowery. But when we go out together, we're on my time and we stay together until we call it quits for the night. Understand?"

He understood. The trip to Fire Island, which Joyce had been wanting for a long time, was Guy's way of saying "I'm sorry."

"Guy, why are you staring at me like that?" Joyce asked.

"Oh, nothing, honey. You know, you really are beautiful."

She slapped him on the wrist and made a tsking noise with her mouth. "You're crazy. What's gotten into you? The hormones in the air affecting you the wrong way?"

"No, I'm serious, Joyce. You have a gorgeous face *and* a fabulous body. I can't understand why you go out of your way to hide them. If I were you, I'd show off my assets."

"Like you do, huh? And look what it gets you."

"Yeah, the pick of the bunch. If you like my kinda fruit."

"Very funny."

"Really, though, you should do something with yourself."

"He's right, sweetheart," Leon said, coming up behind them and kissing each of them on the cheek. Leon was their host. Monsieur Leon to the patrons of Monte's Park Avenue Salon; Leon Feinstein of Bensonhurst, Brooklyn, to his family.

"I hope you don't mind my saying so, but your raw material is just divine. You've got the glow, no doubt about it. You won't believe what I could do with that hair and those eyebrows," he said, leaning over and touching her face and the edges of her hair with his delicate fingers. His gold bracelets jangled.

"Stop it, Leon."

"*Chérie,* please, *pour moi.* Humor me, Joyce," Leon whined. "I'm *très* depressed. The forecast's for rain tomorrow. I'm sick of charades and Scrabble and bloody marys. Let's do you tomorrow. Pleeeze."

"What's he talking about, Guy?" Joyce asked suspiciously.

"Relax, darling, it's nothing dirty. 'Do you' means 'make you over.' Leon *is* one of the most creative and exclusive hairdressers in the city. You should be very flattered."

"Hairdresser! Listen, cowgirl cunt, don't you ever call me a hairdresser. How dare you! I'm not just hair, I'm eyes, nails, lips, legs—the works. The total you. Leon can transform you. Leon guarantees it."

Joyce started to protest out of hand, then stopped herself. The five years *were* up. Maybe it was time she stopped going through the motions and started really living. When she left Stanmore, she was a hormonally unbalanced girl/woman without a uterus, ovaries, or hope. Now she was bronzed, shapely, enjoying life, and ready to consider her future.

"Why not?" she said. "I'm game. As long as it rains, you've got a date."

On Saturday morning, Leon was beside himself with excitement. If the sky hadn't opened up on its own, Monsieur Leon would have seeded the clouds himself.

When Joyce woke up and stumbled down the stairs for a cup of coffee, her mouth dropped. The bungalow's entire living room had been transformed into an operating room cum beauty salon! The rattan couch and chairs had been moved into one of the corners and in their place sat a single wooden and canvas director's chair, illuminated by two 16mm movie spotlights on tripods (to be used as makeshift makeup lights) facing a large three-way mirror. In preparation for the delicate operation, glistening steel equipment and beauty paraphernalia—scissors, combs, brushes, hair dryers, hair sprays, curlers, creams, lotions, dyes—were all laid out meticulously on a glass worktable beside the mirrors.

"Good morning. Good morning," Leon said, greeting Joyce with an assertive kiss on the cheek and shoving a cup of hot coffee topped with whipped cream and cinnamon into her hand. He was wearing his beautiful white Monte's smock with his name, Mr. Leon, embossed on the pocket, and nothing but bikini shorts underneath.

"Now you all know how serious I am about this," he said as he wrapped a barber's drop cloth around Joyce's neck and led her to the sink to wash her hair. "Sweetie, only for you would I wear these hideous tortoiseshell prescription glasses. Now *I* can see, but no one will give *me* a second glance. Those butch Italians don't like me in glasses, you know, and won't sit on my face. They're afraid the glass might break and cut their tushies!" He screamed with laughter at his own humor.

"Joyce, don't be grossed out by Leon, it's a genetic disorder," Guy said, coming down the stairs. "He was born a trisexual— he'll try anything!"

Everyone laughed, but in no time Leon's mince and limp wrist had turned to firm resolve. He assumed a serious, professional demeanor. Monsieur Leon was in control and about to give the performance of his career.

He started on her hair. After the radiation treatments, it had become so dull and limp that she'd looked like Joan of Arc. Now she wore it loose and a little unkempt.

When her hair was clean and wet and she sat before the mirror looking like a dishrag, the rest of Leon's crew came in. There was Raymond of Halston, Harold from Elizabeth Arden, and Vinnie, also from Monte's. They jabbered endlessly and in hushed tones about the shape of her head, the best style and color for her hair, what they should do with her eyebrows and her nails, how they could highlight her cheeks, and the best kind of makeup. In the background, the top-forty station quietly played Gilbert O'Sullivan singing "Alone Again (Naturally)," Neil Diamond's "Song Sung Blue," and Dwight Sharon's "Honky Tonk Man."

Underneath the white tent around her that exposed only her face and her hands, Joyce sensed her own body. As skinny as Twiggy back in 1964, she'd become *zaftig* by 1968 due to the hormone treatments. In the four years since, her waist had become tiny and streamlined, her tummy flat, her hips shapely, and her breasts very full. Greatly enhanced, she had everything a girl could want, except her ovaries and her uterus.

She closed her eyes, embarrassed and flattered by all the attention. She was enjoying being their guinea pig. She couldn't turn back now, even if she wanted to. So she thought pretty thoughts, kept her eyes closed, crossed her fingers, and let Leon and his pals have their way with her.

* * *

Despite the sweltering New York summer heat and humidity outside, inside the Russian Tea Room the chic clientele and perennial Russian Orthodox Christmas decorations sparkled coolly. Seated in his usual booth, No. 2, with his arm resting on the banquette, David nursed a club soda, waved and blew kisses at the familiar faces around the room, listened to the sounds of "Sweetie, baby, cookie, honey" spoken at nearly every table, and checked his pocket watch. He was growing impatient.

Now that she was late, he was having second thoughts. It wasn't that he didn't want to see her; on the contrary, he enjoyed Joyce's company so much that he'd been pleased and gratified when she left London and tied on with the New York film company he'd recommended. And they did have business to discuss.

It was just . . . well, it might have been better to meet somewhere else. Her usual getup—work shirts and sneakers—wasn't exactly uptown attire. But she'd insisted on the Russian Tea Room.

Over the past few years, he'd taken to frequenting places like the Four Seasons, "21," Sardi's, Wally's, Frankie and Johnny's, Joe Allen, and the Russian Tea Room as a way of building his recognition factor and creating the illusion of power. Not because he'd simply become an opportunist, enamored of the trappings of success, but because he worked in an industry built on illusions and superficialities, where power was based on perception.

He'd had his share of successes over the past few years, of course, due in large part to his ever-growing relationship with Brandon. As a result of the unbelievable popularity of the Silverfish in the States—fueled most recently by their *Immaculate Conception* tour, record, and forthcoming movie—and as a result of the dramatic growth of L.O.L., David had seen his own star rise perceptibly. Add to that Hedy's film successes and the remarkable rise of Dwight Sharon, who'd become probably the single most popular recording artist in both the U.S. and the U.K., and it was clear that David Barry and his clients were on a roll.

He wasn't the only one. Thanks to Dwight and the Silverfish, Thane Crawley and Apollo had climbed to the top of the heap. Although David didn't take any personal pleasure in Thane's rise to princedom in the record industry—they weren't exactly compatible—he had to hand it to the guy. Thane had an infallible ear and a faultless marketing touch, and deserved the lion's share of credit for the level of financial success achieved by both Sharon and the Silverfish.

He remembered a strange conversation he'd overheard last week in London at a charity benefit. He'd been standing next to Goddard Lieberson of CBS when Swisstone's aging monarch, Philippe Phochet, came up beside them and put his arm around Goddard. "Goddard, you're to be congratulated. I've seen the figures on CBS's market share and new catalog. Clive Davis is one of the most gifted men in the world of recorded music. What he's done for you is remarkable and you're to be congratulated for your perception in choosing him and your good fortune in keeping him in your fold."

Goddard had smiled and proceeded to return the compliment. "But, Monsieur Phochet, on the contrary, it is you who should be congratulated. You and Swisstone had to start from scratch in the U.S. market, and look what *your* man has done! From practically nothing, he's built Apollo into a major force in the record industry. He's becoming a legend in the music business, Monsieur Phochet. I congratulate you."

"Ah, yes, you are right," Phochet answered. "What Dr. van der Rogdt has done for us in America and the world has been most admirable."

David looked at Goddard who registered shock on his face.

"But . . . but, Monsieur Phochet, what about Thane Crawley?" Goddard asked in dismay.

"Ah, yes, the young lawyer who works for van der Rogdt. I hear good things of him. If you'll excuse me, gentlemen . . . "

David was still puzzling over the significance of that odd conversation when he looked up from his drink and caught his breath at the vision near the doorway.

She was beautiful and refreshing. Regal in her bearing, with delicate features and a cool, ethereal radiance that reminded him of Audrey Hepburn, except with curves—and what curves! Dressed in a pale yellow jacquard dress that clung to her hips and outlined more than a little of her very full, taut breasts, the woman at the front of the restaurant talking to the hostess was an absolute, drop-dead, to-die-from ravishing knockout. Her hairdo and makeup were subtle and ultrachic, and she wasn't wearing a single piece of jewelry to distract from her exquisite face. She looked like a Modigliani painting, with large blue-green almond eyes that were luscious, intelligent, sparkling, sultry—and even in some way familiar. They seemed older and wiser than her face or the sensuous body that showed suggestively through the silk. Her very posture glowed with strength and assurance.

David was smitten. A sudden surge of desire embarrassed him, considering that his only affairs were business affairs. He barely counted the regular one-nighters with ambitious young actresses or aspiring groupies who threw themselves at him. Not one of them was ever a friend. Lonely nights had been, and probably always would be, part and parcel of his life.

As she walked down the aisle, all eyes turned and a low mumble rippled through the throng of beautiful people. David remembered Leslie Caron's entrance as Gigi into Maxim's with Louis Jourdan and was in a reverie. . . .

"Hello, David." He heard a low, sexy voice and felt her presence beside him.

He was speechless.

"Well, aren't you going to say hello and ask me to sit down?"

Still at a loss, and embarrassed at having mentally undressed her only moments before, he finally stood up and took her hand. "Joyce, I'm so sorry. I . . . I didn't recognize you!" He stepped out of the booth and let her slip in beside him, feeling the rustle of her dress against him. Pulling the carefully folded handkerchief from his breast pocket, he wiped his brow.

"I'm glad," she said, taking a napkin and folding it in her lap. "I would've been terribly disappointed if you had. You know, I don't think I've ever seen you so discombobulated?"

"Well, you'd be surprised, too, if one of your oldest friends walked through the door suddenly transformed into Elizabeth Taylor. Not that you weren't lovely before, I mean," he stammered, trying not to put his foot any farther into his mouth. "It's just that . . . you look stupendous! What happened?"

"First things first. Tell me about Rick. Have you seen him? How is he?"

David shrugged. "I don't know, Joyce. He's still playing around England and writing, but . . . I don't see much progress. I asked Dwight Sharon to look him up. Maybe it'll help. But come on, don't keep me in suspense. What the hell's going on?"

"My five years are up. The doctors have given me a clean bill of health. I thought it was time for a change."

"That's wonderful news. I'm so happy for you," he said, signaling for the waiter. "Champagne. This *is* a celebration. But you still haven't told me exactly what happened." David was curious. He knew Joyce hadn't had a mother around as a model, and her aunt had never bothered to teach her any feminine arts. Even if she had, Joyce wouldn't have been interested back then, and in fact she hadn't displayed much interest in her appearance in all the years he'd known her.

"I had a sex-change operation, thanks to Mr. Leon and his group of Fire Island Henry Higginses. It was high time I stopped being a tomboy and came to terms with my femininity, don't you think? After they did my hair, my face, and my legs, they taught me how to apply my own makeup, how to dress, how to walk, how to sit, how to talk and act. I felt kind of silly, like Eliza Doolittle getting ready for the opera, or Annie Oakley gettin' spiffed up to meet Wild Bill Hickcock. But they were so sweet and understanding, and really it was fun—the first time I'd played dress-up since I was a little girl. Tell me, truthfully, do you like the new me?"

"I love the new you, Joyce."

"Joy. I'm Joy from now on. Okay?"

"Okay, Joy." He handed her a glass of champagne and raised his own. "Here's to your future. Untold beauty and success."

"And happiness."

"And happiness, whatever that is," he said, touching his glass to hers. He leaned forward to sip his champagne, but with his eyes riveted on her fine features and soft, radiant skin, he spilled a few drops on his suit.

Joyce laughed joyously and raised her napkin to tenderly pat the drops from his jacket. With that smile and that gesture, David flashed back to Joyce's Stanmore experience and suddenly realized how remarkably transformed she really was—and how remarkable she was in all respects.

After lunch, David turned the conversation to the movie business. Her rejuvenation, and the strange, almost frightening surge of emotion coursing through him, had set his mind clicking.

"When does your movie wrap, Joyce—I mean, Joy?"

"Next week."

"And after that?"

"I'm not sure. I don't know if I want to stay in New York. Maybe I'll go back to Rick in London. . . ."

"Don't do that. I've got a better idea."

"You and your ideas. What's it this time?"

"Hollywood. Beverly Hills. The big time."

"What are you cooking up in that shifty brain of yours?"

"Some people I know in Hollywood are looking for a bright young producer. I gave them your name," he said, stretching the truth. He *would* give them her name, though.

"Without even asking me? You've got some nerve!"

"That's not all I've got. Brandon and I have plans. Big plans for L.O.L. and for you, if things pan out." He pushed away his plate of salad, sipped at his coffee, and looked at her pensively, lowering his voice. "If I'm right, I see a major opportunity for L.O.L. to expand into America, in the record and film business. The kind of thing we tried to do with *Immaculate Conception*— the blending of music and film, and your use of video replays on the set—I just think there's tremendous growth potential in the merging of those markets and technologies."

"What if *Immaculate Conception* bombs, as I expect it will?"

"That won't matter, believe me."

"So where do I come in?"

"I want you to be my eyes and ears in Hollywood. I'll put you on secret retainer from L.O.L, as a consultant, and I want you to report to me regularly on everything going on in Beverly Hills and on the Coast, and to keep me posted on any film studio that might be on the market or amenable to a take-over."

"You mean you want me to shmooze the entertainment crowd, work the Polo Lounge, that kind of thing?" she asked incredulously.

"You got it. A regular Mata Hari disguised as a producer. It'll do wonders for your career. With my introductions and your brains and looks, you'll go places, baby," he said, imitating Jack Black's voice.

"I don't know. It's not me."

"But there's a new you, isn't there? Come on, let me arrange some meetings and interviews. Go out to the Coast, take a look. You've got nothing to lose."

When they got up to go, David walked out of the Russian Tea Room proudly, parading her on his arm. She was still unused to, and a little scared by, the attention she attracted. After so many years of cultivating an appearance that was asexual and unobtrusive, the adjustment wasn't easy.

They walked east on Fifty-seventh Street until David stopped in front of Tiffany's window. "What did they teach you about jewelry?"

"Who?"

"Your boys."

"Don't wear it unless it's real. If it's real, I can't afford it, so they didn't bother to teach me about jewelry."

He put his arm around her waist. "Come on."

"Where to?"

"In here," he said, leading the way.

"Into Tiffany's? What do you want in there? Oh, I know—you want me to help you pick out an expensive present for one of your beautiful girlfriends," she teased. "The gossip columns are full of your exploits."

"Don't believe everything you read in the papers and don't ask so many questions. Let's look. It'll be fun. You said you liked dress-up, didn't you?"

Inside the store, Joy giggled and gaped as they moved from

counter to counter and David, playing the suave millionaire, had her try on wildly expensive diamond bracelets, sapphire rings, and ruby necklaces. He held a double-strand necklace of graduated pearls up to her throat appraisingly.

"We'll take this," he said to the salesman. "It's on a charge."

"David! What are you doing?"

"It's obvious, isn't it? I'm buying you pearls."

She blushed.

He laughed and rested his arm on her shoulder. "For the new Joy Heller, woman and movie mogul. Every woman needs basic pearls—before swine!"

She couldn't refuse without hurting him. And for the first time in her life, she didn't want to. If she was really going to be a woman, she had to learn to receive as well as give. She stepped up on the toes of her new spike heels and kissed David tenderly on the cheek. "Thanks. Thanks for everything."

"Do me one favor, okay?" David asked.

"What's that?"

"Forget Joy. It's not becoming. I much prefer Joyce."

She hesitated for a moment. "Really? Crappy old Joyce?"

"Really." He nodded.

"Well, I wouldn't do this for just anyone. But for you, David . . . okay. Joy is dead. Long live Joyce."

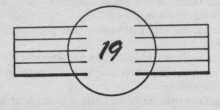

1972

7HANKS TO YET ANOTHER LATE BUSINESS DINNER AND several quiet hours of work at the office, it was well after midnight before David made it home to his duplex apartment.

The original three bedrooms had been gutted to become one vast room with high molded ceilings, a brick fireplace, and tall windows that looked out from the fifth floor of the double-width brownstone over tree-lined Sixty-ninth Street. Except for the corner Steinway and the framed music posters covering the walls, the flat gave away little of the man. In style and arrangement, the furnishings were impersonal and methodical rather than warm and homey, suggesting the owner spent little time and little or no emotional energy there.

Hanging his Savile Row suit neatly on the electric pressing valet, David donned a Sulka silk robe and mixed himself a vodka and tonic. Lately he'd been finding it harder and harder to slow down his overcharged and overactive brain. Between his Silverfish responsibilities and his kvetching clients, he was always "on," always the one expected to be cool and detached under pressure. It was let's pretend, hide your thoughts, seem in control, day in and day out. Somehow, though, the edge was wearing off. It was all becoming too easy, as if his life had plateaued and he was looking out over an endless flatland of more of the same. He'd pretended to feel so often that he wasn't quite sure what the real thing was anymore.

Settling down on the deep blue sofa, he picked up the brief for tomorrow's court appearance. He glanced over the arguments but couldn't concentrate, his attention diluted by the mixture of vodka and his vivid memories of Joyce.

She'd found a chink in his armor, broken through, and touched him, and the nerve was even deeper and more raw than he'd imagined. He didn't want to admit that he was lonely and unfulfilled; that David the lawyer—dispassionate, objective, yet sensitive and clearheaded; conscience, alter ego, and big brother to his clients—was neither a success nor a real human being in his own eyes. Pretending to yourself was the hardest.

Until now, he'd cultivated a flock of followers and surrounded himself with petulant, creative children because he needed to be leaned against, relied on, needed to be needed. It was his way of living: He and his clients fed off each other and David lived through them, vicariously, holding the loneliness at bay, filling his moments but not his life.

Now, thinking back to his conversation with Rick, and remembering the touch of Joyce's lips on his cheek, fear and doubt began to well up inside him. Was there something more to life, something he was avoiding? Was it merely business, part of the master plan, that had made him urge Joyce to go to California, or was there an ulterior motive, prompted by an irrational fear of confronting his own feelings? Had he really been thinking of Joyce's welfare or had he urged her away because he couldn't face wanting her? Was he afraid to feel, just as he was afraid to lose, hiding behind the risks taken by his clients?

The ring of the phone saved him from digging any farther. He didn't think he could bear another whining artiste, but he lifted the receiver anyway.

"Hello?"

"David?"

He recognized the familiar transatlantic echo.

"It's Kevin Singh. Sorry to bother you so late." The accent

was upper-crust West End with a touch of Eton. There was a long silence.

"What's up?"

"He's gone and done it," Kevin said, his voice choked with emotion.

"Done what? What are you talking about?"

"We've lost him. I can't believe it." Kevin's voice cracked and he began to sob uncontrollably. He dropped the receiver to the office floor, sank down from the chesterfield sofa onto the Persian rug, and buried his head in his hands.

"Kevin? Kevin! Are you there? What's the matter?"

Kevin heard the faraway voice calling to him. Finally, he cradled the phone in his hand and leaned his ear down near the receiver. "I'm here," he said quietly.

"It's Brandon, isn't it?"

"How could he do this to me? What am I going to do?"

"He's dead then?"

The quiet sobbing at the other end answered David's question.

"Take it easy, Kevin. Take it easy. It's a horrible tragedy, but there's only one thing you *can* do. You're going to go on, just like Brandon would have wanted you to. I'm sorry, but it was bound to happen, sooner or later. You knew that as well if not better than I did."

"That doesn't make it any bloody easier, you know."

"Look, just stay calm. I can make a plane tomorrow night and be there in twenty-four hours. Have Miss Gwens take care of all the arrangements."

"Don't you even want to know how it bloody well happened?" Kevin asked indignantly.

"No, I really don't. Not now, at least. All that matters is that Brandon is gone and we have to be strong enough to pick up the pieces. There's a company to run and we have to put our best face forward to the world. I'll do anything and everything I can to help. You know that."

Kevin wasn't sure what he knew. Except that David was a cold fish.

When he hung up the phone, David picked up his drink and jealously watched the beads of sweat roll, like tears, down the side of his crystal glass. He'd lost a mentor and his main client. If he'd wanted a crisis, he'd found one. But no matter how much he wanted to cry, he stayed cool and dry, as always.

* * *

The anger started growing as he made his way through the portable boarding ramp at JFK and into the first-class section of a TWA 747.

"I said no, didn't I? Nothing. Just leave me alone and don't wake me till we arrive," he snapped at the stewardess who was offering him champagne, candy, and hors d'oeuvres. Tonight there was no sign of David's usual courtesy, sensitivity, or charm. He washed down a blue Valium with club soda, adjusted the pillow and blanket, then fixed the black eyeshades over his eyes. The whine and rumble of the engines filled his ears.

David hated night flights to Europe. He hated unplanned trips anywhere. But most of all, he hated feeling out of control. "You pathetic prick. You asshole, Brandon," he mumbled to himself, loud enough to raise the eyebrows of the elegant white-haired lady seated across the aisle.

In the end, Brandon had proved even more selfish and self-indulgent than David had expected. Of course, if it hadn't been this drug mix, it would have been another, and no time would have been a good time. But David still felt personally affronted. Brandon had left a life, and a company, in disarray. Promises to be kept, lives to be salvaged, shit to be cleaned up. The Silverfish's five-year record contract with Swisstone was about to expire. The master plan for the U.S., the plan *he'd* developed, was barely off the drawing board. And David was left holding the bag.

He couldn't stay angry, though. Not when he remembered the man's pain and suffering.

The first time he'd seen that look in Brandon's eyes—the deranged glitter, the slight lack of focus, the halfway mark between twinkle and glaze—David had felt a chill. Brandon had unreliable, vulnerable eyes. Eyes that were stoned and looked out with a kind of madness. Eyes that were incompatible with personal happiness, in a body that was a walking testament to his inability to find within himself the necessary resources for contentment. Eyes that betrayed a lifelong struggle. Eyes filled with such self-hatred and self-loathing that David could barely look into them.

Although relatively young, Brandon had aged prematurely because of his inability to accept himself. By all traditional standards, he was tremendously successful: possessed of extraordinary intellectual and material means; never lacking in courage or interest when it concerned others. But he was totally without the courage of conviction when it concerned himself.

He had lived his life vicariously through his "lads." He wanted to be them. When they no longer needed him, when they slipped out of the nest, he found he had no more to do, no more mountains to climb, no more streams to ford, no more wrongs to right. He became insensitive and immune to the aesthetics of music, art, and the simple and obvious glories of life. He suffered terminal ennui. He sat for endless hours staring at nothing with his wild eyes, posed in a lotus position as though meditating. Actually, he was simply incommunicado with the world, slowly starving to death his brain, his body, and his soul.

Because of his wealth, his faithful servants, and his notorious reputation, he was deemed eccentric and was protected from the usual, predictable humiliations of mortals. He was a man possessed—by demon drugs, by alcohol, by anything he could take to hide who he really was. He became the first pharmaceutical potentate, ingesting and inhaling his fortune away as he tried to artificially induce personality changes and mood swings that he couldn't bring about on his own.

If only he could have remained as courageous and brazen as he'd been on that first Silverfish tour. If only he could have held on to that sense of satisfaction. If only he could have continued to feed on the approving smiles he saw on their faces when he'd delivered them another great deal or was proved right after another bout of complaints.

"But, Brandon, why do we have to wear these suits?" they asked.

"Because it's good for your image and your career. Because you want the mums out there to like you so they'll give their kids a few quid to buy your album. Maybe next year you can wear blue jeans and open shirts like Derek Robertson. For now, you're going to be four little gentlemen, whether you like it or not."

"Why do we have to drive all over and visit the jocks at the stations and answer the same bloody stupid questions again and again?"

"You have to give those blokes interviews to make 'em feel like they have a personal relationship with you. Then they'll break their asses for you. Then they'll kill for you. That's why."

"But, Brandon—"

"Trust me, boys."

They questioned the cashbox on the road and the blow for the tooters and complained about doing charity gigs. They couldn't understand why he limited their answers at press conferences and sometimes even answered for them.

Slowly, however, the boys began to see the method behind Brandon's madness. They learned the "biz" of show biz from Brandon. They learned about chutzpah and *putz* and how Yiddish was the official language of rock-and-roll. They learned about the critical importance of sound checks. Unlike the Beatles, he made all four of them write and disguised each album cut, never revealing who wrote which tune or who produced which cut. And he insisted that each album released be four sides, two LPs.

Brandon was obsessed with details, and there was nothing too insignificant when it came to his boys. He fought with club owners and concert promoters, theater and arena managers, so that everything was just right. He made sure there were enough security guards, that the wires were grounded so they didn't get shocked, that the lighting was perfect, that the paper stock for the posters was high quality, that the advertising was consistent with the Silverfish image. He fought daily for more record promotion in Leeds, in Manchester, on the Continent. When record sales slumped, he personally bought thousands of records to keep them looking good.

He led them through the hellhole called "the road," through a war zone of hotels and motels and crummy clubs, even through fucking awful Hamburg and the Reeperbahn. He provided penicillin when they got the clap, and sprang them from the drunk tank when hookers rolled them for a few deutsche marks. He held their heads down and helped them throw up when they mixed bad drugs and bad booze. He gave them hangover remedies.

And Brandon did something else. He made their adrenaline flow. He could muster a performance out of them with a three-minute, preshow rap and by simply sitting down front looking up at them adoringly. When they missed cues, couldn't hear the monitors, were in a funk, he came backstage and laughed, encouraged them, cheered them up. He kept them calm, kept his counsel, kept his sights on the big picture, and kept his head when all the others around him were losing theirs.

He put up with all their shit; all their birds; their paternity suits; their drug experiments; their aggrieved parents, sisters, and brothers; their whims; their fads; their astrological/mystical crap. He did it all for them. Four times over for each of them and for all of them, individually, collectively, in every permutation and combination.

After all those years of his doing for them, of putting up with them, believing in them, trusting them, financing them, loving them, they owed him more than his one-fifth share and they knew it. The band loved Brandon for fighting their battles, for making them more than they were, for believing in them and seeing something more in them than they had ever seen in themselves. They trusted him, and he proved himself right. And the more right he was, the more they trusted him.

So they tolerated his drug stupors, his drunken slurry speech, his staggering out from the wings during their show. They tolerated his interrupting their performances, sitting on the stage, his studio antics when he played at producer, his percentages of their record deals, his overrides. Whatever Brandon did, the Silverfish accepted. He'd earned it, and it was now their turn to take care of him. He was the fifth Silverfish, after all. He ain't heavy, he's their brother.

So he was late. So he called, ranting and raving, in the middle of the night. So he staggered through life and lived off them. So what? They had so much more than he did. They were human, they cried and felt; but Brandon, he was on the edge, with no one to share anything with. The more material things he accumulated, the more alone he felt and the more depressed he became. But he never admitted to the pain or the loneliness. Never opened up or confided in anyone. He remained frozen and isolated.

Poor Brandon never had any family other than the Silverfish. Despite the success of L.O.L. and his enormous power and wealth, they were his life. When they began to drift, so did he. It was only a question of time—and now the time had come.

In his tranquilized half-sleep, floating over the Atlantic, David sensed the parallels between his life and Brandon's: the vicarious living, the need to be needed, the underlying lack of self-satisfaction . . . the loneliness. He shuddered suddenly with fear. There but for the grace of God . . . If nothing else, there had to be a lesson for him in Brandon's life and dissolution. But what was it?

When David finally opened his eyes to see the plane touching down at Heathrow, it was just past 7:00 A.M. London time. Still groggy from the Valium and the time change, he shuffled through customs in a haze and boarded the L.O.L. limousine to Claridge's, on his way not to praise the emperor of rock-and-roll but to bury him.

It took several cups of black coffee, a hot bath in the massive sunken tub of the elegant deco bathroom, followed by a cold shower and half a Tenuate diet pill, before he began to shake off the heavy jet-lag lethargy. By 9:30 he was dressed and ready.

As the limousine approached the Georgian town house off Curzon Street in the heart of Mayfair, David ordered the driver to pull over. He walked the final half-block, waited until another limousine appeared at the curb to distract reporters and photographers, then deftly slipped past them through the massive front door with the L.O.L. logo on the shiny brass plaque.

Admitted past the uniformed guard, David entered a lovely wood-paneled anteroom that smelled of old pine and freshly brewed strong English coffee.

"Good morning, Mr. Barry. So good of you to come," Virginia Gwens said, looking up from the tooled leather Asprey's clipboard of "names" resting on her elegant eighteenth-century partners' desk. The words were proper—the tone showed more tolerance than respect. A middle-aged spinster with a severe, even distasteful, manner, Miss Gwens had been Brandon's personal secretary and protectress. Like a jealous mother hen, she'd guarded and insulated Brandon for many years.

"Hello, Miss Gwens. An unfortunate occasion. I assume you're taking care of the funeral arrangements in your usual efficient way," David said, noting the list.

"Of course, sir. I'm coordinating with the Levy family." Her voice was tinged with hostility. She had never been friendly to David, always treating him like an outsider who was horning in on her territory and coming between her and her master. Only Brandon, and Kevin (after years of charming the woman), inspired her devotion.

"Will the lads be attending?"

"We're not sure yet. None of them is here presently. Colin's off in Nepal somewhere and we haven't been able to reach him yet. The others have been informed but won't commit on attending. Typical, wouldn't you say?"

David forced a brief smile.

"Is there something you'd like me to do, Mr. Barry?"

"No, nothing right now, thanks. I'll just look over some of the papers in Brandon's office," David answered, feeling the chill.

When he opened the door to Brandon's massive office, he was surprised. Not by the elaborate, even pretentious, furnishings, which he'd seen often enough in the past. Not by the cherubs on the fifteen-foot ceiling; the elegant Chippendale table and chairs; the forged copy of Caravaggio's *Seven Acts of Mercy;* the finely woven Persian carpets; or the pièce de résistance, Brandon's nine-by-four-foot antique French desk, with its deep burr elm veneer and ornate ormolu mounts.

Rather, David was surprised by the appearance of Kevin Singh sitting behind Brandon's great desk, deeply engrossed in a pile of confidential files as if he, too, were one of Brandon's props. From the odor of cigarettes and the pile of Davidoff butts in the ashtray, it was obvious that Kevin had been there for some time.

Nice of that bitch to warn me, David thought to himself. It was starting already. With the body still warm, sides were being drawn. And Kevin, consort to the deceased—who'd never reviewed a company file in his life, unless it was a juicy personal dossier on one of the celebrities he was about to meet or entertain—was obviously positioning himself for upward mobility.

Kevin raised his head. "I say, old man, bloody good to see you." He stood up and walked around the desk. Of medium height, with a sharp nose, black hair, and the dark brown skin of a merchant-caste Indian, Kevin had a Brahmanlike posture. As usual, he was perfectly fit and eminently proper in a Kilgore's suit and pastel Turnbull & Asser shirt. This morning, though, his tie was askew, his suit jacket rumpled, his eyes red and watery. He was wearing his best but looking his worst: overcaffeined, overnicotined, overextremed in all regards. His handshake was particularly wet and weak, and his gray eyes latched on to David intensely, as if looking for a clue to his intentions. Kevin was unsure how David would fit into the void and puzzle created by Brandon's death.

"You do look a touch done in. Rough flight?"

"Rough enough," David answered, thinking the same thing about Kevin. "How are *you* holding up?"

"The piss-ass press has been hounding me. Did you see them out there, vile piranhas!"

"It is sickening, isn't it? Have you made a statement?"

"Just the usual rubbish," Kevin said in his cultivated West

End accent. "No official statement will be issued until after the meeting of the board."

"And when will that be?"

Kevin eyed David warily as he walked back behind the confines of Brandon's desk. He was trying to stay calm, but he couldn't stop his hand from shaking and quickly lit another Davidoff. Although he didn't actually dislike David, he felt threatened by the man's dispassionate, take-charge attitude. That was one of the reasons he'd spent so many hours poring over the files. If he was going to keep the outsiders at bay and run L.O.L himself—as he hoped to, considering that he was the only one of the five board members who functioned internally, within the company—he needed to sound savvy and knowledgeable about company business.

"The board meeting is scheduled for tomorrow after the funeral. I'll have to check with the others, but I do believe you're invited for the tail end. Strictly as an adviser, of course."

David read the spirit and the letter of the comment. He *had* no official standing of any kind within L.O.L. No portfolio, no stock in the company, no officership, directorship or board membership. His power, if you could call it that, had developed behind the scenes, as a result of his personal relationship with Brandon and the Silverfish, and their trust in and reliance on his counsel.

"I wanted to review some of the files on the Silverfish contract, if I might, Kevin. You know it expires in just a few months and Brandon had some specific plans regarding the start-up of a U.S. operation. I feel sure the board will want to discuss the matter thoroughly."

"Yes, yes. But wouldn't it be better to wait till after the board meeting? Just to be all proper, on the up and up, you understand."

David immediately sensed Kevin's insecurity, bred deep from his being a minority and a foreigner in his own land. The last thing David wanted was to battle with Kevin and the other vultures for the remains of Brandon's corpse.

He was about to comply with the request when, surprisingly, despite his weariness and depression, he felt a surge. Damned if he was going to roll over and play dead while this fop eased him out and made a shambles of the L.O.L. empire. He'd worked too hard and too long for Brandon and L.O.L. to let it slip away without a struggle. If panic overwhelmed the company now, as it had NEMS after Brian Epstein's death, all the organization and momentum that Brandon had instilled would dissipate in a matter of months.

It wasn't that he had anything against Kevin. The man was eminently likable and good at what he was—nursemaid to Brandon, glorified social secretary, Silverfish representative to the upper classes. But when it came to running an empire, a position to which Kevin seemed to be aspiring, David believed he was sorely ill-equipped and deeply over his head. As far as David was concerned, Kevin lacked the discipline and the vision to run the Levy Organization, even if he had the intellect and style.

On the other hand, there were few alternatives. The board would undoubtedly sell the company before it brought in someone completely new and threatening. And David couldn't fathom the idea of sticking his own neck out and putting it on the line. That was the one thing he'd never done and the real reason he could stay cool and not sweat: He lived in the background, far from the front lines. What he could do, though, for the moment, was keep Kevin on his feet, stay in the background, watch and wait.

"If that's what you'd like, Kevin, of course. I just thought you might like me to prepare a brief for you on the status of all Silverfish business, including a list of outstanding pending matters, in order of priority, with recommended actions and alternatives. Something *you* could present to the board, if you so chose." David stressed the *you*. For some reason, he decided not to present the document he'd prepared on the U.S. operation. Not just yet.

Kevin puffed at his cigarette pensively. Maybe he *was* acting a bit paranoid. For the moment, there was no reason not to use David in just the way Brandon had, as helpmate and consultant. As long as he was careful. Lord knows, he needed all the help he could get.

Yes, he would do as Brandon had done. He would seek David's concise, logical appraisal of the situation, study the alternatives, and spout it all out before the board, regurgitating the digested thoughts in his cultivated accent and manner. The board would have no choice but to be impressed.

"Bloody good show. Why *don't* you prepare me such a schedule. In trying times like these, we must all do our utmost to ensure that the Silverfish and the Levy Organization flourish.

Brandon would have wanted it that way. So glad I can count on you."

Awaiting the entrance of the other board members, Kevin paced anxiously around Brandon's office, chain-smoking and sipping cup after cup of black coffee. His shirt was damp and slightly disheveled from the warm August shower that had fallen intermittently over the somber funeral service.

Kevin was having trouble bearing the pain and holding back the fear. He'd lost the most precious thing in his life, the very ground of his existence, and like a drowning man he was grasping for something solid to hold on to. No matter how hard he tried, he couldn't wipe the picture of Brandon's blank, ashen face from his mind. But he had to think.

He had some savings—a tiny piece of the Lock and Loll Library, a piece of an art gallery, a percentage of a smart restaurant on Beauchamp Place—but not nearly enough to maintain him in the style to which he'd grown accustomed. His whole life and life-style had depended on Brandon, from the breakfasts at the Connaught, the lunches at the Ritz, the dinners at San Lorenzo, to his table position at Morton's and Annabel's; from his L.O.L. title to his car and driver and credit card.

His connection to Brandon and the Silverfish was everything. It was because of the tales he could tell about the lads that he was courted by the rich and titled, able to enter homes which would otherwise have been closed to him on account of his color and low-born status. Because he could gossip discreetly about the Silverfish—their music, habits, drugs, witticisms, and infidelities—and because he was so genuinely stylish and charming, Kevin had become a regular on every "A" list. He always said just enough to titillate his audience, but never so much as to embarrass the boys. Kevin's presence was a coup. He never accepted an invitation too soon, never acted too anxious. He had made himself socially acceptable. The titled, bored rich adored him, and he represented the Silverfish in a way the outrageous Brandon, with his erratic, embarrassing behavior, never could.

Kevin had come to function as Brandon's surrogate and as unofficial social ambassador for the Silverfish. Acting as a buffer, he filtered the flow of information to the world. The public persona of the lads was due in large part to the transmogrification their very real, very human, sometimes very sordid lives received through the silken lips and tactful, artful, facile tongue

of Kevin Singh. By reciting little confidences about the boys at
the tables of the opinion makers of the world, he was guarantied
those "confidences" would become matters of public record. In
his way, he did more than anyone to sustain the band's image
and increase their stature and publicity.

He had trodden a long, hard path to reach that point, though.
No one on the board knew that his father and mother were
greengrocers in Leeds (he was always vague about the "family
after Indian independence," implying he would have been a
rajah if born sooner). Nor did they know that he'd studied for
years with a dialectician and grammarian to develop an accent
that sounded convincingly "to the manor born." They knew
nothing of the years of playing lover and nursemaid to Brandon.
How he scored the drugs and the boys for his emperor when
nobody else would; how he hired guards to protect Brandon
from himself, bailed him out of jail, held him when he cried and
got sick, loved him selflessly day in and day out, and successfully
delayed the actualization of Brandon's self-fulfilling prophecy of
doom and death.

It didn't matter whether Brandon's death was accidental.
Between the Mandrex, the Ritalin, and the booze, it was bound
to happen. All that mattered now was that he keep Brandon's
memory alive, keep himself afloat, and not lose the perks that
had become part and parcel of his life. The only way he could
do that was by convincing the board that he was suitable to
handle the reins of L.O.L.

Kevin sipped coffee from the blue Wedgwood service as his
eyes scanned Brandon's elegant office. Lap mats and napkins
woven by Porthault were laid out for tidbits. The Latin inscrip-
tion on the crest of ormolu mounts in the great desk read: *Omnia
labor vincit improbus*—"Hard work conquers everything." As
long as he was careful and played his cards right, all this would
be his.

He'd worked hard on his homework: reading the pertinent
files, David's brief, even the dossier on David himself. He had
to be careful not to say too much. By showing his grasp of the
superficial basic material and dropping occasional esoteric
minutia, he would intimidate the board from challenging him.
Only David was a question mark.

Despite David-the-lawyer's show of cooperation, Kevin was
nervous. David knew what he was all about. By using his close
working relationship with the Silverfish and his far deeper

knowledge of company business, David could throw a wrench into Kevin's appointment. That is, *if* he wanted to, and *if* he had the balls to take him on.

No matter how nervous he might be, Kevin would appear sharp, charming, and in control for the board, just the way Brandon had always been. Even though it was the last thing in the world he wanted, he had no choice but to live Brandon's life without him.

"I say, do come in, come in. Damn good of you to join us."

David walked through the huge doors into Brandon's office. Seated around the room were Kevin and the four other board members.

"I believe you've met these gentlemen," Kevin said from his strategic position behind Brandon's desk. "Emil Zoltan of Barclay's, John Peters of Arthur Young, Harold Jennings of Linkletter and Paine, and, of course, Michael Reese of Polygram." Kevin was smiling broadly. He had made an Academy Award presentation to the board and everything was looking rosy.

David reached to shake each one's hand and took a seat to one side on the chesterfield sofa.

"The board has been discussing a range of matters, David, and I believe we'd like your opinion."

"Yes, Mr. Barry. We've been considering all options, from possible sale of the company to growth and expansion, and we'd like your view, as one close to Mr. Levy and the entire L.O.L. operation, on the future of the Levy Organization," said Mr. Zoltan, the chubby, ruddy-faced British banker.

"Well, gentlemen," David began, sitting forward on the couch, resting his elbows on his knees, and forming his fingers into a pyramid, "in my opinion, L.O.L. is ideally positioned for future growth and development. As you well know, not only is the company financially sound at the moment but I believe that, properly managed, the Levy Organization can move into the forefront of the entertainment business. Now is not the time to sell but the time to grow.

"Brandon is gone, but he's left behind a legacy and plans for the future. It is my opinion that the top priority for this company is the development of an American branch of L.O.L., a full-fledged record company to handle the Silverfish and the other recording artists currently in the Levy stable. With the Apollo contract expiring, and Silverfish business growing, it was Brandon's fervent desire *not* to renew that contract but to put every effort into forming his own American record company."

David chose not to mention anything about his and Brandon's plans regarding the film industry, emerging technologies, and the amalgamation of film and music. Rather, he opened his briefcase and distributed bound copies of a document entitled "L.O.L. in America."

Behind the desk, Kevin nervously lit a cigarette. The lawyer *had* been holding out on him.

"The document I am distributing provides a detailed analysis and cost breakdown for the development of the American branch of L.O.L. As you can see, the proposal has been substantially researched and start-up funds already budgeted."

The board members reviewed the document and talked at length about the pros and cons of the proposal. Kevin was silent for most of the discussion, his fingers tensely rubbing against his chin.

"Mr. Barry, let me ask you a personal question, if you don't mind." The speaker was Michael Reese from Polygram, the rest-of-the-world record distributor for L.O.L. product. "How do you see yourself fitting into the future of our organization?"

Kevin leaned forward in his seat.

David sat silently for a moment. It was the very question he'd been pondering for the last twenty-four hours, as he thought about Brandon on the plane trip and when he watched the remains of his strange friend lowered into the earth.

If he tried to remain totally in the background now, in a strictly advisory capacity, he'd be jeopardizing his future, the future of L.O.L., and everything he'd worked for with Brandon. But if he stepped too far forward, he would be making a commitment, risking failure, doing the very thing he'd been trying to avoid in every way, in both his personal and professional life, for so long.

He thought of Brandon and of Kipling and searched his soul. "If you make one heap of all your winnings, and risk it on a turn of pitch and toss . . . and lose, and start again . . ." He felt the surge and knew the answer long before he spoke.

David didn't believe in Kevin's ability. And he knew what Brandon would have told him to do: Seize the opportunity. Yet he wasn't ready to implement a strategy. Not just yet. He wanted to wait and see the lay of the land. So he decided on a dramatic but temporary step forward, a very substantial but reversible move into the front lines. It would be a new challenge, as well as an opportunity to move within and keep tabs on Kevin. And, deep down, he knew it actually constituted a plan and a strategy worthy of the great Brandon.

"I would like nothing better than the opportunity to oversee setting up the Levy Organization in the U.S.," David answered. "Temporarily, of course, until the operation gets on its feet. After that, I see myself resuming duties as counselor and adviser to L.O.L., if my services are still required."

"But do you have the hands-on record-company experience for such a job?"

"Of course not," David answered. "But I have the corporate expertise and I would hire the best record executive available to run the day-to-day business."

"And who, Mr. Barry, do you see as the best man to run L.O.L. as a whole?"

He looked dramatically around the room. By asking for the American operation, he knew there was only one possible answer. "Why, I don't think there's any question that Kevin Singh is the most qualified man for the job. And the last thing we want is an outsider running our company. Don't you agree, gentlemen?"

The board members murmured in agreement.

"I believe I'm speaking for the group," Mr. Zoltan said, after looking around and exchanging nods with his fellow board members, "when I say that the board would be delighted to have Kevin accept the position of chairman and chief executive officer of the Levy Organization. Kevin?"

Kevin couldn't help smiling. It had worked out even better than he'd hoped. America was the best place for David and the last place he ever wanted to go. Not when he had so much going for him in the U.K. He felt relieved and vindicated. He deserved it, after all. For all the services he had performed for the Silverfish, for the company, and for Brandon, this was his just reward.

He rose from his chair. "Why, gentlemen, I'm flattered by your vote of confidence. No one, of course, could fill the shoes left by Brandon. But I'm prepared to take the helm of this company and see that it weathers this storm and sails out into the open sea again. With Mr. Barry at my side as head of the new American branch of L.O.L."—he nodded his head toward

David—"I believe we're on a firm course for even greater success and prosperity."

"Hear, hear," Mr. Zoltan said.

David stood up from the couch and walked over to Kevin. "Congratulations," he said warmly, taking Kevin's hand in both of his. "I'm glad it's over."

But David was pretending. Pretending the drama was over when he knew it was simply the end of Act I and that the plot was just beginning to unfold.

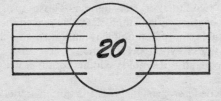

20

1972

𝒲 HEN THE DOUBLE DOORS OF THE PALATIAL APOLLO office swung open and Hans van der Rogdt entered, Thane was all smiles. He came out from behind his finely carved desk and firmly grasped the man's hand. "Welcome to New York, Hans. I'm so glad you could make it. How long has it been?"

"Too long," the Dutchman answered, returning Thane's grip firmly and aggressively and taking the proffered seat on one of the Louis XV needlepoint chairs.

"Can I get you something? Champagne, perhaps? To celebrate our latest financial figures."

"Yes, that would be quite nice, thank you."

Thane leaned over and pushed the buzzer on his intercom. "Sally, have Reynolds bring us some champagne."

Van der Rogdt shifted in his chair to take in the full view. "Your office is really quite remarkable. Every time I visit, you seem to have more beautiful *objets d'art.*"

"I picked up a few goodies: The Sèvres ware in the breakfront over there and the Pre-Raphaelite grouping on the far wall are all new."

The side door of the huge office opened and an older black man in a formal butler's uniform entered, carrying a Lalique ice bucket and two fluted crystal stemmed glasses (prechilled) on a nineteenth-century silver Tiffany tray. He placed the tray quietly on a side table and ceremoniously uncorked the champagne.

"That's fine, Reynolds. I'll pour."

"Very good, sir," Reynolds said, not quite bowing but retracing his steps.

"Louis Roederer Cristal, 1961. It's quite wonderful. I'm sure you'll like it." Thane carefully poured the champagne and handed the first filled glass to the Dutchman. If his intuitions were on target, as they usually were, the newly appointed CEO of Swisstone hadn't come all the way to barbarous New York just to discuss contracts. Even the approaching expirations, and expected renewals, of the Dwight Sharon and the Silverfish five-year contracts weren't sufficient to draw this maggot out of the woodwork.

"To Swisstone?" Thane proposed, raising his glass.

"By all means. To Swisstone," Hans answered softly, taking a small sip, then setting his glass down on a leather coaster on the edge of Thane's precious desk.

Thane quaffed his quickly and walked back toward the bucket.

"Thane, I can't tell you how much we appreciate what you've done for Swisstone these past years. You've turned Apollo into one of the giants of the American recording industry."

And he had. Between the Silverfish signing and his discovery and nurturing of Dwight Sharon, Thane had single-handedly put Apollo on the world-class recording-industry map. But he hadn't stopped there. Along with the big names, he'd conscientiously developed an extensive line of artists across the musical board, from rock, pop, and R&B, to country, classical, and middle-of-the-road. He'd cross-pollinated the American scene with European artists and built a modern empire, with offices in New York, L.A., Chicago, and Nashville. Swisstone management could not have asked for more, nor could they have expected as much. He promoted the artists and the company almost as much as he promoted himself.

"Thank you, Hans. I've done what I thought was necessary to enhance Swisstone's reputation in the United States." Thane could taste the coming promotion almost as clearly as he could taste the crisp, cold, dry champagne on his palate. Now he would control not only the U.S. but worldwide international operations, with a chance at the vacant post of chief operating officer—and probably heir-apparency to the aging van der Rogdt himself. He lifted the bottle once again.

A dark cloud seemed to pass over Hans's face as he followed the American's movements with his eyes. "And that's just the problem."

Crawley stopped and turned, his brow suddenly furrowed, his heart pounding, the champagne bottle poised at a forty-five-degree angle in his hand. "Excuse me? What problem, Hans?"

"I'm sure this will come as a shock to you, but I'm afraid there have been some questions raised by the board, concerning—how shall I say it?—your business practices."

Thane tipped the bottle the rest of the way and refilled his glass. "More champagne?" he asked very calmly, holding the bottle out questioningly toward the Dutchman while consciously keeping his voice well modulated.

Van der Rogdt politely covered his glass with his hand, indicating moderation and a less happy mood.

"I'm afraid I don't understand?" Thane said, taking a seat facing Hans. He didn't know what van der Rogdt was up to. For all he knew, it was another of the clever Dutchman's sadistic tests, perhaps a final challenge of wits before the real reward.

"No doubt you've heard the rumors about American government inquiries into the record industry. Grand-jury investigations and so forth. Well, Philippe Phochet is quite concerned about Swisstone and the family name. He recently initiated a special internal company audit. Unfortunately, Thane, this investigation has given rise to some rather unsavory allegations regarding your business ethics and improper use of the U.S. company's funds."

"You're not serious? Surely you can defend me against such slander."

"I'm quite serious. And so are the charges."

Thane's jaw tightened and his hands came together. He was glad the delicate champagne glass wasn't in them. "Well? Are you going to tell me about these ridiculous accusations or at least ask me to explain the audit findings?" he asked indignantly.

"To begin with, there are reports of possible tax fraud. Are you familiar with any illicit cash reimbursements used to raise money to 'entertain' your artists? Or with illegal cash payments to independent radio promoters?" Hans asked somberly, his eyes staring past Thane and out the window at a building across Fifty-seventh Street.

Thane began to laugh and turned up his palms in a shrug. "Illegal cash payments. Illicit reimbursements. So?"

"So! Please, do not make light of these charges. The board is most disturbed."

"The board, Hans? The board? Correct me if I'm inaccurate in my recollection, but you knew all along about our need to raise extra cash—about the phony receipts and the employee cash reimbursement plan. You knew as well about the skimming of certain numbers of 'clean,' unmarked records to raise cash. The cash keeps our clients happy. It pays off independent promotion men to ensure air play for our artists. No air play, no sales. No sales, no profits. It's as simple as that," Thane said, somewhat heatedly. "Or didn't you want Apollo artists to have American air play?"

"Yes, yes, but I had no idea of the extent. I never realized you were fraudulently avoiding taxes. I never authorized you to cheat the U.S. government!"

"Cheat? Who's cheating? We did what had to be done, what every record company does. It's part of the business, and you know it. It was you, Hans, who said, 'Take care of business, Thane. Do whatever has to be done to make Apollo competitive, Thane.' Or have you forgotten that conversation?"

Suddenly, Thane felt the champagne going to his head. His mind was reeling. No company in its right mind would turn against a man who'd worked the kind of miracle and turned the kind of profit he had! This had to be a test of his composure.

"There's more, though. Much, much more. I wasn't aware that you were supplying drugs to your artists. I didn't know *our* limousines were carrying tanks of nitrous oxide to musicians at the Beverly Hills Hotel. I didn't know *our* courier service was carrying marijuana and cocaine and peyote tabs, mescaline, and God knows what else in demo-record pouches."

Thane tried to smile and not show his exasperation. "Come on, Hans. You're a pro. You know what has to be done to keep this business going. Every company's got a Mr. Fixit who helps artists secure their goodies. It's standard operating procedure. No happy artists, no record company, remember?" he said, almost cutely.

"There are also charges of unauthorized use of the company plane and . . . diversion of corporate funds for personal use," Hans said, holding his palm up and out to indicate the office.

At that, Thane shot up from his chair. He stood tall, like a Viking in arms, in front of the seated van der Rogdt. His face was flushed with anger. "What the hell is going on here? For five years I've been making money hand over fist for Swisstone. Your eyes were open all the time. You knew goddamned well what was going on. Up till now, you didn't seem to give a damn. Suddenly, out of the blue, you're hurling contrived accusations at me like I'm some sort of common criminal. I don't—"

Van der Rogdt stood up and put both his arms around Crawley's shoulders. "Thane, please, sit down, calm yourself. You're a brilliant executive. I've nothing but respect and admiration for you. And you know by now that I love you like a son and wouldn't do anything to harm you. It's just . . ." He sighed. "It's Philippe. He's very concerned about Swisstone's reputation. He's of the old European school; he's not familiar with America or with today's modern business practices or the standards of the industry. Come, pour me another glass of that delicious champagne," he said, holding out his glass.

Thane refilled it warily, surprised that there was almost none left. He needed all his will power to control the maelstrom of his emotions. Anger at the Jew's patronizing tone. Righteous indignation at being forced to defend himself when he'd done nothing wrong. Resentment at van der Rogdt's daring to scold him as if he were a child after lulling him into doing all he did with the man's tacit consent. Gnawing doubts about the truth or sincerity of the Dutchman's remarks.

"Oh, Thane, *I* know how much you've done for Apollo. Maybe, considering the fact that we are an old Swiss company and family-controlled, I should have warned you to be more discreet. In any event, I believe I can take care of the matter to everyone's satisfaction, including Philippe's. I owe you that much."

"And just how do you propose to do that?"

"Give me a personal, handwritten note asking me to conduct an independent study of Apollo finances. With that in hand, I'll employ a top auditing firm to sniff around. I'll tell the board how concerned you are about the accusations and that you've initiated an independent investigation, under my supervision.

"I'll see to it that the audit turns up nothing except a few minor irregularities on very low levels. You'll immediately announce strong housecleaning measures, fire a few people, and the board and the family shareholders will be impressed by your swift, decisive action and satisfied that the problem has been nipped in the bud. Then you can get back to the business of running the best record company in the United States."

Thane couldn't think clearly. He was crushed by the burden of accusation and the wild turn of events. How could he have been so wrong? Still, maybe his dreams of glory hadn't yet evaporated. Maybe Hans could take care of the problem. In any event, he didn't seem to have much choice.

"All right, Hans. I don't understand what all this fuss is about, but if you think it's necessary . . ."

"Please, trust me. It's necessary. I'm going to initiate the investigation immediately. Do you like Rio?"

"Very much. Why?"

"Because I'd like you to take a vacation there, commencing as soon as possible. We'll call it a business trip, to check out our South American operation. Plan on being gone for several weeks. By the time you get back, the investigation will be completed and the whole affair will have blown over."

* * *

There is no place like Rio and no one in the world like the sensuous, life-loving, naturally beautiful locals, the Cariocas, with their combination of delicate northern features and Indian and African tones. Their skin ranges from cream to dark, the color of strong tea tinted with gold. Tall, lithe, and catlike, the Cariocas love fun and folklore, the mountains, seas, jungles, and beaches. Whether poor or rich, their love of life is childlike and infectious. When in doubt, they drink a few *batitas* and dance the samba. They are open and seductive, wise and, above all, happy.

Two of these local goddesses, his companions for the last several days, graced Thane's arms as he wandered toward the terrace bar that looked out at Guanabara Bay and Sugar Loaf Peak. A warm October breeze rustled the gnarled trees and filled the air with a soft, sweet smell. Finally, after nearly two weeks of sun and relaxation, Thane felt fit enough to attend a business party: a celebration in honor of the opening of Jorge Machado's latest movie.

There'd been no word from van der Rogdt in New York. But

then, he hadn't expected any. Although he was enjoying himself in Rio—there was no place more civilized—he couldn't stand being away from the hub any longer. In spite of what van der Rogdt had urged, he would definitely return to New York in a day or two, maybe even tomorrow. After he'd had a little more fun and games.

"Drinks all around, please," Thane said to the tall, blond bartender. Then he spotted Jorge. "If you'll pardon me ladies. . . ." He kissed each of the luscious beauties softly on the cheek, then slid away after the guest of honor.

"Jorge?"

A tall, perfectly tanned gentleman in his mid-fifties looked around. His dark, chiseled features; strong, masculine bearing; and bright, open eyes labeled him a Carioca.

"Ah, Mr. Crawley," Jorge Machado said, turning effortlessly from the man beside him and putting his arm casually around Thane's shoulders. "I'm so glad you could make it. I would offer you something, but I see that, as usual, I am too late." He looked at the drink in Thane's hand, then turned his eyes toward the two beauties by the bar. "Like a true international businessman, you have adjusted to my country's customs with relative ease."

"It was a great struggle, but I managed."

"Yes, yes, all of life is a struggle, is it not? A struggle we do our best to forget. And that is why we make movies and music, no?"

Thane smiled.

"You, of course, have helped to spread much beautiful music. While I—I make only what you call *schlock* movies. The low-budget trash thrillers for the masses. But they do entertain—and they do make money. So how can I complain? I leave that to the critics."

"Jorge, I wonder if we could discuss a little business. Apollo is interested in the sound tracks of some of your recent and upcoming movies. If you don't mind my asking, what are your commitments regarding the soundtrack rights to your future pictures?"

Jorge knit his brow. He looked at Thane with a mixture of confusion and wonder.

"Is something wrong? Have I broken some Brazilian rule by mixing business and pleasure?"

"No, no, not at all. Not at all. I would love to talk about

a new record-distribution deal for my soundtracks. It's just . . ."

"Yes?" Thane said, completely perplexed by Machado's behavior.

"I thought . . . Today in the paper . . . "

"Jorge, I'm very sorry, but I don't understand."

"Wait, please. Wait here one minute." Machado turned from Thane and moved swiftly into the luxurious house. He returned in less than a minute with a newspaper tucked under his arm and handed it silently to Thane.

Thane looked down at the paper. It was a copy of a three-day-old *Variety,* folded to a one-column story in the bottom right corner on page one. The headline read: SWISSTONE SHAKEUP. The story followed:

> Thane Crawley, president of Apollo Records, the American branch of the Swisstone Recording Company, was discharged today "for cause," it was announced by Hans van der Rogdt, CEO of Swisstone Worldwide. After an extensive internal investigation, Mr. Crawley was found guilty of diverting company assets for personal use.
>
> Mr. Crawley was unavailable for comment and has been mysteriously absent from Apollo for the past two weeks. It was unclear whether Mr. Crawley's disappearance had anything to do with the Swisstone investigation or the discovery of malfeasance. . . .

Thane's glass slipped from his hand and shattered on the terrazzo. The newspaper fell to the ground, amid the shards, and soaked up the fruity batita punch, the thin paper stock turning dark and sticky. Everyone on the terrace stopped and turned to look at Thane's pale, blood-drained face and the splash of drink on his white linen pant leg.

"Excuse me, Jorge," Thane stammered as he turned away in a daze. He walked over to his two Portuguese beauties, grabbed their arms roughly, and descended the steps of the triplex, the girls clutched tightly to his sides.

Back at the villa, the girls once again slipped into their revealing leather outfits, nipples and pubic hair exposed; laid out the whips, ties, and oils; and prepared for another evening of dominance and submission, Thane Crawley style.

For what the American was paying, they were willing to do practically anything to him—beat him, shove the leather whip handle up his ass, suck him dry, sit on his face and suffocate him—anything, as long as he didn't hurt *them*.

Tonight, though, Thane had a strange glint in his eye. When he tied them both to the bedposts, one on her back, one on her stomach, he told them it was a game he wanted to play with them, to see what life was like from the other side. The girls giggled nervously but went along with it. Unfortunately, the joke was on them.

Standing at the foot of the twin beds, his shirt off, his face and upper body bathed in sweat, Thane looked down at his handiwork and smiled with a dark, almost twisted, gleam. One of them, the dark-haired one, lay naked on her back, her hands twined together above her head, her legs spread-eagled and bound by the ankles to the bedposts. The other, the blonde with the flashing smile and blue eyes, was spread as wide as she would go on the other bed, naked and face down, her hands and feet bound with a selection of multicolored ties.

Like a vampire, Thane drank in the new sensations: the burning in his forearm muscle; the high-pitched, plaintive screams; the sight of deep, red welts raised on soft dark skin. Every time he brought the whip down on their helpless flesh, he felt a glow through his entire body. The sounds of their screams made him high. He'd never had *this* feeling before. Never. But van der Rogdt had changed everything. There were no more rules. He'd been double-crossed and stabbed in the back and he felt suddenly free of all constraints, free of the bonds of duty and morality. His body glowed with a strange feeling of release.

He'd been a fool. A simpleton. An easy mark. He'd stood by naïvely and let himself be disgraced. Let his whole career be ruined. There was no point in trying to fight it. He could issue statements and hurl counteraccusations until he was blue in the face, but it wouldn't undo the damage. No one would believe him. No one would trust him. No one would touch him with a ten-foot pole. He was no better than one of his burned-out clients.

He would never let it happen again. He would see to that. Suddenly, his whole perspective had changed. The idea of submission revolted him. From now on, *he* would dish out the agony, until he heard the whole world screaming around him. From now on, Thane Crawley would make the rules. He would take control and look out for himself, no matter what he had to do.

With the whip dangling in his hand, he raised his arm up above his head and brought it down with all his might. First he lashed the soft flesh of her thighs until tiny drops of blood crawled down toward the sheet. Then he turned around and stung the other beauty's rosy cheeks until she begged him to stop in her beautiful, lilting Portuguese.

But he didn't stop. He got hard, imagined he was beating the Dutchman, and kept on, over and over, harder and harder, until he was too exhausted to continue. The beds were soaked in blood. The two girls lay unconscious.

Finally, in a dark, mindless haze, he showered, dressed, and packed. After tossing a large handful of hundred-dollar bills into the bedroom, he quietly slipped out of Rio, just as the sun was rising over Ipanema Beach and the Cariocas were going to sleep.

* * *

Outside, where the streets were mired in slush, New York seemed anything but a winter wonderland. Inside the Seagram Building, however, in the exclusive but understated Grill Room of the Four Seasons, the winter decor was tastefully festive. The wonder within was not the bevy of beautiful poinsettia plants, or the magnificent forty-foot ceilings, or the solid rosewood walls, or the shimmering wires and gleaming golden rods suspended above the famous bar; instead, it was the coterie of business magnates lunching in the room and the power they exuded.

Just as Thane reached the top step of the wide entrance stairway, the maître d' approached him suavely and nodded. "Mr. Crawley. Your party awaits you on the mezzanine."

Thane felt a sense of exultation as he slowly but assuredly made his way toward the ultra chic upper level, ignoring the staring eyes and hushed, shocked whispers of New York's elite as he passed. Not only was he finally out in public, but his host had honored him with an early arrival, allowing him the opportunity to make an "entrance." It was his first taste of power in nearly two months and he couldn't describe how terribly he'd missed the sensation.

On the mezzanine, Thane surveyed the six widely spaced tables, then walked to table 42, which strategically overlooked the room. A waiter stood at attention, holding a chair out for him to be seated.

"Good to see you, Thane. Glad you could make it," David said.

Thane nodded politely as he took his seat. He had no idea what sort of "business" David Barry wanted to discuss. But considering his own current "untouchable" status in the entertainment industry, and his ever-growing mountain of debts, there had seemed little reason to decline the generous invitation—especially when Barry was sticking his neck out and bucking the establishment by meeting him so publicly. Most of his other business acquaintances and so-called friends had been noticeably unavailable in recent weeks.

They ordered a round of drinks and David wasted no time in getting down to business.

"I wanted to let you know, personally, that I think you got shafted, Thane, and that I'm on your side."

"Thank you. You're in the minority."

"Maybe I know things the others don't. Things even you may not know."

"Such as?"

"Such as that Hans van der Rogdt has taken over the reins of Swisstone himself. And that he's moved to America, 'reluctantly' and 'at great personal sacrifice,' because he's such a good company man."

"Why should that interest me? I've heard it already."

"I just thought you might find it curious, particularly since Hans purchased a house in Greenwich, Connecticut, almost six months ago."

"What!" Thane set his drink down on the table.

"Umm-hmm. Your Mr. van der Rogdt has had a green card for some time. You were set up, Thane, even worse than you imagined. Your Dutch friend wanted a piece of your sweet American action. He was the one who panicked the board and started the investigation. It was van der Rogdt who persuaded the shareholders to go public, in order to neutralize you, to make you a leper, to make sure you didn't raid the company or move to a competitor—to make you unhirable."

Thane let his hands drop into his lap. His mind boggled. Even though he'd run through the permutations and combinations of his ouster a million times—where he'd gone wrong, what he might have done differently—he'd never conceived quite *that* sinister a scenario. The Dutchman had used him even worse than he'd suspected, if that was possible. He'd never forget the living hell of the past two months. Never.

"Where did you get this information?"

"I can't tell you," David said, thinking of Jack Black. "But you can check it out yourself. It's all true."

"Why are you telling me all this?"

"I have a selfish reason. The Silverfish won't be re-signing with Apollo. L.O.L. has decided to open its own American record company and I'll be overseeing the entire operation. I'm responsible for setting it up."

"Really? How interesting." Obviously, Barry wasn't wasting any time now that Brandon Levy was gone. But what did that have to do with him? "Well, I assume congratulations are in order?"

"Not quite yet."

"No?"

"No. First I have to find someone to run the record company. Someone who's a top-notch record executive. Someone who could handle all the Silverfish business. Someone with a platinum ear and a proven track record, great style, panache, and street savvy."

"I didn't know Clive was available," Thane said dryly.

"I've got someone else in mind. Someone who I know to be available, right now."

"I do believe you're offering me a job, Mr. Barry. Are you in the habit of hiring criminals to work for you? I warn you, I have a larcenous streak."

David's subtle smile did not reveal that he wasn't at all sure he liked Thane Crawley _or_ his dry sense of humor. In fact, he was pretty sure he didn't. But if he wanted L.O.L. to succeed, he had to put personal preferences aside and look to the bigger picture.

"Don't be facetious. You're no more a criminal than any of the good record executives out there, and I know it. Believe me, I have no interest in being charitable. I'm simply being pragmatic. I want L.O.L. to become the biggest and the best entertainment company in America. When it comes to recorded music, you're simply the best man for the job. With our resources, your know-how, and starting with the new Silverfish album, we can build a great record empire. Remember, I have another client, Dwight Sharon, whose contract expires at the end of this year. What do you say?"

Thane sat silently, thinking. He should have felt grateful. After all, Barry was offering him his dream: a chance to get back. Instead, a feeling of resentment welled up inside him, a feeling so strong that he had trouble containing it. To have fallen so low that he needed a job and a handout from another fucking one of them. His parents had the Frehmanns, now he had David Barry, in a position to salvage his lost career and do him a favor that he needed desperately. The shylocks! Thane knew just how his father must have felt. Especially since he, too, was about to be crushed by his ever-growing debts. Of course, he was in a lot deeper than his father had ever been. The underworld "boys" he borrowed money from wouldn't hesitate to tear him limb from limb.

He looked David in the eye. "There's a slight question of money. As you and everyone else in New York are so intimately aware, I am accustomed to a rather extravagant life-style—and I must have the tools with which to function properly."

David knew what that meant: access to unlimited money for payoffs—whether in cash, drugs, or hookers; fancy cars, chartered jets, and the other elaborate, dazzling trappings of power and success. He had seen them all. "Money's no problem. I'm prepared to better your Swisstone deal, all perks included."

"Even the illegal ones?"

"We'll write them into the contract even if they cost L.O.L. more, to ensure that it's all legal and above board."

"I'll need a special environment. Very expensive, but, in the long run, a good investment for the company."

"That's no problem. You want a fancy office, fine. I'll give you an open account."

With the Silverfish base, the possibility of signing Dwight Sharon almost immediately, and L.O.L.'s massive resources, Thane was confident he could do for L.O.L. what he had done for Swisstone and do it faster and better. He would also look out for himself better. Not only would he bring himself back from the dead, he'd rub the Dutchman's nose in his own shit. Stealing away two of Swisstone's main clients would be sweet revenge indeed. How could he refuse?

"When do I start?"

1973

*B*ATTLEY WAS LIKE ALL THE REST, EXCEPT BIGGER,
noisier, smellier.

Nearly fifteen hundred this time, mostly miners and factory
workers, sloshing down fish and chips with warm, dark mugs of
Guinness, and joining Rick Firestone in verse after rousing verse
of "Roll Out the Barrel."

After he'd warmed their cold, January bones, Rick slid into
the newly arranged medley of his old hits. Even if they'd known
the old songs—which only a few did—they'd never have recognized them. He'd revamped and reworked them, turned the
shoobie-doos into ooh-waahs, the old finger-snappers into ballads. The material sounded fresh and catchy, and Battley responded warmly to the mellow sound of the chunky American.
He was as good as Val Doonican!

As he stepped away from the piano at the end of his fifth and
final set, the applause was hearty and sprinkled with shouts of
"Good show, laddie!" Embarrassed, Rick smiled sheepishly and

raised his hand to acknowledge the accolades. As usual, the audience's enthusiasm made it almost worthwhile. Almost.

These days, the performance high lasted only a matter of moments. Heading through the crowd, Rick could already feel the brief spark, like his soul, passing out of him and the shadow of darkness taking its place. Joyce had returned to the States. Hedy had flown off to her new house in Laurel Canyon. David was too busy for socializing. Rose had stopped writing. Rick was more alone now than he'd been in years. It didn't matter that he was playing bigger clubs, or that he was once again writing music. None of it was leading anywhere.

At times he wanted to stay in bed and hide under the covers. He wanted to give up, but just didn't know how.

The memory of that night on the desert with Hedy haunted him. He awakened in the cold English mornings to the imagined smell of the cool, dry sand and the sweet taste of Hedy's warm flesh. When the filming was completed, he felt the reality of Hedy's absence and cried himself to sleep like a baby, knowing he'd lost a chance he should have taken. Over and over he told himself that she couldn't love him, that she was too wrapped up in herself. But the doubt still lingered, and the sharp pang of the loss felt even deeper than the first cut, from so long ago in Brighton Beach.

With his jacket slung over his sweaty shoulder, Rick pushed his way out into the cold, damp night. The sounds of distant voices from the noisy bar carried across the moonless sky and over the dark moors. He wasn't looking forward to another lonely three-hour drive through the mist in his Mini-Morris, back to a London flat that was as cold and empty as his life.

Headlight beams cut across the dark parking lot and blinded him. Holding his hand up, Rick tried to shield his eyes from the bright glare, but the beams from the slowly moving car followed him as he walked. His knee bumped sharply against one of the parked cars and, exasperated, he called out, "Hey, knock off the light!"

The headlights snapped off. When Rick's eyes finally adjusted to the darkness, he made out the outline of a chauffeur-driven Daimler. The rear door opened and a tall, thin figure stepped out and moved hesitantly toward him.

"Excuse me . . . Mr. Firestone?"

"Yes?"

"Sorry 'bout the light. I didn't want you to get away. You're a mighty hard man to find."

"I am?"

"Yes, indeed. I loved your show."

"Well," Rick said, shrugging at the shadowy figure with the melodic singsong Welsh accent and long furry coat, "thanks. It wasn't anything, really. Were you"—he pointed toward the pub—"inside?"

"No, no. I just sat in my car with the window open. I didn't want to distract the audience. Lord knows what they would have done."

A strange, gawky figure, a Welsh lilt, a limousine parked in front of a workingman's pub near Manchester, out here in never-never land. Another car pulled out of the lot, and its lights cut across the man's face. Rick caught sight of the frizzy red hair, the single dangling earring, the terribly pocked, homely face punctuated by a large nose and crooked teeth. "Dwight Sharon!" he gasped.

"Afraid so. I hope you don't mind."

"Mind! My God, you're the greatest. I love your music. What . . . what are you doing here?"

"I live not far away. I came especially to see you."

"Me?"

"If you wouldn't mind, I'd like you to come back to my house, for some tea. It would be a great pleasure."

"Sure. I . . . I'd love to," Rick stammered.

"Why don't you just leave your car. I'll send someone for it later. Come on," Dwight said, touching his hand to Rick's shoulder and directing him into the back of the limousine.

"Please, make yourself at home," Dwight said, leading Rick into a comfortable drawing room with several cushioned chairs, an old gray couch, and a huge Bosendorfer piano, all settled around an orange-flamed fireplace. He removed his fur coat and tossed it casually onto a chair, revealing a flowered shirt and baggy pink trousers.

Rick walked around the perimeter of the drawing room, running his fingers along the mantel and admiring the interior of the sprawling seventeenth-century country mansion. He felt like he was back in Rina Constance's living room, when he was too young and afraid to touch anything. "This place is really beautiful," he said, with a touch of wonder.

"Go on, take a seat. Make yourself comfy. I'll just pour us some tea."

Rick sat, and sank so far into the fluffy couch that his feet barely reached the floor. Looking across the coffee table at his seated host, he had trouble reconciling the frazzled hair, awkward features, and effeminate outfit with the elegant, tasteful, understated decor around him. He didn't have any idea what he was doing there, in the home of a superstar like Dwight Sharon. But the room was cozy, and Dwight so friendly that Rick pushed the doubts and fears from his mind.

"Do you live here alone?" Rick asked innocently, thinking about the huge house.

Dwight stopped the ritual tea pouring and shut his eyes tightly. For a second he thought he might drop the teapot. But he recovered quickly. "Yes. Very much so. All alone. I travel a lot, so I'm not home much."

"Yeah. I know what it's like," Rick said sadly, noticing the wrinkles of pain around Dwight's made-up eyes.

"Do you?"

Rick shook his head and chuckled. "Yeah. I know what it's like from the top and from the bottom. I'm an expert. What could be lonelier than playing a dive like Battley?"

"You really were good, you know. I especially liked the 'Bye-Bye, Blackbird' arrangement and the way you segued into 'Tipperary.'"

"Don't make fun of me, please. I know how bad it is."

"I wouldn't make fun of you. You're an entertainer and you showed the audience a good time. That's what counts. You were an inspiration to them just like you been to me for all these years."

"Me? Come on, Dwight," Rick said, using the star's first name as he'd been asked to.

"You don't think so?" Leaving his tea, Dwight walked over to the piano and started playing. He proved his fealty by running through a quick medley of Rick Firestone's hits, then moving effortlessly into some of Rick's more obscure songs from early albums that only a Firestone aficionado would know.

"See, I used these chord changes as the basis for my first hit, 'I'm a Sad, Lonely Man.' I have every one of your records. It's why I've been looking all over for you."

"I don't know what to say. I'm really flattered. But I . . . I don't understand."

How could he explain it to Rick when he could barely explain it to himself? He'd been a fan for years and had been inspired by Rick's music. But somehow inspiration had turned into obsession. After five double-platinum albums, three sold-out world tours, and countless wild concerts, Dwight was at a crossroads. Despite his unbelievable string of successes and the pandemoniac reaction of his fans, he felt even more repulsive, even more unloved and unlovable, than he had as a child. Just like at the circus, no one could take their eyes off the freak, but no one ever loved the sad, lonely man locked within, the man yearning to break free.

His star was burning ever so brightly, but his heart seemed drained and empty. With his five-year Apollo contract having just expired, Dwight had set out on a quest to find Rick Firestone, as if Rick possessed some mystical Holy Grail that Dwight needed to touch for regeneration. And now he'd found him, thanks to David Barry's information. It was fate, the way David's call had come at just the right moment.

"Will you join me?" Dwight asked, moving to one side on the piano bench.

"Sure," Rick answered enthusiastically. He put down his sweet tea and took his seat beside Dwight.

Tentatively at first, then more and more passionately, they played four-handed piano. They alternated between Rick's songs and Dwight's classics, toying with the rhythms and the tempos, one playing counterpoint to the other. A blues, a ballad, a driving rocker—they inspired each other to interpret and invent each song anew.

At Dwight's prodding and over Rick's shy objections, they tried singing together, quickly blending into an easy harmony. When they decided to try "How Can I Go On Without You?" Dwight told Rick about singing the song in Aberystwyth, after his mom had died, and how it had helped him resolve to come to the States. And Rick told about writing the song. How it was for Hedy and how he sang it at his Gypsy Grandma's funeral. In no time, both men had become tearful.

Provided with food and wine to sustain their musical revel, they laughed and played music with an abandon that caught them both by surprise. Their fingers side by side on the keys, they shared the notes of their craft and revealed themselves to each other intimately through their music. Not since Hedy had Rick felt such a musically kindred spirit.

They played through the night, lovingly reviewing and revising the history of pop music, demonstrating to each other their comprehension of what others had done before them and its significance and influence on them. When the first rays of the sun began to beam through the beveled, leaded-glass windows, refracting into millions of tiny rainbows, Dwight put his tired arm around Rick's shoulders and stood up from the piano. The closeness of Rick filled his nostrils and practically made him swoon, but Dwight closed his eyes, took a deep breath, and kept his feelings to himself.

"Rick, would you play something for me?"

"Anything you'd like. How about something from the top of the 1973 charts? Like 'Long-Haired Lover from Liverpool'? Or something from Elton's new album?"

"I was thinkin' of your new material. The stuff you've been writing," Dwight said, remembering David's comment about Rick's new songs.

The smile drained from Rick's face. The new songs were so personal—songs he'd written for no one but himself this time—that he hadn't even imagined playing them for anyone else. They were songs about his pain, about his Hedy, about his audience who once loved him and now had left him. He wanted to say no, to tell Dwight that the songs were just rough sketches, that he couldn't do it, but something stopped him. Maybe it was the hurt he could sense in Dwight's eyes as he waited for an answer, or the feeling that he owed something to Dwight Sharon for tonight, or the realization that a refusal was simply an act of cowardice. Whatever it was, he turned to Dwight, pursed his lips, and shrugged like a shy little boy.

"Here goes nothing," he whispered.

Dwight sat back on the couch, an audience of one.

One after another, Rick played the new songs, including "Let Me Back into Your Life," "Tears Keep a' Rolling," "Look, I'm Still Here," "Did You Ever Really Love Me?" and "Please Tell Me What I Did." They were songs dredged up from his soul and his guts, written the way Grandma Becky had urged. Everything he'd learned at Juilliard, everything he'd learned from working and crying and suffering and hating, was in his new music. This time there were no little angels or teen queens or shabooms, only haunting, devastatingly beautiful songs about pain and loneliness, love and betrayal, fortune and hope—the group of songs the historians referred to as the "second collection."

They were love songs to Rick's public. Songs about his betrayal by the fans, how their love for him had ceased, about how he wanted to get back into their lives, asking them if they really had loved him the first time around. He asked, musically, what had he done wrong?

The final song—"Can I Make You Love Me One More Time?"—was unfinished and Rick had to stop in the middle of a verse, dangling a musical phrase.

"I don't know where to go with this one. It just doesn't sound right to me," he said, turning away from the piano toward Dwight for the first time.

To his surprise, the Welshman was sobbing. Somehow the pain and the hurt of Rick's songs had touched a chord in the ugly-duckling superstar.

Rick quickly stood up and came over beside Dwight on the couch. Despite the contrast in their careers, his heart went out to Dwight Sharon.

"The songs are wondrous, Rick. More beautiful than you know."

Rick hung his head in embarrassment.

"Thank you," Dwight whispered, the tears sliding down his face like notes on a descending scale. "Thank you for opening up to me. That's the most intimate thing anyone's ever done with me. I'll never forget it."

After all the years of searching, he'd finally found his Holy Grail. But deep down, Dwight knew just how unattainable it really was.

It was nearly evening when Rick finally awakened. Rising out of the luxurious four-poster bed in an upstairs guest room, he stretched his tired arms, warmed himself before the hot coals in the baronial fireplace, and stared out the window. The muted orange ball of the sun was sinking quickly into the hazy green horizon and filling the cloudy sky with streaks of color. He felt exhilarated by the sight, and by the memory of the previous, magical evening and the validation afforded by Dwight's appreciation of his new music.

Showered, dressed, and invigorated, he headed down the winding staircase in search of his host. After wandering vainly from room to room until he was practically lost, he finally heard the distant echo of a piano. From the top of the basement stairs, he recognized the tune: It was his song, "Can I Make You Love Me One More Time?"

He followed the sound until he found an incredibly elaborate mini–recording studio, filled with soundboards and sophisticated recording equipment, tucked away in the basement of the English country house. Rick was awestruck.

At his approach, Dwight turned from the piano and waved. "Rick. Come on in. I'm afraid you caught me. I was takin' a crack at finishin' your song. I hope you're not mad."

"Mad? Don't be silly. I could use some help with that one."

"Well, what are you waiting for? Sit down and help us out, will you."

In a matter of minutes, they were immersed in the song, going through it note by note and word by word.

"How about this phrase?" Dwight suggested, playing a soft melody in a minor chord.

"Or this," Rick offered, adding to and elaborating on Dwight's idea.

"That's it! Move from this chord to this one, and then . . . " Dwight played another section.

"I like that. Yeah. And modulate up."

Their ears were in such sync and their chemistry was so right that they played off each other, laughing, disagreeing, compromising, creating. Their only substantive disagreement came over the last three words of the song: whether they should be "one last time" or "one more time."

Putting that dispute aside for the moment, Dwight cranked up the studio equipment and starting laying down tracks. Between the two of them, they played piano, drums, guitar, and synthesizer, until they had the sound they wanted, the sound of a fully produced master recording.

Rick was in seventh heaven, and Dwight was savoring each moment as if it were his last.

After a 4:00 A.M. kippers break, they moved on to recording the vocals. Rick ran through it once himself but wasn't satisfied. "It just doesn't sound right, Dwight. I need you to sing it with me. You wouldn't want to make it a duet, would you?"

They started out singing harmony like the Everly Brothers, with Dwight carrying the high notes. Then, with practice and experimentation, they moved into tighter harmonies, varying pitch and tone until they were in perfect unison. Then they overdubbed time and again, filling out the mix so they sounded like six beautifully precise voices—like Les Paul and Mary Ford. On the final overdub, Dwight insisted on singing "one last time" in falsetto, as Rick harmonized "one more time" one octave and one third below. The song ended with a fade of those three words, in both versions, repeated over and over again.

When they played back the tape, Rick and Dwight sat side by side on the floor, listening, exhausted and exhilarated. When it ended, there was silence.

"Did *we* do that?" Rick asked, amazed at the completeness, precision, and beauty of their creation.

"I can't believe it either," Dwight whispered. Tentatively, he rested his head on Rick's shoulder. He cherished the moment and the closeness, but knew it wouldn't last. Rather than risk rejection, he immediately lifted his head again.

"You know what we have here, don't you?"

"What do you mean?"

"Rick, my boy, this isn't just a song or a record. It's a hit record. And first thing tomorrow morning, I'm going to take it to London, to our friend David Barry and to Mr. Thane Crawley, the new boss of L.O.L. Records. They're both in town this week and, I tell you, they're going to flip. I guarantee it."

"Thane Crawley! But he's the one that dropped me—"

"Rick, please. I want to do this. For you. More than anything in the world."

Rick pursed his lips, then burst into a smile. "Okay. If you really want to." He reached out awkwardly and put his arms around his tall, skinny friend. "You're really something, Dwight. Thank you."

In an office reserved for visitors, Thane sat across the oak desk from David, sipping tea and looking his usual smug self. David hadn't wanted to make this trip to London, but he'd felt it necessary, to introduce Thane to the board and allay Crawley's fears about his pulling a "van der Rogdt." He also wanted to talk to the long-delinquent Dwight Sharon.

As threatened, the haughty Crawley had created an office back in New York that made Brandon's look like a vestibule. David would have to do some fast talking to the board to explain the cool million Thane had already spent decorating his New York "environment." He'd rejected the company's plans for his suite on the twentieth floor of the newest building on Fifty-sixth and Sixth Avenue, insisting on his own scheme. When it was finished, it was clearly the standard by which all future executives would measure their deals, their goals, their ultimate perk.

Just stepping off the elevator into L.O.L.'s New York headquarters, even before entering the office, visitors knew they were in for something special. The reception area had stenciled and softly patinaed hardwood parquet floors accented with strategically placed, rare Persian carpets. Everything was brass and leather and rich woods. There was Chippendale and Hepplewhite furniture, export china, ecru rubbed walls of eighteenth-century *boiserie* stripped from homes in England and rebuilt in New York City. All very English, very traditional, very Gentleman's Club, with no rock-and-roll posters or *Billboard* magazines. In the background, one heard Bach fugues playing quietly and saw original oil paintings of hunts and nineteenth-century racehorses elegantly illuminated by muted lights that created a hushed atmosphere. Subtle and intimidating.

The intimidation lost its subtlety and became memorable, if not overwhelming, once one entered through the massive double wooden doors into Thane's office. One-upmanship and self-indulgence were redefined by Thane Crawley.

His principal office was forty foot square with a twenty-foot ceiling. He'd re-created a grand English country house setting with carved architectural panels and a spiral staircase leading up to library walks and library ladders on polished brass railings. Hundreds of exquisite, leather-bound rare editions towered over the visitor, who, of course never realized that the books were not real but *trompe l'oeil;* Thane could push open a panel in the "library" and escape to the twenty-first floor for a rest, use of his private bath, shower, and dressing room, or as an exit *privé.*

Most of the furnishings had been purchased at auction from the sale of the Rothschild home, Mentmore. In 1878, the fifth earl of Rosebery had married Hannah, the orphan daughter of Baron Nathan Rothschild. Her grandfather had founded the London branch of the famous banking house and she was the richest heiress in England. Among other things, she inherited Mentmore, a house that Rothschild had built and furnished when he was the wealthiest man in the world. Since he'd been interested in magnificence rather than beauty or convenience, it was furnished in the most dazzling, intimidating, and memorable fashion.

Treasures for the dauphin (son of Louis XV), the writing desk of Marie Antoinette, marquetry from Holland and Brussels,

Etruscan artifacts and Sèvres porcelain, Savonnerie carpets, Gobelin tapestries . . . Nothing was too good for the richest man in the world—or for Thane Crawley. That a WASP anti-Semite now owned some of the great Jewish family's possessions was an irony hardly lost on Thane. What mattered to him, though, was that he create a suite of offices so opulent and grand that they would become known throughout the industry as Crawley's Palace.

David hadn't complained about the extravagant expenditure. In fact, he was actually pleased that he had chosen such a Byzantine, scheming, power-hungry man to head the L.O.L. record division. He especially liked Thane's rationale for the office.

"The music industry, David, is made up of poor people who've made good. People desperate to be accepted, people easily impressed by old money and class. They're paranoid and afraid of being cheated by fly-by-night operations.

"My office will make them feel secure. Like the Bank of England, it will look as if it's been here for a long time and will remain just so for many generations. It's a prop, pure and simple, but in the long run it will make back much more than the million it cost to build.

"The lawyers, the agents, the managers, the artists, they'll all be thrilled to toast their deals with champagne there. They'll consider it a privilege to have their photographs taken there when they sign their contracts. Ultimately, the office will help us close deals and make deals cheaper. Because it looks so respectable, the auditors and accountants will think twice before they dare to file a claim or question a royalty statement. The walls shout out in high dudgeon, 'How dare you question our honor!' "

David was pondering Thane's Machiavellian rationale when he was interrupted by the buzz of the intercom.

"Yes?"

"Dwight Sharon to see you, sir. He doesn't have an appointment—"

"Send him in. Send him in immediately."

When Dwight entered, David stood up and went to greet him. "Dwight, so good to see you." He warmly grasped the skinny artist's gloved hand.

"Good day, David. Thane." He nodded to them both as he removed his long fur coat and white leather gloves and dropped them onto the corner love seat. His face had a calm, almost resolute expression, in contrast to his usual hyperanimation.

"We've been trying to get in touch with you for weeks, Dwight. Is everything all right? I was beginning to worry."

"Yes. Yes. Everything's fine. Your ex-friend Mr. van der Rogdt, he's been tryin' to reach me as well."

"No surprise there. Apollo's dying to re-sign you. That's why I'm so glad you called. We really *must* talk about a new contract."

"That's not why *I* called, however. I have something else for you. Do you have a reel-to-reel machine?"

"Of course. Have you recorded something?" David asked eagerly. It was just what he was hoping for.

"Sort of. Play this now, will you?"

David took the tape from Dwight's hand and threaded it through the empty reel. He looked around at the two men and pressed the "start" button.

Suddenly, the whole room was filled with the chilling strains and solid melody of the harmonious duet. For the next three minutes, David and Thane sat mesmerized until the song faded out on the repeating three-word chant.

"Is that you and Rick?" David asked in disbelief.

"Umm-hmm."

"Did *you* write it?"

"We finished it together, but it's mostly his song."

"Well, Thane, what do you think?"

"I think it's absolutely fabulous," Thane said. "Incredible. The best new sound I've heard in years. With melody back in the music scene and the kids buying soft rock again, this is a surefire hit. It doesn't even need to be remixed."

Thane knew platinum when he heard it. Not only could this song launch L.O.L. and make the label instantly hot, but, overnight, it could reestablish his own career and his own credibility. It was such a sure thing, he might even be able to swing a deal with the "boys," exchanging a share of record sales for a reduction in his debt. "You'll do a whole album together, of course."

"No. Absolutely not. Just this single," Dwight said firmly. "But make it the lead cut for a new album of Rick's. He's easily got an album's worth of material, all of it just as good as this. I suggest you sign him right away."

David couldn't believe it. Rick was finally going to be rejuvenated, and David himself could be instrumental in overseeing his friend's career and in reawakening an entire new generation and audience to the Firestone magic. He would put the full resources of L.O.L. behind this one. With the duet—a virtual sceptered blessing by the reigning king of rock-and-roll—Rick was bound for a new life. And L.O.L America, David's L.O.L. America, was bound for glory, without relying exclusively on the Silverfish.

"But what about you, Dwight? What about your next record, and a new contract?"

"Not now, David. Right now I only care about Rick Firestone. I'll do everything I can for him, and I want you to do the same. There's been time enough for Dwight Sharon."

After the sweet showers of early spring had cleared and a rainbow arced across the sky, Dwight emerged from his country house into the sunlight. Glass and bottle in hand, dressed in a white linen suit and panama hat, with whitish makeup and rouged cheeks, he walked into the pristine garden. Yellow crocuses were poking their heads up from the earth and the forsythia was already in bloom. He spread a white cashmere blanket on the lawn, sat down, and sipped at the dry champagne.

He hadn't planned on Rick Firestone. He hadn't planned on finding something and someone to live for, after all this time. Even in his quest, he'd never dreamed of really finding someone to love. But he had. All the feelings he could identify—passion, need, selfless caring, an aching lust—they all pointed to love.

In the three months since they'd met, he'd done everything he could for Rick. He'd recorded promo tapes, done publicity photos, given interviews. He'd told *Rolling Stone* that Rick was "the chronicler of the hearts of our generation." Now 300,000 records were pressed, en route to stores and radio stations throughout America. Nothing could stop the momentum or interrupt his legacy.

Despite the pain, there was a measure of happiness. It didn't matter that he was fated to carry out his original plan. At least now he had the memory and the sensation of love to savor. In his heart, he knew that his one and only love was doomed to remain forever unrequited. Rick would never know, which was as it should be. For he could never understand.

Dwight had had it all in five years. Fame, money, adulation. Everything except love and happiness. Even before Rick, he'd known there was nowhere to go, no more to give, and little more to say. He would always be a freak. And with no one to share the inevitable fall, he refused to watch his own steady decline and seedy aging, to watch himself fade into oblivion, to see himself slowly self-destruct in the public eye until there was nothing left but the shell of his former self, an oldie-but-goody. The utter loneliness was more than enough; there was no need to add the pain and humiliation of a fickle public. Rick's songs had clearly and incisively told him *that* degrading, painful story.

Downing another glass of champagne, he pulled the small vial from his pocket, flipped the top, and scattered the capsules before him on the blanket. His plan was proving to be even more perfect than he'd hoped. Having brought Rick Firestone back from the dead, not only would he bow out gracefully and theatrically, just as he'd lived, but his very death would ensure the success of Rick's album and guarantee Rick's resurrection.

He grasped the first sleeping capsule between his thumb and forefinger and, without hesitation, washed it down with a swig of champagne. One after another, he placed them in his mouth, until the pile of capsules grew smaller and smaller. In the distance, he could hear their duet playing yet again, piped up from his basement studio. The song mingled with the sounds of chirping birds.

As he lay his head down on the soft blanket, he felt himself sinking into an invisible mist and heard his own voice blending over Rick's. He watched a purple butterfly glide above his head and, with a deep sigh of relief, felt the famous sad and lonely man finally breaking free. His eyes closed. He fell into a dreamless sleep. He found the peace and the love he had always been searching for.

The blinds in David's office were pulled shut, despite the unusually sunny afternoon. Across from David, Rick sat on the stiff love seat, his head bowed, his eyes red and swollen. For the two old friends, the shock of yesterday's news was beyond expression. In contrast, Thane sat on the far couch, absentmindedly filing his manicured nails.

Rick was struck worst, at the very moment of triumph. His thoughts were a jumble of pain and confusion.

"It's my fault, I know it is. I don't understand how, but I feel responsible," he said, his voice cracking with frustration and grief.

"Come on, don't be silly. There was nothing you or anyone

could have done. He'd been planning it all along." That didn't make it easier for David, though. He wasn't sure he could bear yet another rock-and-roll casualty.

"But working on the duet, he seemed so happy. If only I'd known him better, if only I could have seen it coming . . . "

"Stop berating yourself. Dwight was deeply troubled. You know as well as I that this was no spur-of-the-moment decision. He'd never planned on signing a new contract. The suicide note makes it all clear. Do you want to read it?"

"I don't know if I can. Would you read it to me, David?"

"All right." He unfolded the letter and looked down once again at the fine script. It was addressed to David Barry, Esq. He cleared his throat and began to read:

Dear David,
    By the time you read this, I will be free at last of this life of pain and misery. Grieve not. It was a willing choice, the only civilized finale for a performer.
    I have made music, and my final notes were sung with Rick. That song and all the rights to that song are part of my legacy to him.
    I ask you, David, as the executor of my estate, to protect the sanctity of my death. I want no circus, like the ones that surrounded the deaths of Jimi and Janis. My life was enough of a freak show. Therefore, I ask—rather, I demand—that my body be cremated privately, without funeral or fanfare. And I bequeath to Rick Firestone the rights to the masters of all my recordings. I rest in peace knowing that he will be my custodian, that he will protect me and honor my memory, guarding me from the crass, commercial exploitation of the industry.
    With no one to whom I can honestly leave my estate, I ask that you give my entire fortune to UNICEF, so that the poor children of the world may be a little richer as a result of my having lived and died. Maybe then I can make someone love me, one last time.
                          Dwight Sharon

Rick buried his face in his hands. He kept flashing back to those two magical evenings in Manchester, when their souls had touched. "My God. It's unbelievable. Can he really do that? Can he leave me his masters like that?"

David nodded. "I didn't think anything of it when he asked me about the masters a while back. It's true, though. On the expiration of his contract with Apollo, all rights reverted to him. He owns the masters and can do with them as he pleases."

"What should *I* do with them?" Rick asked solemnly, looking David in the eye.

Thane looked up.

"I can't tell you that, Rick," David replied. "You have to make that decision yourself."

"Well, I know what Dwight didn't want. He didn't want a whole series of memorial albums and compilation albums. He didn't want anyone exploiting his death. I feel responsible for his memory. He told me to protect him and that's just what I'm going to do. I'm going to lock those masters away in a vault and forget them. I have no choice," Rick said resolutely.

"That's a brave decision, Rick, and I think you're doing the right thing. I think it's what Dwight would have wanted."

Thane couldn't believe his ears. The masters were gold, they were worth millions, and that asshole Firestone was going to stick them away in a vault! With David Barry's approval! Thane kept his mouth shut but resolved to get his hands on those masters, one way or another, when the time was right.

"You don't mind if I make a business call, do you?" David walked over to his desk and picked up the phone. He smiled mysteriously toward Thane. "Get me Hans van der Rogdt at Apollo Records in New York. I'm returning his call."

Both Rick and Thane looked perplexed until, a minute later, the phone rang.

"Hans. Good to hear your voice. . . . Yes, yes, very sad indeed. A tremendous loss. . . . Umm-hmmm. . . . Well, I'm afraid you've got a problem there. The contract is crystal clear. Apollo's rights lapsed after the delivery of Dwight's fifth album. You're not entitled to any new product. . . . That's right.

"In addition, all Apollo distribution rights terminated upon Dwight's death and all the masters of his records revert to his estate. . . . I'm afraid so, Hans. Not only can't you do a remix or a 'best of' anthology or a compilation album, you can't even rerelease the five albums you produced. . . .

"Of course. Of course. Check with your legal department. But it's in black and white. I'm very sorry. . . . Sure. Anytime."

David hung up the phone. "No doubt that conversation makes you very happy, Thane."

Thane bowed his head in appreciation.

Thinking about the masters, Rick suddenly had an inkling of what Dwight had been trying to do. Since his own life was so unfulfilled, he'd resolved to make Thane happy, to make David happy, to make Rick happy. Unfortunately, Dwight had underestimated the love of his friends and his fans. Already, the worldwide outpouring of grief was thunderous. Surely it was only a matter of days before the duet reached the top of the charts, propelled by morbid, grief-stricken fans all over the world, who got chills hearing Dwight's perfect falsetto announce prophetically, "One last time, one last time, one last time."

Now when Rick heard the song, chills of sorrow ran down his own spine as well, as he remembered Dwight insisting on those final three words. If only there'd been someone for Dwight, someone who could have said "I love you," maybe he wouldn't have felt compelled to sing "one last time."

No matter how hard he tried, Rick couldn't savor his moment of triumph. He had a new recording contract, a new life, a new career. It was happening for him "one more time." But for Dwight, it would never, ever happen again.

1973

22

"**G**ENTLEMEN, WE'RE NOT MAKING ANY PROGRESS. WHY don't we break, and reconvene in a half-hour?"

David didn't wait for the indecisive board members to second his suggestion. Instead, he simply stood up, stretched his legs, and walked out of the grand room that everyone still thought of as Brandon's office. By standing and taking the initiative, he was sending out just the kind of signal he wanted to send. He was acting in control. Of course it was all for effect. It always was now.

The board meeting was proving even more interesting than he'd expected. Faced with what he'd always known would be the fiasco of the *Immaculate Conception* movie, the group was suddenly skittish about L.O.L.'s future and more than a little disgruntled with Kevin's performance. Little wonder. In the fourteen months since Brandon's death, Kevin had redecorated the offices, ordered new stationery, changed the logo, taken three holidays, and spent more than 125,000 pounds on travel and entertainment. He'd played it so close to the vest that he'd accomplished nothing of significance: no new film deals, no new albums, no tours, no policy changes. L.O.L. profits were considerably diminished and there was little reason to expect future improvement. The company was merely subsisting on catalog sales and passive residual income, and the board knew it.

David, however, remained untainted. During the same period, L.O.L. America had been off and running. Between Rick Firestone's blockbuster album and the American release of the *Immaculate Conception* sound track (which sold well despite the box-office failure of the movie), the U.S. company, astonishingly, was already in the black. And David's controversial hiring and support of Thane Crawley had paid off. Like a man possessed, Thane had worked relentlessly—harder and more vigorously than any of his competitors.

Dwight had been right, of course. His dramatic death had put a bullet next to "Can I Make You Love Me One More Time?" It shot quickly to the top of the charts for ten consecutive weeks, revitalizing Rick Firestone's career. From there, Rick had taken over on his own.

The American record company had revitalized David as well. The one thing he'd always feared had actually come to pass: He'd let his law practice slide so far that his colleagues had picked up the slack and made him dispensable. But, strangely, he didn't care. For the first time, he was tasting the fruits of victory in the competitive trenches, and he was finding the taste to his liking.

Even though Dwight was gone, Brandon was gone, and Hedy in seclusion, the presence of Rick and Joyce around him again, just like in the old days, gave David a new feeling of security.

The pain of Hedy's fall still weighed heavily, though. The movie had hurt everyone involved, including the director and the Silverfish. But no one as deeply as Hedy. Just as she'd feared, the critics had laced into her, lambasting her performance and turning her into the laughingstock of Hollywood. When she'd lashed back at them with her salty, virulent tongue, the industry had turned nasty.

Is *Immaculate Conception* faithful to the album of the same name by the group who named themselves after vermin? Well, it's no more faithful to the original than a hooker is to her pimp! Speaking of hookers, the star, Miss

Hedy Harlowe, performing as Mary Immaculate, is the tramp of camp and finally has found a role that stretches her minimal talents beyond all elasticity, just like her eyelids! Well, friends, this aging prima donna has bored us long enough with her smart-ass but obviously well-rehearsed off-the-cuff remarks, which she tries to pass off as extemporaneous epicene bitchiness. . . . How droll this troll is, trying to make us believe that these *bons mots* just pop into her head like all those poppers do in her rather inflamed nostrils. . . .

After a rash of reviews like that and with nowhere left to turn, Hedy had locked herself away in Laurel Canyon, refusing to talk to anyone.

"Excuse me."

David turned from thoughts of Hedy to the short, pudgy merchant banker standing beside him in the L.O.L. hallway.

"Could we talk, David? In private?" Emil Zoltan whispered.

"Of course, Emil. Why don't we go for a walk."

"Lead the way."

They moved a good distance from the L.O.L. building, into Berkeley Square, with David setting a brisk pace. The air was cool and the ground scattered with various-hued leaves, signs of the changing season.

"A little slower," Emil pleaded, red-faced and puffing for breath.

David ignored him.

Breathing heavily, Zoltan finally stopped before an empty bench. "I must sit down. Please."

David noticed the beads of sweat collecting on Zoltan's balding forehead. He took a seat beside him on the wooden bench. "What would you like to talk about?" David asked, although he knew full well what the banker wanted.

"Between you and me, David, I'm concerned. Kevin can't handle the company. We need real management and financial guidance. We need to reduce overhead, stop the cash drain, and initiate capital gains for the shareholders. This company clearly cannot continue on its present course."

"Are you recommending we sell?"

"I don't see any alternative. I think we should fold L.O.L. into a friendly company—somebody with the resources and experience to handle the operation. I'm going to recommend it to the board and I'd like your support."

"You may be right. Still, it's a shame, isn't it? Do you have a particular company in mind?"

"No, no. I'm just thinking as a fiduciary, about what's in the long-term best interest of the company and its stockholders."

"Really? You know, that's funny, Emil, because I have the strangest feeling that you aren't thinking about anybody but yourself." Sitting on the park bench, he turned his entire body toward the banker and stared him hard in the eyes.

Zoltan bit his lip nervously and felt his face flush an even deeper shade of red. "Why, David, what's gotten into you? Why would you think such an absurd thing?"

"Because you're a swine and a liar, Zoltan. You're no fiduciary. You're only thinking about what's in your own best interest." David's voice took on a sharp edge, the anger controlled but just below the surface. He reached into his inside coat pocket and flipped out his small leather notepad. He turned the pages until he found what he was looking for.

"June eighteenth. July fourteenth. August seventh. And then again, just last week, on September eleventh and twelfth. Unauthorized, unreported meetings by you with board members of EMI."

Funny how Brandon's paranoia had paid off, even from the grave. No one had bothered to cancel the slew of information-gathering private detectives he'd kept on retainer as part of his modus operandi. When the reports came in, filled with fascinating tidbits, David soon saw the wisdom of Levy's ways.

"How dare you talk to me that way!" Emil said indignantly, the color now draining from his face.

"Cut the pretense!" David's anger was showing now. "What's your payoff? A directorship? Stock options? Warrants? And all *you* had to do was deliver the Silverfish on a silver platter, right?"

Zoltan stood up smartly from the bench. "I don't have to listen to this slander! I've done nothing wrong." At the sound of his raised voice, the park pigeons flew away wildly.

David opened his palms. "Have it your way. But I think the board will find the detectives' files very revealing. The secret meetings with EMI. Your desperate financial situation. And the tape-recorded conversations . . . "

Zoltan dabbed at his face with a handkerchief. "Be reasonable. It's L.O.L.'s only hope. You can't imagine how much money they're offering. Everyone will be better off."

"You know, Brandon thought you were a toad. Now I know firsthand. You're an even bigger villain than he thought."

Zoltan crumpled back down onto the bench. "What do you want me to do?" he asked quietly.

"Resign, eventually. For the moment, just keep your eyes open. When the time is right, you'll know what to do."

In the shadow of the Caravaggio, David studied the faces of the board members and fingered the ivory pawn in his jacket pocket. It had taken him this long, but he finally understood the legacy of the chess set.

When the will had been read and Brandon's estate divided, he'd been surprised. Not about the money and the stock, which Brandon left to his mother. Or about the town house bequeathed to Kevin. But, after all they'd been through together, he couldn't fathom why Brandon had willed him nothing more than a simple ivory chess set.

In the heat of battle over the past year, he'd all but forgotten the legacy. Until last week, when Joyce had called to tell him about MCA's internal problems and their possible availability. Then he remembered the chess game.

It was back in '69, when the movie studios were jockeying for position and panting after the Silverfish. On the very day that David had arranged for them to lunch privately with key executives of MCA, on condition that Dr. Jules Stein, the founder of the company, be present, Brandon at the last minute skipped lunch and went for a cruise to Santa Barbara instead.

David had been flabbergasted. After all his persuading and planning, he couldn't believe Brandon's rudeness and irresponsibility. He complained bitterly about the seemingly pointless power play, the boorish and embarrassing behavior, until Brandon, over a game of chess, explained several points of strategy in his usual oblique fashion.

Opening a large envelope, he said, "Take a look at this, David. It's something I picked up last week for a hundred thousand pounds sterling."

David studied the series of photographs. They pictured an expertly crafted leather and wood Chippendale sales trunk that contained miniatures of the entire Chippendale furniture line.

"It's magnificent. I didn't realize you were a collector," David said, wondering what this had to do with MCA.

"I'm not. But Dr. Stein is."

The ballet had been perfectly orchestrated. When Brandon's spies had informed him of Stein's weakness for Chippendale, he'd located and purchased the unique and exquisite piece, then arranged for a New York antique dealer to "offer" it to Dr. Stein. The one condition: that Stein fly to New York to conclude the deal in person.

Although he offered a quarter of a million pounds sight unseen for the trunk, a disappointed Dr. Stein refused to budge from L.A. and miss the Brandon Levy/Silverfish meeting. That was how Brandon had learned just how badly MCA really wanted the deal. He knew just how hard to push for "final cut" and the precedent-setting "gross" percentage points. By rudely standing up Stein in favor of yachting, Brandon was simply manipulating the corporate chessboard to stay one move ahead of his commercial adversaries.

David recalled the lesson and the moral: Stand apart and look down with perspective on the game board called "business"; manipulate the pieces and stay one step ahead of your opponent; risk losing and still have the courage to return to the board; be patient enough to let your opponent self-destruct. And after victory, never gloat; instead, turn the vanquished into ally. So, after signing the deal with MCA on Brandon's rough terms, Brandon magnanimously made a gift of the Chippendale trunk to Dr. Stein.

Now David understood. The chess set was Brandon's way of urging him to rise to the challenge and become one of the players in life's game.

"David, all of life is a chessboard," Brandon had said, "but few of us are ever the players because we usually are being played. I'm a player, David, and you are my knight. Others are pawns. I'm always prepared to lose—"

"And start again at the beginning?" David interjected.

"Exactly. Study the board carefully from above, David. It's a microcosm of life, which is just a bigger game with bigger stakes. But yours is the world and everything that's in it. . . ."

David smiled to himself at the memory and listened to Kevin Singh begin to speak

"Gentlemen, before we begin, I'd like to make a statement."

Conversation in the office ebbed and everyone looked at

Kevin. There were circles under his eyes and he looked distraught.

"I've thought a great deal about this morning's conversation," he said quietly. "In view of the company's current financial trend and the questions raised about my 'effectiveness,' I would like to offer the board my resignation."

"Please don't be hasty," John Peters interjected, just as Kevin had been hoping.

Kevin raised his hand to quell the objection. "This company's leadership is up to the board. Should you wish me to continue at the helm of L.O.L., I will, of course, acquiesce to your wishes. Considering the current problems, I think we should all think long and hard about the management of the company." The appearance was just right. How diplomatic. How noble.

The board nodded with approval, impressed by Kevin's selfless gesture. He smiled wanly in return, breathing a sigh of relief.

For the next hour, the board discussed future options for the company, carefully skirting the issue of the presidency. Despite the board's requests for direction, David remained silent through most of the meeting. His mind was wandering.

The game and rules were always the same: Don't let the world know what you're thinking; don't let them perceive you as threatening; act a little less forceful if it accomplishes your goal; as long as you're really still in control, that's all that counts. Play it the way you know best. Become a master at disarming, charming, and lulling potential adversaries into dropping their guard without realizing that they're losing control of the situation. Such were the bylaws that David Barry lived by, laws that made him a prime candidate for a successful corporate mogul.

With the L.O.L. board and the Silverfish, David must not be seen to attack. He disposed of Kevin simply by allowing him to self-destruct.

Up to now, David's demeanor had been impeccable and he'd ended up just where he wanted, about to act out the final scene in the drama. But he had to win over Kevin. Remembering Brandon and Dr. Stein, he realized it was crucial to his plan that Kevin be kept from festering with anger.

Finally, when the time was right, he broke his long silence. "Gentlemen, as I see it, there are three alternatives: one, sell the company and give up what Brandon and all of us have worked so hard for over the past years. This is an alternative favored by some of you. Without a doubt, the stockholders and the Silverfish would come out ahead for the moment, but they would lose the opportunity for future growth and development.

"Two, maintain the status quo. Cruise along as we've been doing and let the company slowly but surely run out of steam and money.

"Or three, plow back our earnings and build a *real* company. A company that no longer relies primarily on the Silverfish for its income. And in view of the failure of our film, I don't expect we can rely on the Silverfish to continue generating windfall profits. L.O.L., however, has the resources and the wherewithal, the momentum and the leverage, to move beyond a simple artists' managerial company. We've started doing that now with L.O.L. America, and I believe that with proper direction Levy Operations Worldwide can expand into new areas and become a vertically integrated entertainment conglomerate."

Everyone in the room sat forward and listened intently. The atmosphere of stale cigarette smoke suddenly seemed to have cleared.

"Do you have a plan for such growth?" Michael Reese asked.

"Yes, I do. I believe Levy Operations should purchase a Hollywood film studio and become a vital part of the U.S. entertainment industry. We should deal in the hard currency of the dollar and not depend on the pound sterling, which will be devalued. With a combined force in the audio and visual media worldwide, L.O.L. would be well positioned for the predictable technological developments of the Seventies and Eighties."

"I'm not sure I understand what you mean, David."

"Music is changing, gentlemen, and I believe that film and video are going to play important roles in that change. Movie sound tracks, contemporary musicals, even visual presentations of rock songs and concerts are more than oddities and promotion tools. These are things I see as the wave of the future."

"You can't be serious! Look at the failure of *Immaculate Conception.*"

"A failure of execution, Harold. Not of idea. Look at what's happening to *Jesus Christ Superstar*! Rock fans are dying to see their stars, any way they can. Theater and rock are merging. Film and rock are merging. We made a pretentious, overblown, three-hour religious drama without the Silverfish. We were on the right track—Brandon's instincts *were* infallible. I'm only carrying on with his vision."

David went on to outline his detailed plans for the growth and development of L.O.L., fielding questions from the board, conveying his enthusiasm. He didn't bother giving all the pros and cons, the pluses and minuses of his plan. Instead, for the first time, he put on the very blinders he'd always shunned, let the cool fade and the heat rise, and whipped himself and the board into a no-lose frenzy.

When he'd finished, it was Emil Zoltan who spoke first. Now he knew what David had meant. The time was right.

"Gentlemen, in view of David's remarkable, courageous vision for the future of this company, I would like to make a motion."

Kevin nodded his approval.

"I move that the board unanimously offer the position of chairman and chief executive officer of L.O.L. Worldwide to Mr. David Barry."

"Yes, indeed," John Peters said. "I second that motion."

Kevin quietly crushed his still-lit Davidoff into the Baccarat ashtray. "All in favor?" he asked as chair of the meeting, his voice trembling slightly.

One by one, the hands went up around the room, until only Kevin was left. His arm felt as heavy as the marble in the Taj Mahal. But finally and reluctantly, he, too, raised his hand, but only barely, a mere few inches above the desk.

"David, the board is pleased to offer you the chairmanship of Levy Operations. For the good of the company, we urge you to accept," Emil Zoltan said, a little too emphatically.

David leaned back in his chair. Even though he wasn't really surprised—it was the logical culmination of his strategy—the reality was now staring him in the face. For a moment he was scared. But not so scared he'd dream of backing off. His fingers rubbed the smooth surface of the pawn in his pocket. He thought of how quickly the past months had flown by and how satisfying they'd been. And he remembered his grandfather's advice about listening to his heart. He took a deep breath and spoke.

"Gentlemen, I'm appreciative of your offer and your vote of confidence." He turned his head and looked at Kevin. "Despite all the current problems, I think Kevin deserves our sincere thanks for his extraordinary efforts in the aftermath of tragedy. He's done a remarkable job in maintaining stability and preserving the integrity of this company."

"Hear, hear," Harold Jennings piped in.

Kevin wanted to crawl away and hide. He was numb.

"Therefore, gentlemen, I am willing to accept the leadership of Levy Operations. But there's one condition."

The whole room tensed up. Kevin's ear tuned in to the voices around him.

"The condition being that L.O.L. finance a separate, co-owned public-relations unit, with Kevin Singh as its head, to represent the Silverfish, our other clients, and third parties with the press. A good business, with a good and trusted friend who can cross-pollinate with our activities."

"Jolly good idea," John Peters said. "All for it."

The board consented, and in a matter of minutes it was over. Details and contracts would be forthcoming, as would David's written proposal for L.O.L.'s ten-year plan of expansion.

Buzzing with excitement, the members shook David's hand and exited the office. Emil Zoltan bowed slightly, smiled mischievously, and hurried out. Only Kevin stayed behind.

"I don't know how to thank you," he said, his voice choked with such emotion that it almost reverted to its uncultivated roots.

Flush with the excitement of the moment but still very much under control, David clasped him warmly around the shoulders. He knew he'd done the right thing. He'd taken the plunge headfirst and the feeling was heady. "None necessary. It was the least I could do. I know how good you'll be for us."

It was an auspicious beginning. He hoped Brandon was watching.

BOOK 4

The Troubadour

23

1981

*A*LL THE SIGNS WERE THERE. FROM THE BRISK CHILL IN the air to the crisp blue sky and the scent of chestnuts roasting. The dog days of summer had burned off and the Big Apple was back in fall gear.

It was a fall when the Stones were due on their '81 tour; when Twyla Tharp's new ballet, *The Catherine Wheel* (music by David Byrne of the Talking Heads), was set to open at the Broadhurst Theater; when the city was still in shock over John Lennon's murder and the sentencing of his killer.

Emerging from the St. Moritz onto Central Park South, Rick felt as alive and vibrant as the city. After an early-morning jog through Central Park and a quick swim and sauna at the Athletic Club, he was ready for anything and anybody, including Thane Crawley.

He waved off the doorman. Today he didn't want a limousine. He wanted the feel of cement under his feet and the chance to savor old memories of Manhattan: of Juilliard, of the Brill Building, of Rose and Hedy, David and Joyce, and Grandma Becky. No need to worry about a mob scene—New Yorkers were too sophisticated to fuss over a star, especially one who'd been out of the public eye for as long as he had and who was returning to his old haunts so miraculously transformed.

Not that he wasn't a superstar. His mellow sound *had* captured the hearts of the Seventies, yielding four platinum albums from '73 to '79. The last two albums had begun to slip, however, and it was going on two years since his last release. But that was about to change.

Walking down Sixth Avenue toward the L.O.L. Building, Rick felt more relaxed and self-confident than ever before. His inner strength, bolstered by the incredible music he was about to present to Thane, was reflected in his new look. Instead of mounds of flesh, straggles of hair, and the sallow complexion that had followed him through the Seventies, Rick was now thin and wiry, nearly fifty pounds lighter, with a healthy tan and a buoyant, effervescent step. For the first time in his life, he was at peace with himself and ready to take on the world.

As he rode the elevator up to Thane Crawley's palatial office, he flashed back to an earlier ride, when the words *Didn't you used to be somebody?* had echoed through the elevator and burned into his brain like the tag on a "Twilight Zone" episode ("Room for one more, honey"). Now he *was* somebody again, but, ironically, was glad not to be recognized.

"Can I help you, sir?" the beautiful redhead asked as Rick approached the opulent reception area.

"You sure can. I'd like to see Mr. Crawley."

"Do you have an appointment?"

Rick smiled with delight. This was going to be fun. "Well, I thought so." He looked down at his watch. "Let's see, it's eleven-thirty in the morning, Wednesday, September twenty-third. I believe he knew I was coming. . . ."

The secretary's mouth dropped. "Mr. Firestone! I . . . I'm so sorry, I didn't recognize you. Please, go right in. Mr. Crawley's expecting you." She showed him through the double doors into Crawley's Palace.

"Rick! Is it really you?" Thane said, more shocked than he'd expected by Rick's appearance. Despite the reports, he was still amazed to see his delinquent star again. When Rick had retreated to the desert, Thane was convinced he would never come back, that he was over the hill once and for all, of no more use to him or L.O.L. "You look terrific!" He hugged Rick, then stepped away, gawking and shaking his head in wonder. "Don't hold out on me, now. What was it? A doctor? A spa? Whoever or whatever it was, I want the name."

Rick smiled enigmatically and looked around at the Crawley collection of fabulous antiques, paintings, and *objets d'art,* and up at the twenty-foot ceiling and the spiral staircase leading to the library walks. He knew it was only a set—Thane's method of getting the upper hand—and the funny thing was, for the first time he wasn't the least bit overwhelmed or intimidated. The frightened little boy who'd gaped at the houses of Rina Constance and Dwight Sharon had finally grown up.

"Sit down, please. I want to hear everything. All about the desert and what you've been up to."

Actually, Thane already knew quite a bit—thanks to his all-around spy and hired gun—and he didn't give a shit about Rick, his personal life, or what was left of his fading musical talent. There was only one thing he wanted from Rick Firestone, and he wanted that so bad he could taste it: the Dwight Sharon masters. After years of trying, he still hadn't persuaded Rick to release the tapes. Worth millions, they were languishing in a vault, gathering dust, forgotten by practically everyone. Except Thane.

He was willing to do anything to get his hands on them. Although he'd done more than David Barry had expected— directing L.O.L. to the top of the record heap—and had regained and even enhanced his own stature in the industry, Thane was in a tight spot once again. Between his ever-increasing heavy debts to the mob and the current industry doldrums, he needed a blockbuster album, one he could hand over to the mob, and he needed it soon. The boys were losing their patience. That's why he'd resurrected Derek Robertson and foisted him on Firestone.

Unfortunately the plan wasn't working. All that time in the desert and Derek still hadn't come up with anything. Thane couldn't wait any longer; he'd had his fill of that burned-out case. Now he had to formulate another plan, sweet-talk Rick, threaten him, anything to get those tapes. Considering Rick's new image and attitude, he might be able to string him along, encourage him, then crush him, tell him his new music was shit, stomp on his fragile ego, make the release of the Sharon tapes

a condition for the release of a new Firestone album. But it was
damn risky.

He leaned forward to press the intercom button. "We can talk
over lunch. I've had Reynolds prepare your favorite: chateaubri-
and, *pommes frites,* salad, and Haut Brion '66. Looking at you,
though, I'm afraid you're going to want steamed veggies and
granola."

Rick held up his hand. "Please. I'm not into food right now,
I'm into music. And there's really nothing to catch up on. The
last two years are all in my head. There's only one way I can
share them with you or anyone—and that's why I'm here."

Thane barely hid his exasperation. "Anything you want."

Rick walked over to the corner Steinway, lowered the top, and
took a seat. "I'm going to play you my new material," he said
in a take-charge voice. "I want you to hear it live."

Thane loathed the idea. He hated watching people perform
music. Despite the recent debut of Warner's Music Television
Network (MTV) and David Barry's commitment of L.O.L.'s
film and music divisions to the video industry, Thane still believed music was meant to be heard and not seen. He especially
resented the prospect of playing nursemaid to an aging star and
submitting to his ego trip. Even though Derek had told him
about Rick's new material, Thane had no confidence in Rick's
commercial appeal.

Still, he couldn't refuse. Maybe the desert *had* changed and
rejuvenated Rick. Everybody changed, after all. Thane had only
to look inside himself to see that.

"Well, this *is* a treat. To reveal your product to me live,
without any embellishment . . . you must have tremendous
confidence in your new material."

Rick said nothing. Instead, he simply rested his fingers gently
on the keys and began to play, eyes closed, without interruption.
The new songs warmed his insides, as if they captured the hot
desert sun in their every note and transported him back to Palm
Springs. . . .

It had begun as a simple escape but ended up as something
far more profound. After five long years at the top, he had begun
to feel old and tired: drained from the work load, still alone,
unfulfilled despite his string of fading successes, his creative
juices drying up. Memories of '64 haunted him. Barely forty-
one, he'd been about to plunge into a full-scale midlife crisis.

At Joyce's urging, he spent a week alone in Palm Springs at

Barry Manilow's house. To his surprise, he loved the colors, the smell, and the solitude of the desert. Even though "the Springs" was practically Malibu-in-the-desert—a winter place where entertainers and entertainment moguls hid, visibly and all together—Rick felt drawn to the dry sand and the patches of snow-topped mountains. So he made a resolution: to find a private, monastic retreat near the Springs where he could hide from his public, from his friends, from his music, *and* from himself.

He needed someone to take care of all the secret arrangements and locate the perfect spot. At Thane's virtual insistence, he hired a man who'd been on the L.O.L. payroll for a number of years, a man who, like himself, was a onetime casualty of the rock world, who had died in the Sixties and, miraculously, was still alive in the late Seventies: Derek Robertson.

Rick hardly believed his ears or his eyes when Thane introduced him. There was no denying that Derek had sunk to the bottom in the early Seventies, selling and shooting enough smack to fill a coffin. With the smell of death around him, though, he supposedly had bellied up, dried out, and turned over a new leaf. At least that was how Thane and Derek told it. And Rick, good-hearted as always, and convinced that a snob like Thane wouldn't hire a shady or unreliable character, took them at their word.

Surprisingly, Rick and Derek hit it off reasonably well. With pasts that crisscrossed in so many places that their connection seemed almost fated, Rick agreed to hire a willing Derek as his part-time assistant.

David had been bemused, but not Joyce. She'd objected strenuously. The idea of Derek scared her, and the idea of Derek working for Rick scared her doubly. She would never forget the old hurt and Hedy's bitter tale. When she met him, though, Derek seemed mellowed, almost burned-out, and far from threatening. He was still blond and beautiful, and she would never trust him, but Rick laughed off her fears, saying he felt sorry for Derek and could take care of himself.

Considering Rick's fragile ego and his bevy of self-doubts, Joyce decided not to push. The past was so long gone to a self-confident Hollywood mogul like Joyce Heller that, really, Derek seemed harmless enough, an insignificant and insubstantial shadow from the distant past.

Entrusted with the sensitive job of locating a desert house,

Derek succeeded beyond Rick's fondest dream. The house became Rick's Shangri-la. Hidden in a valley surrounded by hills,
just seven miles from town but approachable only by helicopter,
the large Mexican-style hacienda had a tile roof, a 1930s old-
Hollywood air, and was enclosed by a huge, gated courtyard for
maximum privacy. The pool, the grass tennis court, the interior
garden, the view of the mountains—everything converged to
make Hidden Valley a perfect retreat.

Rick couldn't have been happier. No phone, no television, no
press, just perfect weather, fresh fruits and vegetables from the
local Indians, natural spring water. For the first time in his life,
he didn't *have* to do anything. He didn't have to write, record,
perform, create, even dress for anyone. Every minute was his
own and he thrived on the solitude. He didn't grow bored or
fidgety, or sleep endless hours. Rather, he filled his days with the
mundane activities that brought pleasure to normal people and
from which he'd been so long removed: reading and walking,
cooking and cleaning, gardening and mountain climbing. He
listened to music, tended the flowers, studied the stars.

Flying in and out on a regular basis, Derek quietly and unobtrusively helped Rick in every way he could. In fact, he came
more often and stayed longer than he was asked. In order to
accomplish his mission, it was essential that he remain by Rick's
side and worm his way into the star's confidence. Thane Crawley's instructions were clear: "Stick to Rick, make yourself indispensable, watch him like a hawk. Bide your time until the opportunity presents itself. I don't care how you do it but get
something on him, something juicy, something that I can use
against him." He never deigned to tell Derek why, but Robertson figured it out soon enough: Thane wanted blackmail ammu-
nition so he could snatch the Dwight Sharon tapes.

Derek was fed up with being a lackey, fed up with doing other
people's dirty work, with cleaning their shit and feeling their
pity. After all the dues he'd paid and all the painful, bitter years,
his ship was long overdue, ready to come in any day. He was
desperate for recognition, fame, fortune—for the sweet fruits of
success that the Thane Crawleys, Joyce Hellers, and Rick Fire-
stones enjoyed, the glories he deserved but had never reaped. For
the time being, he would do whatever Crawley wanted. After all,
it was Crawley who'd saved him from the mob when he'd gotten
in over his head, and Crawley who'd promised him a new re-

cording contract and a new career, when he finished with the dirty work.

Although they barely saw one another for the first six months, Derek did everything he could to maintain Rick's privacy and run the household smoothly. He shopped, took calls and messages, oversaw the maintenance. Slowly but surely he became Rick's eyes, ears, and hands to the outside world.

At Rick's behest, Derek made arrangements for the final purchase of the house, at a cost of several million dollars, with title taken in Derek's own name to confound the curiosity seekers. He arranged for a Nautilus gym to be built in the basement and began to lead Rick in daily workouts, beginning every morning before the searing desert heat overwhelmed the day. Sit-ups, push-ups, jogging, swimming . . . Derek coached the singer through his first taste of muscle and stamina. He videotaped the workouts and reviewed them for form and feedback. With a deft combination of encouragement, demonstration, and admonishment, he made Rick work his body until the muscles toned and tightened, the waist thinned to thirty-two inches, the weight fell from 190 to 140 pounds.

After nearly a year of solitude, a year completely away from his music, Rick felt himself growing in ways he'd never dreamed possible. Not only physically, but mentally and spiritually. Before, there'd always been someone around to shelter him even from himself, whether it was Rose or Joey, Hedy or Joyce, David or Dwight, show girls or entertainment people. Now for the first time, after all these years, he was taking the time to come to terms with his feelings and getting to know himself. Maybe he wasn't such a bad guy after all.

He spent his evenings writing and meditating, reviewing his life, thinking about his family, mulling over his relationships, his hopes and dreams. He thought about Rose and his sisters, glad that he'd reconnected with them. When he'd returned to the old neighborhood, he had hugged his haggard mama, forgotten the bad times and remembered the good. Although he'd barely kept in touch when he was in England—the bitter taste of Joey still overwhelming his senses—on his return to the States, a star once again, he'd finally had the nerve and the confidence to face Rose and Brighton Beach.

The more Rick thought, though, the more he dreamed of Hedy.

One night, after a particularly strenuous day of training, Rick invited Derek to dinner. Over a hearty meal of brown rice, vegetables, and a bottle of Chablis, Rick screwed up the nerve to pry.

"Can I ask you something personal, Derek?"

"Of course you can. Joyce or Hedy?"

Rick smiled. "Fuck you," he said lightly. "All right . . . Hedy. What happened with you two in San Francisco?"

Derek shook the blond hair off his tan face and looked across the table. "That was a heavy trip. I was desperate, trying to hang on to my music for dear life. I was fucked up and she was my lifeline. It only lasted a few months, and then . . . well, we missed Monterey, I got busted, and, poof, she kicked me out. What can I say? It was a lifetime ago."

Rick noticed the bitterness. Despite his calm exterior, Derek harbored a hidden intensity that flashed up on occasion through his deep eyes.

"Been thinking about her, huh?"

"I guess so," Rick said truthfully. "We were pretty close once. It's been almost seven years since anyone's seen her. I know it's stupid, but I feel kinda responsible." There were times, like now, when Rick wished he had a real friend he could talk to. He toyed with the idea of calling Joyce or David—they used to talk regularly, until he retreated to the desert—but they were always so busy with business, they didn't have time for him anymore.

He thought back on the roller coaster of his life. Sometime in the future he would contact Hedy and let her know he was there if she needed him. If only he hadn't walked away from her that night in the desert . . . Maybe that was why he loved the desert so much: It always reminded him of *Immaculate Conception* and the Heavenly One.

"Don't blame yourself, Rick. You know, the cliché's kinda true. You can't help those who aren't ready to help themselves."

Thanks to the desert and the solitude, Rick was beginning to understand. He and Hedy; they wouldn't have worked. At least not in '72. He couldn't have saved her any more than she could have saved him.

"I guess you're right. But, you know, it sucks. Usually it's the ones who can't help themselves who need it the most."

Sometimes Derek couldn't believe Rick was for real. He'd never met anybody so sincere. Despite Thane's badgering, Derek was dragging his feet, procrastinating. Obviously, Rick was lily-white. There were no skeletons dangling in *his* closet. Every day the assignment was looking harder. He would have to trick him, drug him, manufacture something from scratch. But Derek was strangely comfortable in the desert. To his own surprise, he was enjoying the responsibility, taking pleasure in working for and being with Rick. Nobody had ever been so kind to him before.

When the urge finally hit him, Rick couldn't wait to get started. Suddenly, he was aching for music. Instruments were brought in, including synthesizers, an organ, and a Steinway grand. Contractors were hired to build a mini–recording studio in the basement, modeled after the one Dwight Sharon had in Manchester.

He locked himself in his basement and let music once again become his consuming passion. The emotions triggered by his introspection and solitude were now channeled into musical sounds and words. He began composing and experimenting day after day, working with the new tunes and sounds that he was hearing in his head. The excitement and energy of creation took over his life.

The new material was delicate and sensuous, with simple, rapturous melodies inspired, as Grandma Becky had urged, by the likes of Rachmaninoff, Tchaikovsky, and Puccini. Digging deep into his classical roots and into his heart and soul, Rick collaborated with his own past to create a new, wondrous, haunting sound that was more a celebration of life than simple music. Every song felt real and honest. Every note led him back to Hedy and to a reawakened passion for his one and only love.

He wrote it as a piece, calling it the *Firestone Fireside Symphony,* with prologue, movements, a musical interlude as gentle as a caress, dramatic climaxes, and a finale as quiet as a goodnight kiss. He imagined kids necking in their cars, his songs on their cassette; and their parents, curled up in front of the fire, his music in the background.

And so did Thane Crawley. When Rick played the final notes, the usually glib record executive was struck dumb. It was several moments before the magic faded enough for him to regain his voice.

"Rick! I'm speechless. I'm incredibly moved."

"You're the first one on the outside to hear this material. I need to know if you really like it. Please, don't bullshit me."

"Like it! It's exquisite, it's delicate, it's beautiful, it's original. Nothing compares. McCartney's 'Yesterday,' Lennon's 'Imagine,' they don't hold a candle to it. It's more powerful than the

'Can I Make You Love Me?' duet. Believe me, Rick, you're going to turn the entire music community on its ear!"

Thane's voice was filled with excitement and his golden ear was vibrating. This was the once-in-a-lifetime opportunity. The new sound, like Elvis or the Beatles, that would make music history. The groundbreaker he'd been waiting for. Fuck the Dwight Sharon masters; they could wait. Rick's album would be worth far more to him. First he would milk every last dollar out of Rick Firestone. Then he'd find a way to turn the screws and get the Sharon masters. For once, Thane had been dead wrong. Rick Firestone was anything but over the hill.

Rick glowed with self-confidence. He'd been right.

"When can you start recording?"

"It's already recorded."

"What? But I haven't seen any studio bills, musician contracts, union payments. You've been holding out on me."

"I did it all on my own, recording it in my basement studio. I just completed the mixing and sweetening."

"Where's the master? When can I have it?"

"Hold your horses, Thane. I don't want this marketed the usual way. It's a concept album. No prereleased singles. The album stands as a whole, on its own."

Thane's marketing wheels were turning. "It won't work. We have to release a single and then let the momentum build for six to twelve weeks to prime the market for the LP. There has to be time for demand to build."

"No. I won't do it that way," Rick said adamantly.

"Look, be reasonable. You've been away a long time. Your name's not exactly on the tip of the public's tongue. The radio market has changed. It's all FM now, and the market's segmented. Even with the help of the independent promoters, we still need over a hundred stations to break a record, and over two hundred to make top twenty. It's a new world. After all your work, you don't want to get frozen out."

"No. That's not the way I want it done." Rick stood up dramatically from the piano. "I want you to invite everybody in the entertainment business to the Troubadour in early December. I'm going to play the album for them there, live."

"I hope you're kidding."

"I'm dead serious." Rick began pacing back and forth, deep in thought, his face radiating energy. "I want them all flown in.

All the press, every key radio programmer in America, the key rack jobbers, the critics . . ."

"You're crazy!"

" . . . all my old friends, all the big stars, all the oldies-but-goodies. Put 'em all up at the Beverly Hills Hotel. Give 'em the royal treatment: limos and flowers and fruit and wine. A big reception, full of press and photographers, so they all feel like stars."

"That'd cost a fortune."

"Charge it against my royalties. My catalog will cover the cost."

"Have you been snorting coke?"

"Come on, Thane, use your imagination. We'll create a media event the likes of which hasn't been seen in Hollywood since Louis B. Mayer. Every major performing artist in the last twenty-five years all in one place. You're gonna dress 'em up, ship 'em to the Coast, treat 'em like royalty.

"Imagine the media coverage: *People, US, Newsweek, Time, Life.* The eyes and ears of American music focused on the Troubadour. Rick Firestone sings his heart out to the stars."

"And if you don't pull it off? Imagine the damage to your career and mine. If we release the usual way, we're guaranteed a moderate success and we could still have a blockbuster."

"You heard the music. You want this record to be big, don't you? Well, I'm ready to stake my professional life and my own money on this material. If you are."

"You believe in it that much?"

"Yes. That much. It's me. I want to perform the *Fireside Symphony* live, in front of my peers. I want to give them something back. Trust me. I'll build a word-of-mouth for this record that'll shoot your sales through the roof."

Thane looked out the window across Sixth Avenue. The risk was tremendous, but his ear and his instinct told him Rick was right on the money. The material *was* dynamite. And with Rick playing it live, it was irresistible.

If Firestone actually pulled it off, who knew how many units Thane might move? Enough to pull L.O.L. America out of the doldrums. Even enough to line his own pockets, repay his debt to the mob, and set himself up for life. Instead of letting them bootleg one of every four, he could up the ante and give them two of the first 3 million units. God, what a killing that would be!

But to do it, he needed the master tape. And he needed it soon.

He turned from the window, walked over to Rick, and clasped his hand. "If that's what you really want, Rick, then I'll go along with you. I'll see to all the arrangements. But I need the master immediately."

Rick shook his head. "Not yet. I don't want this music leaked to *anyone* before the Troubadour. You just get everything ready. Don't worry, I'll give you enough lead time so you can press and distribute the day after the Troubadour."

There was no point in arguing. There was no need to. He had an ace in the hole. The two men shook hands, and Thane was once again alone in his Palace.

He flicked the switch on his intercom. "Wilma, get me Derek Robertson in Palm Springs."

"Derek, Thane. Listen, about the plan. Put it on hold. I've got something else I need you to do right away. Something much more important."

* * *

It took him a couple of weeks, but Derek delivered.

With Rick off in New York for a weekend, Derek snatched the *Fireside* tape, flew into L.A., and rendezvoused with Thane in the parking lot of Holly Park in Inglewood.

"You're sure it's the master?"

"Hey, what am I, stupid? I told you I was sure. Labeled and everything."

"And Rick doesn't know?"

"Didn't see me take it; won't see me return it. He'll never know it was missing."

Thane ripped the flap off the folder and turned over the tape in his hand. "Okay, I'll meet you back here at four."

"Wait just one second." Derek stuck his hand out and slid his thumb back and forth over his fingers. "Aren't you forgetting something?"

"How could I forget you, Derek? A job well done deserves a generous reward." Thane reached into his inside coat pocket, pulled out two brown envelopes, one thin and one thick. He held them up in front of him, teasing Derek, making him reach for the goods like an animal being fed at the zoo.

Derek snatched them out of his hand. He opened the thin envelope and counted out ten one-hundred-dollar bills. "Is this some kinda joke, Crawley? That's it? A measly grand? Who the hell do you think you are? Why, I—"

"Take it easy, Derek." Thane knew damn well who and what Derek was. An unreliable scum. A scum with a mouth who had to be watched and kept quiet, who had to be kept down and under his thumb. "Check out the other envelope. It's worth a pretty penny. A special treat, direct from Columbia. As pure as the driven snow."

Derek unsealed the flap and looked down at a large Ziploc of shiny white rocks and flakes. He pulled the seams apart, reached in, and scooped out a sample in his nail. The light reflected off the powder. He bent his head down, gingerly raised his finger to his nostril, and took a sharp snort. Then another and another.

"Nice buzz, huh? It's primo stuff. Top shelf. Nothing but the best for you, Derek. And it's just a sample. There's plenty more where that came from." Thane started up the engine. The meeting was over. "Go out and enjoy yourself. You deserve it."

Derek felt his nose burn and the sweet, numb feeling in the back of his throat. It had been so long he'd almost forgotten what it was like. Almost but not quite. "Thanks. But what about the other thing? You know, you promised that when I was finished you'd sign me up, give me a contract, let me record."

"Patience, Derek. Give me time. I'm a busy man. You didn't deliver the original goods, after all. But don't worry, you can trust me. We'll talk about it later. Now, I'm in a hurry."

1981

TAGGERING OUT OF BED AT 6:00 A.M., JOYCE WAS MET
by the riveting odor of freshly brewed coffee. Blindly, like a
zombie, she followed the entrancing scent into her kitchen that
overhung the Santa Monica Mountains, then poured herself a
large mug of automatically timed, ground, and brewed coffee.
Thanks to the miraculous Hammacher Schlemmer contrap-
tion—a thoughtful gift from her friend and boss David Barry—
she no longer had to wait like an addict for her morning caffeine
fix.

After she'd mainlined the first mug, her pressure jumped and
her heart began to pump. She slipped into her sweat suit and
sneakers, downed a final few gulps, and headed out the door for
her strenuous morning jog up Benedict Canyon Drive to Mul-
holland and back.

More than mere exercise, the morning ritual was practical and
therapeutic: a time to clear out the cobwebs, take stock, and
make plans. With the opening of *Carnival in Rio* approaching,

and five other projects in various stages from pre- to postproduction, these morning jaunts represented her only time alone.

This morning's was even more necessary than usual. After nearly three years as head of production and senior operating officer of L.O.L. Films, and a string of moderately budgeted winners that had rocketed her and her company to the forefront of the movie business, Joyce was suddenly caught up in a double helix of pressures and emotions.

Generally, she was all radiance and magnetism, with a sense of power and purpose surrounding her like an aura. Although she could pass as one of her own starlets—with flowing black hair, high cheekbones, and a curvaceous body—she was anything but. Not only did she walk the sets and talk turkey with the crew, but she had a keen eye for detail, a sound financial head, and an understanding of people and production, all of which combined to make her a dynamo of a movie exec.

She gave good meeting *and* she delivered product—a rare Hollywood combo. On top of that, she was a workaholic and one tough cookie, projecting a sometimes frightening confidence and control from her piercing jade eyes.

Today, however, her knees wobbled slightly as she took the first hill, and her stomach flip-flopped inside her. Struggling to snatch her concentration away from her tiring body, she tried to analyze the strange jumble of feelings.

Clearly, the opening was partly responsible. She'd gone out on a limb for this one, risking a far bigger budget and predicting record receipts for box office and sound track alike. When she'd read Jeski's book, it had struck her musical chord, the way Nik Cohn's *New York* magazine article had struck her back in '76.

It was before L.O.L., when she'd been working for Jorge and trying her hand at independent production. She'd read the article, "Tribal Rites of a New Saturday Night," had seen the possibilities, and tried to sell MCA on a development deal based on the article. They'd turned her down cold, only to pound their heads against the wall when another producer and another studio picked up on the idea and did a hundred million on *Saturday Night Fever*.

Up till now, she'd shied away from musical-related material, reasoning that movies like *Saturday Night Fever* and *Grease* had glutted the market. Until her gut told her the time was ripe.

Carnival in Rio had all the right elements: box-office stars; a driving rock-and-roll track; crisp editing and direction, thanks to Christopher's nod to the new rock-video style; sharp dance numbers and a hip tone that was right-on with the adolescent market; and, most important, strong characters and an upbeat story about the romance of a mature Brazilian man and an aspiring young dancer from New York. Meeting at the carnival in Rio, they unfold a touching story of spiritual and sexual awakening, of love and self-discovery.

Obviously, that was part of the problem. Even a blind man could see it. The bittersweet memory of Jorge still burned brightly for Joyce, and the story hit too close to home.

The first two years, '74 and '75, had been strictly business. Thanks to David's Hollywood intro, she'd hired on as an executive producer with Jorge Machado's highly profitable B-movie factory, helping the suave Brazilian crank out low-budget horror/disaster flicks like *The Valley of Baboons, Bloodsuckers,* and *Tidal Wave.* He was like King Midas: Everything he touched looked like shit but, through alchemy, turned to gold.

Despite the *schlock* content of his movies, she admired everything about the man: his open, easy manner; his unerring commercial instinct; his firm but trusting way with people. He was a rare commodity in Hollywood, thanks to the Carioca in him. He inspired trust and genuine loyalty—and unlike the characters in his pictures, was true to his word and never stabbed anyone in the back.

After only six months on the job, she'd cemented their working relationship by alerting Jorge to the corruption rampant in his studio.

"Jorge, look at the figures for negatives. You're paying one to two hundred thousand dollars more than you should, per film. At ten films per year, I'd say you were being screwed to the tune of one to two million per year. You could make a whole film with that money."

At first, Jorge had been reluctant to believe her. Despite his expertise in the business, he was too honest and trusting.

"So efficient but such a worrier you are, Joyce. Each film is audited. The directors earn a percentage of each film, and certified negative cost is something they care about. Their lawyers, their accountants, their auditors, all of them check it carefully. The crucial starting-off point to measure break-even and profits is the negative cost. No one could cheat that much."

"Give me a chance to prove it."

"I believe you are mistaken, but I give you a free hand to

investigate. Carte blanche for an internal audit. You realize you may ruffle some feathers?"

"I'm willing to take the risk. I don't need corrupt friends."

"Where will you begin?"

"I'll check the relationship of the production people with the unions, suppliers, and contractors; examine the hours per picture the union drivers claim they're used and compare that figure with the hours it takes to make the picture and the mileage charges. I'll see who buys all the surplus ordered for each film, the little things like towels, linens, dishes. I'll examine the volume of wood ordered per picture for construction and compare that figure with the volume ordered by other studios and independents.

"I can tell you now what I'll find. That Machado Studios is the major supplier of wood to a thriving lumberyard in Woodland Hills. That the lumberyard is owned by one of your directors. And that your film budgets have subsidized and even built numerous patios, porches, house wings, and guest houses.

"I'll also show that certain company cars, which are supposed to be functioning full-time, have been signed out in the name of nonexistent employees and leased, for cash, to a rental agency near LAX. And I'll be curious to see just who owns that car-rental agency. In fact, this whole place is crawling with people from the new union, IAGKT—the International Alliance of Gonifs, Knaves, and Thieves—whose motto is, 'Everyone does it, so why not me?' "

She was right, of course. With Jorge's support, she was instrumental in cleaning up the studio and increasing its profit margin.

After two years and seven pictures, Jorge had finally invited Joyce to his exclusive Malibu Colony home for a private tête-à-tête before one of his extended Brazilian trips. From the outside, the house looked like any wood and glass contemporary. The inside, however, was brimming with style: French impressionist paintings, a Calder mobile, a Henry Moore bronze nude looking out over the Pacific. When she caught sight of the Louis Comfort Tiffany wisteria, standing practically seven feet high, Joyce couldn't help gasping.

"Never believe your eyes, darling. It is merely a copy," Jorge said, materializing beside her. He was tall, nearly six-three, silver-haired, with a beautiful, sharp-boned face and a firm, sensuous body more appropriate to a man of thirty-five than one of sixty.

She eyed him skeptically and bent over to feel the side of the leaded glass for the Tiffany mark. "Bullshit, if you'll excuse the expression. It's real and you know it. Why pretend it isn't?"

He smiled expansively. "Real? What is real? Is Tiffany glass real? Are the movies we make, the illusions we create, real?"

She laughed at him. "Yeah, real crap. Now cut it out. You know what I mean." A few months ago she wouldn't have dared be so casual. But recently they'd spent more time together and become more comfortable, even though his presence still sent a chill down her spine. And not because he was her boss.

"Of course I do. But, for me, only one thing is real: what is in here." He pointed to his heart. "Come, let's sit on the deck." His fingers gently wrapped around her elbow as he led her out through the sliding glass door and into a front-row seat for the sunset. No gossipy Hollywood party and screening for Jorge Machado—he liked his privacy, the outdoors, and real human contact.

Without even asking, he handed her a delicious rum cocktail, then sat down beside her. They talked business for nearly an hour, reviewing current productions and future projects. Finally, Jorge stood up, both his large hands holding empty glasses. "Enough of this nonsense," he said. "We only do this for me, so I feel involved. You don't need me to tell you how to make pictures anymore. Of Joyce Heller, the consummate professional, I have had my fill. But the real Joyce Heller, the woman, her I have yet to meet."

She watched him, the last rays of light illuminating his face, as he returned with two more drinks and lit the grill. She'd never met anyone quite like him. A studio executive with barely a trace of Hollywood. A sensitive, caring man with a fiery Latin temper and a heightened sensibility. A strong, masculine odor and a charged sexual aura, both of which terrified her.

She'd yet to come to grips with her sexuality. After the Fire Island transformation, she'd been scared at first by her own beauty and uncomfortable with the way men suddenly reacted to her presence. Sex hadn't been on her mind for years. She was numb, emotionally and physically, anesthetized to feeling, protected from hurt and humiliation. She wanted no part of love affairs, dependence, anguish.

The fear was behind her now, but she hadn't sloughed off the feeling that she was still internally defective and unworthy, even incapable, of loving and being loved, of experiencing real, passionate love. She wouldn't and couldn't take the chance of disappointing a man and thinking less of herself. Up till now, work had been her only bedmate.

"A cruzeiro for your thoughts," Jorge said after they'd polished off the steaks and salad and were sipping strong Brazilian coffee.

She blushed. "I was thinking about you," she answered honestly. "You're a very complex man."

"Complex? I should be insulted, no? Behind all the illusions, there is Jorge Machado, unveiled, like a statue, for all to see. Men, they are simple creatures: They pretend to be strong, but they are shot full of holes. Women like you, on the other hand . . . they tell a complex story, full of plot twists and surprise endings. But Jorge, he knows a little about the script."

"I'll bet."

"He knows, for example, that there was great pain and sadness somewhere in your past."

"And how does he know that?"

"From the paleness of your flesh and the dark, tight circles around your beautiful irises."

She shivered in the cool breeze. "You can read the past in my eyes?"

"Not like the old women in Rio. But some."

Joyce was silent and Jorge didn't press the inquiry. Instead, he began to talk about himself. About his wife and children in Rio, about the hardships and poverty of his youth. He talked, too, about his moviemaking, and the feelings inspired by his financial success and critical failures, and the ways he maintained his own self-respect.

Under the half-moonlight, touched by his gentle compassion and honesty, and ignoring all the warning bells tolling inside her head, Joyce let down her guard and started talking. She skirted the crux for as long as she could, until finally she broke down and told him about the cancer, as if it were the ultimate skeleton in her life's closet.

He held her in his arms, deeply moved by the story of suffering and rejuvenation. She was an even more incredible woman than he'd imagined, a volatile mix of strength and vulnerability. It tore at his heart that she still punished herself and shut out the life-giving passion. If only she would let him, he would move inside her and open her up like a flower.

When the breeze rose off the ocean, she followed him inside, before the fire. The casual touch of his fingers seemed to sear her flesh. His whispers and caresses—soft and reassuring at first, then sensual and erotic, filled with lust and desire for *her* lips and *her* breasts and *her* body—shocked and amazed her. She hadn't believed anyone could really desire her. And never imagined she could feel the heat again, deep inside and down between her legs, where surely she was dead and buried.

But she did. Oh, she did indeed.

As he undressed her, her nipples hardened and her breath came sharp and staccato. She heard her own quick moans and felt herself growing moist. She saw the passion in his eyes and in his hard cock, and squeezed her eyes shut when, inch by inch, slowly, as if she were a virgin, he entered her and she screamed with joy. Empty for so long, she suddenly felt full with the strangeness and began to sob like a baby.

Jorge kissed away her tears as he rocked her, inside out, until the tears turned back to moans and then to shrieks and they came together, on the floor, that first time.

It was the first of many nights. Nothing permanent—they both knew that from the beginning. But certainly something substantial, something that touched them both deeply.

When the end came, it was as unexpected as the beginning. One minute he was with her, preparing for another trip to Brazil. The next he was gone, never to return, his private plane down somewhere in the Brazilian mountains. She'd cried at the loss, more for his family than for herself. After all, he'd brought her more happiness and feeling in one year than she'd ever thought possible or dreamed she deserved. Still, it was another in a long string of losses that began with her mother and carried through to Brandon.

As he would have wanted, she took over the studio and, soon afterward, folded Machado Enterprises into L.O.L.

Little wonder, then, considering the personal relevance of the plot, that *Carnival in Rio* stirred up unusually strong feelings in Joyce.

Still, even that didn't explain all the free-floating anxiety and the unfamiliar pain in her chest and her legs as she pumped up and down the hills of Benedict Canyon Drive. Jogging was her unerring psychic barometer: The harder the run, the deeper her psychological strain. There had to be more.

There was the potentially unpleasant lunch date that afternoon with the director Tony Christopher. She hated having to turn down his movie—he was so talented and he'd done such a good job on *Carnival*—but the property just wasn't up to snuff and definitely not right for L.O.L. She'd have to orchestrate it just right, so his reputation wouldn't be damaged.

And there was Rick. When he'd called yesterday, he'd sounded desperate to see her and she'd squeezed him in for early tonight, although she couldn't really afford the time. He'd been unusually hyper for a desert fox, naturally revved up about the upcoming Troubadour show and the new album, but strangely nervous and reticent. It wasn't like him to be so edgy, and she was concerned.

She could also add to the mix her growing doubts about Thane. With all the hype over *Carnival in Rio,* she couldn't figure his marketing strategy for the sound track. Even though his advertising budget seemed enormous, she'd learned that he was pressing under half a million units. For the life of her, she couldn't understand why he was being so conservative. When she'd pushed him on the phone, he'd just oozed with his usual bullshit; then, uncharacteristically, had blown his cool.

"Who said anything about a half-million units? I'm pressing enough to cover the initial demand," he said. "If it hits, we'll know right away. Don't worry so much, Joyce. Two days, that's all it takes to press up another batch and distribute to the record stores. Record sales are down, my dear. I just can't risk taking a wash on this one."

"Two days can be an eternity. Most sales go in the first wave. Look, you've got your best artists on this sound track. We've even got solo cuts from each of the old Silverfish. Hype the Silverfish angle. Even if the movie bombs, you can still—"

"Look," Thane said, cutting her off contemptuously, "you run your end of the business and I'll run mine. When I want your advice on my projections, I'll ask for it. Until then, stick to making movies and keep your nose out of my affairs!"

"Well, fuck you," she'd said aloud to the dial tone. What the hell had gotten into him? He was a scumbag, everybody knew that. But she'd always thought he was a sharp operator. A bitchy, defensive tone and an ultraconservative approach weren't encouraging signs in an L.O.L. record mogul, however.

When she finally reached her driveway, she stopped dead, panting, and bent over with her hands at her waist. She felt an urgent need to talk to David, who was out on his yacht again, doing God knows what, playing incommunicado. She resolved to call him tomorrow.

After catching her breath, she trudged up the steep driveway and back into her kitchen. She was wet and sticky from the run. The muscles in her calves and thighs ached and her temples throbbed. She downed a quick glass of water, then poured herself another cup of the hot coffee elixir, carrying it from the kitchen to the bedroom.

In front of the bureau mirror, she stripped the CARNIVAL IN RIO sweat shirt up and over her head, releasing her firm breasts from the hot, steamy flannel. Her cheeks had a deep red flush and her hair was damp and straggly.

Suddenly, two strong hands grabbed her from behind and wrapped around her breasts! Terrified, she struggled free and spun around, her nipples grazing against the hairs on his chest.

"Jesus Christ, Mark, you scared the shit out of me! What the hell are you still doing here? I wasn't kidding when I told you to be gone before I got back."

"Hey, I'm just a struggling cowboy turned actor on the make. I can't take no for an answer," the stud said. He was no more than twenty-two, with light brown hair, a dirty-blond moustache, and lots of muscles. Another typical one-nighter that barely occupied her thoughts or satisfied her body.

"You won't even get a screen test if you don't gitty-up outta here lickety-split, cowboy."

"Come on, baby, one more time. I'm not beggin' for a part. I want it all. All of you, sweetheart."

"Cut the macho shit. I'm in no mood for games and I'm in a hurry," she crackled. Picking his clothes and boots up off the floor, she tossed them in his direction. "Outta my town, pardner. Now." She marched into the bathroom and locked the door.

Between the run and Mark the stud, Joyce felt horribly dirty. She hadn't wanted meaningless sex with another beautiful, faceless boy. When the party had gone late, though, she just hadn't been able to bear the prospect of a cold, empty bed. Ever since Jorge, there'd been nothing and no one even close to real.

Sitting cross-legged on the bathroom carpet, Joyce removed her Adidas jogging shoes and socks, then stood up, released the knot in her sweats, and stepped out of her pants and into the glass-enclosed shower.

The shower-massage pounded against her neck and back. Then she switched the head and turned, so the hot water prickled in fierce tiny streams against her front. She soaped her breasts and her flat stomach, then began to wind the lather around her pubic hair. Her finger slid in between her lips and circled the tip of her clitoris.

As her mind wandered erotically, she rubbed gently, in tiny figure eights, her eyes closed, the hot water streaming against her nipples. She moved to little circles, then pressed harder and moved her two fingers up and down, up and down, along the lips, until her breathing came faster.

It was only then that she realized whom and what she'd been fantasizing. And it wasn't Mark, or Jorge, or any man she'd ever had. This man was lying over her, his face just above her, his pelvis thrusting wildly, his dark hair and features so very familiar. He was sexy and powerful, but, oh, so very vulnerable. She wanted to make him come inside her. She wanted to see his face twisted in ecstasy.

As Joyce's fingers vibrated against her wet, pink flesh and she felt her whole body tremble with pleasure, she realized, with a flash, the source of her fantasy *and* her anxiety. My God, she was dreaming of David!

She turned the shower on cold, soaped her body once more, and forced her mind back to reality—back to business.

Sunset Boulevard never changed. It was consistently ugly and slapdash, alternating exotic buildings, statues of Bob's Big Boy, gas stations, and imitation-château apartment houses. Driving down the boulevard, Joyce barely noticed the bizarre scenery. En route to her lunch at Le Dôme, she was thinking of Tony Christopher and how best to stage the scene.

Earlier in the day, she'd placed a personal call to the maîtresse d'hôtel of Le Dôme.

"Stephanie, darling, hi, it's Joyce. I'm coming in for lunch today . . . Yes, I've got a reservation. But I want to be in a very heavy traffic area. That's right. No privacy, no back room. Not today. A prime table and very visible. And I want the works, the royal treatment. Dom Perignon chilling on the table, the best waiter fawning over Mr. Christopher. A phone at the table. . . . Umm-hmmm. You got it. I want us to be *noticed*. You're a doll."

She'd told her secretary to call her table four times during lunch. Everything was set.

Joyce pulled her car up to the parking valet and met the

gray-bearded Tony Christopher in the restaurant's alcove. As they walked in, Stephanie greeted them and escorted them to their table.

The restaurant was cheerful, elegant, and very chic. A lot of etched glass and polished brass with pink tablecloths thrown over floor-length striped fabric. The leafy wallpaper pattern was gold leaf over green. The carpeting was deep green. The fixtures art-deco.

Joyce smiled to herself. Their entrance was perfectly timed, just late enough so everyone else was settled in, white-wined and Perriered. The only empty table in Le Dôme—conspicuously prominent and unoccupied—was so well lit that she thought Jules Fisher had been flown in from New York to do the lighting. All the diners eyed it expectantly.

With her arm through Christopher's, they made their entrance and the restaurant buzzed. The nods, the smiles, the little waves. She looked around at all the wonderfully sincere "dear" friends—the ones who secretly rooted for *Carnival* to bomb, just because it wasn't theirs—and listened to their predictable cackle. Listened to the "So divine, darling." "Sweetheart, darling, baby, call me, let's lunch." To the "Sweetheart, do join us in Puerto Vallarta this season." The "precious" do this, the "sweetie" do that, the "honey," the "cookie," the "baby." She'd heard it all a million times before and it was as hard to swallow as a Vaseline sandwich. This was L.A., where the license plates had more to say than the girls. Still it was her world, her milieu, her chosen life.

By five o'clock the whole town would know that Joyce Heller and Tony Christopher had lunched. And everyone would be jumping to all sorts of conclusions, just as Joyce wanted.

Moments after they were seated, the elegant service began. Beluga caviar with hot toast and the appropriate condiments. Stolichnaya, in a block of ice and wrapped in a white napkin, poured into two beautiful crystal shot glasses.

As Joyce and Tony drank a toast, the forty tables in the restaurant watched in complete silence for several seconds (like an E. F. Hutton commercial), amazed at the lunch partners and simply dying to know what hot new project the two were discussing. Christopher's whispered conversation actually sounded like this:

"What the fuck are you pulling on me?" he asked through clenched teeth and a fixed smile.

"I viewed the rushes of *Hallelujah.* L.O.L. is *not* going to distribute your movie, but I wanted to keep my promise to help you and talk to you sensibly, in a place where you couldn't throw one of your famous tantrums."

"I hate you, Joyce Heller."

"No you don't. If I went through the motions of releasing your picture and not marketing it properly, then you'd hate me. But you don't hate me for being honest. For not buying a picture that you and I know isn't worthy of you."

Joyce felt a touch of regret, but she had no choice. It was business. They'd helped each other over the past year, and now it was time to move on. When *Carnival* had been floundering in production and she'd fired the original director, she'd offered the job to Christopher when he was so cold and unbankable that no one else in town would be seen with him or even return his calls. David had supported her to the hilt.

Not only was Tony famous for budgets so inflated that one of his recent flops had brought down a studio, but he'd mortgaged his entire personal fortune to open his own studio, vowing never again to direct for anyone else, never again to relinquish complete creative control. Unfortunately for Christopher, his own studio was on the verge of bankruptcy.

Joyce knew he was an inept producer and a bad businessman. But he was a very talented director and she'd needed him to save *Carnival.* She was confident that if she oversaw the project herself, she could keep him in line. The question was how to entice him to L.O.L.

She had gone all out. At her direction, L.O.L. had bought up Tony's mortgage, his pledges, and his notes from Wells Fargo Bank. In exchange for his directing *Carnival,* Joyce offered him the one thing nearest and dearest to his heart: the chance to keep his studio. She agreed to put a two-year moratorium on all the papers held over his head. By turning out a box-office smash for L.O.L., he would help himself and help her stay on top.

There was one further condition: that she consider Christopher's own most recent picture, *Hallelujah.* If she didn't like the finished product well enough herself, she promised to help him look good on the street. Lunch at Le Dôme was her way of paying off on that promise. She was glad to help him out. He'd been good on *Carnival,* almost as good as she'd hoped. He overshot a little and had to be watched constantly because he shot a little too slowly. He was a million over, but the finished product was damned slick and commercial.

They stared at each other with unwavering smiles, then looked up to see Anita Habsburg sauntering past their table with an expression of feigned shock.

"Well, well. Dahlings. Who would have imagined! Joyce Heller and Tony Christopher. Still discussing *Carnival?* A little late, isn't it? I do hope the opening next week goes well," Anita croaked in a voice made gravelly by too many Lucky Strikes and martinis (so her vocal cords were both pickled and smoked).

Her entire appearance was dictated by Hermés, Cardin, St. Laurent, Blass, Gucci, and Cartier. She had logos and initials and trademarks on everything and every part of her body. She was very social, very rich, very in, very indiscreet, very Hollywood. Her free time (which was all her time) was spent playing backgammon and dishing ice cream along with all the Hollywood deep-dish "dirt." If she were back in Brooklyn, where she was born Agnes Blatt, she would have been a yenta playing Mah-Jongg and eating Carvel.

She was made to order for Joyce's scenario.

Joyce squirmed in her seat and clutched a script, beautifully bound in green leather, so firmly and secretively to her breast that her knuckles turned white with the effort. The maneuver attracted Anita's very curious and probing eyes.

"Yes, we hope so too, Anita," Joyce responded, smiling.

The waiter appeared with their chicken in champagne sauce. Anita said her "cookies" and "sweeties" and prepared to move on to another table. Joyce unfolded her napkin, and the script just happened to fall to the floor. She bent quickly to pick it up. Anita squatted down as if to help and caught sight of the embossed L.O.L. logo and the embossed title jumping out from the green leather. It read: *Hallelujah.* Thanks to Anita, Joyce knew the story would make the gossip column of tomorrow's trades, if not page 6 of the *New York Post.* Her plan was working to perfection.

As Anita walked away, her curiosity sated, Tony practically burst out laughing. He began to relax. He knew Joyce didn't have a shooting script of *Hallelujah* and that the leather-bound script was simply a prop. Obviously, this was her way of "helping."

Between bites, Joyce leaned over and whispered advice. "Listen, Tony, have your agent tell all callers that we're in negotiation. That you can't be disloyal, your head can't be swayed, especially after all L.O.L. did for you—believed in you enough to hire you for *Carnival.* That'll really turn them on. You can't get anywhere in this town unless you make the competition think they're pulling a coup. The other studios will jump at the opportunity to snatch the film from me—to screw me. They'll all be hot and bothered to steal *Hallelujah* and give my studio a pain in the ass. So, ultimately, you'll be 'seduced' away and sell your picture."

Tony shook his head in wonder. "Jesus, you really know how to make this bullshit town work for you, don't you?"

"You gotta learn the rules and pander to their standards. Smile and keep aloof, but remember, the winner is the one whose stiletto slips in first. You're a talented guy, Tony. Win, lose, or draw at the box office with *Carnival,* you're a fucking A-one person and a great director. I hope everything works out with *Hallelujah.*"

"It's been a long time since someone I respected complimented me without jiving or sucking up. Thanks for telling it straight. You're a gem."

Thanks to Etta Leake, keeper of the vast collection of L.O.L. props and interior decorator *par excellence,* Joyce's studio executive office was warm and tasteful, more like a comfortable living room than a trendy movie set or pretentious "environment." Reflecting Joyce's character, the space was relaxed and businesslike rather than stuffy or intimidating. The walls were a muted beige linen with a heavy textured weave. The carpet was cream-colored pile. Dominating the room were three plush gray couches arranged in a U around an antique manteled fireplace and facing a square polished travertine table piled with scripts. Two graceful wing chairs covered in rich crewel flanked the fireplace, and the burgundy-and-green crewel pattern reemerged on the throw pillows and the window valances.

Alone in the office, coffee in one hand and papers spread out before her, Joyce sat behind her small corner writing table surrounded by built-in bookcases housing scripts, books, stereo and video equipment, recessed refrigerator and sink. Gracing the shelves and the side tables were art objects, including a Mayan clay pot, a delicately painted Chinese vase, and a cachepot that held a white amaryllis bulb.

It was early evening and she hadn't begun to slow down. After spending the morning reviewing all the L.O.L. development deals and the status of the films in preproduction, she'd spent an hour on the set to find out why production was stalled on the latest horror film—this time it was cocaine rather than simply star ego—and another hour with the star (as well as with her agent, manager, and lawyer). Then the lunch with Christopher, script reviews and critiques, hair and nails, more phone calls.

She pressed the intercom.

"Yes?"

"Janet, take a memo for me. For general distribution in sealed envelopes, marked 'Confidential.' Are you ready?"

"Shoot."

"To all studio personnel. Re: Mr. Christopher's film, *Hallelujah*. Quote: Please observe absolute silence regarding the *Hallelujah* project. All inquiries, direct or indirect, should be channeled to my office. Discretion is crucial if L.O.L.'s position on this project is not to be compromised. Unquote. Got it?"

"I've got it."

No one in the studio would know what the hell she was talking about. But word would get out soon enough about a secret deal in the works on *Hallelujah*. Inquiries would be made from the outside and they'd all be met with "We're not allowed to talk about it" or "I don't know, and even if I did, it's against L.O.L. policy to converse on the subject."

She was creating a truly delicious mystique.

She pressed the intercom again. "Janet, be a doll and get me Jack Bifton at the network."

The phone light pulsed.

"Evening, Jack. Well, what did you think of the extra *Carnival* footage?"

"Fabulous, Joyce darling, simply fabulous," Bifton answered.

"So, what do you say? How does three hours of prime time carried over two nights sound, instead of a simple two-hour movie? A different cut for television with new scenes, never before seen in the theaters. An extra eighteen minutes of commercial time. Jack Bifton, hero and innovator. Do we have a deal?"

Jack's brain had been clicking madly since Joyce suggested the expanded format. The extra footage and surplus scenes were all exquisitely shot. They could turn the TV version of *Carnival* into a blockbuster miniseries. As long as the picture hit at the box office, he was in like Flynn.

"All right, what's the catch?"

"Catch? There's no catch. Except, if two hours are worth five million, then three should be worth seven and a half, don't you think?"

The red light on the phone board blinked again.

"Excuse me, Jack, can you hold?"

"Sure, sure."

She punched "hold" and then depressed the flashing button. "Yes, Jan."

"Rick Firestone to see you."

"Send him in. And, Jan, go on home and put the calls on service. You were a big help today. Thanks a million."

She released the "hold" button. "Sorry, Jack. Where were we?"

As she looked up from the desk, she saw the new-model Rick Firestone, svelte and tanned, enter the office. Holding the phone away from her ear, she raised her eyebrows in resigned exasperation and pointed him toward the fireplace.

He smiled hesitantly, waved a silent finger in hello, and plopped down on one of the gray couches.

"We were talking about seven and a half million dollars. Come on, Joyce, that's out of the question."

"Okay. I'll give you a break. I'll take a measly additional one million if you exercise your option to utilize the extra footage. If the movie breaks out based on our usual success formula, though, you agree to lift the lid from fifteen to twenty mil maximum."

"I'll get back to you."

Joyce hung up the phone and smiled. She was sure he'd bitten. Not a bad hedge, to lay off Christopher's wasted footage on the network and reduce her downside.

Her eyes turned toward Rick, who was thumbing through scripts on the coffee table. She stood up from her desk, walked over to her old friend, and kissed him on the cheek. Then she sat down beside him on the couch.

Rick stretched his arms around her and hugged her long and hard. "How's my best girl?" he asked.

She returned the hug, leaned back, and gave him a thorough once-over. "Stand up, you hunk."

He complied, turning front to back like a model.

"I can't adjust. Maybe I liked you better fat. Less competition."

"Bite your tongue, woman! I couldn't compete with you in a million years. You're far and away the most beautiful studio head in Hollywood."

"Gee, thanks. Big, beautiful group. Don't go out on a limb or anything."

"Okay, I won't."

She stood up and headed for the bar. "You drinking?"

"Yeah, maybe I'd better. How about a beer."

"What, no Perrier? No carrot juice? You haven't fallen off the health wagon, have you?"

"No, not exactly." His shoulders suddenly slouched and his body seemed to sink, in depression, into the couch. "I wouldn't mind being a little inebriated, though."

She pulled out a Dos Equis from the fridge and poured it into a tall glass. Then she fixed herself a white wine spritzer, carried the drinks to the coffee table, and took a seat facing her old friend. "You're not having second thoughts about the Troubadour show, are you? 'Cause if you are, and you want to play me the music . . ."

Rick took a long swig from his beer then leaned back against the couch, one hand on his hip, his eyes fixed accusingly on Joyce. "No, I'm not having second thoughts. And, no, you can't con me into a private performance, no matter how hard you try. You're going to have to wait a week for the Troubadour, just like everyone else."

"You don't love me anymore, is that it? You can tell me, I can take it."

But Rick's face suddenly turned glum and his head sank down toward his chest.

She immediately read his gloom. "What is it, Rick? What's the matter?"

He sighed deeply. "I think I've got a problem with Derek."

Jesus Christ. Not Derek again, after all these years. She was afraid to find out. "I knew it. What's that shit up to now?"

"I don't know. All of sudden, the last month, out of the blue, he started acting crazy. Now he's been calling me, making all these strange, vague threats. Says he's not going to take it anymore, that he's not going to get screwed this time, that I'd better take him seriously or else. Insists I see him right away. I don't know what the hell he's talking about. I think he's cracking up."

"Sounds pretty familiar. Knowing Derek, I'd wager drugs."

"Really? Yeah, I guess you're probably right. Gee, I feel bad for the guy. He really was a help out in the desert."

"Any idea what he's talking about?"

"Haven't the vaguest. Of course, the house *is* in his name. I know—you don't have to say it. I should have listened to you. You told me so. So, call me *pisher.*"

"Under no circumstance are you to take any crap from that guy, Rick."

"I don't plan to. I've got too much on my mind right now, what with the upcoming show and album."

"What do you think he wants?"

"The usual. What everybody wants. Money, fame, anything he doesn't have."

Rick finished off his beer, got up, and snatched himself another from the refrigerator. He began pacing behind the couch. "What should I do?"

What could she tell him? That the evil spirit of Derek Robertson had returned to haunt yet another of her dear friends? That he was a fool to have befriended him and an idiot to have hired the shmuck? "Where is he now?"

"Hidden Valley."

"Go right to Palm Springs and tell him to get his fucking ass out of your house and off your property. He can't hurt you. David will take care of any legal hassles. Just don't let him use you the way he used me."

"Christ, how the hell do I get myself into these situations?" Rick stopped his pacing and sat on the edge of her desk, one foot on the floor, his mouth resting against his fist. "You're right, of course—again. I have to tell him to get out. I just don't know if I've got the nerve or the heart."

"You've got too much heart, that's your problem. Want me to do it? I'd consider it a privilege."

"No, I'm not *that* big a coward. But, Jeez, I can think of a lot of things I'd rather do."

"Yeah? Like what?"

"Like go see Hedy."

Joyce turned around on the couch, her mouth open. "Why, Rick Firestone! Still?"

He nodded. "Can you believe it? After all this time, I still haven't gotten her out of my system. When I was working on the *Fireside Symphony,* I was thinking about her. If I hadn't chickened out and gotten cold feet, maybe I could have had her, for real. I had my chance, thanks to your little setup in the desert—and don't give me that innocent look."

"I confess. She wanted you bad back then. But she was really on the edge. It wouldn't have worked."

"I know."

"You could try calling her."

"I tried. Her phone's been disconnected. And she never responded to the Troubadour invitation. If only things had been different," he said reflectively.

Joyce stood up, walked over to Rick, and rested her hand on his knee. "Come on, cheer up. You never know what the future holds." She pulled out the cold bottle of Stolichnaya from the refrigerator and poured two generous shots. "Enough of this wimp stuff. How about a real drink?"

"All right. Let's get down." He took the glass from her and held it up. "To old times," he toasted.

"To the *Fireside Symphony!*"

They downed their shots and Joyce impulsively threw her shot glass into the fireplace, where it smashed to pieces. Rick was startled, then followed suit.

"Okay, Joyce Heller, time's up. Here I am spilling my guts out and you're Miss Cool Silent Movie Mogul not giving away diddly-squat. Start talkin', lady, or I'll make you talk." He rubbed his hands together in sinister fashion. "I've got my vays, you know," he cackled and panted in poor imitation of Peter Lorre.

"I'll talk. I'll talk. What do you want to know?"

"The dirt."

"Okay. Let's talk about David."

"David, huh."

"Yeah. What's he doing out on that yacht of his?"

"Wheeling and dealing. Dreaming and scheming. Who can tell with David. Why do you want to know?"

"You'll laugh."

"Jo-oyce. Come on, tell. I promise not to laugh."

She pursed her lips. "Well, I just can't seem to get him out of my mind," she blurted. "No matter who I'm with, I keep seeing David's face. It's really weird. Just the thought of him makes me tingle. I don't even know when it started. Just sort of snuck up on me."

Rick burst out laughing and Joyce slapped him hard on the arm. "I'm sorry . . . I'm sorry," he said, between giggles. "It's just funny, that's all. After all this time. You and David . . ."

"Pretty stupid, huh?"

"No, no, not at all. It's perfect, in its way. It just scares me. I mean, you're my two best friends. If you guys were to have an unhappy love affair . . ."

"Listen to you. I tell you I'm thinking about David and you've already put us together and broken us up. Christ, that was the fastest affair I ever had!"

"Are you sure?"

"Hey, shut up!" she said, smiling.

"Seriously, Joyce, I couldn't imagine anything more wonderful."

"Yeah, but there's nothing I can do about it. I'm not about to throw myself at him and jeopardize our friendship and I'm not interested in joining his stable of 'Barry girls.' Anyway, I guarantee I'm the last one he'd ever think of like that."

"Don't be so sure."

"Well, I *am* sure. He's my boss and my friend, for Christ's sake. And I couldn't bear losing him as a friend. That's what would happen. It always does. Anyway, he's got a shell around him as thick as the walls around Fort Knox. I'd never be able to break through."

"Sure, he's got a tough exterior. He's got more money than he knows what to do with and he's running a company worth practically a billion dollars. But, deep down, he's lonely and unfulfilled, and you and I both know it. Why the hell else would he go cruising by himself on that gigantic yacht?"

"Lonely, probably. Unfulfilled, I don't think so. His whole soul is wrapped up in L.O.L., just like *my* whole life revolves around the studio. If either of us ever had a chance at a normal life, it passed us by years ago. I think it's too late for both of us."

"It's never too late."

She looked at him and read his mind. He was thinking of Hedy. And how it *was* too late.

"Well, at least we still have each other. The musketeers, now rich and powerful, still endure."

Comrades-in-arms, they raised imaginary swords in the air and prepared to return to the fray.

1981

$\mathscr{A}$S THE HELICOPTER SKIMMED OVER THE DESERT AND approached the Hidden Valley compound, the dying sun flashed azure, amber, and burgundy across the flat sand. Rick, his nose pressed against the cockpit window, looked down at the Springs and the nearing hacienda. Like the multitude of colors spread across the horizon, Rick's emotions covered the psychic spectrum, from elation to trepidation. He loved Hidden Valley and everything it meant to him; but the prospect of confronting Derek terrified him.

When Rick jumped from the chopper and crossed the courtyard, Derek was waiting for him, looking thin, frazzled, and wild-eyed. Dressed in his usual outfit of sandals, white button-down shirt, and white beach pants, with his blond locks flowing Christlike to his shoulders, Derek seemed anxious and jumpy.

He took the bag from Rick. Despite the heat, his hand was cold and clammy. "Glad you made it, man," he shouted over the din of the blades.

The helicopter blades wound down. The silent calm of the desert reasserted itself. Rick raced into the house, changed into his bathing suit, and plunged into the pool. The cool water energized him as he swam lap after lap in the early-evening air.

When he emerged from the pool, wet and panting, Derek handed him his terry-cloth robe. "Feels good, huh? Just the thing to wipe away that L.A. grime. Come inside, I'll make you a drink."

Rick followed Derek into the glass-enclosed living room, side-stepped the video camera set up in the corner, and took a seat on the wicker couch. He watched Derek fix two tall rum drinks and bring them over.

"To the *Fireside Symphony*, Rick. It's gonna do great things for both of us." Derek clicked his glass against Rick's and took a long swallow.

"Thanks. But how do you mean 'both of us'?"

"You know. It's gonna send both our careers flying. We're gonna be sittin' pretty. Yes, sir, I can taste it already."

He wasn't making any sense. "Derek, level with me, will you? You look terrible. What the hell's going on?"

Derek's expression lost its faraway, dreamy look and turned suddenly dark and threatening. "Going on? You know damn well what's going on. I'm not gonna stand around and let myself get screwed. Not by you, not by Thane, not by anybody!"

Rick looked perplexed. "What are you talking about? Nobody's trying to screw you."

"Yeah, right. Everybody wants to help me. Lend a hand to a poor, lost soul. Well, forget it, I don't want handouts. I'm wise to your tricks."

"Tricks? What tricks?"

"Finally I'm seeing things real clear. There's only one way to get what's comin' to me." He ran his hand back and forth nervously along the arm of the couch. His mouth was dry as the desert, and his tongue, like a lizard's, flicked continuously at his parched lips.

"And just what *is* it you want?"

Derek began to laugh demonically. He was as charged as a live wire. "What I want? You want to know what I want? I want as much as I can get."

"Meaning . . . ?"

"Meaning you're going to give me exactly what I deserve. Co-producing and co-songwriting credits on the album. Fifty percent of the royalties generated by the *Fireside Symphony*. And you're going to introduce me at the Troubadour as your musical collaborator."

Rick's eyes practically popped out of his head. "What! You're kidding, of course."

"No joke, Rick. This is real life. It's time you woke up."

Rick looked closely at Derek and noticed the telltale signs: the demented glaze in his darting eyes, the absence of eye contact, the burning intensity in his face. All these plus the sudden mood swings and the revved-up edge to his voice told him Joyce had been right. Derek was into cocaine, at the very least. His monkey *was* back. "Is that all? You sure there's nothing else you want? You sure you don't want the shirt off my back?" Rick pretended to unbutton his shirt.

"Don't be a wise guy."

"So, tell me, Derek. I was under the impression—obviously mistaken—that the *Firestone Symphony* was *my* creation. Would you mind giving me one good reason why I should just hand over half my life to you?"

Derek reached down and picked up the remote control from the coffee table. Silently the monitor flicked on and the VCR announced PLAY. Lines of ghostly static disappeared and a picture emerged.

Rick sat forward on the couch, his eyes glued to the monitor.

Suddenly he was looking at himself on the screen, stark naked, on his own bed, with Derek's naked body beside him. Derek was hunched over his lower body, his mouth wrapped around Rick's genitals. Rick's eyes were closed. Cut. The position changed. Rick on his hands and knees, Derek appearing to enter him from behind. Flicker. Cut. The two men, face-to-face, Derek's tongue lingering on Rick's lips and sliding in and out of his mouth.

"Son of a bitch!" Rick shouted, jumping up from the couch and running to the monitor. He ejected the tape, picked out the black plastic box, and smashed it down violently against the wooden arm of the couch. Once, twice, three times he crashed it against the wood, until finally the plastic split. He grabbed the black tape and pulled at it until it dangled lifelessly from the mangled box, floating limply toward the floor. Rick's hand was bruised and bleeding slightly.

Derek looked on, smirking. "Rick," he said condescendingly, "I'm surprised at you. You could hurt yourself like that. You don't think I'm stupid enough to show you the original, do you?"

Rick took a deep breath. He tried to take hold of himself. What was he doing, overreacting like a madman? That was Derek's game. He had nothing to fear and nothing to hide. He'd done nothing wrong. Still, he couldn't stop his mind from racing through vague memories, trying to dredge up the event.

He walked up beside Derek and looked him in the eye. Derek dropped his gaze. "I don't know what you're up to and I don't care. If you think for one second that you're going to blackmail me with some trumped-up, fabricated, simulated sex video, you've got another think coming. No one's going to believe that crap. You don't scare me and you're not going to intimidate me."

"No?"

"No."

"Aren't you even curious to know how I did it? Come on, sure you are. Really, it was a cinch. I should have done it long ago. I don't know why I ever waited, but I'm damn glad I did. Remember the night a couple weeks ago, the night we were celebrating the album, when you got so drunk you passed out cold? You had a little help. A couple Quaaludes dissolved in your wine. Then I rigged up the video cam and—with your help, of course—put you in just the right, compromising positions. What'sa matter, don't you remember?"

After he'd been paid off by Thane in October, Derek had started thinking. He was sick of being jerked around like a puppet on a string, made to dance at Thane Crawley's whim. The more he dug into the nose candy, moving quickly from snorting to freebasing, from freebasing to shooting, the more Derek's mind churned. He was flying high again, just like in the old days. Thane wasn't going to make him a star. He was just stringing him along, taking him for a ride, just like the first time, back in the sixties. Derek Robertson wasn't anybody's fool. He had to find another way.

And he found it, right in front of his eyes. The goose that lays the golden eggs. Why let all that time and energy go to waste? He'd laid the groundwork. All he had to do was carry it through. Not only didn't he need that prick from L.O.L., he was better off without him.

The setup was Thane's idea, from long ago. And it was twisted and sinister as only Crawley could be. Knowing Rick's relationship with Dwight and his dearth of relations with women, Thane figured Rick for just enough sexual insecurity, figured he was vulnerable in just this area. And he was right. Even though Derek had to swallow more than his sexual pride, it was worth it.

"Come on, Rick. This is dynamite stuff and you know it. Now, what do you say we talk turkey?"

Rick's head was spinning. He felt weak and nauseous. The entire surreal scene whirled through his brain like an image from a bad dream. This couldn't be happening. God, if only he'd listened to Joyce's warning.

"You're not getting anything out of me. Not a penny. Just get out of here before I call the police."

"Sure, Rick. Take your time. I'm in no hurry. I've got the house. But I want a guaranteed income and I want my career back. And you're gonna help me get them. You're my meal ticket, man. Thanks to you, I'm finally gonna get the credit I deserve. You're gonna introduce me at the Troubadour and make me a star. Oh, yeah, I almost forgot. I want the Dwight Sharon masters, too. They must be pretty valuable. They might come in handy."

Rick backed away and sank down onto the couch. His head dropped into his hands. Derek was so wired he was spooky, almost inhuman, and he gave Rick the creeps. "Just tell me why, Derek? I never did anything to hurt you. I thought we were friends—"

"Don't give me that sentimental bullshit."

"You don't have to do this. I *am* your friend. I'm willing to help you. I'll help you get off the coke. I'll help you find gigs, if that's what you want. You don't need to do this. Don't be a fool, Derek, you'll never get away with it."

Derek shook his arms so violently, like they weren't part of his body, that Rick flinched back, afraid he was about to be attacked. But Derek didn't move. Only his voice, frantic and high-pitched, seemed to career around the room. "You think I'm gonna fall for that? You don't give a shit about me. Nobody gives a shit about me. Everybody's out to get me. This is the only way. Thane finked out on his promise. He won't do it for me. You're my only hope, man. Sorry, but I've got to look out for myself or I'm gonna get screwed."

No matter what Rick said, Derek wasn't going to pass on an opportunity like this. This was it. The chance of a lifetime. The chance to get everything he'd ever wanted. What did Rick Firestone care about him? What did anyone care about him? He had to look out for number one.

Rick took a deep breath. "You don't scare me, Derek. I feel sorry for you. You never did break your old habits, did you? All you think about is using people. You must be very unhappy." Rick's voice was firm and quiet. "I don't understand you at all. I hired you, let you live out here with me, even let you play guitar on a couple of my album cuts. And in return, you do this to me. I've had it with you. Now get out, before I really call the police."

Derek had known that was coming. Even if he hadn't made the tape. Rick didn't need him anymore. The desert was behind him; Hidden Valley was a thing of the past, and Derek's services would no longer be required. The star was off to greener pastures and it was time to toss Derek Robertson out once again, like a dirty, used rag, to face the emptiness and the abyss one more time.

Well, this time the scenario was going to be different.

He had Rick hooked and there was no way he was going to let this fish get away, no matter what he said. Not after he'd lost Joyce and Hedy and his career; not after he'd watched Hendrix and Morrison and the others lose their lives. Not after he'd groveled in the dirt for ten years. He'd finally found someone else to use—and this time he wasn't going to let him slip away.

Derek raised his hands to his shoulders, palms out. "Okay, okay. I'm going. Just think it over real carefully, Ricky. Give it some good, long thought. Remember what it was like last time, when your career went downhill? Remember how you suffered? Think of what happened to Hedy. You wouldn't want the same thing to happen to you, would you? What's a little credit and a little dough compared to losing your whole career again? When you lose it this time, you won't come back. That'll be it, forever. You're getting off easy. Otherwise"—Derek made a tsking noise with his mouth—"I'm afraid you'll be real sorry. And I wouldn't want to see that. After all, you've been pretty good to me."

Rick listened too carefully, trying in vain to blot out the horrible scene and the implications of Derek's cruel words.

Derek headed for the door. "And, Rick, don't be stupid. No police, no hotshot friends. You'll just get me angry. You wanna be my pal? Help me out. Do what I say."

* * *

Looking out from the bow over wave after endless blue-green wave, David felt the pitch and toss of the yacht. Mesmerized by the variety of white-crested swells, he felt a cold chill down his spine. With the misty wind blowing against his face, he imagined himself falling into the sea, the bow breaking around him. Even though he was on top of the world, he felt as though he were sinking to the bottom of the sea.

By all rights, he should have been happy. After all, he'd accomplished more than he'd ever hoped or expected. Thanks in large part to his careful and clever series of acquisitions, and his constant replowing of capital back into the business, he was head of a still-growing $2-billion empire. Over the past seven years, springboarding off the now-defunct Silverfish, he'd pursued vertical and horizontal growth for the company with a monomaniacal passion. Not only had L.O.L. become a giant in the entertainment industry—with record, film, and video divisions around the world—but David had structured Dutch holding companies and elaborate chains of Antilles/Cayman Island/offshore banks that kept L.O.L. cash-rich and debt-free.

Even now he was embarked on his largest project yet, a project many labeled "David's folly." Digging deep into the L.O.L. cash reserves, he was single-mindedly buying up twenty-year exclusive licenses on video and synchronization rights for all the major recording artists. If MTV-type rock videos were ever to capture national or international attention, L.O.L. would hold the corner on the world market. In addition, David was in the process of acquiring ROW (rest-of-world) home cassette rights from the major motion-picture studios, banking that the real future of the video market lay outside the United States, in media-hungry Europe, South America, and Asia. Only the future would tell whether he was right.

The risk was tremendous, but David was shot through with confidence. Over the past years he'd shed the wary, detached lawyer's skin to emerge, free-flying like a butterfly, as a daring entrepreneur. He'd developed the fanatic energy and drive, the no-lose mentality blind to all obstacles, the pathological self-belief that characterized all entrepreneurial giants. In his business persona, David Barry had become ballsy and innovative, a single-minded workaholic, a man aroused by deals and passionately devoted to success.

With everything going for him, the despair had sneaked up and caught him unawares. Even though the video venture was in full swing, he'd suddenly realized that he still wasn't satisfied. That in fact he was *never* satisfied. Like an addict, he kept seeking greater and greater risks, needing larger and larger deals. There was no ultimate gratification in any single gain, no clear end to justify the means, just as there was no reason *not* to take the plunge, and no one to play it safe *for*.

His life seemed empty. Money and power, balance sheets and earnings, what were they but dust on the path toward death? Everything he'd done seemed mere vanity, a mere whiling away of time, since there was no one to share his success or his failure. He was jealous of Joyce and her string of young lovers. He was even jealous of Rick and his heartbreak over Hedy. He wanted his own heart to be breaking. And it was—but not over love.

That was why he'd run off to the yacht. To escape the frenzy and reason out the despair, the way Brandon used to do. To feel the sharp bite of his loneliness and run away from the never-ending game of "let's pretend."

But no amount of intellectualizing, rationalizing, or self-pity could help. Only the call from Joyce had crystallized the void. Her voice, coming to him disembodied over the sea and airwaves, begging him to come back to L.A. and to his two dearest friends, had touched him where he was so untouched: in his heart, which he now realized was anesthetized beyond reviving.

Joyce. Her voice and image intruded on his thoughts until he was compelled to concentrate and dredge the picture into consciousness.

There she was. Walking into the Russian Tea Room. Her green eyes flashing. His own mind undressing her until she was naked and beckoning. Joyce, he said to himself. "Joyce," he whispered aloud.

But it was impossible.

He couldn't love or be loved. He couldn't care or be cared for. He felt loneliness even when someone was beside him in bed. No matter how much the idea of Joyce appealed to him, the reality was something he was too frightened to confront. No matter that he was a fearless entrepreneur and a loving friend . . . when it came to a personal, one-on-one commitment, he couldn't take the plunge. Although he'd taken risks and chances right and left in his business life, with Joyce he had to play it safe. He was afraid to spoil the precious friendship they shared, afraid of being rejected and hurt, of paling in comparison to the young studs who peopled Joyce's bed, afraid of dropping his defenses and probing the depths of the real David. That was why he had thrown himself into work and let business take over his soul.

It was too late, pure and simple. It had taken him forty years, but he saw it clearly now. He would never have those simple, human things. He'd taken the pitch and roll and had won—he was on top. But the price of power and glory was that he'd made a heap of all his emotions and sacrificed them, along with his heart and the chance for real happiness, love, even "relationships."

He could barely use the word *relationship* for any of his numerous affairs. The gossip columns were full of news about his string of "Barry girls"—each of them gorgeous and classy, paraded like jewelry for a night or two on the arm of the powerful empire-builder, David Barry. And then, having displayed them to the world, he sent them off with a kiss into the beds and lives of other rich and powerful men, men more capable than he of relationships, marriage, even love.

By reputation, he was the ultimate ladies' man, glamorous and sexy, *the* eligible bachelor. So great a lover that one of the gossip columnists had written about the secret acronym that women used to describe his prowess. "IPIP," they would whisper, to indicate their membership in the Barry fold: Infinite Pleasure, Indefinitely Prolonged.

What the columnists didn't know, and even Barry's mates didn't seem to comprehend, was the totally one-sided nature of David's erotic life. He was an orgiastic pleasure-giver, devoting himself exclusively, like a master artist of the erotic, to leading his partners to unexplored heights of passion, while he himself refused anything in reciprocation.

His tongue was his primary instrument. Strong, sensuous, sinewy, and sinful, like a serpent, his sharp, moist tongue slithered from one erogenous zone to another, until his victim was moaning and shuddering uncontrollably. Starting on her lips, he would move to her earlobes, her neck, her armpits, her nipples—lashing, sucking, caressing, all the while whispering erotically, describing what he was going to do and how he was going to do her.

His tongue and fingers played her body with intensity, shooting an electric charge out from his soul through his flesh and into the very tips of her nipples and the lips of her hungry, aching sex. When she tried to reach out for him, he pushed her back firmly onto the plush carpet, whispering for her to lie back, like a goddess, while he worshiped her on his knees. His magic tongue wandered up and down her thighs, around her pubic hair, sliding in and around her moist lips, until it plunged into the depth of her secret, dark, soft womanhood and she screamed out with unbearable pleasure.

Her body tingled all over as blood rushed to her head so fast she felt like someone was placing poppers in her nostrils. Her skin was taut, her nipples so stiff and tight and hard and red that they quivered like mini-erections as millions of nerve endings sent shock waves of ecstasy through her body.

As his teeth nipped at her red labia and his sharp tongue flicked and pressed against her swollen clit, his fingers roamed from her breasts to her buttocks, pinching her flesh until it burned, sliding into her buttocks and her cunt. When the first wave came, she shuddered and screamed in an agony of pleasure. Then he pressed on even more passionately, his tongue working faster, his mouth devouring her, his fingers probing deeper, until the pleasure became practically unendurable and she came again and again and again, for a seeming eternity, sobbing and shaking and shivering in erotic delirium, carried outside her own body. At that moment he owned her, and she would never be the same again.

When it was over, he covered her with the red fox blanket and kissed her forehead gently, the way a father would kiss a sleeping daughter. Infinite Pleasure, Indefinitely Prolonged.

But not for David Barry. The woman felt overwhelmed: sexy and ravaged and shaky and special. In return, David asked and felt nothing. In fact, insisted on nothing. All his pleasure was vicarious, derived from the feelings and pleasures he bestowed so unselfishly.

He managed to carry it off so smoothly and suavely that none suspected the deep-seated fear that motivated him: that he couldn't feel the way he was supposed to, and couldn't perform as he was meant to. It was as if he'd lost touch with his own organ, as if the nerves between brain and cock had been severed, and he no longer remembered what real passion was like. Without warmth and love, power had become his passion, and business the only mate that could make him hard.

Even though he hadn't committed himself to return—telling Joyce he would try but never really intending to; still clutching to an overwhelming need to be off by himself—he *was* anxious to hear about the problem Rick was having, which Joyce had hinted at but had refused to elaborate on by phone. He *was* anxious to hear about Thane, whose pressing of half a million *Carnival* albums made no sense in view of his advertising budget; and to hear more of Joyce's gossipy tale, picked up years ago from Jorge, of Thane beating up several girls in Rio.

But that was only part of it. Joyce's *Carnival* opening was only a few days off. Rick's Troubadour show was fast approaching. Maybe his friends really did need him.

He made his way from the deck down to the large pine-paneled study. Yes, it was time, he resolved. He picked up the phone. "Get me the captain. . . ." His fingers drummed impatiently against the desk. "Captain, turn her around, will you. We're going back to L.A. That's right. Full steam ahead."

26

1981

*F*ROM AFAR, WITH BLUE SPOTLIGHTS ILLUMINATING ITS
pink adobe dome, the infamous Beverly Hills Hotel looks more
like a Spanish mission or an Islamic mosque than *the* chic
Hollywood club. The pink and green Spanish theme, the eclectic
movie-back-lot architecture, and the eternally flaming gas fire-
places offer nary a clue to the legendary wheeling and dealing
that take place within its confines.

Around the pool and cabanas, the Polo Lounge and the exclusive bungalows, the beautiful, rich, and powerful of the entertainment industry "work" the hotel like the consummate artists
and politicians they are: playing kiss-kiss, mingle-and-scheme,
see-and-be-seen.

The family management fuels the fires with their smooth,
personalized service. A dossier on each and every regular guest
lists current position in the industry, credit rating, favorite suite,
preferences, and intimate peccadilloes. The entire staff—from
telephone operators to bell captains, from doormen to valets,

from pool staffers to waiters—is briefed so thoroughly on each guest that they know whose film is dying and whose has legs, which singer has a bullet and which doesn't, who is on the up and who isn't. They bow and scrape accordingly, the warmth of their welcome proportionate to the status and generosity of the star.

Today, Thane Crawley was king of the hill. The entire afternoon was precisely choreographed for slick, orderly elegance, as befitted the man himself. Thanks to his careful planning, his demeanor, and the hundred-dollar bills he'd tossed about to prime the hotel pump, the staff was abuzz with obsequious efficiency. The poolside reception for the *Fireside Symphony* was the chicest and most "informal" party of the year. Thane had seen to that.

Taking Rick's cue, he'd gone all out to promote the event, the album, and, not incidentally, himself. The most prestigious Beverly Hills PR firm had arranged the optimum date (Saturday, December 5) and the guest list for the afternoon reception and evening Troubadour show. Rick's face and new body, captured by Scavullo, already graced the covers of countless magazines. The cost of the entire operation, including Thane's $2,000-a-night bungalow, was exorbitant. But who cared about cost. L.O.L. and Rick Firestone were footing the tab.

By keeping an airtight lid on the music while promoting the forthcoming show and album to the hilt, Thane had whetted media appetites and rippled advance word through the recording world. The stars, the press, the new and old greats of the music business, they were all there. No one wanted to miss this social and musical happening.

Walking toward the pool area, Thane smiled with deep satisfaction. The sun was still bright, the last guests were finally leaving, everything had gone according to plan. If, for a moment, he'd ever doubted he would slough off the stigma and leave behind that horrible dark period to return from purgatory, he had only to look around. The same men who had once turned their backs on him were now groveling at his feet. Apollo Records was in the dumps and Hans van der Rogdt back in Geneva in disgrace, while Thane Crawley was on top, with a spotless reputation, about to rake in as much power, glory, and money as he'd always wanted and deserved.

First *Carnival in Rio* and now this. Thanks to that efficient bitch, Joyce Heller, *Rio* was breaking box-office records and pushing the sound track to the top of the charts. As he'd hoped, the half-mil hadn't made a dent in the stores, leaving more than enough room for the next half-million units he'd helped the mob bootleg, as well as another pressing for L.O.L.

The whole bootlegging operation was so laughably simple that he'd jumped at the opportunity some years back. Especially when it promised financial windfalls for himself and a chance to screw his kike boss, David Barry, out of L.O.L. profits. Duping the vinyl was a piece of cake. The art was trickier, but not when a copy of the album art was lifted from the color processor and handed over. No one could tell the difference after they cut the parts from a "mother" in the stamper.

Finished product in hand, the mob simply undersold the record company by offering perfect replicas to the stores at substantial savings. With no one the wiser, everyone but the artist and the record company stood to profit: the mob; the record-store owners, who garnered larger profit margins; the public, who could buy the record at a discount price; and especially Thane Crawley, who received substantial kickbacks.

Timing was everything, though. The contraband couldn't sit for too long without attracting attention, so the sales projections had to be on target. Already burned several times in the past, Thane couldn't afford another setback. The *Fireside Symphony*, fueled by the Troubadour, was just the sure thing he'd been waiting for. This time he'd gone all out—thanks to Derek's early delivery of the master—pressing the first million and handing the next two to the mob on a "platinum" platter. Thereafter he would share the market with the boys on a one-to-one ratio. And he'd taken care of Derek, in case he had any ideas, providing him with enough uncut blow to keep him strung out and in line.

Thane was out for a killing, counting on Rick's album to break the sound barrier. It was all coming down today: the album shipped to the stores, Rick doing the Troubadour, Thane himself presiding like a king over the Beverly Hills Hotel. The excitement and danger were thrilling, making him ready to slip away from the party to his posh bungalow and savor the flesh of the black Amazon with the whip who awaited him in one of the bedrooms.

Unlike Stigwood, who preferred the huge 10, or Clive Davis, who opted for the tasteful 5, or the distant 12 once favored by the reclusive Howard Hughes, Thane Crawley asked for, and received, the newly built Bungalow 7. Its large living room and dining area were done in yellow-and-black California Chinese with yellow chintz screens and antique mirrors. There were three baths and three bedrooms (each with its own door leading discreetly to the outside), direct access from Crescent Drive (so guests never had to pass through the hotel), and soundproof walls, making No. 7 perfect for the elusive Thane Crawley.

Usually Thane used Herb Armstrong's stilted hill house on Sunset Plaza Drive or Phil Waters's Santa Monica beach house for his private "sessions." In return, he took care of his manager friends, inflating the figures on their deals so they'd get an extra twenty-five grand (more than enough to cover their legal fees), or signing a few of their unknown artists for a half-million advance, twenty-five percent of which went directly into Herb and Phil's pockets. All easily justifiable and certainly within the customary and acceptable boundaries of the recording industry.

But today was different. Today he had no time to slip away.

As Thane entered the bungalow and locked the door behind him, his mind began to conjure and his member to swell. He could smell her damp, dark skin and imagined the way she would lower herself down onto him, her lips grabbing and squeezing him like a vise. He could feel the tip of the leather whip burning into his flesh and could taste her taut, brown nipple in his mouth. After a few hours of his black beauty—after she'd beaten him and eaten him and sucked him dry—he'd be ready to face the music. Let Rick Firestone play his heart out and drive them wild. When all was said and done, it was Thane Crawley who would triumph.

*   *   *

The atmosphere outside the Troubadour was electric, charged with the energy of an opening night. The line of limos stretched around the block, fans desperate to stargaze shoved against police barricades, flashbulbs popped furiously as celebrities paraded up the red carpet into the theater.

Inside, the heavies of the music and film business, decked out in sparkling (rented) jewels and dazzling evening attire, strutted their stuff en route to their seats. Greeting each other with ostentatious displays of insincere affection, they checked each other out and bitched, in catty undertones, about friends, seat locations, and tablemates. To the naked eye, the space looked as overcrowded with stars as the Milky Way.

Front and center, at the prime round table before the elevated stage, Joyce sat radiant beside Rose Feuerstein. Regally garbed in a black velvet evening gown, Joyce had taken special care with her appearance, recalling all the tricks Monsieur Leon had taught her long ago on Fire Island. Her coal-black hair cascaded over her creamy bare shoulders, and her neck was circled with a double strand of pearls—the ones David had bought for her a lifetime ago at Tiffany's.

Despite the inner tension roused by the excitement and trepidation of Rick's opening night, Joyce was aglow with success. The *Carnival* numbers were surpassing even *her* expectations. Thanks to her expert maneuvering, Tony Christopher had signed a three-picture deal with another studio and had laid off the total cost of *Hallelujah*. And David had returned.

"I'm so excited I could *plotz*, Joycie. All these stars to see my *boychik*. If only Becky could see him now!" Rose bubbled excitedly. At sixty-seven, the once buxom platinum blonde looked worn and haggard, with deep wrinkles in her thinning face and a slight hunch in her posture. After all the years, and notwithstanding Rick's comeback, Rose still bore the scars of Joey Gold's betrayal.

Joyce smiled and tenderly patted Rose's arm. The happiness in Rose's face made her doubly glad that Rick had returned to Brighton and reconnected with his family. Roots were important, for those lucky enough to have them.

As Rose looked around to gasp at the celebrities, Joyce turned once again to search the crowd for David. Although he'd promised to escort her, he'd bowed out at the last minute. Another crisis, another unavoidable meeting. She knew what it was like and, of course, excused him without giving an inkling of her disappointment.

Then she spotted him across the room and her heart raced.

It seemed to take him forever to wind his way through the crowd, shaking hands and greeting associates. When he finally reached the front table and their eyes met, he looked so strong and handsome that she wanted to fall into his arms. Instead, she kissed him lightly on the cheek.

He drank in the odor of her hair, her body, her perfume. His wandering eyes riveted on her bare shoulder. She was hypnotically beautiful.

"You're breathtaking tonight, Joyce. You really are," he whispered. He leaned behind her to greet Rose, then took his seat beside her.

"Thank you, David. You're not so bad yourself." In fact he looked quite dashing in his dark blue suit.

"About tonight . . ."

"Forget it. I know the credo: business before pleasure." She felt her stomach flutter and took a deep breath. "I don't know about you but I'm nervous as hell. Imagine having to perform in front of all these people. Poor Rick! You really think he'll pull it off?"

"He'll bowl them over. I can't wait to hear the new music."

The band members began to wander into place on stage, rechecking their instruments, plugging in, getting comfortable. Joyce leaned over and whispered into David's ear. "Listen. We've got to talk."

"About Thane?"

"Yeah, that too. But that can wait. About Derek."

"Derek Robertson?"

"Yeah, remember Derek the shit? The one who bounced me like a rubber ball? The one I thought was long dead? Well, I think he's been revived, in a new alien body. And he may be out to get Rick."

"You're kidding."

"Afraid not."

"What's up?"

"I don't know for sure. Rick won't talk about it. He had some big confrontation with Derek last week in Palm Springs. He seemed very upset."

The lights slowly dimmed and the noise level in the audience gradually decreased. "I'll tell you about it later," she whispered, resting her fingers tenderly on his forearm.

The room darkened completely. Then a single quartz beam shot intensely onto the piano, bouncing off the shining surface and making it glow like a painting in a museum. Over the loudspeaker, the announcement was simple and straightforward, just as Rick had requested. "Ladies and gentlemen . . . Rick Firestone!"

Despite the thundering ovation, Rick didn't emerge on stage. Instead, he suddenly materialized behind the crowd, making his way up through the throng of friends and celebrities. With the follow spotlight on him, he shook hands, kissed cheeks, called out "Hello's" and received words of welcome and good luck. He brushed by Thane and shook his hand. Then he stopped at the center table, bent over and kissed his mom and then Joyce, and squeezed David's shoulder.

Beaming with joy, Rick finally made his way up onto the stage. The applause ebbed, but the crowd continued to buzz at the sight of the formerly roly-poly Rick Firestone, now tanned, muscle-toned, and practically a sex symbol in his svelte-fitting formal black tails.

As he took his seat at the bench and rested his fingers dramatically on the keys, the spotlight softened and the audience hushed. He looked back toward the band, whispered, "One, one, one two three," and burst into his first songwriting hit, "You're the Devil in My Life." Still catchy and singable, the old material was part of everyone's past, and Rick cleverly warmed the audience by doing fifteen minutes of nonstop Firestone hits, a medley of all his top-ten singles from 1958 to 1964. He followed with a medley of an additional fifteen hits spanning the years '72 to '79, giving each number less than a minute before flawlessly segueing into a new tune.

Each song was a dazzling reminder of just who and what Rick Firestone was, his place in musical history, his up-down-up-again career, and the professionalism and success that he was daring to try and top. After nearly thirty hits, more than most artists could hope for in a lifetime, Rick was putting it all on the line one more time.

When the warm and respectful applause died down, Rick addressed the audience. "Thank you, thank you very much. I'm not much with words, so I won't even try to tell you how happy I am that you're all here to share this night with me. I'll leave that to my music." His fingers played lightly and nervously over the keys.

"That first set was a little history, in case you'd forgotten who Rick Firestone was." The audience laughed. "Now I'd like you to sit back, close your eyes, and think of someone you love. In fact, don't think at all, just feel if you can, and let the music carry you away. Now you'll see who Rick Firestone has become.

"I'd like to dedicate this performance to someone who couldn't be here tonight. Someone who many of you knew in the past and who holds a very special place in my heart . . . This is for you, Hedy."

Eyebrows raised around the room and the crowd murmured in surprise. Rose hung her head. Joyce, secretly pleased, exchanged a "How do you like that!" look with David.

When Rick's hands touched the ivory keys and he began the overture, the inanimate object beneath him suddenly came to life. The sound that emerged from the piano was like a caress or a romance, so warm and loving and sensual that it aroused even the most stonehearted in the audience.

In ten self-contained but integrated songs, ten wondrous movements of music, Rick presented the *Fireside Symphony* to the Troubadour with the theatrics of a Coco Chanel presenting her spring collection. Using his voice as a brush and his music as the oils, Rick painted a picture of love and sharing, loneliness and despair, emptiness and fulfillment, that even the blind could see.

No one in the audience could resist the fluid, embracing sounds that sneaked into their hearts and ravaged their souls. The music was so pure and universal that it broke through the barriers of even the most guarded listeners. It forced them to react spontaneously, naturally, unselfconsciously, as they had when they were children, before they'd been taught how they were supposed to react, before they'd learned to fake and temper their responses.

The magical sounds eradicated all thoughts of deals and royalties, money and jewelry, hits and misses. Instead, the hypnotic chords and heartfelt words touched the audience directly, making their hearts beat with feeling. For those precious few moments, they were returned to the innocence of childhood, to a time gone by when they felt need and hunger that no worldly goods could satisfy, when love was their fix, their business, and their pleasure.

Rick's music was violating the audience almost indecently, forcing them to lower their guards, cutting through their hypocrisy, touching them to the quick.

For thirty minutes, the audience sat entranced. When he played the final chord of the symphony, Rick didn't let them react but jumped from the soft strains of the *Fireside* directly into a totally revamped, bluesy, almost a cappella version of "How Can I Go On Without You?"—singing his heart out one more time for Hedy and Grandma Becky.

After the music stopped, the sound lingered in the room and in the hearts of everyone present, like the spirit of a departed loved one. The crowd sat still, almost afraid to move and break the spell. Then, slowly, they began to clap. As if lifted by a giant magnet, they rose as one and cheered wildly, screaming out their thanks and appreciation. In an uncharacteristic display, they whistled, shouted, and stamped their feet. Cold, hard, vicious vipers of business wept openly for the first time in their professional lives. The blasé music critics, who shunned public reaction, were swept along with emotion. Everyone looked around, aware that they were sharing in a magical, historic moment.

Standing beside his piano, Rick looked out over the crowd. He saw that he'd moved them, not just his tried-and-true fans but his peers, the most famous names in the music business, his fellow composers, producers, recording stars, executives, friends. His heart practically burst with love. His gamble had paid off: The *Fireside Symphony* was working.

The crowd kept up their applause. They wouldn't stop and they wouldn't sit down. They shouted over and over for more, until Rick realized he had no choice but to play again.

He'd planned no encore. He had nothing more to play and no more to say. Whatever he did would be anticlimactic.

His thoughts turned to Becky. What more was there inside him that he could turn to? What was left in him that he had to share?

Then, like a message from the gods, the inspiration came to him and he knew what had to be done. Although it had been nearly twenty-five years, he trusted his instincts. He asked his musicians to leave the stage and signaled for the lights to dim. A single pinspot illuminated the piano. Confident their wish was about to be granted, the audience finally quieted in anticipation.

He didn't play or sing a new song. He didn't reprise "How Can I Go On Without You?" the way Garland used to encore with a second rendition of "Over the Rainbow." Incredibly, Rick managed to astound them again. He managed to gild the lily and blow the unblowable minds of the overindulged, jaded professionals who filled the Troubadour.

Taking a deep breath, he closed his eyes, imagined he was in a recital hall, and let his fingers recall long-gone nerve endings. He attacked the keys impeccably, passionately, musically, as a pianist rather than a piano player, the way he'd done for Frances Goldstein and for Juilliard, throwing himself into an inspired performance of the *Fantasy Impromptu* by Frederic Chopin.

Except for Joyce and David and Rose, the audience had forgotten or had never known about Rick's background. They knew him as a pop singer, not as an accomplished, classically trained musician. Knocked back in their seats, the audience thrilled to the passionate, emotional, unexpected virtuoso performance.

This time, when he finished, he simply stood up and drank in the ear-shattering applause. He grinned and blew kisses to the audience. Then he bowed formally and walked off the stage. The revelry continued unabated, but Rick never returned.

When the lights came on, the crowd inside the Troubadour resembled the audience after a Greek tragedy. They stood still, emotionally drained, unable or unwilling to return to real life and come back down to earth.

To one side, Thane began wandering through the crowd, accepting congratulations for his star, his flesh tingling, his heart beating faster. It was everything he'd expected.

At the center table, Joyce hugged Rose tightly and turned to David to feel his strong arms wrap around her. She cried softly into his chest, and he felt it as well, remembering Sheepshead High and Juilliard and Grandma Becky. Rick had come such a long way. If only he, David, were capable of traversing that same emotional and spiritual path.

In all the tumult, no one noticed the blond-haired man in the caftan sitting in a dim, back corner of the theater. With his eyes staring straight ahead, Derek Robertson sat motionless, glued to his seat. His teeth were numb and clenched. He squeezed the drink in his hand so hard that the glass cracked.

If that's how Rick wanted it, that's how he'd get it. Nobody, but nobody, fucked around with Derek Robertson and got away with it.

1981

"OH, MY GOD!" JOYCE SAID ALOUD, ADDRESSING THE empty space of her kitchen and the early-morning light.

Her run completed, she was relaxing at the breakfast table, sipping her coffee and skimming the trades, just like everyone else in Beverly Hills. Until the front-page column in *Variety* jumped out and practically kicked her in the groin.

Hollywood, Dec. 7—Out of the frying pan and into the fire? That's where the red-hot Rick Firestone seems to have jumped. Flush from his dramatic appearance at the Troubadour and the release of his toasty new album, the mellow pop star and former teen idol finds himself embroiled in a palimony suit that might just quench some of his female fans' fires.

Seems that one Derek Robertson (Sixties flash-in-the-pan rock and sex symbol, more renowned for his tight bulge and erotic poses than for his music) is about to file papers in California Superior Court claiming he is the common-law spouse and gay lover of none other than Mr. Straight, Rick Firestone!

Robertson, who worked as Mr. Firestone's "assistant" and "live-in helper" during his Palm Springs retreat, claims that the romantic *Fireside Symphony* was actually written to and for him, as a testament of love and affection, and that he collaborated on the writing and producing. He is seeking co-songwriting and co-producing credit and half the revenue generated by the album. Looks like Rick wasn't so alone in the desert after all. Better fire up those new muscles, Rick, to jog a retreat from your pursuing Mary.

Additional scuttlebutt: Did you know that Rick darling dedicated his Troubadour show to the former Tramp of Camp, Hedy Harlowe (may she rest in peace, *please*)? The long over-the-hill prima donna hasn't been seen or heard from in nearly seven years, thank God, but she and Rick were reputed to be quite a number once, back in the Sixties. Of course, that rumor might be just another media lie to smoke-screen Rick's true sexual propensity. After all, he was very close to the late, great Dwight Sharon, and we all know what kind of "man" Dwight was. With Derek's pretty blond hair in his face, who knows, but Rick Firestone may be following Hedy's footsteps down the path to oblivion. Doesn't it burn you that these stars are such hypocrites that they won't come out of the closet until they're forced out?

Today's gossip quiz: What hotshot movie-studio head used to be Derek Robertson's old lady and was responsible for taking the infamous erotic cover shot for Derek's "Looking at the Face of Love" single? That's right, she's a she (meaning Derek's at least AC/DC) and, hint-hint, she works for supermogul David Barry. She may seem cool and tough, but beneath that thick skin beats a hot-blooded mama who loves to carnival. Send in your responses today. As usual, no entries will be kept confidential!

She picked up the phone and dialed David's private number. It rang five, ten, fifteen times.

"Come on. Come on, David," she urged. "Pick up the fucking phone."

On the eighteenth ring, the phone clicked and a voice materialized.

"Hello?"

"David, it's Joyce. Where the hell have you been?"

"In the shower. Why? What's the matter?"

"Obviously, you haven't seen the morning papers."

"Not yet."

"Remember that talk we were going to have about Derek? Well, forget it, we're too late. Just fetch your *Variety* and be sure you're sitting down when you read it. We've got ourselves a problem."

* * *

"I'm all right, really I am, Joyce."

"You're sure you don't want me to come over?"

"Positive. Don't worry so much. Everything's gonna be fine. I've gone through too much to let some crazy drag me down."

"That's the spirit, Rick. You're terrific, you know that?"

Despite the slander, Rick was still too elated from the Troubadour show to let anything bring him down. He was flying high, feeling calm and in control. The reviews and advance word on the *Fireside Symphony* were tremendous. Indications were that the album could surpass *Songs in the Key of Life, Rumours,* even the *Saturday Night Fever* sound track. His time had come and he could deal with anything, including Derek Robertson's idiotic lawsuit and some gossip columnist's bitchy slander. Even though he'd been shocked by Derek's action and by the column, and outraged at the nasty gibes at Hedy and Joyce, and the reference to Dwight, he wasn't going to let himself get upset.

Most of all, he tried to forget the videotape, tried to block it from his mind just as he had all last week, even though the naked images wanted to haunt and mortify him. The prospect of Derek making the tape public terrified him. Still, he couldn't bring himself to tell Joyce and David. Any more than he'd been able to tell them about Derek's threats. Instead, he hoped against hope that Derek would reconsider, that he wouldn't sink that low or be that mean-spirited. Regardless of the consequences, Rick refused to capitulate, refused to be blackmailed into giving up what was rightfully his.

"David thinks maybe he should talk to Derek's lawyer, see if we can settle out of court and avoid the publicity."

"I don't know. Can't we just ignore the whole thing and let it go away of its own accord? No one's going to take that nut seriously. If we settle, it'll be an admission of guilt and, goddammit, I haven't done anything wrong!"

"It may not be that easy. You're gonna get some heat, I guarantee it. The media's bound to play this up. It might get pretty uncomfortable."

"I'm not scared of the press or the public. They're more interested in my music than in some fake, souped-up scandal about my life. They know me and I trust them."

"I think we should follow David's advice on this one."

"Whatever you think is best. I trust you guys completely."

"We'll do everything we can."

"I know he's desperate. Maybe you're right. Maybe if we offer him something, he'll be reasonable and forget the whole thing."

"Don't count on it. The guy's over the edge. Always has been, always will be. I should never have let you hire him—"

"Stop with the guilt trip. You sound like a Jewish mother. It doesn't fit your image, now that all of Hollywood knows you're a hot-blooded mama!"

"Shit. How the hell am I supposed to run a movie studio with everyone laughing at me?"

"Beats me," Rick answered, making his best effort at a laugh.

*   *   *

The tape was the coup de grace.

If L.O.L. had hoped to contain the Firestone scandal as a mere brush fire, Derek's release of the video turned the brush fire into a raging conflagration. Rick's *Fireside Symphony* was suddenly fuel for a hotter, juicier story.

It happened on that Monday afternoon, the seventh. Derek's lawyer wasn't interested in talking settlement, not quite yet. Instead, he released the videotape to the general press, along with additional gory, fabricated details. Starting in the *Variety* column, the story spread to the tabloids and the national wire services, was picked up by television and carried in the national magazines.

Instead of a minor story about yet another employee stirring up a scandal to extort money from his star boss, the media now had something they could sink their teeth into. Something they could play for all it was worth. They had pictures of Rick and Derek, seemingly engaged in explicit sex acts. And they ran lurid headlines like

FIRESTONE PHOTOS FUEL FIRE
FIRESTONE PALIMONY SUITOR UNVEILS
   XXX TAPE
FIRESTONE SYMPHONY—GAY LOVE SONGS?

The official denials and countersuits merely stoked the fires of controversy. What could Rick say, that he'd been set up, raped, duped? Who would believe him?

By Tuesday Rick was a mess. He didn't get up in the morning. He was so afraid of the throngs of reporters and photographers that surrounded his Malibu house that he didn't dare venture out or answer his phone. He washed down his bitterness with Cognac, and popped Valium to numb the anger and humiliation. After two years of healthy desert living, his body was unused to fending off such an assault. For the life of him, he didn't understand what was happening.

Even though he'd known it was coming, the tape jolted him. Derek's timing couldn't have been more perfect, or more sinister. To Rick's dismay, the scandal was knocking the *Fireside Symphony* off the front page. At first, he was boiling with anger and indignation, feeling victimized, wanting nothing more than to get his hands on that slime, Derek Robertson. But, soft touch that he was, Rick began to harbor doubts and fears. Derek's premeditated viciousness shook his newfound confidence. He started looking for explanations, blaming himself, as if he were somehow responsible, as if he'd let it happen.

The booze and tranquilizers jumbled his mind. His memory dredged up shadows of the fateful night and, ashamed, he seemed to remember his own complicity. He thought back to Dwight. Derek and Dwight converged in his thoughts and he imagined that Derek's insanity was merely the flip side of Dwight's suicide. Self-destructively, he began reviling himself.

He was lying on the living-room couch in his pajamas, drinking Cognac and watching "General Hospital," comparing his life to the lives of the soap-opera characters, when he heard the insistent knocking. For a second he thought it was merely another visitor for Luke and Laura. Then he realized it was his own front door.

"Go away," he whispered. "Leave me alone."

When the knocking continued, he slumped down under the blanket and buried his head in the pillows. "I don't hear anything. I'm not going to talk to anyone."

Despite the feeble attempt to block the sounds, he heard the sudden click of the lock and the distinctive squeak of the front door opening. He sat bolt upright on the couch. "Who is it? Who is it?" he screamed. "Get out of here or I'll call the police!" Like a little boy, he pulled the blanket up to his chin.

"Rick, it's us," Joyce called out. "It's David and I. It's all right."

David, Joyce. He released his clutch on the blanket and let it slide down into his lap. Part of him was bathed in relief, and part was ashamed for his friends to see him in this condition. He jumped up, intending to run to the bedroom for clothes, but wobbled and fell back onto the couch just as David and Joyce entered the living room.

Seeing him stumble, David leaped forward and grabbed Rick's arm. "Are you all right?"

"I'm okay. I'm okay."

As he helped Rick straighten up on the couch, David could smell the alcohol on his friend's breath. He heard the voices on the TV, noticed the pajamas and the sloppy condition of the house. His heart wanted to break. It was worse than he'd expected. So bad that he had second thoughts about going through with the conversation. He was no longer sure that they were doing the right thing, or that he had the courage to tell Rick.

"Maybe we should come back another time," David suggested.

"No, it's all right, really. I just got up too fast and got a little dizzy. I . . . I was taking a little nap." He looked at their faces and then around at the room and realized what they were thinking. "I told the maid not to come in. I didn't want anybody around."

"I'm really sorry, Rick," Joyce said, setting down the pile of unopened letters and newspapers that she'd picked off the front stoop. "We didn't want to break in, but we had no other way to reach you."

"I took the phone off the hook. I guess I've been incommunicado. Like David." He managed a weak smile. "How *did* you get in?"

She held up the key. " 'Member? You gave it to me for safe-keeping. We were worried about you."

"About little old me? Nothin' to worry about. I'm tip-top. Couldn't be better. Just needed a little time to myself."

"How about some coffee? I think we could all use a caffeine fix." Without waiting for an answer, she headed for the kitchen.

David picked up the remote control and Rick nodded to him. "Please. Turn it off. It's giving me a headache." Then he stood up slowly from the couch, gathered a few stray pieces of clothing off the floor, and headed for the bedroom. "Be right back," he said in an unconvincingly cheerful tone.

Joyce returned with three mugs of hot coffee just as Rick, now dressed in jeans and a work shirt, made his way back into the living room. With David seated in the rattan chair, Joyce sat beside Rick on the couch and draped her arm affectionately around his shoulders.

"So?" Rick said, sensing that this was more than a social visit and that his friends were uncomfortable and reluctant to speak. "What's up?"

"You're sure you can focus?"

"Spill it, David. What the hell's going on?"

"You haven't seen the trades or the other papers, or watched the news today, have you?"

"No. I don't need the hassle."

"Well, things have gotten a lot worse. Joyce and I think you should go away for a while, get out of the country, get away from this media zoo."

Rick sipped his coffee silently, then looked up. "I don't want to go away. I'm fine here. This whole thing'll blow over any day now and then everything'll be back to normal."

"Listen to me, Rick. I have to level with you. It's not going to happen like that. The press is out of control on this Derek affair and there's nothing we can do. It's not rational and it's not pleasant, but that's the way it is. The public's turned against you."

"I don't believe it. My public still loves me. They love my music. When they hear the new album, they'll forget about all this crap."

"They've heard the album—it's been on the radio—and they're making fun of it. They're twisting your words and making up vulgar symbolism, reading in all sorts of gay connotations that you never intended. It's become 'in' to make jokes about you. It's horrible but it's true."

Rick didn't say a word.

"You have your health. You have money. Please, for your own good and our peace of mind, take a long vacation, let it all pass. Then, when the time is right, you can come back even stronger."

"Stop trying to scare me, will you. You're making a mountain out of a molehill. It's not nearly as bad as you think. I've been through all this before. I know what it's like. I was down and out and came back. The music is what brought me back last time and the music will bring me back again. The music stands on its own. The public will listen to it and realize how terrific it is. It's the ultimate love feast. It's about the love of another human being and the love of life. Don't underestimate the public, David. They're smart. They'll know it has nothing to do with Derek Robertson."

David shrugged and looked to Joyce.

"He's telling the truth, Rick. God, believe me, I wish it weren't true and I wish I didn't have to tell you. No one's taking the love songs seriously. The public feels angry and betrayed. There's an antigay backlash against the album. It's become a circus. It's got nothing to do with your music anymore. They're laughing at your songs, and no amount of money, pull, or power is going to reverse that now. Nothing."

"No. No! It's not true," Rick insisted.

David took a deep breath. "It's true, dammit. And for your own good and the good of L.O.L., I've decided to pull the album off the market. We've stopped shipping it. I'm sorry."

"Pulled the album?" Rick said, his eyes wide with shock and grief.

"I had no choice. The stores don't want it. They refuse to carry it."

"Please, let us make arrangements for you to go away until this blows over," Joyce repeated.

Rick hung his head. "For how long?"

"A month, six months, a year? However long it takes. You have to swallow your pride and have the courage to disappear."

"Shit, that's not courage, that's cowardice. I just got back and I'm not going to run away again, no matter what you say. I know you're my friends and mean well, but I refuse to throw in the towel without a fight. I don't believe I've lost. I *won't* believe it!"

Rick said passionately, trying to talk himself into the delusion. Inside, though, he was sick to his stomach and scared shitless.

"Then at least get out of this house and move in with me for a while," Joyce offered. "Don't stay here alone."

"I like it here."

"But the press is camped out on your doorstep. It's too depressing to be by yourself."

"You guys are more depressed than me," he lied. "Cut out all the advice, will you? I'm stronger than you think. And to prove it, let's all have breakfast at the Beverly Hills Hotel. Show the world that I don't give a fuck. That this whole thing is a bunch of bullshit. Let 'em all see me. Lct 'em see us smiling together at the Polo Lounge. They can laugh and point and stare all they want, but they're not gonna scare Rick Firestone and drive him into seclusion. Well, whatta ya say?"

Joyce leaned over and kissed him on the cheek. "We love you, Rick. We truly do. If that's what you really want, then you got it. Right David?"

David didn't believe him. Judging by Rick's appearance, he doubted his friend was anywhere near as strong as he claimed. That was why he was trying to negotiate a settlement and a full-scale denial with Robertson's lawyer. So far, however, their demands were ridiculous. Still, if Rick could put on a good enough show for this all-show town, and keep it up, maybe—just maybe—the whole rotten affair would disappear sooner than he expected.

"You got a lot of guts, Firestone. The Polo Lounge, huh? All right, we'll pick you up at 8:30 tomorrow morning. Bright and early."

"Make it Thursday morning. That'll give me a day to get my act together."

"Okay, Thursday it is."

"Now both of you get out of here and leave me alone or I'll have you thrown out for breaking and entering," Rick said, standing up and giving Joyce a playful shove. He couldn't keep up the front much longer. He needed to be alone.

* * *

Maneuvering his Mercedes through the traffic on Santa Monica Boulevard, Thane gripped the leather steering wheel fiercely and shoved his foot down on the accelerator.

Fucking Derek Robertson! When he got his hands on that

blond faggot, he'd strangle the life out of him. What irony, that a nonentity like Robertson, whom he'd salvaged from the gutter, could turn the tables on him. Thanks to Derek's double cross, Thane's plan had backfired in his own face, foiling his moment of triumph and putting his very life in jeopardy! Somebody was going to pay for the two million useless "boots" the mob had on their hands. And that "somebody" was Thane Crawley, unless he performed a miracle.

He had to think now, clearly, and come up with a pile of money or a brilliant plan before the mob came down on him. That was why he was headed for Robertson's hideout. To get him out of town . . . to make him drop the suit . . . to force him to issue a retraction. Anything to take the heat off and defuse the situation. Anything to save the album.

The first day's consumer sales had been spectacular and it was only a matter of time before the bootlegs could have been unloaded safely onto the market. When the shit hit the fan, the bottom dropped out, L.O.L. stopped shipment, and the mob was stuck with a big investment and two million *Fireside Symphony* albums.

He'd been careless and stupid, so cocksure that nothing could go wrong. There was no way in the world he could raise the cool millions demanded by the "boys." If only he could run away and feel the sharp, relentless whip searing his flesh, maybe then he could think. But there was no time.

He'd come too far to let it all slip away. Not now. Not when he was on top of the world. After what had happened at Swisstone, he'd do anything to keep from falling again.

As he made the turn onto Pico and approached the U-shaped group of garden apartments, Thane noticed the ambulance parked out front. He pulled the car to a stop several houses down and walked the sidewalk toward Derek's apartment, No. 3.

Then he saw it. The crowd of people. The door to No. 3 open. The gurney emerging. The hospital personnel surrounding a white-sheeted body.

"What happened?" he asked one of the attendants.

"O.D."

"Is he . . ."

"Yup, stone dead. The syringe was still dangling from the poor sucker's arm."

Thane turned white and walked briskly back to his car. The bonus had been too good. Now the fuck had gone and O.D.'d at the worst possible moment. What the hell was he going to do now?

He revved the engine and pulled away from the curb just as they were lifting Derek's body into the ambulance.

"There has to be a way. There *has* to be a way to move those units!" Thane said aloud, vehemently.

When the idea came, like a flash of lightning in the dark sky, Thane practically jumped out of his driver's seat, as if brought to life by the brainstorm. There *was* one way. A surefire, time-tested way. One that had proved itself over and over in rock history. Not only would he save himself, but he'd make an even bigger killing than he'd planned. It was absolutely perfect. All he had to do was sell the mob on the idea.

He picked up his mobile phone and frantically punched out the number.

"Yeah," the gruff voice answered.

"I'm trying to reach Mr. Catina."

"Yeah. Who are you?"

"I'm Thane Crawley."

"Hold on."

It was nearly a minute before someone came to the phone.

"Mr. Crawley. So nice to hear from you. You've raised all the money and you just wanna know where to drop it, right?"

"Not exactly, Mr. Catina."

"What the hell does that mean, Crawley? You got a short memory or a death wish, or what? Don't you remember what I told you was gonna happen if you don't deliver?"

"I know, I know. It's just . . . I've got a better idea. A way for you to unload all the units you're storing, just like we originally planned. And maybe even more. That'd be best for both of us, wouldn't it?"

"Okay. I'm listening. But it better be good."

"Oh, it's good, all right. In fact it's better than good. It's brilliant."

* * *

After David and Joyce's visit, the next twenty-four hours were pure hell for Rick.

Betrayed by his beloved fans, with the lifeline of his music ripped from his hands, he felt strangely out of control. Pretending that he was seeking facts, when actually only hungry for self-recrimination, Rick turned manic, frantically rummaging through all the papers and trades, clipping and underlining the many vicious articles about himself, spreading them out like a collage across the living-room floor. It was his equivalent of Joyce's photographic journal of her year in Stanmore.

He read about the lawsuit and the claims of community property. He read and heard Derek's vengeful interviews accusing him of hypocrisy, of trying to hog the glory, of being gutless. He read line-by-line dissections of his "faggot" love songs, and violent letters from ex-fans, who reviled him as a sham and a fake.

Every word he read beat him farther into the ground and took away another breath. The very public who had brought him to life and then revived him were now burning him at the stake once and for all. He felt overwhelmed with hopelessness, and stupid for not having taken Derek seriously, for not paying him off.

By Wednesday afternoon he'd been awake for twenty-four hours straight, pumped with the burning energy of doubt and misery. The Courvoisier and Valium made hardly a dent in his frantic nightmare. Regardless of what he'd told David and Joyce, he was no longer sure he had the strength to endure the humiliation, show his face, hold his head high. He was afraid he was down for the count and would never come back again, just as Derek had threatened. Without the public behind him and without Hedy to turn to, there was nothing left to live for.

Walking into the bathroom, he looked at himself in the mirror. He saw bloodshot eyes, stubble on his wan face. Then he seemed to see the strong, hot Rick Firestone—the name and image that he'd created so many years earlier—dissolve before his very eyes and turn back into the chubby cheeks and receding hairline of little Richie Feuerstein.

How could he start from the bottom yet again? That was too much to ask of any man. Maybe there was no point in trying. Maybe . . . maybe he was better off dead. Then his public would be sorry.

If he took twenty Tuinal and drank four or five glasses of Cognac, it could all be over in no time at all. No more press, no more bulbs flashing, nobody laughing at him anymore. Peace at last.

Hesitantly, he reached out his hand and slid open the mirrored door of the medicine chest. His reflection disappeared and his fingers wrapped around the bottle of Tuinal.

A chill went down his spine. No more Rick. Ever, forever.

Nothingness, for eternity. No more music, no more friends, no more life. His mother would die of shame. David and Joyce would wallow in guilt and disappointment. If there were any fans left out there, they'd hate him for giving up and taking the easy way out.

When he turned the plastic bottle around, he saw it was empty. Such a nebbish, he couldn't even kill himself properly.

"Who am I kidding anyway?" he said aloud. "I can't go through with it. I don't want to die." He remembered Joyce telling him about contemplating suicide at Stanmore. He wasn't any more ready to die than she had been. "I just want to make music and make people happy. Why has everything turned out so goddamned rotten?"

Of course he would keep his promise and his resolve. He would meet David and Joyce for breakfast tomorrow. He would put on a good front. He would be strong and brave. It was the Firestone way. The way of the three musketeers.

He shuffled back into the living room, his bare feet stepping on the newspaper clippings, the inky words clinging to the balls of his feet. He picked up the phone and dialed the number of the Malibu Pharmacy.

"Is this Fred? Hi, this is Rick Firestone." The phone line clicked oddly. "Look, Fred, I gotta get a good night's sleep. Can you send me over a couple Tuinal? . . . That's right, just two. I don't want any more." The line clicked again. "And make sure the delivery boy uses the back entrance. . . . Yeah, Jimmy's okay. . . . Within the hour? All right. Thanks. You're a lifesaver."

He lay down on the couch and dozed in and out of a restless sleep until the knocking at the door woke him. He jumped up and hurried to the back door.

"Who's there?"

"Delivery. Malibu Pharmacy," the voice answered.

Rick unbolted the door.

"Delivery for you Mr. Firestone," the young man said. He was wearing overalls and had a dark Latin complexion.

"You're not Jimmy. Fred said he was sending Jimmy."

"Jimmy got delayed. Fred didn't want you to wait, so he sent me instead." He held out the Malibu Pharmacy paper bag.

"Well, I guess it's all right. There still a crowd out there?"

"Oh, yeah. Lotsa press guys."

"Be sure you don't talk to them." Rick handed him a twenty.

"Sure thing. Thanks."

Rick shut the door and bolted it, then leaned back against it for a moment, perplexed. Finally he shrugged and went back to the living room. On the way to the couch, he picked up a glass of water and set it down on the coffee table beside the nearly empty bottle of Courvoisier. Plopping down onto the couch, he removed the bottle of Tuinal from the bag. He flipped the top on the pills and shook the two blue-and-orange capsules into his hand. He sipped at his water. He felt bone-weary and exhausted. "I have to sleep. Everything will look better after I've slept."

He reached out, picked up one of the capsules, and placed it on the back of his tongue. He washed it down, did the same with the second, then lay back on the couch and closed his eyes.

Please, God, let me sleep. And he closed his eyes and was out like a light.

At 8:30 sharp the next morning, David and Joyce rang the doorbell and waited. They rang again and again, but there was no answer.

"Maybe he's showering or something," Joyce suggested. "What should we do?"

"Use the key."

Joyce reached into her purse and emerged with Rick's key. She turned the lock and pushed open the door. "Rick?" she called out, stepping into the house with David close behind her. "Rick?"

As she came around the corner into the living room, she saw him and gasped. "David!" she whispered frantically, reaching back to clutch his arm.

He moved quickly in front of her to see Rick lying passed out on the couch, his arm dangling over the side, his fingers brushing against the floor. Holding hands, they ran forward and bent over their friend. David touched Rick's wrist. It was cold. His face was white and bloodless. His eyes were closed. There was no sign of breathing.

"Oh, my God, Joyce."

"No, Rick! Please, no!" Joyce cried out as she fell to her knees beside Rick's lifeless body and dropped her head onto his chest. She folded his heavy, limp body into her arms and hugged and rocked him, sobbing wildly. "Call an ambulance! Hurry, David!"

David looked down at the coffee table. All the signs were

there. An empty bottle of Tuinal, a near-empty bottle of Cognac. He reached for the phone and dialed 911.

"Wake up, Rick! Please, wake up!" Joyce mumbled.

Dropping to his knees beside the couch, David rested his hand gently on Joyce's head. She looked back at him, her eyes wet with tears, her chest choked with sobs. "It's not fair. He can't leave us. Please, God, don't let him be dead. I'll do anything you want, but don't let him die!" Then she leaned her head back down on Rick's still breast.

They sat there side by side on the floor, waiting, not speaking, until the distant wail of a siren filled the silence. Soon they would take away his body as well and leave only emptiness. A part of them was gone—the best part—and they both knew that nothing would ever be the same.

1981

$\mathscr{C}$LIMBING THE STEPS FOR THE SECOND TIME THAT DAY, David entered the somber carpeted hall of the Beverly Hills Funeral Parlor. Past the director's office, he turned into the chapel where Rick's service would be held the next morning.

The flowers were arranged just as he'd ordered. No sprays mounted on wooden frames, no gladiolus, nothing white. Instead, a rainbow of exotic lilies, birds-of-paradise, fabulous red and purple orchids. Pink, yellow, and red gel spotlights shone down on the smooth raised coffin. By David's design, the area looked more like a stage than the front of a funeral chapel.

He walked up the aisle and stopped before the closed teak coffin. After taking a deep breath, he leaned forward and raised the upper lid.

He blanched. Christ, what the hell had they done!

Carefully lowering the hinged cover, he turned and marched resolutely down the aisle. When he reached the director's office, he knocked on the glass and barged in.

"Why, Mr. Barry. I didn't realize you were here. Follow me, please. I'll show you the arrangements we've made," the pudgy director said in a thick Jewish accent. With considerable effort, he leveraged himself up from behind his desk.

"I've already seen them, and they're not at all satisfactory, Mr. King."

"No? What seems to be the trouble?"

David led the way back into the chapel, with King following, breathing heavily. He pushed open the coffin and pointed to his dead friend. "Look what you've done to him! What do you think you're doing, getting him ready to audition for *La Cage aux Folles?* The makeup is horrible. The pancake is way too thick. His eyes look like Theda Bara's. And what the hell's he doing with rouge?"

"We were only trying—"

"Listen to me, King. This is Rick Firestone you've got here. His soul may be gone, but you're sure as hell not going to make an embarrassment out of his body. Now get this slop off his face and let his tan show. I don't care if you have to bring in Bud Westmore from the studio, but I want my friend to look natural. And get rid of this white fluffy silk and satin crap! I want a gray flannel pinstripe lining with a solid gray silk pillow. Do you understand?"

"Of course, Mr. Barry, of course. Anything you want."

"I want this coffin open tomorrow morning, and if there's one snicker or one snide remark about Rick's appearance, I'll hold you personally responsible. And I promise you, Mr. King, even *your* business can suffer a reversal!"

"Hold on to your hat, Mr. Barry. I'll see to it right away."

"You do that. I'll wait. I don't have time to make another trip."

"Please," King said, pointing his open palm toward the hallway, "wait in my office. It will take only a few minutes." He hurried away.

David watched the round man disappear and felt a pang of remorse. It wasn't like him to vent his anger and frustration, to let his passion bubble to the surface. But he couldn't control it any longer. He'd been in control his whole life, and what had it gotten him besides a dead friend and an empty bed?

The day wasn't half over and he was already tired. The morning had been spent making countless calls—including the horribly painful call to Rose—handling the funeral arrangements in his usual cool and efficient way, arranging for security and other precautions to ensure the privacy of the ceremony and prevent Rick's last rites from becoming another circus.

The media was already swarming and the fickle public beginning to pine for the singer whose coffin they'd helped nail shut. This was just the beginning, though. Besides tomorrow's ordeal and the never-ending business problems raised by Rick's death and the many crises that had to be dealt with at the office, David still had to make the dreaded trip to Laurel Canyon to inform the reclusive Hedy Harlowe of Rick's final request. To face the burned-out "chanteuse" and, yet again, be the bearer of bad news.

Walking back out of the chapel into King's office, time seemed to stop for David Barry. He looked at the bare walls and wondered how many tears, heartaches, and sobs of desperate sorrow were buried in the wood around him. And how many more would be added tomorrow when his friend was laid to rest.

David had pulled strings to rush the coroner's report, and the investigation had been quickly completed. Soon it would be official: Rick Firestone had died of a lethal mixture of sleeping pills and alcohol. As with the deaths of Jimi and Janis and Jim Morrison, no one could say for sure whether it was suicide or accident. David couldn't believe it was either.

If only he hadn't been so blunt with Rick on Tuesday. Or had kept a closer watch, been more supportive, acted more decisively. If only he hadn't been so consumed with business, maybe he could have seen that Rick was fragile, breakable enough to take his own life. If he'd been there when Rick needed him, maybe his friend would be alive today. He spent so much time being Mr. Big Business, Mr. Unfeeling, Mr. Cool Take-Charge that he'd fucked up his priorities—lost sight of what was really important and what was just bullshit. Big-cheese David Barry, who could build an empire reading the minds of strangers and predicting the economic future, couldn't read the signs of desperation and need in one of his two best friends.

Reaching up to a shelf in King's empty office, David lifted one of the cheap black rayon yarmulkes off the pile and placed it gingerly on the back of his head. He bowed and tried to remember something in Hebrew, rummaging through fragments of his bar-mitzvah ceremony and his grandparents' seders, but he came up blank, his mind too filled with questions and self-recrimination. Why Rick, Lord? Why not me? Tell me who, if anyone, is to blame? Me? Derek? The public? The business? Rick himself? Speak to me, tell me. Give me a reason to explain this insanity. Tell me where it's all leading. Make it worthwhile.

But the Lord was silent and David turned more deeply inward. He still couldn't believe that Rick had taken his own life. He refused to believe it. It just didn't fit. It went against everything he knew about his friend. It wasn't like Rick to crumble under pressure and turn to drugs, like so many others in Hollywood, to anesthetize the hurt.

But then, what did he really know about Rick, or about anyone? Everyone was a mystery. Including himself.

It was only a matter of time before it would be his turn, before the fragile thread broke and he, too, was returned to nothingness—ashes to ashes, dust to dust. At least Rick had brought joy with his music and was leaving behind more than a few grieving friends to mourn him.

What have I done for anyone, and what will I leave behind when they pile the dirt over my corpse? David wondered. Cold cash, an impersonal business, a legacy of passionless dreams that, in retrospect, make my life seem like a living death? Ironic, isn't it, that Rick couldn't endure the pain, while I can barely feel it, and have to live knowing that ice runs through my veins.

"Mr. Barry, we're ready for you," Mr. King said, popping his head into the office and interrupting David's ruminations.

David followed King through the corridor and back down the center aisle of the chapel, past the empty pews. This time when he looked into the open coffin, he saw his old friend, finally looking like himself: relaxed, natural, at peace. Impervious to the slings and arrows of a crazed druggie, a cruel public, and a vicious, sensationalist press.

He nodded to the director, who smiled and tactfully made his exit, closing the double doors quietly behind him.

David stood over the coffin, resting his hands on the teak lip, and looked down at his friend. They were alone now, for one last time.

"I'm sorry, Rick," he whispered aloud. "I let you down and I'll never forgive myself. I lost sight of what really mattered. I loved you. You were part of my life, and losing you . . ." David's voice quavered and the words stopped coming. His body shook violently and, like a dam bursting, the tears began to flow, slowly at first, then uncontrollably. His chest heaved with racking sobs—he could barely keep his balance. His nails dug into his palms. He cried out in bursts of agony and leaned his head against the coffin edge.

For once, he didn't care what he looked or sounded like. He didn't think, he didn't hold back, he wasn't performing or pretending. At last, there was no audience to perform for. If he hadn't cried for Rick, he would never have cried. If he hadn't felt now, then his feelings would surely be dead and he wouldn't deserve to be alive.

The tears flowed until his body grew weak and the hysteria subsided. When he finally caught his breath, his body tingled with a strange new feeling of release. Somehow, the barrier that had surrounded him for a lifetime seemed weakened. He could feel it inside and out. This was the cry he'd been suppressing for a lifetime, the cry of feeling, passion, and emotion that, bottled up inside him, had been aching for release. He felt the pain of Rick's death like a needle through his heart—but *he felt,* and that was Rick's most profound bequest.

He raised his head, looked down at the corpse and smiled. "You owed me nothing, Rick, but you left me something priceless. I can feel it, here, deep inside. Maybe I was wrong. Maybe it's not too late for me. Maybe, through you, God actually *has* spoken. I don't understand it, but somehow, in dying, you've made me see and feel things more clearly. Now I realize how much you meant to me. Finally, I feel like a human being, with the courage to face myself and the future. Don't worry, Rick, I'll do everything I can to clear your name and preserve your memory, just like you did for Dwight."

David reached up and gently lowered the cover of the coffin. "Goodbye, old friend. You're not alone and neither am I. I won't forget you."

By the time David steered his Lagonda up the winding Benedict Canyon driveway, it was well past midnight Thursday. Although emotionally and physically drained and with every intention of driving home, he'd ended up driving to the canyon. Tonight he couldn't face the prospect of an empty house. He needed to be with Joyce.

His legs felt like lead as he trudged up the steep steps to the front door and rang the bell. His hand clung to the railing for support.

"Who's there?" an anxious voice asked over the intercom.

"Joyce, it's me, David."

He waited on the steps in the warm December night, looking down at the smattering of Christmas lights on the houses below. When the porch light came on and the door opened, he turned and saw her. After Rick and Hedy, she was like a breath of pure air, a living, breathing vision, with her white blouse tied at the waist; her soft, faded blue jeans; her bare feet; her jet-black hair falling around her gorgeous face.

"David! My God, are you all right?" she asked, immediately noticing the deep lines in his face, the crumpled suit, the tired slump in his posture. She reached out and hugged him. They embraced spontaneously, as two mourners, finally able to share the burden of their tragedy.

"Sorry to barge in this late. But . . . I don't know . . . I just had to see you. I didn't wake you, did I?"

"God, no. I just got back from the office." In his embrace she felt his need as she'd never felt it before. "I'm so glad you're here. I've been in shock all day." Their bodies drifted slowly apart. "Come. I'll fix you a drink."

She held his hand and led him into the warmly lit living room, sitting him down on the soft red sofa. She poured two stiff snifters of Chivas, handed him the larger, then sank down close beside him. The *Fireside Symphony* was playing softly in the background.

Choking back her tears, Joyce ran a hand roughly through her hair. "God, I must look a mess. Every time I put on makeup, I just cry it off. My secretary wanted to bring in the makeup man to fix me up. You look pretty done in yourself."

"I feel like I lived a whole lifetime today." He looked up into her eyes, the whites reddened from tears.

"I can't believe he's gone. My God. If only I hadn't let him hire Derek, hadn't pushed him back to Palm Springs. He knew all along, but he couldn't bring himself to tell us. If only I'd had more time for him . . ."

"Shhh, Joyce. There's no point. I've been doing the same thing all day." He put his arms around her and she laid her head comfortably on his shoulder. He could feel the heat of her body and the rise and fall of her breasts against his chest. They had so much in common, knew and cared so much about each other, shared so much compassion and affection.

If only it were a different world. And he were a different man.

Joyce felt his arms around her, inhaled his masculine odor, and sighed in resignation. No matter how close they were, there would always be a space they didn't dare cross. They both had too much of a stake in L.O.L., in their careers, in the walls they'd built up around them, in each other. Although they were both risk takers, neither could bear to risk losing the friendship, even if the payoff could mean happiness.

"One musketeer is gone. But we still have each other," Joyce said, pulling gently out of David's light embrace. "Is everything taken care of?"

David jumped on the question, hoping to still his throbbing heart. "The press; the funeral home twice; Rose; the cemetery. Then three hours at the office to deal with ten urgent crises. Unless I fucked up, though, everything should be set for tomorrow."

"Stop worrying. You never fuck up."

"Right. Not on the little things. Only where it counts." He took a long swig of his drink.

"Have you listened to the radio?" she asked.

"No."

"They've been playing his songs all night. Holding candlelight vigils across the country. Suddenly Rick's a martyr and everybody loves him again. The fickle public's already clamoring for the album."

"I can't stand the idea that we'll be profiting from his death," David said soberly. He was suddenly anxious to tell her about his afternoon. "I went to see Hedy."

"I wish you'd taken me along."

He shook his head. "You wouldn't have wanted to come. It was pitiful. Worse than you could have imagined. The whole house was a pigsty, and Hedy . . . I hardly recognized her. She looked so old, I thought she was her mother. All the spark was gone and she looked like a fat old bag lady. Her hair was dirty and gray. Her eyes were dull and washed out. The whole place reeked of drugs and booze."

"We should never have left her alone. Poor Hedy. Another good soul fucked over by the business. God, it's horrible!"

"When I told her about Rick, she collapsed dead away. Scared the shit out of me. I carried her to the car and drove her to that fancy nursing home in the Valley."

"Is she all right?"

"The doctors checked her out immediately. They don't think anything's seriously wrong with her. At least nothing that drying out from booze and Quaaludes wouldn't cure."

"Do you think she'll come to the funeral?"

"I don't know. I can't believe she will. She was still groggy when I left. I bought her some decent clothes and made all the arrangements, but it'd take a hell of a lot of guts for her to show up in her condition in front of all those people. And even more to fulfill Rick's final request."

"Request? What request?"

David leaned his head back against the couch. "It was part of Rick's will. He requested that Hedy sing at his funeral."

"Hedy sing! She'll never do it. Not with all those entertainment people there. Not after what they did to her. It's been nearly eight years. Anyway, she lost her voice, didn't she?"

"So they say." David turned toward her and rested his hand lightly on her arm. "The coroner's report is in." His voice was soft and mournful.

"Suicide?"

"Cognac and Tuinal."

She circled the glass with her hands and closed her eyes. "I don't believe he did it on purpose. It doesn't seem possible. Not after all we'd been through together in London. God, I must have been blind."

"Sometimes we can't see the very things that stare us in the face."

"I suppose so."

"You're right, though. It doesn't add up. All day I've been rolling it over and over in my mind. Every explanation stinks. Fuck the coroner's report, I don't buy suicide *or* an accident. The whole business smells. It's too reminiscent of all the others. Of the deaths of Joplin and Hendrix, of Morrison and Presley, even of John Lennon. Mysterious circumstances, cause and motive never firmly established . . ."

"What are you getting at, David?"

"I don't know what I'm getting at. But neither of us believes that Rick killed himself. And an accident . . . Rick didn't even *take* drugs."

"You think Derek had something to do with this?"

"I don't know, but I intend to find out."

"How?"

"Hand me the phone."

Joyce stood up from the couch, cradled the phone, and set it down on the coffee table in front of David. He quickly and decisively punched the L.A. phone number with his index finger, then waited, tapping his fingers nervously against the glass tabletop. Someone picked up on the seventh ring.

"Jack. It's David. Sorry to bother you so late."

"No bother, man. Listen, brother, I just heard about your friend," said the deep, familiar voice on the other end. "He was a good kid and I feel sorry for him. I want you to know that I had nothin' to do with it. I didn't know what was gonna happen and even if I did, there was nothin' I could have done about it."

"Tell me what you know."

"It was business, pure and simple. Economic. Nothin' personal."

David's head started swimming. His mind fumbled over Jack Black's words and he struggled to turn them into sense. "Are you telling me . . ."

"Yeah, man, you read it. It's no jive. But I can't say more over the phone. Just remember, David, things like this happen for a reason. They don't happen without help. Ask around your own joint. You'll see what I mean."

David clutched the receiver. He could barely control the maelstrom of his emotions. "Jack, don't hang up, please! I've got to know what happened. He was like family to me. Except for Joyce, there's nobody in the world who means more. I've got to know. Tonight. Please. You owe me this one."

There was silence on the other end. Finally, Jack spoke. "This is some heavy shit, man. I shouldn't be doing this. But for you, David, as a favor . . . let me see what I can do. Meet me in the parking lot of Chasen's in a half-hour."

The phone clicked dead. David stood stock-still, the receiver dangling in his lowered hand. His mind, numbed for a moment, began whizzing, reviewing and analyzing the information.

"What is it? You look white as a sheet," Joyce said, coming up behind him.

He turned to her, his hands suddenly cold as ice. He had to swallow hard before he could speak. "I think Jack was trying to tell me that organized crime had some hand in Rick's death. That maybe he didn't commit suicide, and that it was no accident, either."

"What about the pills? The coroner's report?"

"He said it was 'business, nothing personal.' If the mob _was_ involved, they could have taken care of everything."

"What are you saying? That Rick might have been murdered? My God, David!"

"The whole thing doesn't make any sense. I mean, why would the mob be interested in Rick? He didn't owe money. He wasn't into drugs or gambling. He was an innocent. Unless . . ."

"Unless what? Derek?"

"No. I don't think so—but what do I know? Jack said it was 'economic' and that I should ask around my own joint. That it didn't happen without help. Maybe . . . But it can't be."

"What?"

"Maybe he meant that Rick's death had something to do with the record business, with my company."

"How could it?"

"I don't know. But goddamn, we're gonna find out!"

He slammed down the receiver and began pacing. Rick murdered? Possibly for some commercial motive? It was too heinous to imagine. The company could only stand to lose by an artist's death.

Or could it?

"Let's go," David ordered.

Joyce rushed into the bathroom in another vain attempt to fix her face. But she gave up after only a few seconds. "Come on. Let's get out of here."

It was nearly 2:00 A.M. by the time David pulled the Lagonda into the empty parking lot of Chasen's, cut the motor, and doused the lights. Silently, the two friends sat side by side, waiting. David's fingers drummed against the wooden dash.

When the maroon 1954 Rolls-Royce convertible pulled up beside them, David stepped quickly out of his car and slid into the front seat beside Jack Black. After several minutes, he opened the car door and motioned to Joyce. She emerged from the Lagonda and took a seat in the rear of the sleek Rolls.

"Jack, this is Joyce Heller."

"My pleasure, darling," Jack said, turning around to nod.

The light at the edge of the parking lot cast an eerie shadow over the faces of the men in the front seat. As Jack turned around, Joyce saw the outline of his strong, dark figure and the fresh flower in his lapel. His hair, a short natural afro, was silver at the temples.

"What can you tell me?" David asked anxiously.

"I made a few calls. It's a long story and one you're not gonna like."

"Go ahead. I have to know."

"You gotta be real cool about this, though. Mum's the word. We never had this conversation, understand?"

"I gotcha," David answered.

"You too, beautiful."

"My lips are sealed, Jack."

"All right. Let me talk about your friend's death." Jack leaned back in the driver's seat and rested his left hand lightly on the steering wheel. The other glided through the air as he spoke. "It fits the pattern like a glove. Rock star, under stress, can't cope with the pressures of stardom and decides to slide out the easy way. The public turns him into a martyr. The fans can't get enough of their dead hero. Think of Elvis, or Jim Morrison.

"Sometimes, when a rocker's star is on the decline, he can be worth a lot more dead than alive. Look at how the Doors' albums are still selling, ten years later. Why? Because of the mystery around Jim Morrison's death. Take Lennon. He was over the hill until he was shot. Then the fans made him a martyr and sales of his albums skyrocketed. Check out the scene after Elvis kicked. The King's more popular dead than alive.

"Rick Firestone falls into the same category. Alive, he wasn't about to sell shit. But dead—man, that's a whole different kettle of fish. His death could be very profitable for your record company."

"What are you saying, Jack? That L.O.L. Records will benefit from Rick's death?"

"You bet, baby. Think about it. Yesterday the *Fireside Symphony* was untouchable. Tomorrow, everybody's gonna want a copy. They'll want to buy Rick's entire back catalog. They'll be dying to purchase every compilation album, best-of anthology, memorial collection that your Thane Crawley releases. That's not even counting the increased value of his music publishing."

"Then it points back to me, to the company. We're the only winners from Rick's death." But how could that be? He was ultimately responsible for the entire company.

"Not exactly," Jack said. "A couple of other parties could stand to benefit."

"Like who?"

"Like the mob, for one."

"The mob? How could *they* benefit?"

"Let me tell you a little story. Just hypothetical." Jack's hand waved expressively in the air. "Say there's a hot artist about to release a hot double album. That product's as good as cash. The record company's gonna wholesale the album to the record stores at $6.98, but the street might be selling bootleg units at four bucks apiece. Why not? The street doesn't pay royalties to the artist or profits to the company; they don't owe songwriting or publishing royalties; they don't pay taxes. It costs them practically nothing to reproduce the album, so at four bucks a unit, they're making a pretty penny.

"So what happens? The stores pick up copies from the street. They'd be nuts to refuse. Every "boot" they sell nets them an extra couple of bucks over and above their usual profit margin. They mix in the contraband with the real thing and nobody's the wiser. In fact, they can't lose. If the album suddenly bombs, the record stores ship back the unsold albums, fake and real, to the record company for credit against future purchases. Heads they win, tails they win. They're not even crap-shooting."

"Yeah, I know about the rip-off," David interjected. "It started with some of the Beatle albums. There were supposedly big contraband sales for *Frampton Comes Alive,* and the *Saturday Night Fever* and *Grease* sound tracks."

"Right on. But do you know what happened to the sound track from the Bee Gees' film version of *Sgt. Pepper* in '78?"

David shook his head. But Joyce remembered the picture was a flop.

Jack nodded. "The word on the street was dynamite. Coming on the heels of *Fever* and *Grease,* the movie was supposed to be a sure thing and the record company overpressed and overshipped the soundtrack. The mob did the same thing with their bootleg albums. To everyone's surprise, the movie died and so did the soundtrack. Millions of unsold albums were shipped back to the record company for credit. So many that the record company ended up with more albums returned than they'd originally shipped!"

Jack held up his hand. "I know. I know. So what's the point? You're wondering. The point is, the mob doesn't like to get burned. So let's just speculate:

"What if there *were* plans for the bootlegging of the *Fireside Symphony*—and the huge advance publicity made it a prime target. Something goes wrong, though. That little prick, Derek Robertson, he fucks up everybody's plans by shooting his mouth off."

"What are you getting at?"

"Patience, dude, patience. So the question is, what to do? Say the mob has two million bootleg copies of the album ready to hit the stores—"

"Two million!"

"Right on, two million. All of a sudden, L.O.L. stops shipping the album. The market disappears overnight and the boys are stuck with a major headache and a big fuckin' loss. So they do the only thing they can to put new life into the album. They dispose of the star. But make it look like a suicide."

"Are you telling me that Rick was murdered?"

Joyce caught her breath and reached up to grab tightly to David's shoulder.

"Your friend wasn't the suicide type, was he? Check out the timing. Convenient, hey? Just at the moment the album was dead. By tomorrow the public'll be clamoring for it."

"I don't understand. How could they have done it?" Joyce asked.

"Easy. The pros know all the ropes. His phone was tapped. His call to the pharmacy for a couple sleeping pills was intercepted. The delivery boy was switched and the prescription altered. Your friend only wanted a good night's sleep. He got more than he bargained for. The pills were laced with a lethal dose of curare."

"Curare!" Poor Rick. Murder. For the first time David keyed on the concept, something he'd been avoiding all night. "But the coroner . . ."

"The coroner was on the take. The autopsy report was fudged. You know, Rick wasn't the first to go this way. Your friend's in good company. Think of Marilyn Monroe. Think of all the other rock superstars' reported suicides/O.D.'s. I didn't say it but . . ."

"But what?"

"There've been other times when it's been expedient to accelerate the demise of a rock star."

David didn't know whether to feel shock, anger, or relief. He tried to think of something positive. "At least Rick was a _mensch_ after all," he said to Joyce. When all was said and done, he was still their Rick, the man they'd known and loved. Only now they knew he'd been murdered, in cold blood.

"Tell me this, Jack. What made the mob think they could move two million units? That's a hell of a lot of albums."

Jack pointed his finger at David. "We're just speculating,

remember? But that's a good question. Tell me, how many units of the *Fireside Symphony* did your company press?"

"I don't know offhand. But I can find out."

Jack picked up the mobile phone in his huge hand and passed it to David. "Find out."

"Now?"

"Now."

David depressed the seven numbers.

"Thane, David. Sorry to wake you, but this is important. How many copies of Rick's new album were shipped? . . . Umm-hmm. And returned? . . . Right. . . . No, I can't tell you now. Tomorrow. . . . Yes, I'm aware of that. We can talk about rereleasing tomorrow. After the funeral. Goodnight, Thane."

David turned to Jack. "There were 1.2 million shipped—and .6 million returned."

"Half a million albums in two days. The market for the *Fireside Symphony* was much, much heavier than 1.2 million. And your record-company president knew it."

"The *Carnival* album," Joyce said aloud, remembering her concern about Thane's conservative pressing of the soundtrack. Suddenly, everything was falling into frightening place.

"Are you suggesting that Thane intentionally underpressed and undershipped Rick's album in order to give the bootleggers room to fill the gap?" David asked.

Jack's silence provided the answer.

"Why? Why?"

"Your president lives far above his means. He's one rotten apple. Bitter, angry, corrupt, he's been on the take, fuckin' over you and L.O.L. for years. Sorry I didn't warn you sooner, David, but I didn't know. Your company's outside my turf. Crawley's the one who provided the advance artwork to the mob. When Rick's album flopped, Crawley's neck was on the line. *He* was the one suggested the setup. He had the most to lose when the album died—"

"And the most to gain from Rick's death." David's blood began to boil.

Jack held his palms open in front of him in a gesture that suggested he was sorry but there was nothing he could have done.

"Thanks, Jack. You've gone out on a limb for me. I'll make it up to you."

Jack nodded. "Be careful now and take it easy, man. Don't do nothin' rash."

David opened the car door.

"Nice meeting you, Miss Heller. Too bad the circumstances weren't better. See you in the morning."

Joyce and David got out of the car and watched, in a daze, as the classic Rolls pulled away.

"Jesus Christ!" Joyce whispered, biting her lip and reaching out to touch David's arm. "I can't believe it."

"Believe it." David raised his hands to his hair and squeezed them against his temples. "God Almighty, Joyce. *I'm* responsible. L.O.L. is *my* company. I should have known what was going on. I hired him. I gave him free rein. If I'd been on top of things—"

"Cut it out, David. Stop feeling sorry for yourself," she said sharply. She'd been through it all and she knew when to be strong. "You can't be everywhere. You can't see inside Thane Crawley's head. No one could have predicted this."

He looked at her, his angry eyes filled with admiration. God, she was quite a woman.

"You're right. This is no time for self-pity. We have to go out there and put on a good show, for Rick. Afterward, though, I'm going to make Thane Crawley crawl. I swear to God I'm going to kill him. If it's the last thing I ever do."

Arm in arm they slid into the front seat of the car. Although exhausted, they didn't have the time or the desire to sleep. Not when they had to lay their best friend to eternal rest in only a matter of hours. Not when his name was mired in scandal and his murder was still unavenged.

1981

7HE PRIVATE, EARLY-MORNING CEREMONY AT THE chapel—attended only by Rick's relatives and closest friends, and merely the preamble to the huge public ceremony planned for the grave site—was mercifully brief but filled with the anguish of a classical tragedy. With his body resting prone in the coffin and the haunting strains of his music played on the chapel organ, Rick's presence eerily pervaded the room. Memories were too fresh for anyone to believe that he was really gone forever.

When the ceremony was over and the attendees filed past the open coffin, Rose, looking down at her son's body, collapsed at the foot of the casket, beating her breast and keening at the mysterious workings of the Lord. Helped up by Joyce, she was led out of the chapel and into the first long, black Cadillac.

David and Joyce shunned the limousine and slid into the sleek Lagonda, taking their place in the funeral procession. They were both wiped out and on edge, crushed by the fact of Rick's murder, exhausted from sleeplessness and responsibility, tense with anger and recrimination.

Headlights blazing, David drove the route to the cemetery in a silent daze. As they approached the gates of Mount Hebron, Joyce gasped. "David! Look."

The outskirts of the cemetery resembled the scene outside a mega–rock concert. Thousands of frantic fans milled about the gate, dying for a glimpse of a celebrity or a last look at their late, now suddenly great, hero. Hawkers offered everything from Rick Firestone candlesticks to incense to memorial T-shirts. The area crawled with TV cameras and press. Even through the closed car window, David could hear the sounds of sobbing fans and the pounding of Rick's music emanating from ghetto blasters. No matter how much he'd wanted to avoid a circus atmosphere, the fans had their way and there was nothing he could do about it.

Inching through the throng of screeching fans and past the horde of security guards, David wound the car down the long path until he reached the grassy knoll near Rick's plot. He turned onto the grass and shut off the motor.

Joyce smoothed the lap of her black cotton dress and checked her face in the mirror. She reached over and straightened David's tie, then tenderly brushed the pocket of his charcoal-gray suit. She took a deep breath. "Ready?"

"As ready as I'll ever be."

They emerged from the car and looked out at the spectacular array of stars and moguls walking slowly toward Rick Firestone's grave. They were the "sweeties" and the "babies," the "cookies" and the "honeys." Everyone who was anyone in the entertainment business was there, to see and be seen and, only incidentally, to pay their last respects to a man who only a few had enough heart or selflessness to care about.

"Let's wait here, in case Hedy comes."

Catching sight of Thane's tall, arrogant figure striding across the field, David struggled to control his rage. There was no doubt in his mind: Thane Crawley had murdered Rick Firestone, just as if he'd strangled him with his own hands. David clenched his fists, his hands eager to mete out the same fate to his record-company president.

He knew he couldn't do it, though. The man deserved to be tortured. No punishment was severe enough. But what could

David possibly do to him that could make up for what he'd done to Rick?

Across the road, David noticed the driver of a dark Cadillac waiting expectantly, holding open his rear door. When no one emerged, he touched Joyce's arm. "Over there. Come on."

They walked up to the limousine and David nodded to the driver, then bent down and leaned into the back seat. He offered his hand to the large gray figure seated within. "I'm so glad you could make it, Hedy. It's what Rick wanted more than anything."

Grasping David's hand, she emerged into the sunlight, wearing a large hat with a veil, dark glasses, and a puffy steel-gray dress. David held out his arm and she took it, hesitantly. Then Joyce came around beside her and lovingly supported her other arm. For a moment, Hedy looked bewildered. When Joyce smiled, though, the haze cleared and Hedy recognized her old friend.

"He loved you, Hedy. Always. And we love you, too."

"Thank you, honey. I needed that," Hedy whispered back.

As they escorted her through the throng—to the curious murmurs of the crowd—Hedy's step lightened and she lifted her head proudly. They took their places before the open grave, beside the tearful Rose—and Thane Crawley.

By the time the ceremony began, the crowd was a hundred deep all around. The rabbi, standing over the grave, rocking forward and back as if drawn to and then away from the open hole, read long passages from the Bible, then translated them into English.

As if mesmerized by the melodic chanting, David heard the sounds but not the words of the ceremony. Instead, his mind cut across time, back to Brighton Beach, to Grandma Becky, to the old, vibrant Hedy Harlowe, to Sheepshead High. He *had* succeeded, beyond his wildest dreams and beyond the expectations of even his high-school chums. But at what price? He thought of all the casualties. Of the young, fragile Joyce. Of Derek the shit. Of poor Hedy and the many lives of Rick Firestone. Of the once buoyant, idealistic David Barry. Of Brandon and Dwight.

The idea came to him, triggered by the memory of Dwight Sharon. A plan crystallized in his mind that was even more perfectly formed than Thane Crawley's plan. A plan that actually made David smile to himself. If only he could make it through the funeral ceremony . . . His hand reached out and squeezed Joyce's fingertips.

When the rabbi spoke aloud the special words, David's ears perked and his attention turned back to the funeral.

"If Miss Hedy Harlowe is present among us, will she please step forward and fulfill the request of the deceased."

The crowd buzzed at the name. Everyone looked around, straining to see, anxious for a vision of a corpse resurrected: the long-gone Hedy Harlowe come back from the grave.

For the longest time, there was nothing. Surreptitiously, David touched his hand lightly to Hedy's elbow. "Come on, you can do it," he told her. Joyce kissed her on the cheek for encouragement.

When she finally stepped forward nervously, David's heart went out to her. Joyce squeezed his sweaty palm. They were both pulling with all their might for Hedy, as nervous as if they themselves were on stage, mere schoolchildren about to perform before a fearsome audience. Only this time no one was faking or pretending. This time, it was for real.

At the sight of the large, gray figure inching toward the grave, the crowd gasped as one. "Honey, that isn't Hedy Harlowe, is it?" someone crudely asked. "My God, *look* at her!" came a voice across the flatland.

She stood motionless at the grave site, looking down at the wooden coffin. Slowly, she raised her head and lifted her veil. She waited dramatically until the crowd hushed. Her chest expanded as she took a deep breath and opened her mouth.

Then, miraculously, spectacularly, Hedy Harlowe began to sing, and the sound that emerged was as vibrant and clear as a cloudless sky. Her voice rang out over the cemetery and across the field, the voice that had thrilled a generation, singing Rick's song, the song he'd written for her, asking "How Can I Go On Without You?"

For three minutes the entertainment industry barely took a breath. Only Rick Firestone, in his performance at the Troubadour, had been able to move them like this. The song was Hedy's paean to Rick, the story of their love, longing, and disappointment, a living tribute to her only true love and a thanksgiving for her rebirth and reawakening. She was singing again, thanks to Rick, and this time she'd never stop.

When she sang the final note, the crowd stood still, shocked and overwhelmed. The sounds of sobbing filled the air. Suddenly

Rose, tears running down her face, ran up to Hedy and hugged her. Standing together, arm in arm, they watched as the workmen, at the rabbi's signal, began to lower the coffin into the ground. Then the two women reached down together, picked up the lone shovel, and, hand in hand, tossed the first pile of fresh soil over Rick's corpse. As they backed away from the grave toward David and Joyce, others followed, with handfuls of dirt, until the entire crowd had filed past the final stage and began to disperse.

David raised Hedy's veil and kissed her on the cheek. "Thank you, Hedy."

"Don't thank me, thank Rick. I owe it to Rick."

"You're right. We should all thank Rick," Joyce said.

"I'm going to take Hedy home," Rose said. "We're going to stay together for a while. Catch up on old times."

Joyce smiled. "That's a good idea." As Rose turned away, Joyce whispered into her ear, "Take care of her, Rose. She needs a mother—maybe even a manager."

"Mother, maybe. Manager, no way," Rose answered.

Joyce watched them walk away, then moved over toward the grave and knelt down on the damp ground. "I guess this is what friends are for, in the end. You're the best, Rick." She closed her fist around the dark earth, stretched her arm toward the empty space, and let the dirt slide through her fingers.

When she stood up, he was standing there, right beside David. Thane Crawley! She pushed to her feet and hurried to David's side.

"A terrible tragedy, David. I'm so sorry it turned out this way. That day he came to play the symphony . . ." Thane shook his head. "He was so happy, so alive."

As the workmen hovered around the grave and began to shovel the earth back into the hole over the coffin, the menacing, final sound of dirt striking wood echoed through the air.

David scowled at Crawley. His hands were rock-steady, but his nails dug vengefully into his own palms. "I've made my decision about the album."

"Yes? It's sad they couldn't appreciate him when he was alive. But now . . . well, at least his music will live on. As soon as we rush release—"

"We're not going to rerelease," David said evenly.

Thane's face lost all its color. "What? You mean, not today."

"Not yet. Not for some time. Not till a civilized period has elapsed. I'm going to preserve Rick's memory intact. I refuse to distort it or exploit it commercially. The *Fireside Symphony* will not be re-pressed or rereleased until *I* feel the time is right. And the same goes for L.O.L. releases of any Firestone memorial material or compilation albums."

Joyce grabbed David's arm with a fierce, almost triumphant energy. He *was* going to make Thane crawl, by giving him a taste of his own medicine. What could be more fitting!

"David, you're out of your mind," Thane said, his voice raised and frenetic. "You're talking about millions and millions of dollars. The public is dying for Firestone material! You can't do this to them. You can't do this to me!"

"I can and I will," David spat back. "Regardless of the consequences to anyone and everyone. Don't forget, I'm not only the chairman of the Levy Organization, I'm also the executor of Rick's estate."

Joyce wrapped her hand around David's wrist and together they abruptly turned their backs on Thane Crawley—leaving him stock-still and numb—and walked across the grass toward Jack Black.

"That was wonderful, David," Joyce whispered.

When they came up beside the sartorially splendid Jack, he smiled at the couple. "Tough day, sweetheart. If there's anything I can do . . ."

"You already did it, Jack. But I've got some news you're not going to like."

"Yeah, what's that?"

"I'm putting a freeze on the shipment of all Rick's albums, including the *Fireside Symphony.* I'm afraid the LPs not going out."

"That's pretty ballsy of you. I admire that. But the boys— they're gonna be real unhappy. There could be trouble."

"There'd better be trouble. For Thane. Right now they owe me for Rick. Thane's *their* problem, not mine. When Rick's death has been avenged, I'll make it up to the boys in my own way, and you know I keep my word. The album will be rereleased. And I have lots of other ways, including my video ventures, to keep the boys happy. Tell them not to worry."

"Oh, they won't worry. They never worry. You know what they'll do to Thane?"

"Take their losses out in blood, I hope."

"You got it."

"My heart's breakin'."

"I always said you was cool, Barry. Now I know it. It's a pleasure doing business with a man of integrity." He tipped his hat. "David. Miss Heller."

They watched him walk away. And looked across at Thane still standing in the same place, his eyes flicking nervously back and forth as he observed the meeting with Jack. Then, hand in hand, David and Joyce made their way back to the Lagonda.

"When did you come up with *that* plan?" Joyce asked. Even though it was the perfect retribution, she still felt a chill down her spine.

"A little while ago."

"When you squeezed my hand?"

"Umm-hmm. When did you start reading my mind?"

"Always could. So, what now?" she asked.

"Back to the office. What else?"

Joyce shook her head and smiled. "To work on a strategy to clear Rick's name and start the wheels turning on L.O.L.'s newest and hottest movie and recording artist?"

"Are you thinking what I'm thinking?"

They said it aloud at the same time: "Hedy Harlowe!"

"She was fabulous, unbelievable. We owe it to Rick to put her back on top."

"To Rick?" Joyce asked skeptically.

"Yeah." He looked her in the eye and had to speak the truth. "And we owe it to ourselves."

" 'Cause we can't go on without the business, huh?"

"I guess not."

"What a pair," she said with resignation as she leaned her head gently against David's shoulder and he drove the Lagonda out of Mount Hebron Cemetery, back toward Hollywood.

ABOUT THE AUTHOR

Freddie Gershon received his education at the Art Students League, Hunter Playhouse, the Juilliard School of Music, Queens College, and Columbia Law School.

In the course of the '60s and early '70s, he acted as attorney for such emerging talents as composers Neil Sedaka, Marvin Hamlisch, and Lesley Gore, as well as performing artists Eric Clapton, Chicago, Phil Ochs, and Bette Midler. In addition, he was special counsel to several theatrical ventures, including *House of Blue Leaves, Lorelei,* and *Joseph and His Amazing Technicolor Dreamcoat.*

In the early '70s Gershon began to manage legal affairs for the Robert Stigwood Group, Ltd., helping to produce Broadway's *Jesus Christ Superstar,* and television's "All in the Family" and "Sanford and Son."

Mr. Gershon began to function as a teammate of Stigwood with the film *Tommy,* which initiated his relationship with Allan Carr, with whom he would later produce the hit stage musical, *La Cage aux Folles.*

In 1976 Gershon became Stigwood's partner and, in addition to overseeing RSO's worldwide record operations, was responsible for its Film Division, which produced *Saturday Night Fever, The Fan,* and *Grease I* and *II.*

Gershon retired from active business in 1981 but remained Vice Chairman of the Stigwood Group until 1983. Since retiring he has begun lecturing on entertainment law and has started his writing career.